Changing The Game

By the Author

Royal Rush: 75 Days to Fall in Love

Changing The Game

Changing The Game

by

Lissandra Rowe

2026

CHANGING THE GAME

ISBN 13: 978-1-63679-997-1

This Trade Paperback Original Is Published By
Bold Strokes Books, Inc.
P.O. Box 249
Valley Falls, NY 12185

First Edition: April 2026

Credits
Editor: Cindy Cresap
Production Design: Susan Ramundo
Cover Design By Tammy Seidick

Dedication

To all those around the globe who keep
women's sports alive and thriving: Thank you.

To my family and friends: Thank you for believing in
me and supporting me to see this story through.

To Jordyn: You are the greatest gift of my life.
Whether you bounce a basketball, pick up a paintbrush
or pen, or bang on the drums, I'll always be beside you.

PART I

THEN

Chapter One

The gym was electric as the cacophony overflowed from the maple bleachers. Northwoods College had possession of the ball with fourteen seconds left on the game clock. The scoreboard's red digital numbers stood tall and unblinking behind the basket, a glowing reminder that Northwoods College had the last shot and were down to Van Mars University by a single point.

Fourteen seconds Emersyn Tanner dribbled confidently near center court and surveyed the scene before her. Late afternoon sunshine filtered through a thick glass skylight along the roof of the gymnasium, throwing drifting spots of golden light along the smooth hardwood. It was all part of the background to her, a background that she had known practically since she could walk.

One point down and one chance to take it. Emersyn quickened her pace and dribbled left. Her defender was on her as soon as she crossed half-court, the opposing guard's arms spread wide as she leaned closer and kept up with Emersyn step by step.

Emersyn turned to her left, reading the swipe that her defender threw toward the ball before her arm was even fully extended. "You really think I'm going to turn it over?" she said with a grin. "Yeah, right. You haven't played me one-on-one enough."

Strands of hair that had fallen from her ponytail stuck to her temples as beads of sweat rolled down her forehead and neck, disappearing beneath the thick hem of her Northwoods College jersey.

"I know you aren't going to pass the ball," her defender muttered back knowingly. "Everyone knows you hog that shit too much and don't get your teammates involved enough. It's right there on the scouting report."

The trash talk was all Emersyn needed as she straightened confidently, jab-stepping to her right and then speeding to her left as her defender stumbled. Coach Kay Hanlon had drawn up a smart play.

"Swing the ball to Savannah, who will cut around the basket to the right wing." Emersyn recalled Coach Kay's urgent, quiet tone during their final timeout. *"She has the hot hand tonight and we want her taking that last shot. Savannah, get a good look. Get the ball out of your hands as soon as Emersyn passes it."*

Emersyn knew that Savannah Sanchez was one of the best three-point sharpshooters in the NCAA and she had one of the quickest releases, with the ability to shoot the ball with precise accuracy as soon as it hit her hands. Like clockwork, she spotted Savannah taking off from one side of the wing to the other as her defender became stuck behind a screen from Mia DiCorro, their power forward.

She dribbled confidently toward the free throw line, her own defender lost as she toyed with the ball and bounced it between her legs with the sort of poised expertise that only years of living, breathing, and playing basketball could teach. Emersyn wanted to eat up as much clock as possible to avoid giving Van Mars even a one- or two-second possession at the end.

Nine seconds. Another defender ran at Emersyn, but she didn't even look at her—or the ball—as she surveyed the court once more. She had been perfecting her handles since the fourth grade and could dribble in her sleep. She glanced around sharply as she noted their lanky center, Erica Owen, jostling with two opposing players beneath the basket. The easiest move would be to get the ball to Erica and let her lay it in, and it appeared that was the play Van Mars was anticipating.

Can't get it to Erica. A pang of mild frustration rose in Emersyn's chest. *They have her too covered.* The rhythmic lull of the ball pounding against the floor in time with the squeaking sneakers across the hardwood, the shouts and cheers from the crowd, and the quick movements of the coaches along the sidelines blended into a comfortably familiar din at the back of her mind. Emersyn was laser-focused. She wanted this shot and she was going to win it for her team.

Six seconds. Time for action. This was the part of the game that Emersyn loved; no, that she *lived* for. Out of the corner of her eye, she could see Savannah. With Erica double-teamed beneath the basket, she was wide open. Emersyn knew that leaving Savannah that open was a grievous error by Van Mars, given her teammate's impeccable shooting. Savannah's feet were firmly planted behind the three-point line, and she crouched with her hands open and ready to catch the ball.

The noise in the gym seemed louder and more pronounced as it echoed in time with the seconds on the clock ticking by in seemingly slow motion. Emersyn was undeterred. She had been playing—and winning—this game for as long as she could remember. It was part of her DNA now, just as much as the fact that she was one of the shortest point guards in the NCAA at just five feet, four inches tall or the fact that she was one of the top five highest scoring female basketball players in Northwoods College history. She wasn't used to playing in what was often referred to as "garbage time," the tail-end of a game played out by the bench players because the lead and the W was secure.

This is to be expected. Emersyn scolded herself. *This season hasn't exactly gone according to plan. Besides, Coach Hanlon may not believe in captains or hierarchies because she says we're all one team, but it's clear I'm the leader. The starting point guard. The number one playmaker.*

Emersyn smiled. She knew what to do. Without so much as a glance at Savannah, she pump-faked toward the basket. Erica twisted beneath the hoop, brief confusion shadowing her face, as she tried to free herself from her defenders.

"Sanchez!" Emersyn could hear Coach Hanlon's voice bellowing from the sidelines. "Tanner, she's got a wide-open look! Get the ball to Sanchez!"

With five seconds left on the clock, Emersyn pump-faked again and opened just enough space between her and her defender.

"What's the matter, you afraid to shoot now? You're eating too much clock," Emersyn's defender hissed as she quickly recovered.

"Pass it to Sanchez!" Coach Hanlon's shouts floated above the noise of the crowd. "Now!"

Emersyn snapped back into the present. Using her sharpened basketball instincts, the same natural skill that her mother affectionately dubbed her "basketball brain," Emersyn's eyes darted to Savannah again for just a second. The shooting guard grinned and gave Emersyn a nearly-imperceptible nod that relayed she was ready to take the shot.

Forty-six percent three-point shooter this season, Emersyn recalled from a Wisconsin sports pamphlet that had practically fallen over itself with praise throughout the year for Savannah. Her heart pounded as she turned her shoulder away from the open pass to Savannah, the easy bucket, and the near-perfect play that Coach Hanlon had drawn up.

Without acknowledging the trash talk, Emersyn fixed her defender with an icy stare. She could still hear Coach Hanlon yelling at the top of her lungs somewhere at the back of her mind.

"What the hell are you doing, Tanner?" she shouted. "Pass it!"

The next three seconds were a blur as Emersyn tore toward the hoop. Every fiber in body screamed at her to slow down, get rid of the rock, and let Savannah win the game. Instead, she ignored her instincts and rose up into a heavily-contested mid-range jump shot just inside the free throw line. She knew she wasn't exactly open, but it didn't matter. She had sealed plenty of games before, even while double-teamed.

As Emersyn shot the ball, a sudden pinch of electric pain from somewhere deep in her lower back spiked up her spine. She froze as the ball left her hands and fought to keep herself from squeezing her eyes shut against the searing tremors, but it was too late. As soon as it was out of her hands, she knew the shot wouldn't go. Instead of watching helplessly as it clanked loudly against the backboard and then rolled off the rim, Emersyn tried desperately for a second chance.

Draw the foul. Two free throws and we can still win it.

As she came down, she bit her lip against the sharp pain and threw herself forward in hopes of landing against her defender. The Van Mars point guard was too astute, too quick, for Emersyn's last-ditch flop attempt and threw her arms straight up before stepping back once.

Emersyn landed on the hardwood in a heap of dizziness, sweaty arms, and cramping muscles. She hoped against hope for a late whistle but closed her eyes instead as a loud buzzer sounded from somewhere high above to signal the clock had expired. Just like that, the possession was over and the game was finished.

I blew it. A sick feeling turned her stomach as the opposing team gathered at the other end of the court in a sea of forest-green to celebrate their tough road win. Emersyn sat up and rested her elbows on her knees for a long moment as she closed her eyes once more against the whirlwind of dizziness and pain. With the game over, she was all too aware of the chaos and noise around her. She had wanted to prove herself, to show her team that she could still be *the one*, and instead sat on the waxed hardwood with the stinging knowledge of a preventable loss.

Emersyn glanced up and blinked as she met Savannah's brown eyes across the court. Her unreadable gaze held Emersyn's for a long moment. She didn't look angry or surprised, though Emersyn wouldn't have blamed her if she was. Instead, hurt flashed through her dark eyes before she turned and stood behind the rest of the team in the handshake line.

Emersyn glanced down at her white Nikes and bit her lip, surprised by the deep ache in her chest. For a moment, the realization that she had hurt Savannah felt as though it was splitting her in two and she wasn't entirely sure why.

She's gorgeous and you can't stop thinking about her. The thought zinged through Emersyn's mind, unwelcome and sudden. *Even if she did hijack your team while you were out all last season recovering from injury.* Emersyn rolled her eyes as she quickly shook the thought away, hurried to her feet, and gingerly rubbed her lower back. The sting of the loss was still acute as she trudged to the handshake line and refused to make eye contact with her defender.

"I know you aren't going to pass the ball. Everyone knows you hog that shit too much." The trash talk replayed in her mind and Emersyn hated that she had proven her right.

She glanced up as the opposing team's center leaned down to give her a quick high five.

"Good game," she said with a nod, barely concealing her grin at their win.

"Good game," Emersyn echoed with a sigh.

One stupid point. Game over.

Chapter Two

Emersyn watched as the court emptied slowly and the crowd dispersed from the bleachers into the buzz of post-game chatter. She lifted her arms over her head and winced at the ache in her muscles as she tried to stretch out the pain. It was the swell of disappointment coursing through her veins, though, that she felt much more keenly.

We lost. That's it.

Emersyn hated losing. She disliked everything about it, from the subdued air that settled over the team as they trudged back to the locker room to the sighs and critiques from Coach Hanlon after they showered and changed clothes. The prickly disappointment of losing was not a familiar one to Emersyn and she remembered why she despised it so much.

Usually, we're the ones cheering on the sidelines and recounting every awesome play. Emersyn glanced at the group of forest-green-clad players clapping one another on the backs and laughing loudly as they faded into the visitors' locker room. *Especially for a home game. What happened this season?*

Instead of following her own team into their locker room, Emersyn dropped onto the bottom row of bleachers and stretched her left leg out with a wince. It was wrapped from her calf upward in a skin-tight white leg sleeve, though her muscles still felt leaden and heavy. Cool air prickled against her sweat-soaked jersey, and she shivered as she leaned forward.

Suddenly, the waning sunlight was partially blocked and Emersyn glanced up from her seated position at the figure who stood over her. Savannah shot her a wide smile that Emersyn noticed with part-annoyance and part-intrigue seemed to light up her entire face.

"You hit the ground hard," Savannah said as she raised an expertly-tweezed eyebrow. "You okay?"

Emersyn swallowed hard as she kept her eyes trained on the hardwood before her. "I'm fine," she replied quickly. "Shit happens sometimes."

She felt Savannah's gaze on her and, for some reason, it made her heart pound in her chest like it was the last fourteen seconds of the game all over again. She glanced up, trying her hardest not to notice how Savannah's brown eyes were framed by impossibly long, dark eyelashes or that her tanned, toned arms were on full display as she crossed them thoughtfully in front of her.

"You've been overdoing it again, haven't you?" she asked.

Emersyn didn't answer, though the beat of silence felt oddly comfortable. "Look, I know I blew it," she finally said.

Savannah sighed, her eyes never leaving Emersyn's face. "You played hard," she said gently. "We all did. Besides, we win as a team and we lose as a team. That's it."

Emersyn bit her lip. "Not when I jack up a bad hero shot like I'm the second coming of Diana Taurasi."

Savannah laughed. The sound was soft and unexpected in the cavernous gymnasium and Emersyn felt that same heart-pounding tickle deep in her stomach.

"It wasn't *that* bad," Savannah said. "I've seen you make mid-range jumpers practically in your sleep during practice."

Emersyn swallowed hard as their gazes locked for just a beat too long.

God, she's beautiful. The thought crossed Emersyn's mind before she could stop it. She was annoyed that she was thinking that *now,* in the midst of one of her worst moments of an already-disappointing final season of college basketball. Still, she couldn't help but memorize the laugh, the big smile that tugged at her impossibly full lips, or the trickle of sweat that slid down her neck and disappeared beneath her jersey.

"Yeah, but this wasn't practice," Emersyn finally said.

"No, it wasn't, Savannah said gently. "But it's also not the end of the world."

How is she completely non-plussed by this loss? Our team lost by a single basket to a group of girls that has been consistently mediocre for the last three years. We played March Madness my first two years here and made it to the Sweet Sixteen my sophomore year! Not that Savannah was here for any of it because she hadn't transferred to Northwoods yet, but still.

Savannah stuck out her hand. "Come on," she said. "You know Coach will have a fit if you're not in the locker room soon. Want to walk back together?"

Emersyn stared at her outstretched palm and shook her head quickly as she tried to ignore the dread of having to face her other teammates and Coach Hanlon. "I'll be there in a minute to face the music," she said dryly. "I'll catch up."

Savannah didn't push. Instead, she nodded once and turned back toward the locker room.

After a moment, she turned again as if considering an afterthought. "Hey, Emersyn," she called back to her. "So, um, my parents are in town this weekend and they rented this really cool cabin out near the woods. Most of the girls and I were going to hang out there tonight and take advantage of the grill and hot tub. Want to stop by around, like, eight?"

"Can't," Emersyn said as she pushed herself off the bleacher. "I have plans."

She tried not to acknowledge the sliver of guilt or the ache that sliced through her chest as Savannah's face fell.

She quickly recovered and smiled. "Is it a guy?" She pressed as she paused outside the locker room door. "Because you're more than welcome to bring him. I think Erica is bringing her new girlfriend Kayla and Mia is bringing that guy Ryan she's been seeing. It'll be fun."

Emersyn swallowed hard at the mention of a boyfriend as another sick feeling swept through her. *So much for my goal of coming out before graduation.* An icy but familiar wave of anxiety gripped at her chest. *But who knew how much could change in a year and a half?*

Emersyn shrugged as she followed Savannah into the locker room before ducking down an aisle of lockers. She twirled the combination on her blue-painted locker with one hand and reached behind her head with the other to pull out the tie that held her hair in a tight ponytail for the last three hours. Emersyn took a deep breath and shook out her sweat-matted hair. She stood on her tiptoes to grab her Northwoods College hoodie from the locker's top shelf and considered her lack of height. She knew full well that for what she lacked in inches, she made up for with IQ and speed on the basketball court. She could dart easily from one side to the other and was much faster than most of the taller girls.

And let's be real. Almost every girl is a taller girl.

"You're not going to Savannah's thing at the cabin tonight?" Erica asked. Her voice was muffled as she pulled a soft gray Northwoods College T-shirt over her head. "It's going to be fun."

Emersyn sighed as she dropped her blue basketball shorts and compression sleeve on the scarred wooden bench between them before stepping into a pair of black track pants. "Yeah, I know," she said sarcastically. "She said that too. I mean, duh, right? If *she* says it's going to be fun, it must be fun."

Erica rolled her eyes and laughed as she smoothed the thin black braids that spilled over her shoulders. "Look, I know you're in a mood because we lost—"

"I'm so *not* in a mood—" Emersyn started.

Erica laughed harder. "Yeah, okay," she said. "We've played ball together since we were freshmen. I know how you get when we lose a game. And I know you don't like Savannah. Hell, *everyone* knows you don't like Savannah."

Emersyn shook her head as she pulled a fitted white T-shirt over her head. "I never said that."

Erica squeezed lotion into her hands and rubbed it over her calves. "You don't have to," she said. "You refuse to talk to her more than you have to, even when socializing with the rest of the team. Which you do less and less these days, by the way. Oh, *and* you let it get in the way of your game today and you made a dumb decision."

Emersyn stilled as Erica fixed her with a pointed stare. "What do you mean?"

"We all watched you try to play hero and completely ignore the play that Coach drew up," Erica said. "You had ample time to get the ball to Savannah. She didn't have a single defender on her because *I* was fighting the double-team and you know she would have made that shot. I'm not saying we lost because of you, Em. I mean, our game was off after halftime. It is what it is. But you sacrificed *our* last chance to get the W because you didn't want Savannah to get the glory." She shrugged.

Emersyn swallowed hard as she tied her black Converse low-tops. Despite the warmth of the locker room, outside was still the beginning of March in northern Wisconsin and Emersyn knew full well the contrasting temperatures of gymnasium and outside took years to get used to.

Erica wouldn't meet her eyes, so Emersyn finally glanced at the floor. "Everyone's mad at me, aren't they?"

Erica sighed as she dabbed Chapstick over her lips. "No, Em," she said gently. "But they're not thrilled with you either. I know Coach Hanlon is disappointed. I'm sure she'll talk to you. We can be a great team—"

"The best in the Midwest," Emersyn said with a smile. "Remember? That's what all the newspapers called us after our surprise Sunday Selection for March Madness two years ago."

"Right." Erica nodded. "This year, it's like something happened to us. I know this isn't how we expected to go out our senior year. Not winning the division, not being chosen in the Sunday Selection, whatever. But we're still a great team that should be playing the right way. Something happened to our chemistry…"

Emersyn rolled her eyes. "Yeah, the Great and *So* Amazing Savannah Sanchez transferred to Northwoods for her senior year. And she completely screwed up our team's synergy. She should've just stayed at Arizona State. Did the athletic department really have that little faith in me coming back strong after my injury?" The words felt bitter on Emersyn's tongue.

Erica closed her locker hard and stared at Emersyn sternly. "I don't think the problem is Savannah," she said. "She's one of the top NCAA female basketball players in our division. Just like you. We're lucky to have her, even if it's just for a season. Besides, I'm sure *she* didn't anticipate her senior season being spent on a losing team. But you know what? You'd never know, because she's a *really* nice person too. Maybe you would get that if you gave her half a chance."

Emersyn shook her head. "As far as I'm concerned, the season is almost over. And then we graduate, and I never have to see her again. Right now, my focus is on finishing out the school year strong, figuring out what the hell I'm going to do with my life since my pro ball prospects are pretty much gone after this injury, and celebrating graduation with my favorite teammates. I don't need a new friend, Erica. I need to make it out of college without going insane."

"She reminds me of you, you know," Erica said and then blinked. "Savannah. She reminds me of you two years ago. When you were happy and loved life and basketball was the most natural thing in the world to you. When you weren't so…*withdrawn* and angry all the time."

"I'm *not*…" Emersyn started defensively, but Erica shook her head knowingly.

"You two are remarkably alike, actually," she said. "You're just too blind to realize that."

Erica's words cut Emersyn to her core. She smiled, but it was without humor. "Well, no wonder I don't like her then," she deadpanned as she slammed her locker door shut. "I can barely stand myself most of the time, let alone another me."

Erica sighed and leaned against her locker. "I wish you would talk to someone," she said. "I wish you would talk to me or Coach Hanlon or *anyone*. It can't be healthy to keep all that stuff about the accident inside."

Emersyn hated the sour feeling that coursed through her as she slung her messenger bag over one shoulder and pulled a tube of lip gloss from her hoodie pocket.

"I'm going home," she finally said. It felt unnecessary. "Have fun tonight."

Emersyn quietly made her way through the locker room as she dabbed the gloss over her lips. She paused as she passed Savannah, Mia, and their small forward, Arissa Johnson. They were talking animatedly near the door, but a hush fell over them as she walked by. Emersyn could feel the eyes on her back.

It wasn't all that long ago when I *was the one surrounded by teammates, laughing and making evening plans.* She pushed open the heavy wooden door and threw a glance over her shoulder. The other girls had resumed their excited chatter, but Emersyn froze as her gaze met Savannah's across the tiled hallway. She swallowed hard as Savannah seemed to hold her in place for a long, charged moment. There was a sort of confidence in her as she seemed to regard Emersyn as though she was some sort of challenge she was determined to crack. A shiver ran down Emersyn's spine as the locker room suddenly felt small and the air temperature seemed to spike with heat and electricity.

Would it be so bad to let her get closer? Emersyn didn't have time to dwell on the thought. Coach Hanlon poked her head out of her office door and cleared her throat pointedly.

"Tanner, are you on your way out?" Coach Hanlon's stark tone made the question sound rhetorical.

Emersyn straightened her spine, hoping to blink away the tingles of something electric that had made her chest flutter. She glanced in the direction of her coach before stealing another glance at Savannah, who had turned away and was pulling on a pair of suede, toffee-colored heeled boots.

Emersyn's annoyance with her flooded back. *God forbid Savannah doesn't dress like a supermodel for one day. She really thinks she's too cool, I know it. And, most obnoxiously, so does all of Northwoods College.*

"Yeah, I'm headed home for a shower, Coach," Emersyn called back. "Did you need me?"

Emersyn already knew the answer as a sinking pit formed in her stomach. The brief nod from Coach Hanlon confirmed it as she gestured toward her office.

"I want to have a quick chat," she said. "Once the room clears out, why don't you come in and take a seat?"

Mia stood next to Savannah and cracked her gum loudly. "Guess that's our cue to leave," she said as she scrunched her already-washed and teased-to-perfection brown hair. "Is nine tonight okay? Ryan and I were going to see a movie first, but I don't want to miss coming by…"

Her voice faded as the group brushed past Emersyn and out the heavy door.

Great. I can already hear Coach's lecture now.

Erica tucked one of her braids behind her ear on her way out, surrounded by a group of their bench players. Emersyn attempted a smile and was relieved to see her grin back.

Call me later Erica mouthed before she turned and left the locker room.

Emersyn glanced in the long mirror opposite Coach Hanlon's quiet office. It was so smudged with handprints and flecks of dried makeup that she could barely see her face through the greasy blurs.

It's better off. I don't know when my eyes got so dark. Mom used to say they were the most piercing shade of hazel, whatever that is. But I don't think they've been that color for a while.

"You wanted to see me?" Emersyn asked tentatively.

Coach Hanlon glanced up from her computer monitor as her hands hovered over the keyboard. Her office was neat, disciplined, and strategically organized, something that Emersyn noted with mild amusement was exactly how Coach Hanlon operated. Crisp stacks of manila folders with color-coded tabs lined hanging shelves on the wall opposite her L-shaped desk. Emersyn knew they contained game film notes, player development journeys, scouting reports, and precisely written plays. A series of framed photos decorated the top of the metal three-drawer file cabinet at the back of the room. Emersyn's eyes swept over the photo of Coach Hanlon and her longtime girlfriend, Diana Miller, walking along a white sand beach in Florida before settling on a grainy photo of a much younger Coach Hanlon in her college uniform, grinning and raising her index finger in a number one gesture next to the NCAA women's basketball championship trophy. A banner behind her in the photo said "1978 Champions" in big, bold letters.

Emersyn glanced back at her coach as she leaned back in her desk chair and pulled a pair of reading glasses from the bridge of her nose.

"I can always come back later…" she said.

Coach Hanlon rubbed a hand over her face tiredly. She gestured to a hard-backed chair opposite her desk.

"That's okay, I'd like to chat with you now," she said. Emersyn braced herself as she wondered if that was weary resignation she heard. "Please, Tanner. Sit."

Chapter Three

"I'm really sorry about today," Emersyn blurted as her butt hit the chair. "I don't know what happened. I had that shot and I froze. I know it's my fault that we lost…"

Coach Hanlon held up a hand and frowned as the wrinkles across her tanned forehead deepened. Her short, spiked blond hair with its natural streaks of silver and her ubiquitous royal blue Northwoods College polo shirt gave her a no-nonsense air that Emersyn had learned long ago not to question.

"Whoa, whoa, slow down," Coach Hanlon said. "We're a team. That means the things we do on the court are a collective effort. Whether we like it or not, when one makes a mistake, then we all do. Just like when one wins, we all do. We were off today. It happens to everyone. Even the best teams in the world have their good and bad days. You ever see the Spurs crying because of one game? Or the Celtics? Of course not. We couldn't find any cohesion today and that's okay. It was a fair game and the better team won. It's Saturday. We have two practices this week and then next Saturday's game. I'm confident we'll play better."

Emersyn nodded seriously. "Agreed. I'll play better. These girls need me at my best."

Coach Hanlon sat further back in her chair and sighed. "Tanner, that's not what I'm trying to get through to you," she said. "Everyone on that team needs everyone to be at their best. They need you and you need *them*, that's how team sports work. Every player and every position needs the other to work effectively in a fluid basketball game. We don't ride on any one player's shoulders. It's on everybody."

Emersyn nodded, slightly less sure of herself this time. "Got it."

"Do you, Tanner?" Coach Hanlon asked thoughtfully. "I've already decided that I'm benching you for Tuesday's practice. That little maneuver you did in the last few seconds of the game was in no way representative of the team player I've mentored since you were a local high school standout. Why didn't you pass the ball to Sanchez?"

Emersyn's mouth dropped open. "Benching me?" she said incredulously. "Coach, I don't see how that's fair! I know I had an off day and I realize that I choked at the end—"

"You were well aware of what you were doing, Tanner," Coach Hanlon said. "You didn't want to pass the ball to Sanchez because you didn't want her to win the game. She would have made that shot, easy. You didn't want to give her the opportunity and, as one of the main playmakers on this team, that's dangerous and selfish."

"I…" Emersyn opened and then closed her mouth in defeat. She knew it was no use. Coach Hanlon had mentored her since her junior year of high school and Emersyn knew she could see right through her. "I wanted to try and make that bucket," she said softly. "I wanted to show everyone I can still do it. I'm still just as good as I was before the accident, even if I get those spasms and nerve pains. I know Savannah is, like, this unexpected angel from Heaven or whatever and she was one of the top ten female high school basketball players in Arizona…"

"Top five," Coach Hanlon corrected her.

Emersyn crossed her arms and shot daggers at the smooth tile floor. "Well, *I* was the hometown hero here. Everyone in northern Wisconsin knows who I am. I'm still better than most of the girls out there and a lot of the men too. After the accident, this was supposed to be my season to show everyone I can still play at the same level and I can still lead a team to victory. And then Savannah comes in, out of nowhere, and takes over the team? It's *not* fair and I don't get what everyone else sees in her. She's okay, I guess. Nothing special."

Coach Hanlon fixed Emersyn with a knowing look. "Tanner, you know damn well that isn't true. She's a natural on the court and her shot is nearly unguardable. Best of all, she's *passionate* about the game. She's an excellent player and you know that."

"I'm an excellent player too!" Emersyn said. Somewhere in the back of her mind, she was aware she was sounding more and more like a petulant child, but she was too frustrated to care. "We made it to March Madness twice *without* Savannah."

"I know it." Coach Hanlon smiled broadly. "And maybe we'll end the season strong still. *With* Savannah. I'll tell you what, Tanner. What would you do if you were in my shoes? If you had two amazing athletes, but you couldn't get one to work with the other? One who, in fact, momentarily sacrificed her sense of team to make a stupid decision to play hero ball in the last seconds of a winnable game. All because of ego and because she couldn't bear to let someone else shine. What would you do?"

Emersyn shifted in her chair but didn't uncross her arms. "I'm happy when the other girls shine," she said as she wrinkled her nose. "I wanted Erica to get the easy layup, but she was double-teamed. And in the sophomore year season opener against UW Madison? I kept feeding her the ball because I knew she was hot and she ended up with twenty points in the first half. I couldn't talk for days afterward because I screamed so loud for her. I always cheer for my teammates. Every time Mia flattens someone with a screen, every time—"

Coach Hanlon sighed. "You know damn well those girls are good, but they don't usually play at the same skill level as you. Your court vision is the best I've ever helped develop and coach. You know those girls aren't a threat to you; you orchestrate the game for them. Sanchez, on the other hand? Tanner, you know you've met your match."

Emersyn thought for a long moment about her teammate. She recalled a moment in the locker room after a game late in the fall that she tried hard to forget. Emersyn had glanced up at the exact moment Savannah pulled her jersey over her head. Even now, months later, a jolt of electricity coursed through her as she remembered Savannah's toned, golden-tan abdomen or the way her long, dark hair had cascaded down her back.

There's no denying that Savannah is gorgeous. Even I'm not that blind, despite what Erica says.

She thought of the way Savannah's whole face seemed to light up when she smiled and the playful intensity in her eyes that Emersyn realized held a lot more depth beyond what she allowed others to see. She frowned as she tried to guess how tall Savannah was.

At least 5'8". Or maybe it's just those stupid heels she wears. Emersyn crossed her arms tighter against her as a surge of warmth spread through her like wildfire. *Whatever.*

Coach Hanlon studied her face closely and Emersyn wondered for a moment if maybe she was testing her. She rolled her eyes for good measure.

"If you say so," she said as she tried to inject every ounce of boredom she could muster into her tone.

"That aside, I asked you a question, Tanner," Coach Hanlon said. "What would you do if you were in my shoes?"

Emersyn stared at her nails. They were short and unpolished, an unfashionable sacrifice she had made long ago to play basketball. "I guess I would have a long talk with that player," she mumbled.

Coach Hanlon grinned and waved from behind her desk. "Hi!" she said. "We're talking."

Emersyn smiled despite herself. "And maybe I'd bench her for a practice so she could sit back and watch the team instead of trying to let her ego run it."

Coach Hanlon gave her a thumbs up. "Bingo! Tanner, I don't want to see that kind of unsportswoman-like conduct I saw from you today again, you hear me?"

Emersyn nodded. "Yes, Coach."

"Look, I know the accident has been tough on you." Emersyn shifted as her coach's tone became serious. "You lost an entire season of your college basketball career, you spent months in physical therapy, your mom lost her job…Believe me, I know it's hard. I know you grew up in this town and you were a high school basketball standout with pro prospects if you played your cards right. I see the pain in your eyes every time I look at you. It's a lot of pressure."

Emersyn felt the tears before she realized her throat had closed. "It's okay," she said. "With my mom out of work now, there's no way I could leave to go overseas and play after graduation anyway. You're the reason I'm at Northwoods. If it wasn't for basketball, I'd be just another townie at this college."

"No," Coach Hanlon said. "*You're* the reason you're at Northwoods College. I just recruited you after witnessing your varsity seasons in high school and your progression from seventh grade on with your AAU club. You're too talented to not have been given the opportunity, and you've always held up your end of the deal in terms of grades, conduct, and your basketball accomplishments here. Don't sell yourself short, Tanner."

"I just wish…" Emersyn shook her head and tried again. "I keep thinking, like, what if I hadn't offered to drive my mom to the doctor because she had the flu? What if I had left class early and hadn't made her wait until I was out that evening from biology? Or what if she had, I don't know, forgotten her purse and we left three minutes later? Everything would be different."

Coach Hanlon reached over and placed her hand atop Emersyn's. "Tanner, you can't drive yourself crazy with stuff like that," she said gently. "What happened is what happened, and that's unchangeable. It doesn't take away how much it sucks, I know, but this is the reality."

Emersyn sniffled. "But then I'd still have my pro ball prospects, my manager wouldn't have cited that stupid injury clause when revoking his representation, I wouldn't have had to take out student loans to finish senior year because my basketball scholarship was rescinded, my mom would still be working, and money wouldn't be so tight. I'd be looking ahead to the life I've been working for since...well, as long as I can remember. Four years of college ball and then the ultimate goal of going pro. That was *always* the plan." She took a deep breath. "And maybe I wouldn't be so angry and spiteful all the time. I hate myself, Coach. I hate *everything*."

"Tanner, you can't think like that," Coach Hanlon said. "The accident wasn't your fault. You were T-boned on the busiest road in Northwoods by a driver in the midst of an unexpected medical emergency. Nobody can predict those things."

"But maybe if I hadn't been hurrying so I could get my mom and I home from her doctor sooner so I could watch the...the stupid NBA preseason game, I could have seen it coming," Emersyn said. "Or maybe if I'd used the restroom before leaving the house, we would have missed it by five minutes. Or..."

Emersyn bit her lip hard as she tried to blink away the silent tears. Coach Hanlon squeezed her hand comfortingly. "Tanner, Tanner..." she said. "*Emersyn*."

Her head snapped up. She couldn't remember the last time Coach Hanlon called her by anything other than her last name. "It's hard not to think about how much has changed so quickly," Emersyn said. "My entire life has been basketball. I did everything the way I was supposed to. I didn't allow any distractions, I stayed away from social media and the sleazy clothing and shoe reps, and I focused on my grades when I wasn't practicing or playing. And now, because of that stupid accident? I'm lucky to even still be finishing my senior year playing basketball."

"Tanner, you can't let yourself get wrapped up in the what ifs and the maybes," Coach Hanlon said firmly. "I know it's easier said than done, but one day you'll look back and see the well of strength you have inside you that will get you through anything the world throws your way. I see you getting back to yourself more and more. You worked your ass off all last year in physical therapy. I know it's easy to get angry and point fingers, but you can't let what happened define you…" Coach Hanlon paused. "God, I sound like a fortune cookie. Tell you what, why don't you head home, shower up, and get some rest. I heard some of the girls talking about a get-together tonight. It might do you some good to spend time with your teammates."

"Savannah is hosting," Emersyn said crossly. "Her parents are in town this weekend or whatever. I'm going to call it a night."

"Ah, yes, of course," Coach Hanlon said. "All right then. See you on Tuesday. Don't forget about practice. I know you're on the bench, but I still want you suited up and on time."

Emersyn nodded and stood. "Yes, ma'am."

"And, Tanner?"

Emersyn turned slightly, her hand on the doorknob. "Yes?"

"Sanchez really isn't that bad," Coach Hanlon said dryly. "This may shock you, but you would probably even get along with her. I think you two are actually very similar. Take my word for it, kid."

Emersyn tried not to roll her eyes as she gave a short nod. She heard Coach Hanlon's familiar chuckle echo through the locker room as she reached the exit.

Why does everyone keep telling me that?

Chapter Four

Savannah Sanchez sighed as she gently closed the front door of the luxurious cabin on the outskirts of Northwoods that her parents had rented for the weekend. There were just a couple of hours before most of the girls on the team would come by for an impromptu evening hot tub party, but she wasn't as excited to socialize as she expected. After all, the person she wanted to show up for the get-together most had made it crystal clear that she wouldn't be stopping by.

Savannah gently dropped her gym bag onto the rich honey-colored hardwood floor. There was something about Emersyn Tanner that made her ache, first in her chest and then somewhere deeper. It wasn't just the way that Emersyn moved on the court, all precision and laser-focused fire, like she refused to cede control for even a moment. Savannah took a deep breath. That refusal to let go lit a fire inside her that seemed to stoke anytime Emersyn was near. For all her clinging to control and refusal to show even the slightest ounce of vulnerability, Savannah could see beyond whenever she looked into Emersyn's hazel eyes, and she knew the one thing Emersyn refused to do was what she needed to do most. Emersyn carried herself like she'd wrapped every vulnerable piece of herself in impenetrable, untouchable armor.

Savannah swallowed hard as her mind wandered over Emersyn, the guarded clench of her jaw and the stubborn pout of her full lips, and the way she never allowed herself to need anyone. The challenge and the mystery of Emersyn, the delicious desire to slip past her defenses to see who she really was, was intoxicating.

As she padded barefoot through the cavernous living room anchored by a tall stone fireplace, Savannah wondered what it would be like to touch her, to hear her breath catch, and feel her let go under her command. There were fleeting moments when she swore she saw brief cracks in Emersyn's bratty surface. The way the air would feel charged with electricity anytime they were close. The way Emersyn's breath hitched when Savannah looked at her.

God, how I would love to undo her. The thought surprised her. The tantalizing idea of finally getting through all of Emersyn's sky-high walls sent a low jolt deep into her core. She let herself daydream over the idea of gently trailing kisses along her spine and around the curve of her neck, murmuring reassurances against her soft skin as she let go and her body melted beneath Savannah's touch. She wanted to press her lips to the sensitive spot just below her ear and feel her shiver. She wanted to gaze down at Emersyn beneath her and watch those carefully guarded layers slip away until what was left was just breathless, needing, and begging to be hers.

Savannah sighed and grabbed a bottle of water from the stainless steel refrigerator. She wanted to be the one Emersyn unraveled for and the one Emersyn trusted to see her and not look away when she pretended everything was fine.

If she ever surrenders, I want it to be to me. Savannah took a long, slow sip of the icy water. *Because she trusts me enough to fall.*

Savannah shook her head and flipped her hair over her shoulder. "Good luck with that," she muttered to herself.

Savannah walked through the spacious luxury cabin and then pushed open the door to the master bedroom. She knew exactly where her mother would be. She closed her eyes and breathed in the scent of lavender emanating from an essential oil diffuser on the bedside table. Her mother's portable speaker was carefully perched near the window. Traditional Native American tribal music, sounds that Savannah had been familiar with for as long as she could remember thanks to her mother's full-blooded Navajo heritage, filled the room at just a loud enough volume to keep the bedroom from being eerily quiet.

Savannah carefully spread the extra yoga mat that her mother had rolled up behind the door and took another breath. She crossed her legs, straightened her spine, and closed her eyes as her shoulders relaxed.

"Hola, Savannah," her mother said from her seated position next to the bed.

Savannah blinked and glanced at her out of the corner of her eye. *She's so strong and beautiful. I wonder if I'll ever be as beautiful as Mami. Even sitting here meditating, she looks like a vision.*

She glanced at her mother's baggy white linen pants, cinched around her tiny waist by a sparkly gold belt, and her white camisole. She wore a loose white button-up shirt over her top, its sleeves pushed up to her elbows, and her dark brown curls loose down her back. Several thin gold bracelets, which Savannah knew usually jangled with her every move, were silent as she remained still and focused.

"Hola, Mami," she whispered. "Sorry, I thought I was quiet enough that you wouldn't hear me."

A smile played at her mother's lips. "I didn't," she said. "But you're my daughter. I'm one hundred percent in tune with you. I always know when you're near."

Savannah sighed and closed her eyes again. Her arms fell loose and the backs of her hands rested against the cool hardwood floor. They remained silent for several beats. The only noise in the room came from the stereo.

"What's the matter, sweetheart?" her mother asked after another long moment. Or maybe it was many moments; Savannah was never sure when she was meditating. "I can sense that you're bothered. How was your game?"

Savannah breathed in deeply through her nose and let her breath expel slowly before answering. "We lost."

"That's okay," her mother said. "As long as you tried your best and had fun. I'm sorry we didn't make it to this one."

"It's fine," Savannah said. "I know you and Dad had a lot to do to get ready for the meeting with Chris tomorrow. I still can't believe Dad's old manager's son is interested in representing me after graduation."

"That shouldn't surprise you," she said calmly. "You've worked so hard. It's only natural that you'll need a business representative as you pursue pro ball prospects after graduation."

Savannah swallowed hard.

"Are you excited to have the team over tonight?" her mother asked. "You remember what I said, right? Absolutely no funny business, Savy. Partners are allowed, but no sneaking off to bedrooms. No drinking…"

Savannah would have rolled her eyes had they not been closed in meditation. "Yes, Mami, I know," she said pointedly. "The whole team would be in big trouble if any of us were caught doing anything like that, especially since the freshmen and sophomores aren't twenty-one yet. No one is going to risk what's left of our season."

Her mother breathed in deeply and pressed her fingertips lightly together at her heart. "Yes, because I would drag you on that plane with us right back to Arizona."

Savannah giggled. "No, you wouldn't."

She smiled. "You're right," she said. "I wouldn't. But you'd be in such big trouble, it wouldn't even be funny. You wouldn't have a shred of a social life left because I'd find a way to ground you even across the country."

"I don't anyway," Savannah couldn't help herself. "Not since transferring here for my senior season, at least. But don't worry, Mami. The girls and I won't get you and Papa into trouble."

"I know you won't, sweetheart," her mother said. She bowed her head for a moment, her fingertips still pressed together at her heart. With a deep, satisfactory sigh, she unfolded her legs and blinked. "I've never had to worry about you doing things behind my and your papa's backs. And what do you mean by no social life? You've adapted so well since transferring. You're always hanging out with the team. If that's what you call no social life..."

Savannah stretched and stood. She was already four inches taller than her mother. *I definitely got my height from Papa.*

"I know," she sighed. "It's just so different here than it was in Tempe. People are different."

Her mother embraced her tightly. "I know," she said gently. "But the more people you meet, the more places you see, the larger your world view will be. And the wider your heart will stretch. That will be important, given the options I expect Chris to present to us as far as your post-college opportunities. Besides, I'm proud of you how you've adapted to Northwoods this year, Savy." She knelt to gently roll her yoga mat. "You have something special inside you that makes everyone see your light and want to flock to you. You've always made friends so easily."

Savannah frowned at her bare feet. "If that's so true, then why does the starting point guard on the basketball team hate me so much? It's, like, from the first day of training camp, she made up her mind that she can't stand me."

She followed her mother back into the large, open kitchen, where she began slicing fresh fruit and measuring cups of organic juice from the refrigerator.

"If she didn't like you, why would she stay and play with you all season instead of entering the transfer portal before the deadline? She's the captain, no?" she asked. "Sweetheart, you're a basketball natural. I never expected my child to be one of the top recruited high school prospects to Arizona State, but you have a gift. You've been playing since you could walk. And playing *exceptionally*, I might add."

"Technically, she isn't the captain," Savannah corrected herself. "Coach Hanlon doesn't believe in that. She says it creates an unnecessary hierarchy or something."

Her mother nodded as she pressed a button on a tall blender and the machine whirred to life. "Good coach."

Savannah shrugged and watched as the chunks of fruit and ice blended together until only pink-orange liquid spun inside the thick pitcher. "Emersyn is clearly the leader of the pack," she said. "Or she was. I can tell she dislikes me. It exudes from her. The way she looks at me…" she trailed off as she remembered the electric intensity in Emersyn's eyes earlier in the locker room. "It seems so painful for her to talk to me, but she likes everyone else on the team just fine."

"Maybe she feels threatened by you," her mother said. She stood on her tiptoes and pulled three tall glasses from a dark wood cabinet near the fridge. "Especially if she was the leader for three years and then here you come. And you're *so* good on the court…" She took a long sip of her smoothie. "And you just have a way with people, Savy. You make friends quickly and they enjoy your company. It sounds to me like Emersyn Tanner is jealous, plain and simple."

"Jealous of what?" Savannah said. She glanced down at the smoothie that her mother quietly pushed toward her. "Jealous of the fact that I left Tempe the summer before my senior year of college for a fresh start not for my basketball career…" she threw air quotes around the word "career." "… as I let everyone assume. No, because my heart got so shattered by Thalia that I couldn't possibly focus on my final season of college ball there so long as she was nearby. I said good-bye to the friends I'd known all of college to come to Northwoods, Wisconsin, and, come *on*, it's freezing half the year here…"

Her mother chuckled as she leaned back against the sink and watched Savannah for a moment. "Sweetheart, you're the new girl on the team and they thought they lost their chance to recruit you nearly four years ago. Of course they're flocking to you," she said. "Besides, you'll always have a home base in Arizona. Since your father came out of retirement to be a seasonal consultant for the men's baseball team at Southern Arizona, we'll be keeping roots there. You know ever since your papa retired from the MLB, he's been itching to do *something*."

Savannah took a small sip of her smoothie. *God, that's good.* She took another sip. "At least *his* dreams are coming true all over again," she said. "Who knows what Chris thinks my realistic prospects are after graduation. I'm sure it'll mean going overseas for a few years, but I hope at least *one* of the semi-decent EuroLeague teams or someone from the Australian WNBL will be interested in a workout."

Heavy footsteps on the hardwood floor stilled and Savannah turned just in time to see her father run a hand through his shaggy black hair as he dropped his gym bag on the floor with a soft thud. He was tall, muscular, and the dark five o'clock shadow that always seemed to dust his sharp profile could make him appear intimidating, if not for his smiling brown eyes and goofy personality. He had always been a big Puerto Rican teddy bear to Savannah.

"That gym off Main Street isn't bad," he said. "Got a guest pass for the weekend." He glanced at Savannah. "Still going on about Thalia, I hear?"

He grinned and planted a quick kiss on her mother's lips as she handed him a smoothie. "Thank you, amor."

Savannah grimaced at her parents' affection and examined her short fingernails instead. "Sometimes I still think about her, Dad."

"Yeah, I can tell," he said. He pulled out a stool at the marble-topped breakfast bar and took a long swallow of his smoothie. "No one here has caught your eye all year? No girls at all?"

Savannah stared at the shining hardwood beneath her feet and chewed the inside of her cheek. Emersyn's shimmery blond hair and tentative smile flashed in her mind and she felt her heart beat a little faster at the idea of that smile one day being just for her. She thought of their last practice before this afternoon's disastrous game. Emersyn had raced up and down the court and dribbled the ball around bright orange cones at measured zig-zag intervals with practiced ease. Her shoulder-length hair had loosened from its tight ponytail and her smooth, toned calf muscles were on full display as she tore around each one. Pieces of her hair had fallen around her face as she expertly elevated into a mid-range jump shot and completed the exercise. Her unguarded smile lit up her face as the ball swished gently through the net.

Smiling looks good on her. Really good. She swallowed hard. *But she'll never look like that in front of me, not on purpose anyway.* While the idea of Emersyn submitting to her, letting Savannah claim her, and allowing her guards to drop completely caused a tantalizing spark to course through her, she also knew the reality of the situation. *I couldn't make her guards drop no matter how hard I try.*

The thought hurt more than Savannah expected. She pushed her glass forward on the counter resolutely and turned. "Nope," she said quickly. "No one."

Her father smiled broadly. "Good!" he said loudly. Savannah knew her protective papa was only partially kidding. "I can rest easy for a while. At least until Chris tells us where you're off to next. Can't put too many shocks to an old man's system all at once."

Savannah rolled her eyes. "You really think there will be that many options?"

He grinned as he pulled her mother onto his lap. "I know it," he said. "Remember his pops? Mr. Walter? He managed me for nine of my twelve years in the MLB. Made the GM for the Diamondbacks up his offer for my first free agency when he got the Dodgers to send an offer sheet on the first day. He's retired, but Chris took over the sports management business. They're looking to build long-term, homegrown relationships with up-and-coming clients. He really liked what he saw from you at Arizona State, and Walter personally reached out to me from whatever California beach house he's lying around in now to inquire about setting up a meeting between us and Chris."

Savannah took a deep breath. Three p.m. tomorrow. *Two hours to map out the rest of my life. Or at least the next few years.* "I'll be ready," she said. "What are you and Mom doing tonight?"

Her parents exchanged a smile. "We're going to that steakhouse for dinner and drinks later," her father said. "Hopefully, she doesn't make me stop by a yoga studio on the way back to work it all off…"

Her mother burst into laughter and Savannah took that as her cue to leave. "You guys are weird." She threw the parting shot over her shoulder as she hoisted her gym bag over her shoulder and padded down the hallway. "I'm going to shower while I'm here. The water pressure in my on-campus apartment sucks."

"*You're* weird," her father said jokingly. "And go wash that basketball stench off you. I could smell the sweat and heartache all the way from the front door!"

Savannah rolled her eyes again as she closed the bathroom door behind her. She gently twisted the faucet and held a finger beneath the gentle spray that cascaded from the stainless steel shower head to test the water temperature. As she began undressing, she glanced at a decorative mirror neatly hung over a long custom-carved wood vanity. She was pleasantly surprised to see she looked cheerful again.

Sure, our game sucked. And Emersyn still drives me absolutely crazy, even though she hates me for no reason whatsoever. But nothing a little quiet meditation and one of Mom's fresh fruit smoothies can't fix.

Savannah felt better as she turned to the deep soaking tub beneath the shower.

"I am seriously married to the most beautiful woman alive!" Her father's booming voice was filled with unbridled enthusiasm as it echoed down the hallway and beneath the crack under the bathroom door. "Woman, you are amazing. This is by far the best smoothie you've ever made."

Savannah laughed to herself as she pulled the shower curtain swiftly shut. "What a dork," she said to herself.

Okay, okay. I could've gotten stuck with a lot worse when it comes to parents. I'll miss them a lot wherever I go this fall. She took a deep breath and tried to ignore the tiny sliver of doubt that cut through her chest at the thought.

If *I go overseas after graduation...But why wouldn't I?* Savannah stuck out her chin defiantly as she tilted her head back beneath the warm spray. *Whatever. I'm twenty-two now and these have been my dreams since I was a kid. It's up to me and only me to make them happen.*

Chapter Five

Savannah leaned back against the jets of the outdoor Jacuzzi centered beneath a wooden pergola. The sun had begun to set, and the northern Wisconsin temperature was already dipping close to near freezing. Still, the back patio of the cabin provided a stunning view of the late winter sunset along the flat, tree-lined horizon and she was warm beneath the frothy bubbles. An ethereal layer of steam floated above the hot water as Erica playfully splashed her girlfriend Kayla at the other side of the Jacuzzi. Arissa Johnson, fully dressed in a thick hoodie and blue jeans, had taken over the large grill on the other side of the patio and was focused on flipping the burgers that sizzled against the iron grate.

Savannah glanced up expectantly as Mia DiCorro settled into the Jacuzzi next to her. "Thanks for having us over," she said with a smile. "Well, thanks to your parents for letting us trespass into their vacation rental, I guess." She laughed. "Your dad was an Arizona Diamondback, right? *So* cool."

Savannah nodded as she tightened her ponytail. The ends of her hair floated along the warm water as she adjusted her position against the jets. "Thank you," she said. "He played with them for all twelve seasons of his career. I don't remember a time when he *wasn't* a Diamondback. I miss Arizona a lot, but I've had a great time in Wisconsin."

"It's a lot different than Arizona," Erica said. She stretched her long, lean legs over her girlfriend's lap before glancing at Mia. "Did you hear back from Em?"

Mia shook her head. "I checked my phone a few times before getting in the hot tub, but she hadn't responded. That's to be expected these days."

Erica shook her head as a few braids fell over her shoulder. "Good," she said. "I'm really mad at her. She hasn't been the same since…Well, the accident. And after what she pulled at the end of the game today, I don't care to see her tonight."

Arissa sighed as she flipped another beef patty on the grill. "I know you're pissed at her, E," she said. "We've known Emersyn for years. You know that isn't who she really is. She's frustrated me too this season, but I try to put myself in her position and imagine the heartache she's experiencing. And you know what? It reminds me to be nicer."

Erica sighed and glanced quickly at Savannah. "What do you think?" she asked. "You're the one she wouldn't let take the final shot, after all."

Savannah had been watching the exchange quietly and curiously. "I, um…" She sighed. "I don't know Emersyn like you girls do. I guess if Arissa says she used to be different, then I have to believe that."

Mia gasped and threw a wet hand over her mouth, nearly smacking Ryan in the face in the process. "Wait a second!" she said. "You don't really know about the accident, do you?"

"She doesn't," Arissa said. "Nothing personal, Savannah. It really feels like you've been part of the team since freshman year. I always forget that you only transferred to Northwoods last summer."

Savannah smiled. *I like that.* "Thank you, but…" She shook her head. "If it's something Emersyn wouldn't want anyone to know, you don't have to tell me. I just know what everyone else outside Northwoods does. A really bad freak car accident. A broken femur and back spasms that kept her out her entire junior season."

Arissa cleared her throat. "It really broke Emersyn in more ways than one," she said. "How many burgers, Savannah? I've got a bunch almost ready."

Savannah glanced up and blinked. "Oh!" she said. "Um, I'm actually a pescatarian. I have a salad in the refrigerator." She nodded toward the back door of the cabin.

Arissa looked momentarily confused. "Then why…" She shrugged. "Whatever floats your boat. But hey, thanks for letting us cook out since you don't eat red meat."

Savannah forced a smile. *Why* would *someone who doesn't eat red meat get hot dogs and hamburgers for a team get-together? Maybe it had to do with the fact that I overheard Erica and Emersyn talking about their favorite burgers at practice two weeks ago. I thought Emersyn could see*

I'm not this awful person she thinks I am. I should have known she wouldn't show up.

"I'll fill you in," Erica said. She slipped an arm around her girlfriend's shoulders and sighed. "The accident changed Emersyn as a person. She used to be so full of life and she had, like, this endless Energizer Bunny energy. We played in AAU together in high school and she was always one of those people laughing, smiling, social. I'm not from the best neighborhood in Milwaukee. I didn't think we had anything in common. But damn if she didn't befriend me and drag me out of my shell after I moved up here for the AAU club." Erica shook her head ruefully. "Even then, she always had guys from the boys' teams all over her, but she never really went out with any of them. She was about basketball and school, and we all looked up to her. She had it together. Got accepted here on a full-ride scholarship as the local hometown hero, you know?"

"And what happened?" Savannah asked cautiously. She swirled her foot beneath the water and slowly circled the tip of her finger around a bubble that had settled near her arm.

An uncomfortable silence settled over them as a chilly breeze swept through the patio. The girls looked between each other and Savannah with varying degrees of pity and sympathy.

Mia finally shrugged. "Let's acknowledge the elephant in the room, girls," she said. "It's not like Em is going to tell Savannah herself."

Savannah's relaxed feeling instantly disappeared. "I don't understand what I ever did to her."

Arissa rolled her eyes as she joined them and leaned her elbows casually on the Jacuzzi ledge. "It's not you, Savannah," she said confidently. "You two are actually kind of alike. I'm sure if she knew you as a person, you would be really tight with each other. It's *her*. She's been through so much in the last year. And you're easily the best basketball player that Northwoods College has had since, well…*her*."

"I don't want a competition between teammates," Savannah said quickly. "The competition should be saved for opposing teams, not her and I. I play because it's fun and I love it. The last thing I want is to make Emersyn feel worse. That's not what basketball is about."

Erica sighed. "There must've been something in the desert air," she said jokingly. "You really are that kind and compassionate, aren't you?"

Savannah shrugged and glanced down at her lap. *Only when it comes to Emersyn. For whatever reason.* "I don't see the point in being catty or dramatic. It's not me."

"With Emersyn, it's crazy how quickly her life changed, you know?" Mia said. "I mean, we made it to March Madness our freshman and sophomore years. She was getting noticed by some of the bigger sports journalists and bloggers. It was like a dream come true for her and it was exciting for all of us."

"Emersyn's mom was pretty sick with the flu for a few days," Arissa said. "It was right in the middle of training camp and she had practice and then a biology lecture. It was late when she took her mom to the doctor. They were on the way and there's this intersection where the highway meets the main street into Northwoods. The light was red and Em stopped. She did everything right. This elderly driver had a massive stroke while behind the wheel, blew the light, lost control of his truck, and T-boned them on the passenger's side. Totaled their car. She and her mom had to be rushed to the hospital by ambulance. They were both unconscious."

"Oh my God, that's horrible!" Savannah said. The pieces were beginning to fall into place. *And because of her injuries...*

"She lost her scholarship," Arissa said sadly. "Some stupid catastrophic injury clause buried at the back of the contract she'd signed. *And* her representation. Anyway, no other college expressed interest in her entering the transfer portal for a new scholarship. They had all written her off and were convinced she wouldn't return to basketball. So, she stayed here and took out student loans. Worked her ass off to prove everyone wrong, including herself."

"No wonder Northwoods was so eager for my transfer," Savannah said as she chewed the inside of her cheek. "And I was so wrapped up…" she sighed as Thalia's face flashed through her mind. "In my own shit that I didn't think twice about it, because it was far away from Arizona and one of the most highly regarded programs in the Midwest."

Erica shook her head. "Don't blame yourself," she said. "Em knows how to be a better sport than that. She just…She has a lot going on, you know? Her mom lost her job. Nancy's right hip shattered and she fractured her pelvis in two places. The damage has made it really hard for her to walk because it's caused a lot of issues, especially with her right leg. Her dad left when she was young. He hasn't been in the picture in almost two decades. Emersyn had the broken femur that took her out for an entire season, but she also had minor damage to a few discs in her spine and that's been giving her back spasms lately. That accident changed everything for her, her life, her future, everything. She just hasn't been the same happy person the rest of us have known and loved."

Savannah's heart went out to her as she thought of the bright future she had no doubt been excited for and the crushing aftermath of the accident. As a fellow athlete, she knew it must have shattered Emersyn. "It sounds like her life really took an unfair turn," she finally said.

"She blames herself for her mom's injuries," Erica said. She stepped out of the Jacuzzi and wrapped a towel around herself as water poured down her legs and pooled around her feet. "Of course, she never talks to us about anything. Even me. I was only her best friend, you know?" Savannah couldn't help but detect the obvious hurt in Erica's voice. "The only person she confides anything to is Coach Hanlon. They've always been close. Coach Hanlon has mentored Em since high school."

Savannah nodded as she digested it all. *To go from hometown golden child and basketball phenom to discarded and broken, with an uncertain future. No wonder she's disillusioned with the world.* "I'm sure it broke her heart," she said carefully.

And God, what I wouldn't do to put it back together again, to feel her open herself to me.

Savannah blinked as Arissa glanced at her. "And now you know," she said. "Just understand that Emersyn wasn't always the way she is now. I really hope she comes back."

Mia leaned toward Arissa and grinned. "She will," she said. "She's strong. Little, but vicious."

The girls laughed as Ryan pulled Mia onto his lap with one arm and reached for his bottle of Sprite with the other. "Yo, how about those burgers?" he said. "I'm starving."

As the conversation shifted, Savannah stood and braced herself against the rush of frigid late winter air that clung to her wet skin. She wrapped a thick cotton towel around herself and tried not to notice that the goose bumps along her forearms didn't disappear as Emersyn's stoic face and soft, pouted lips flashed in her mind.

"I'm hopeless," she said to herself as she hopped in three quick jumps to the back door to grab her salad. Still, she smiled to herself as she considered the whole new perspective she had gained on Emersyn Tanner.

❖

Emersyn sat casually in the bleachers during Tuesday's afternoon practice and squinted across the gymnasium. She watched quietly as the team dribbled basketballs around cones that had been strategically placed up and down the court. As she leaned back against the riser above her and casually rested her elbows along the ledge, she silently marveled over how different practice sounded from the bench. The thud of basketballs and the squeak of shoes against hardwood seemed further away than usual and she couldn't quite make out the advice and exclamations of her teammates as they focused on their ball handling drills. Coach Hanlon sat at her left and furiously scribbled notes onto her clipboard. Emersyn glanced up every now and then to watch her teammates and wrapped the hoodie she wore over her jersey tighter around her. The cavernous gymnasium was chilly when you weren't running and jumping, she had realized, and the frigid late winter air from outside seeped in through thin cracks under the exit doors.

Emersyn's gaze shifted to Savannah, who was racing up the court with her back to the bleachers. Her long, dark ponytail streamed behind her as she expertly dribbled between and around her ankles. Emersyn couldn't help but notice the smooth muscles of her tanned thighs peeking from beneath her white practice shorts.

Her thighs are practically glowing against those shorts. Emersyn blinked. *Whatever. She needs to work on her mechanics. She may be fast and she may be good on the dribble, but speed can be just as much of a curse as it is a blessing. If she doesn't know how to use it to her advantage, she'll get tripped up.*

Coach Hanlon stood and clapped her hands together twice. "All right, great job, girls!" she said. "I know it's getting late, so let's take a few more minutes and call it a day. Line up. I want each of you to take the ball through the cones and shoot it when you reach the basket. Wherever your ideal spot may be. Try to get through the course and make as many baskets as you can in the next ten minutes."

The girls stopped dribbling and trudged over to where Coach Hanlon had asked Emersyn to line up a zigzag of bright orange cones at the other end of the court. Emersyn watched silently as Savannah walked slowly to the beginning of the course, one hand on her hip. Her neck was slick with heat and sweat, and Emersyn found herself studying the way Savannah's slender fingers curled around her hip.

"Tanner, how was your weekend?" Coach Hanlon's conversational tone jolted Emersyn back into the present. "I take it you didn't see the team after Saturday's game?"

Emersyn shook her head. "I had to get home and make sure Mom ate," she said. "The doctors have her on a new pain medication that's messing up her sleeping patterns. By the time we finished dinner, I was ready for bed."

Coach Hanlon nodded after a moment. "I see," she said. "And how is your mom doing these days?"

Emersyn shifted on the bleacher. "She's in a lot of pain," she said. "The doctors keep switching out her medications and it's taking a toll. They're trying to alleviate her discomfort, but she's had some weird side effects with some of them. I guess they haven't really found the perfect combination yet. She's trying to find a job, you know, but it's been hard…" Emersyn let her voice trail off.

Coach Hanlon nodded again. "What about you?" she asked. "You said you wanted to talk about something today?"

Emersyn sighed and ran a hand through her hair in frustration. She couldn't remember the last time it had been down and around her shoulders, clean and sweat-free, at practice. "I don't know who else to talk to," she said. "I don't even know where to begin."

"I want you and any of the team to feel that it's okay to reach out," Coach Hanlon said. She folded her arms over her chest and glanced at Emersyn. "Talking to someone about things that are troubling you isn't a sign of weakness. It's a sign of maturity. The world isn't against you, Tanner."

Emersyn absent-mindedly scratched her knee. "It sure feels like it is," she said. "And I don't just mean the accident, although the fact that graduation is looming and everyone is off to a new life and career while I'm stuck here does weigh heavily. Let's face it, Northwoods isn't exactly Europe, Australia, New Zealand, or even one of the coasts."

"Northwoods isn't a death sentence, Tanner," Coach Hanlon said gently. "Maybe you would have gone on to play professionally. I have no doubt that you have the talent. But maybe you wouldn't have. Maybe, after a few years, you would have gone on to explore other talents or pursue paths elsewhere. You're twenty-two, Tanner. You have a long life ahead and you can't spend it dwelling on the unknown. You'll drive yourself mad."

Emersyn considered this. *Haven't I been feeling like I'm on the verge of moving permanently to Looney Land lately? Maybe she's on to something. Maybe I need to figure out how to let go of professional basketball. Try to understand how to be okay with my future being wide open for possibilities.*

"There's so many unknowns right now," Emersyn said. "I like knowing where my life is going and how it's going to get there. Basketball has been the plan since I was a kid and I've never deviated from that. I never even considered the need for a Plan B, C, or D." She sighed. "I wish I could look into a crystal ball and see my future. I think I'd be a lot more comfortable knowing that everything will end up okay."

Coach Hanlon scribbled a quick note onto her clipboard and smiled. "That's life, Tanner," she said. "Things happen as they should. It isn't perfect, but it's made for a few bumps in the road. You're a smart kid with a good head on her shoulders. I know you'll be okay."

Emersyn digested this as Coach Hanlon stood and cupped her hands around her mouth. "Erica, that was an excellent block on Mia's layup!" she shouted. "You timed that perfectly."

"There's more..." Emersyn hedged as Coach Hanlon sat and placed her clipboard at her side.

Emersyn took a deep breath. *I can't keep holding onto this secret without telling a soul. Not with everything else that's going on.*

"I...I think I'm a..." Emersyn sighed. *Spit it out! You're a...* "Lesbian," Emersyn finally blurted out. She closed her eyes and felt a rush of pride at saying it out loud. "I'm gay and I've known forever. I told myself that I was going to come out before graduation. And then everything happened and it went to the back of my mind for a while. But sometimes it feels like it's burning inside of me and it's one more thing that I'm sick of keeping inside..."

The words tumbled out, one after the other, as Emersyn tried to explain. "I just...nobody knows and..."

"Are you okay with it?" Coach Hanlon's thoughtful, gentle question quieted Emersyn. "Are you comfortable with yourself and this realization?"

Emersyn cocked her head in thought and finally nodded. "I think so," she said. "I've always known. It scares me. It took *so* long to come out to myself and think the words. The thought of telling anyone else is terrifying."

Coach Hanlon smiled. "You just did."

Emersyn grinned back. "I guess I did, didn't I?"

"I understand the difficulties, Tanner," Coach Hanlon said. "Believe me, I do. It's a process for everyone and time is the only thing that makes it easier. Some people flow right into accepting themselves and living an out life. Some people take longer, years even, to accept themselves after the realization that they're not straight."

Emersyn kicked her sneaker against the bleacher. "I have to tell my mom." She sighed miserably.

"How do you think she'll react?" Coach Hanlon asked. "She's always seemed to be quite supportive of you. Never missed a game."

Until the accident. She tried to clear the bitter thought from her mind.

"I don't know," she said hesitantly. "She's never said anything derogatory that I can remember. She's not very religious. I honestly don't know and that's hard. At least if I knew she was a homophobe or ultra-accepting then I could mentally prepare myself either way. But this? Not knowing and keeping it inside is making me crazy." She paused. "Crazier than I already feel lately."

Emersyn's gaze gravitated like a magnet to Savannah. She jogged to the back of the line as a satisfied smile played at her lips.

"The way I see it, Nancy is going to have to know at some point," Coach Hanlon said. "Whether you opt to tell her sooner or later, there will be a time in your future when you'll come out. Maybe you'll fall in love, perhaps you'll be outed accidentally, or maybe she starts to figure it out for herself and asks questions. But one day? You're going to have to have a conversation with her. Or what? Live a life you know isn't yours with a man you know you don't love?"

"So maybe sooner is better than later," Emersyn said slowly.

"Not if you're not one hundred percent ready," Coach Hanlon said. "I know you and Nancy are very close. If you're not prepared to deal with any sort of reaction she may have, it may be better to wait until you gain that confidence in yourself."

"I *am* confident," Emersyn said. She crossed her arms and glanced at her before sighing. "Well, most of the time."

"What frightens you most about telling her?"

Emersyn chewed her bottom lip in thought. "I've already lost so much in the last couple of years," she said honestly. "If I lose my mom too, I think I'll break. I had a taste of it when we were in the accident. I was injured, but she got the worst of it. The thought that I might lose her, even for a second, was the absolute worst feeling I've ever had."

She could feel Coach Hanlon's eyes on her. Coach patted her shoulder affectionately. "You have a good heart, Tanner," she said. "And I promise you have an entire lifetime ahead of you to rebuild, journey, find love, make mistakes, and live. I'm glad to see you're coming back."

Emersyn considered this as Coach Hanlon stood and clapped her hands together again. "All right, girls," she called. "That's a wrap for today. Pack it in and hit the showers. Great practice. I saw each of you playing as a team and recognizing your collective strengths and weaknesses. That's exactly what we need to continue doing."

The sweaty team trudged toward the locker room and Emersyn tried not to stare as Savannah brushed past her. She appeared to be listening quietly as Mia complained about her arm sleeve. She didn't look at Emersyn once.

Coach Hanlon nodded at them as they filed past her. "Remember, the game against UW Superior is this Saturday," she said. "It's on their turf, so let's be suited up and ready to go by seven a.m. Bus leaves here at seven fifteen sharp. We may not be competing with the best of the best in Tampa for March Madness this year, but we still take pride in every aspect of our game."

Emersyn stood and began following the team. She turned as Coach Hanlon's voice quieted.

"Oh, and Tanner?" she said. "Let me know how it goes with your mom if you do decide to talk to her. It's important that you have people you feel comfortable speaking with. I'd be happy to sit down with you again if you ever want to chat."

"Thanks, Coach," Emersyn said. "I'll figure it out eventually. I have to, right?" She laughed and turned back to the locker room.

This week. I'll tell Mom this week. She should know and this is one less thing I want to keep inside.

Chapter Six

A few days after her benched practice, Emersyn slipped through the front door of her mother's modest split-level home on the outskirts of Northwoods. She paused, unsure which was more surprising—the mouth-watering scent of something being sautéed in garlic and olive oil or the sight of her mother humming happily over the stove to a Van Halen song on the radio.

"Mom?" she asked in confusion. Emersyn walked slowly into the tiled kitchen and glanced at the large tilapia sizzling in a shallow pan. "What are you doing?"

Her mother smiled and rolled her eyes. "Goodness, Em, I may be injured but I'm not completely feeble. I got tired of sitting around this house all day and decided to do something about it. I'm making a special dinner for us."

Emersyn wrinkled her nose. "Why?"

Her mother sighed and leaned heavily on her bamboo cane. "Why not? You're too young to be worrying all the time, Emersyn. There was a sale on tilapia at the store, so I asked our neighbor down the street, you know, Gunther?"

Emersyn nodded.

"Well, you know ever since the accident, he's been kind enough to ask me if there's anything he can bring back from the store for me after his morning stock shifts," she said. "Usually, I tell him no, because I hate to be a bother. But today I decided we're having those fish, so I asked Gunther to bring me back two of the biggest, fattest fish he could find. I already paid him for them, so I don't want to hear another thing about it." She appeared pleased with herself. "With some garlic, butter, olive oil, and just a tiny squeeze of lemon, it'll be like eating out at a fancy restaurant. I used to cook for us all the time, sweetheart. Don't tell me you forgot already."

Emersyn smiled despite her concern that her mother could hurt herself by standing over the hot stove. She glanced again at the pan as melted butter ran down the sides of the nearly translucent fish. "Of course I remember," she said. "You're an amazing chef. Dinner smells wonderful."

"I hope you worked up a good appetite after practice," her mother said. "This fish is going to be divine."

Emersyn opened and then closed her mouth. She decided against telling her mother that she had, in fact, worked up an appetite, especially after being benched for the team's practice earlier in the week and feeling today's a little extra as a result. "I did," she said. "I'm glad you're feeling well today."

Her mother's pale blond hair was rapidly fading to a shining silver, but had been tied back into a neat French braid. Her blue eyes shone with mirth and her skin looked brighter, with less saggy pockets and dark shadows hiding the natural angles of her face.

Emersyn glanced from her mother to the table. It was already set. *Great. The one day that Mom decides to make a special dinner is the same day I'm going to ruin by coming clean about being gay.* She looked over her shoulder at her mother as she happily squeezed a lemon wedge over the fish. Emersyn wondered if she'd still look as carefree after she told her.

"I wanted to ask," her mother said absent-mindedly. She twisted the oven burner off and poked at one of the fish with her spatula. "How's this last semester going?"

Emersyn stiffened as she slid into a chair at the table. "Fine," she said evasively. "Just ready for the season to be over and to get through finals."

Emersyn's mother fixed her with a look as she transferred one of the tilapia to a plate. "I know the basketball season hasn't gone the way you'd hoped," she said. "But you came back and showed everyone that you're still a gifted player."

Emersyn shrugged as her mother sat heavily at the table. "I'm definitely ready to leave college ball behind me."

Her mother eyed her as she cut into her fish. "And how about the boys?" she said as she took a sip of lemonade. "No special dates lined up? You barely even socialize with the team after games anymore. You haven't gone out at all this year to those bars near campus where you used to go dancing with them."

Emersyn's heart sank. *There it is.* Her appetite seemed to vanish. *Perfect way to bring up what I so desperately need to tell her. No, there's no special dates lined up and definitely not with any guys.*

"I..." She coughed once. She fidgeted on her chair and ignored her heart thumping wildly in her chest as the kitchen suddenly seemed impossibly tiny and hot.

Her mother glanced at her as she carefully blew on a forkful of flaky tilapia. "Is everything all right, honey?" she asked. "I'm getting the feeling you're a bit...out of sorts tonight."

"I'm sorry, I didn't think it would be this difficult to get the words out," Emersyn said. She refused to look at her mother as the nerves threatened to close her throat completely. "I don't know why I'm so nervous."

What if she hates you? The sinister thought was illogical but reared itself anyway as her mother put her fork down and squinted at her. *What if she can't bear to look at you the same way? You're her only child and you're about to disappoint her by coming out of the closet.*

Her mother took a deep breath and her eyes narrowed. "Emersyn, I'm going to ask you flat out."

Emersyn swallowed hard as her mother rubbed her temples gently with her fingertips.

Please don't be mad at me. Please don't be mad at me.

"Are you pregnant?" she asked, her tone hushed.

In the surprised beat of silence that followed, Emersyn was sure she could have heard a pin drop. "What?" She blinked and stared at her mother, dumbfounded.

"Oh God, are you?" Her voice reached a shrill pitch. "Tell me the truth. We can figure it out, sweetheart."

"No," Emersyn said after a moment. "No, I'm not." *She really has no idea.*

"Oh, thank God." She seemed to deflate with relief. "You scared me for a second. I've never seen you so nervous to tell me something. I automatically thought the worst, like you were about to inform me I was going to be a grandmother in nine months." She fixed Emersyn with a warning stare. "Which, by the way, I would love to be one day but not right now. Not when you have your whole life ahead of you. Besides, you want to be financially secure and in a healthy, stable relationship. I wouldn't want my grandchild to struggle the way we have after your dad left."

Emersyn wanted to cry as realization set in. *The idea that I might be gay hasn't even crossed her mind. Coming out is going to be way harder than I thought.*

"I get it," she said. A surge of frustration welled up inside her. "You *really* don't have to worry about it."

Her mother took another bite of tilapia. "Well, what did you want to tell me then?"

Emersyn fought to keep the tears at bay, but her vision blurred anyway. "I, um…" She shrugged. "I forgot. It was probably nothing."

Her mother studied her for a moment. "Are you sure, honey? You seem bothered."

Emersyn tried to blink back the tears as one snaked down her cheek. "You know, everyone keeps asking me the same question," she snapped. "I've heard it from you, Coach Hanlon, Erica, my professors…" She ticked the list of concerned people off on her fingertips. "Everyone around me keeps asking if I'm okay. Telling me I seem upset or not myself or bothered…" More tears slid down her cheeks. "You know what? Sometimes I wish the whole world would just leave me alone!" She gestured wildly around the house. "We're broke. I mean, we've always been broke, but now it's a whole new level of poor. You can't work because of me. I had to take out tens of thousands of dollars in loans just to finish fucking school and get my degree. I'm probably not going to have a pro ball career. This stupid accident has done nothing but ruin my life and yours!"

Her mother's mouth dropped open. Emersyn hated how frail and sad she looked as the cane dangled from the back of her chair. "Em, talk to me," she said, confusion coloring her tone. "What is going on with you?"

Emersyn shook her head and pushed her chair back with a loud screech across the tile. "I need to be alone," she said. She hated that she had still somehow managed to ruin the evening and her mother's upbeat mood. "I'm going to bed."

"You barely touched your fish…" She gestured helplessly with her fork.

"Just…Just reheat it for lunch tomorrow," Emersyn said. "I have that game in Superior, so I won't be around. I need to be alone."

Emersyn turned and took the carpeted steps two at a time until she reached her bedroom door. She closed it behind her and squeezed her eyes shut, allowing the avalanche of emotion to overcome her. She slid down the door slowly until she collapsed onto the worn carpet and buried her face in her hands to muffle her sobs.

After a moment, she glanced up at a framed photo on her messy dresser across the room. She and the team grinned, their arms slung around each other's necks and their royal blue jerseys wrinkled after an especially grueling practice, and their faces shone with excitement. Emersyn remembered that afternoon. It was right after Coach Hanlon had shared that they'd officially been chosen in the Sunday Selection and would be playing March Madness in San Antonio that season.

"Whoever said that college is some of the best years of your life was definitely wrong," Emersyn said. She swiped at her eyes. "Being twenty-two sucks."

❖

Early the next morning, Emersyn stared out the window as thick snowflakes fluttered from the sky and sparkled beneath the streetlights before gently landing along the sidewalk. It was still dark outside, but she wasn't sure if it was because of the morning snow or because she was awake an hour early.

She glanced over her shoulder at her mother's bedroom door. It was still shut tightly and there had been no sound of her alarm clock yet, though Emersyn knew one of her pain medications continued to wreak havoc on her sleeping patterns.

Emersyn chewed the inside of her cheek as she pulled up the hood of her sweatshirt. *I can't face Mom. Not after last night.* She slowly hoisted her oversized gym bag and quietly opened the front door.

"This is going to be a seriously wet walk," Emersyn said as she shut the door behind her and locked it carefully. An icy breeze rattled through the tall birch trees dotting the neighborhood. She shivered against an especially strong gust of wind as she ducked her head and walked quickly down the sidewalk.

This sucks. Emersyn ignored the small drifts that had already accumulated along the edges of the concrete. *This...sucks. This...sucks.*

As she reached the corner of the main intersection into her neighborhood, she blinked as a large snowflake landed with a wet plop onto her cheek. She lifted her gloved hand to wipe it away as a loud horn startled her into the present. Emersyn squinted at the black pickup truck that pulled over and slowed to a stop.

Coach Hanlon leaned over the passenger seat and rolled down the window. "Tanner, what the hell are you doing out in this?" she said. "Get your ass in the truck right now."

Emersyn hopped into the passenger's seat, eager for the shelter. "Morning, Coach," she greeted her . "Lovely early March morning in the upper Midwest, huh?"

Coach Hanlon eased the truck back into 4-wheel drive and fixed her with a sidelong look. "And of all mornings, this is the one you chose to walk to the gym?"

Emersyn sighed as she settled back against the warm leather seat. "Things didn't go so well with my mom last night."

"Oh?" she asked. "Do you want to talk about it?"

Emersyn rolled her eyes as she gazed at the dashboard. "There's not much to talk about," she said. "She assumed I was hiding a pregnancy when I told her I wanted to tell her something. The thought that I might be gay really hasn't even occurred to her."

"Then what happened?" Coach Hanlon said. She turned the truck into the gymnasium's vast parking lot, already covered in a thin layer of white. Emersyn watched as a few cars paused in front of the large concrete steps to drop off other student athletes with Saturday games.

"I kind of flipped out," Emersyn said. She stared down at her lap. "We're not really talking at the moment."

"Kind of flipped out?" Coach Hanlon repeated incredulously.

Emersyn grimaced. "Okay, I *really* flipped out," she said. "I think I scared her. I just...I wish I could talk to my mom like I can talk to you. I'm terrified of hurting her and I can't even think about losing her. She doesn't understand what's going on. And I don't want to stress her more than she already is."

Coach Hanlon appeared to think as she pulled a worn Milwaukee Bucks baseball cap over her head and turned off the truck. "You're letting too much eat at you, Tanner."

She exited the truck and Emersyn followed her lead. She waited politely for her coach to continue and glanced at her over the bed of the truck. Coach Hanlon was looking across the parking lot at the drop-off area. Emersyn followed her gaze and her mouth dropped open at the sleek red BMW screeching to a sliding stop. Whoever was driving clearly didn't get the memo about how to navigate through fresh snow.

Savannah stepped out from the passenger's seat and slung her gym bag over her shoulder. Emersyn watched as Mia waved to her from beneath a long overhang at the gym's double-door entrance.

"Hey, Savannah!" Mia called. "Loving this weather?"

Savannah grinned. "It's a little different than the desert."

"Savy!" a woman's voice called from the BMW. It was then that Emersyn realized what, or rather *who*, had caught Coach Hanlon's attention. A short, lean woman stepped carefully from the driver's seat and held a fashion magazine over her head to protect her dark, glossy curls from the falling snow. "Darling, have a great game. Be safe."

Savannah turned and smiled, despite the faint color that brushed her cheeks. "Thank you, Mami," she said. "I should say the same for you, driving back to the cabin in this. Be careful in this rental. I hope the flight back to Phoenix doesn't get cancelled for you and Papa."

She's beautiful. God, if that's what Savannah is going to look like in twenty-something years? Then her future husband... Emersyn's neck flushed. *Or wife...will be one lucky person.*

It occurred to Emersyn that she had never heard Savannah mention an interest one way or the other and that she had never seen either of Savannah's parents before. Her mother was small, toned, and impossibly youthful.

"Noon." Lisa Sanchez nodded. "That's when we're supposed to be taking off, but I wouldn't be surprised if we're delayed. I'll keep in touch. I love you, sweetheart. Have a great game, girls!" She addressed the last part to the small group of teammates waiting for Savannah around the front steps. As she waved, dozens of thin gold bracelets clinked together on her wrists and Emersyn was sure she spotted a French manicure.

She tried not to think about how cute Savannah's blush was as it deepened. Her mother had the same wide, easy grin that Savannah did and her forehead was smooth and free of lines that Emersyn assumed had been expertly Botoxed away in some chic desert med-spa.

"Love you too, Mami," Savannah said as she trudged up the steps. The BMW started toward the parking lot's exit and Emersyn watched as the red sports car disappeared over a hill in the distance.

She turned back to Savannah as she and Coach Hanlon side-stepped snow drifts through the parking lot. "Wow," Emersyn said. She didn't even realize she had spoken out loud until Coach Hanlon took a deep breath.

"Wow," the coach echoed. Emersyn glanced at her and realized she was still glancing over the hill that the little BMW had disappeared over.

Emersyn suppressed a smile. *Who knew? Even Coach Hanlon is human.*

As they approached, Emersyn could hear Arissa asking what everyone was thinking.

"That was your *mom*?" Arissa said loudly.

Savannah shrugged. "Unless my parents aren't telling me something."

Emersyn felt her heart slow and her peripheral vision fade as she caught her teammate's teasing expression.

"Your mom is, like, *really* pretty," Mia gushed. "She seems nice too."

Savannah laughed. "What can I say, she's in her own world most of the time."

The snow fell harder as a drift gently spilled from the edge of the overhang. Mia shrieked and Savannah laughed harder. Emersyn watched as they both sprinted further beneath the protection of the metal roof.

"Hey, Sanchez!" Coach Hanlon said as she and Emersyn reached the concrete steps. Savannah turned at the doors.

"Hey, Coach!" she said. She opened and then closed her mouth before glancing away from Emersyn.

"I had a thought," Coach Hanlon said. "I've been advising Coach Walters on the incoming freshman team for next season. It's getting down to crunch time for her to decide who her starting five should be. You both have contributed so much to this team over the years..."

Emersyn set her jaw and cut in. "No offense, Coach, but the only one who has been on this team for over a year is..."

Coach Hanlon shot her a warning look. "You *both* have contributed so much to this team over the years," she said pointedly. "And I'd really love to pick both your brains on the ride over to Superior. Coach Walters has a pretty good idea of who she wants in her starting five next fall, but I'd like to get your takes on it too. Remember, Northwoods College women's basketball is your legacy you're leaving behind once you graduate."

Emersyn scuffed the toe of her boot against the concrete. *It was supposed to be* my *legacy. Not mine* and *Savannah's*. She thought back to her recent conversations with Coach Hanlon and Erica.

She glanced up and met Savannah's gaze. A slow heat crept through her as they held each other's eyes for a long moment. Her heartbeat quickened as she fought to not look at her full pink lips.

They were right a small voice piped up at the back of her mind. *You should have given Savannah more of a chance instead of shutting her out right away.*

"I think that's a great idea." Emersyn surprised even herself as she rushed to fill the sudden silence. "I think, um, yeah, we could both contribute a lot of thoughts and insights to fine-tune Coach Walters's strategy for next fall…" Emersyn realized she was stumbling over her words but she swallowed and pushed on. "Savannah and I can both spot talent…" She glanced at Savannah again, who was staring at her with what seemed to be a knowing, amused intensity.

"And, um passion," Emersyn continued. *God, where did that come from?* She looked at Savannah again. *Oh. There.* "I think that talent is important, but so is passion. For the game, I mean. And, uh, I think we could help identify those incoming freshmen. With passion *and* talent."

Coach Hanlon opened and then closed her mouth. "I think I got what you're trying to say, Tanner," she said bemusedly. "Why don't we sit together on the bus this morning and talk it over?"

Savannah nodded. "That's fine."

Emersyn's heart was still thumping wildly and she felt electricity working its way up from somewhere deep in her core.

She tried not to stare at Savannah as Coach Hanlon turned and addressed the rest of the team gathered on the wide concrete steps. "Girls, important update," she said and clapped her hands once. "We have a two-hour drive across Wisconsin to UW Superior this morning. I've been watching the weather forecast since last night and been in contact with the athletic director all morning. Right now, we're still playing. Forecast says this snow should clear out by about ten and then we get a break before the winter storm that's predicted to arrive here by six tonight."

"My mom called me all the way from Queens to tell me they're predicting over a foot of snow here," Mia said. "I'm glad my apartment is right behind the gym." She nodded at a nondescript semi-circle of low brick student apartment buildings across Northwoods College's vast soccer fields. "You all are more than welcome to crash at my place later."

Coach Hanlon smiled. "Thanks, Mia, that's a very generous offer," she said and then looked at each of the girls. "Keep that in mind when we get back here after the game. This late-season winter storm tonight is supposed to be bad and what we're getting now is just the prelude. No sense in being at risk if you can spend the night at Mia's."

"Oh, Emersyn," Savannah giggled. "Your tag is sticking straight out."

Goose bumps rose across the back of Emersyn's neck before the flush in her stomach deepened at Savannah's gentle touch. Her fingertips were light but knowing as she tucked the tag of her hooded sweatshirt beneath the thick, warm fabric.

Emersyn realized too late that she had leaned into Savannah's touch as her fingertips seemed to still along her neck. *I don't want her to stop touching me. I'm crushing. Hard. And of all the girls in the world, it has to be on Savannah Sanchez.*

She heard Savannah take a deep, shaky breath and felt her step away as she hugged her black wool peacoat tighter around her. Emersyn was barely paying attention to Coach Hanlon going on about the impending winter storm or the strict time crunch that the game would be on to avoid the team being caught in a blizzard. She hardly registered the sleek white bus with the Northwoods College logo printed proudly across its sides as it pulled up to the curb or her teammates as they nodded along to whatever their lead assistant coach, Jane Connor, had chimed in with. The whole world seemed to blur around her as she turned and met Savannah's gaze. Her expression was intense with something that made Emersyn want to fall to her knees, and she swallowed hard.

Though she tried to recall all the reasons she wasn't supposed to like Savannah, they didn't seem good enough anymore.

"Thank you," she said as she picked up her gym bag and stepped into line with the rest of their teammates. "I didn't realize my tag was out."

With that, Emersyn turned and shuffled toward the bus as the doors swung open with a mechanical whoosh. She could still feel Savannah's gaze burning into her back as she climbed the steps and dropped into an empty seat near the front of the bus.

Let's see if I can make it to Superior without fainting. Or fantasizing about Savannah tearing my sweatshirt over my head and crashing her lips against mine.

Chapter Seven

The game versus UW Superior had started off flowing and cohesive. A sudden synergy seemed to flow through the team as Emersyn easily distributed the ball to her teammates. They ran the same play they'd practiced dozens of times, where Emersyn would sprint toward the basket as though she was going to lay it in and then kick it out at the last second to a wide open Arissa just inside the free throw line or bounce it around her defender to Savannah, who was planted in her favorite spot just outside the arc and on the wing.

By halftime, Emersyn noticed the snow was falling faster. As the rest of the team walked toward the visitor's locker room, Emersyn jogged outside through a heavy door and leaned against the rough brick of the gymnasium. She closed her eyes with a deep, cleansing breath as the frigid air blasted her lungs and she shivered against the thick cotton of her hoodie over her sweat-soaked jersey. Still, she relished the cold air on her face and took another deep breath.

Emersyn blinked as the side door creaked open and Erica glanced at her. "Jesus, Em, it's freezing out here," she said as she rubbed her bare forearms. "Coach wants to have a word with everyone in the locker room before we start the second half. You ready?"

Emersyn nodded and followed Erica into the locker room, glancing at the thick gray clouds hanging in the gloomy sky.

"The blizzard might start before we get out of here," Emersyn said. "It's ugly out there."

Erica laughed. "March in Wisconsin." She shook her head. "I think that's what Coach wants to talk about. It's a shame if we have to wrap early, because this is the first time I can remember all of us playing so well together in a *long* time."

Emersyn nodded her agreement as they lapsed into silence alongside the rest of the team in the locker room. Coach Hanlon held steady at the center and shot a furtive glance at Coach Connor before turning back to the girls.

"All right, ladies, I've spoken to our athletic director and we've been following the winter storm closely throughout the first half," she said. "It's moving a lot faster than the meteorologists expected and it'll be bearing down here in Superior in the next hour or so."

A collective groan rose from the team and Coach Hanlon held up a hand. "We have some options," she said. "There's a clause in the NCAA guidelines that says due to emergency, under which inclement weather would fall, both teams can agree to shorten the game to three quarters instead of four. Whoever wins after the third quarter takes the W. I spoke to Coach Hoffman." She nodded toward the home team's locker room. "She agrees that safety is paramount. She's fine with implementing this clause to make it a rare three-quarter game only. This winter storm is expected to be a beast, ladies. Going against Mother Nature is not something I'm willing to risk. Let's be happy this isn't a playoff game and let's get out there and finish strong, so we can take this W home *safely*."

The team mumbled their agreement and filtered back into the gymnasium. Emersyn grabbed a basketball and tossed up a few practice jump shots. She glanced over at Savannah, who was tying her hair back up into a high ponytail and looked thoroughly uncomfortable.

"First real Wisconsin blizzard, huh?" Erica said jokingly as she walked past Savannah. "Leave it to Coach to scare the crap out of you with all this talk about shortening the game and going against Mother Nature. It won't be that bad, I promise."

Savannah nodded but didn't look entirely convinced. Emersyn took a deep breath, tucking the basketball under her arm, and approached her. *I'm just helping her get her head back in the game, that's all.*

"Catch and shoot," Emersyn said as she bounced the ball to Savannah. "Don't think, just shoot the ball."

Savannah glanced at her in surprise and looked down at the ball hesitantly before arching into a jump shot. It clanged loudly off the rim and she winced as the ball bounced right back into Emersyn's hands.

"It's fine," Emersyn said. "Just get the blood flowing and get back into your rhythm. It's always hard for me after halftime, especially when I'm in my flow state and have to break from it."

She tossed the ball back to Savannah. "Catch and shoot."

Savannah met her eyes for a brief moment and then bounced the ball once before trying a fadeaway jumper. Emersyn didn't miss the smile that played at her lips as the ball rolled around the rim once before dropping through the net.

"See, you got it," Emersyn said. "Try not to think about the blizzard. Coach Hanlon and Coach Connor know what they're doing. If it was really dangerous out, we wouldn't still be here. I've lived in northern Wisconsin my whole life and I've never been stuck in dangerous weather."

Savannah tossed the ball at Emersyn, who bulleted it back to her. "I'm just worried about the long ride back," she said. She watched as the ball sailed through the hoop, barely moving the net. "I thought this morning was bad, but that was just a little of what's coming. Do you think it'll be safe on the bus?"

Emersyn started to answer as she glanced out the large glass window above the gymnasium door. Streams of white swirled to the ground and she couldn't see more than a few feet beyond the thick, fast-moving flakes.

Wow. Emersyn stilled. *Coach Hanlon wasn't kidding about this storm.* She shook her head quickly as she bent to retrieve the basketball. "Wisconsin knows how to prepare for a winter storm," she said as she ignored the visibly worsening weather out the window. "Trust me, you'll be more annoyed than anything that you won't get any sleep tonight because you'll be listening to the plow trucks loudly circling Northwoods all night long."

Emersyn felt a rush of *something* sweet as Savannah finally grinned at her. "I'm just glad my parents got out on their flight home," she said. "There's no way they would've made it out if they had booked anything later."

She was cut off as Coach Hanlon and Coach Connor hurried to their side of the court after speaking animatedly with two referees near the edge of the bleachers. Coach Hanlon clapped her hands together as the sound of chatter and bouncing basketballs faded.

"All right, girls, change of plans," Coach Hanlon said quickly. "The Midwest Conference just put out an official bulletin to all referees in the path of this storm, and I just spoke to the athletic director again. Unfortunately, we'll have to cancel the rest of this game." She paused as another collective groan rose from the team. "I know, I know. I was hoping to get one more quarter in too, but this winter storm is already here. There's no way we can finish this safely, and our safety is my top priority."

"What do we do now?" Mia asked, annoyed. She stared at the basketball between her palms. "Are we getting on the bus right now?"

Coach Hanlon sighed. "Look, I know you're all disappointed," she said. "I am too. We have five minutes to get back into the locker room, change if we need to, and gather our things. I'll share my game notes and some pointers I wanted to bring up once we're on our way back to Northwoods. Let's take five and meet out front. The driver will be doing a headcount and Coach Connor…" She looked around and then shook her head. "Well, I'm not sure where Coach Connor went, but she'll…" she paused again as her lead assistant jogged over to her from the visitor's locker room and spoke quietly into her ear.

Emersyn watched as Coach Hanlon's eyes widened. She opened and then closed her mouth before turning to meet Coach Connor's serious expression. "You're kidding."

Coach Connor shook her head. "Just took another call from the athletic director and I spoke to someone at the sheriff's office to confirm."

The word *sheriff* seemed to get the team buzzing as the girls exchanged furtive glances. Coach Hanlon turned back to them with a heavy sigh. "All right, then," she said quietly to her assistant coach. "I'm not going to argue it. We'll figure it out. You'll start calling around?"

Coach Connor nodded quickly. "Yes, I have a list of nearby places."

Coach Hanlon smiled wearily. "Thank you," she said. She cleared her throat as she addressed the team. "There's been a slight change of plans, but I'll make that announcement once we're all dressed and on the bus." She clapped her hands once. "Come on, let's put some fire under our behinds."

Emersyn stretched her arms over her head as she followed the team back into the visitor's locker room. She glanced over as Savannah fell into stride with her.

"What do you think that was all about?" Savannah said, wrinkling her nose.

Emersyn had a sneaking suspicion that the sheriff had probably put out a bulletin that the roads were unsafe for travel, but it was the last thing she wanted to tell Savannah. "Um," she hedged, cursing herself for being unable to convincingly fib to her. "Maybe one of the Superior girls is in trouble or something?"

Emersyn turned back when she realized that Savannah had stopped, her hand on her hip. "You're totally lying to me."

Emersyn blushed. "You can't possibly tell when I'm…"

She paused as Savannah arched an eyebrow. Her face told Emersyn that she did, in fact, know exactly when she was lying to her.

"Sometimes the county sheriff will put out a warning if they expect the roads to become treacherous or impassable," Emersyn finally said with a sigh. "I mean, it's not always reason to panic…"

"That's what I thought," Savannah said. She took a deep breath and walked into the locker room. "Great. Just lovely."

Before she could think better of it, Emersyn reached out and gently touched Savannah's fingertips. She stilled as Emersyn swallowed at the deep swell of electric energy that rushed through her as her fingertips curled around Savannah's.

"It'll be fine," Emersyn said quietly. "We'll figure it out." She was no longer sure if she was only referring to the blizzard.

Savannah held her gaze for a beat longer before the locker room door opened and the rest of the team spilled into the quiet space. Emersyn dropped her hand as though it burned and glanced quickly at Arissa as she strolled past.

"You better hurry!" she called over her shoulder to Emersyn. "You know Coach Hanlon hates to wait."

"Yeah, plus I want to know what this big, important announcement is," Mia said with a giggle. She grabbed Arissa's shoulder in mock surprise. "Wait, what if we have to sleep on the bus?" She dissolved into loud laughter.

Erica shook her head from where she was changing clothes near her locker. "Oh, *hell* no," she said. "I call dibs on the emergency blanket. The rest of you can dogpile to keep warm."

Laughter floated through the air and by the time Emersyn turned back, Savannah had already slipped down the aisle to her own locker. She gently rubbed her fingertips where they had curled around Savannah's, waves fluttering through her as she recalled the moments just before. Taking a deep breath, Emersyn braced herself for what she anticipated to be a very long, interesting journey back to Northwoods.

Chapter Eight

Savannah plunked into a front seat on the bus and debated if sliding her headphones into her ears for a few minutes of bliss thanks to her mother's meditation playlist was worth Coach Hanlon barking at her to listen up. The soothing music had always been in the background at her house growing up, a soundtrack to her life so far. It relaxed and centered her as the gentle flutes and echoing drums calmed her mind.

I could definitely use some relaxation and centering right about now. Savannah stole another glance out the bus window. She could barely see the cars parked one row over from the bus's designated pickup spot just yards away. Her stomach flipped nervously and she quickly turned away. *This is ridiculous. I'm not scared of anything. And I'm definitely not scared of a stupid snowstorm.*

She glanced up as she sensed someone pause near her seat. Savannah took a deep breath as Emersyn shot her the tiniest hint of a teasing smile. A strange pang ricocheted in her chest. Without a second thought, Savannah quickly scooted closer to the window and patted the vacant space at her side. She hadn't realized she was holding her breath until Emersyn's smile deepened and she plopped down next to her.

"I thought you'd never ask," Emersyn said teasingly as Coach Hanlon and Coach Connor clambered onto the bus behind the last stragglers.

Savannah couldn't resist flirting right back. "I'm glad you decided to sit with me." She arched an eyebrow. "Good choice, Emersyn."

Emersyn's cheeks flushed as she squirmed slightly in her seat. She opened her mouth, but Coach Hanlon cleared her throat loudly from the front of the bus.

"Well, girls, there's no easy way to say this," she said as she drummed her fingers against the metal railing leading down the bus stairs. "I'm just going to come out and tell you what's going on and what our action plan is. Looks like we're stuck spending the night in Superior this evening, ladies."

She paused as a collective gasp rose from the team, followed by murmurs of disbelief. Coach Hanlon sighed and nodded. "I know," she said. "Trust me, I'm not thrilled about it either. But the county sheriff has officially banned all non-emergent road travel until this storm has moved through and their plows and salt trucks have had a chance to do their rounds. They don't want *anyone* on the roads and certainly not a bus packed with a college basketball team."

Coach Connor waved her phone from the front seat across the aisle from where Savannah and Emersyn sat. "I've gone through a list of nearby hotels," she said. "They are sympathetic to our situation, but most are booked tonight and don't have enough rooms available for us all."

There was a short pause and then Arissa wrinkled her nose. "So…" she dragged out the word with annoyance. "What are we supposed to do?"

Coach Hanlon exchanged a brief glance with Coach Connor and then forced a smile. "Remember that Super 8 that we passed about a mile down the road?"

Savannah's mouth dropped open as she watched Emersyn flop back against the seat in disbelief. "This is insane," Savannah said.

"I bet this never happened in Arizona," Emersyn responded glumly.

Coach Hanlon held up a hand. "We've gotten verbal approval from the athletic director to spend the night and charge it to our budget," she said. "They're the only place around with enough space for us all tonight, but we're going to have to double up. Coach Connor and I will share a room and to make this as easy as possible…" She did a quick headcount across the bus. "Perfect. We have an even number. Plan to room with whoever you're sitting with now. The manager at the Super 8 knows we're all together and he'll try to be as flexible as possible to accommodate us for the evening."

Savannah and Emersyn glanced at each other incredulously. *Wait a second. Did Coach Hanlon just say I'm…spending the night with Emersyn Tanner?*

The rest of the team began to call out questions, but Savannah could barely keep up. She blinked as her mind kept going back to one important detail, as if stuck on a loop. *I'm spending the night with Emersyn. We're sharing a room. I'm spending the night with Emersyn.*

Savannah shifted in her seat as heat rose between her thighs. The idea of having Emersyn so close was tantalizing, but she knew Emersyn would have to come to her first—and open herself up to Savannah.

"Look, I know this is far from an ideal situation," Coach Hanlon said. "But there isn't a lot we can do right now. Until the sheriff clears the county for travel, which his deputy didn't expect to be until six or seven a.m. tomorrow, we can't go anywhere. We're lucky we got the sheriff's permission to drive a mile down the road, do not pass go, and head directly to the motel."

Emersyn stared at the floor and shifted again as a shadow passed over her face.

"Are you okay?" Savannah said, worried.

Emersyn took a deep breath and leaned her head back against the seat. "Yeah, I..." She nodded. "Yeah."

Savannah watched her as the bus rumbled to life. "I don't believe you," she said. "You already know *I* know when you're lying to me."

Emersyn shot her a glare. "You think you know everything about me, but you *really* don't," she said tightly.

Savannah rolled her eyes pointedly as she pushed her earbuds into her ears. "La, la, la, can't hear you," she replied loudly, hoping it drove her point home. *Immature, sure. But Emersyn drives me crazy. Every time I think she's* this *close to opening up to me...* She sighed. *And why do I care so much and want to be her lifeline so badly anyway?*

Too soon, the bus pulled into a small parking lot for the tiny, one-level Super 8 motel. The bus chugged to a shaky stop around the back of the building, across from a long-abandoned, snow-covered basketball court in an overgrown field. Savannah stood, pulling her earbuds from her ears as Coach Hanlon and Coach Connor hustled them off the bus and into an underwhelming beige lobby. Its air was thick with the strong, mingling scents of cleaning chemicals and flowery aerosol spray.

As their coaches spoke with the manager, the rest of the team stood awkwardly around the lobby with their heads down and their hands tightly gripping their gym bags. Savannah stole another glance at Emersyn, who stared straight ahead and refused to meet her eyes.

I guess it'll be a silent, awkward night. Savannah crossed her arms. *Fine.* She glanced around the lobby again, wondering if she could switch rooms with Erica. *Surely Erica, who has always been the closest to Emersyn, wouldn't mind swapping with me.*

Savannah bit her lip as she wondered what she was supposed to say without sounding like the biggest bitch of the century. What irritated her more, though, was the fact that she knew deep down she didn't *want* to room with anyone else. The idea of sharing close quarters, even for just a night, with Emersyn made her heart pound with delicious anticipation. A slight shiver ran down her spine as she tried not to think about how right it would feel to have Emersyn warm and safe in her arms.

Savannah glanced up just as Coach Hanlon handed her a white plastic key card emblazoned with the Super 8 logo.

"Sanchez, Tanner," she said. "Room twenty-three. Remember the ground rules I just went over. Call our room or our phones if you need anything."

Savannah nodded, realizing too late that she hadn't been paying attention. She turned the key card over in her hands, feeling uncharacteristically shy and off balance.

"Twenty-three like Jordan," Emersyn said as she crossed her arms. "Maybe this won't be *so* bad."

"All right, you two," Coach Hanlon said. "We're meeting in the lobby at six thirty a.m. sharp for the continental breakfast and hitting the road as soon as the sheriff clears us to do so. Shower up and get some rest tonight."

❖

Barely an hour later, Savannah sat thoughtfully on the edge of a bed facing a rectangular window. All she could see were blurs of white against the pitch-black of the evening. She had figured out that room twenty-three faced the desolate plot of land behind the motel, all of which was cloaked in nightfall and thick, heavy snow. The windowpane was ice-cold to the touch and Savannah wrapped her white Northwoods College sweatshirt tighter around herself. A hot shower had helped wash away the game, but she realized she'd have to make do with sleeping in her oversized sweatshirt that hung loosely over the extra pair of black yoga pants she'd brought. It wasn't ideal, Savannah noted as she popped a chocolate-covered almond into her mouth, but she was clean, comfortable, and warm with the rickety wall heater cranked all the way up.

She listened as the shower squeaked off and Emersyn pulled the curtain to the side to towel off. They hadn't spoken except for a few short words to decide the order of showers and who would take which full-sized bed. Savannah's mind wandered to the meeting she and her parents had with Chris earlier in the week and the contract she'd signed to be represented by his business after graduation. She thought of Thalia, her ex-girlfriend, reaching out with a congratulatory text that had gone unanswered. The news had begun swirling quickly and excitedly amongst their friends, family, and community in Arizona.

It's weird. What I feel when I look at Emersyn is so different from what I felt with Thalia. It was never this...intense. And Thalia always liked attention at all times, no matter where she could get it. Savannah rolled her eyes. *But how deep can it be with Emersyn? I have a crush, sure, but* please. *She and I aren't even talking to each other.*

Goose bumps rose along her forearms as she felt Emersyn gently sit on the bed next to her. She glanced at her and wished she hadn't. Her cheeks were rosy from the steam of the shower and her damp hair looked impossibly soft as it curled along the ends that brushed her shoulders. In her bare feet, her royal blue Northwoods College sweatpants, and a fitted white thermal, Emersyn looked...vulnerable. For a moment, Savannah caught a glimpse of who Emersyn was before the accident, before life had betrayed her, and before she ever knew her. Savannah swallowed hard and glanced down at the bag of almonds in her hand.

It's best that I'll be going overseas to play after graduation.

"You were right." Emersyn's voice was so quiet that Savannah wondered for a moment if she meant to talk out loud. "On the bus. I *was* upset. I remembered that my mom has an eight a.m. physical therapy appointment tomorrow that I'm supposed to drive her to. If we don't even leave Superior until close to seven, there's no way I'll be back in time. And she can't really drive on her own anymore. She's working toward it, but... she's not there just yet." Emersyn shook her head glumly.

"That's all you had to say," Savannah said softly. "You might think I don't know you at all, Emersyn, but I *know* when you're not telling the truth. You don't have to shield yourself from me, you know."

Emersyn glanced up with a half-smile. "I've been angry," she admitted with a deep breath. "And depressed. And lost and confused about *everything*. I figured it's better if I shield myself from everyone, because I don't even recognize myself."

I still see the best parts of you. And what I wouldn't give to shatter you, put you back together, and make you mine.

She held out the bag of almonds instead. "Chocolate-covered almond?" She offered, then grinned as Emersyn's face lit up. "My mom slipped these into my gym bag when I wasn't looking. I'm glad now, given the circumstances and the fact that the rest of the team pretty much emptied the lobby's vending machine."

Emersyn popped an almond into her mouth. "No, your mom is on to something," she said easily. "Chocolate-covered almonds definitely make the world a better place."

Savannah considered this as she chewed another almond. "You're right," she said. After a moment, she glanced back at Emersyn. "You know, I can order a taxi for your mom if she really needs to get to her appointment tomorrow. Don't worry about the cost, I've got it. I'll call one of the campus taxi services now and confirm the pickup."

Emersyn shot her a smile. "That's really sweet of you to offer, Savannah," she said. "But I don't want you to do that. Ever since the accident, I haven't wanted to be that girl who everyone whispers about and feels sorry for." Emersyn flopped onto her back on the soft mattress and blinked up at the beige popcorn ceiling. "Honestly, I just want to be *me* again."

Without a second thought, Savannah dropped the bag of almonds onto the nightstand and flopped onto her stomach next to Emersyn. She propped her head up with her elbow as her hair fell over her arm. She glanced down at her, and a sudden warmth filled her chest. Emersyn smiled up at her from her prone position on her back, her gaze unguarded as she studied Savannah's expression, and it was then that she realized only millimeters separated them. The friction in the small room seemed to spike as Emersyn's gaze lingered along Savannah's profile, her lips, and finally back to her eyes.

I want to kiss her. The thought flared in Savannah's mind before she had a chance to stop it. The overwhelming desire to feel her lips against Emersyn's, run her fingertips along her silky skin, and wrap her arms around her nearly took her breath, but it was Emersyn's next words that made her feel lush and full again.

"Savannah, I… Is it weird if, like, the more I get to know you, the more I feel this…this connection to you? It cuts through *everything* and it sort of scares—"

Emersyn's quiet, wondering tone was interrupted by a loud knock at the room door.

"Maid service!" Mia's voice, still recognizable through the high-pitched accent she bestowed upon herself, called out before dissolving into giggles. Her feet padded down the carpeted hallway and then Savannah could hear her pounding on another teammate's door.

Emersyn closed her eyes, her face scrunched at the interruption, and then she glanced at the door. "Mia better be careful," she said with a shake of her head. "If Coach Hanlon hears her, she's going to rip her a new one."

Savannah glanced out the window into the frost-tinged darkness. *I sort of hope Coach Hanlon does.* She rolled her eyes in response. *Emersyn was finally getting real with me. For a second, at least.*

She flopped onto her back with a heavy sigh and stared at the ceiling in frustration.

Emersyn glanced at her. "What's wrong with you?"

Savannah chewed the inside of her cheek and tried to shake away her annoyance at Mia's interruption right as Emersyn was telling her…*What?* Savannah wondered. *That she feels a connection to me? That she feels this deep, unshakable* thing *between us too?*

Savannah glanced back at Emersyn, who raised an eyebrow. "Are you having a mood swing?" Emersyn said teasingly. "Seriously, are you getting your period?" She arched further into the pillows as she laughed. "Of course I'd get stuck with a PMS-ing roommate all night. I promise you can have all the chocolate-covered almonds!"

Emersyn laughed harder as Savannah twisted on her side. She had never seen this version of Emersyn before, the carefree one with the gorgeous smile that their teammates had promised existed somewhere. Her laugh was real, genuine, and intoxicating as she rolled playfully into Savannah's side.

Savannah feigned annoyance. "Oh, you think that's funny?" she said playfully as she tickled Emersyn's ribs. Her thin white thermal rode up slightly as Emersyn shrieked through her laughter and curled her fingertips around Savannah's hips.

"I'm so glad you found your sense of humor in this crappy hotel room," Savannah said through giggles as Emersyn playfully twisted beneath her hands. The thin flowered comforter was bunched around them and Savannah felt a wave of warmth crash through her as Emersyn's fingertips trailed up from Savannah's hips and tangled into her hair.

"I'm glad my totally uncharacteristic angst is enough to make you laugh," Savannah said as her fingertips gently targeted Emersyn's toned abdomen.

"I mean," Emersyn laughed breathlessly as she squirmed harder. "If you're going to start bleeding, I'm glad you at least gave me a head's up. You're lucky I keep extra tampons in my gym bag, Miss Thing."

Savannah grinned and then finally relented as she collapsed beside Emersyn with a triumphant sigh. The small room seemed to still around their quiet breathing and the electric charge that had ignited them gave way to something softer, more tender.

Emersyn rolled onto her side and faced Savannah, her expression bright. She ran a playful hand through Savannah's hair as their gazes collided. Savannah's hand still rested lightly along Emersyn's ribs, her skin warm and soft through the waffled fabric of her shirt.

Time seemed to slow and settle into something deep and heated. Emersyn's hazel eyes had darkened just enough to appear as though they were practically begging Savannah: *Kiss me.*

Savannah couldn't resist any longer. She leaned in, slow and sure, as she gently pressed her lips to Emersyn's. A fiery thrill snaked up her spine when she realized that Emersyn hadn't pulled away. Instead, she leaned into it and tightened her hand in Savannah's hair as the kiss deepened, as though it was the most natural thing in the world. *Like she's been waiting for me to do exactly this.*

The thick, heady energy in the room was making Savannah dizzy with deep desire that she wasn't even sure she recognized from herself. As their tongues explored and the kiss grew more urgent, Savannah felt an overwhelming, aching hunger surge through her core. Stubborn, beautiful, controlled Emersyn, who held everyone at arm's length and didn't even realize how much she ached to be held, was pressing herself closer in her arms. She was kissing her back with a fervent tenderness that told Savannah she felt it all too.

Savannah pulled her closer, running her hands along Emersyn's spine and lingering in the gentle dip at the base of her back. She shifted as Emersyn snuggled into her and cupped Savannah's face with her hand, still not breaking the kiss.

Finally, Savannah thought as desire pooled through her core. She curled a soft lock of Emersyn's hair behind her ear. *I'm getting through that careful composure and unraveling her. She knows she belongs to me. Emersyn Tanner is mine and I'm not going to let her go.*

Chapter Nine

The wind howled outside and thick snow gathered in the pitch dark against the hotel room window. Savannah pulled back just enough to drink in the way Emersyn's cheeks flushed pink and her chest rose up and down breathlessly beneath her. Still, Emersyn looked back at her sure, steady, and reverently. Savannah's fingers brushed down her face as she tucked another damp strand of hair behind Emersyn's ear. Her eyes fluttered closed at Savannah's touch and when she opened them again, her gaze had darkened with desire.

Savannah leaned down and met her lips again, the ache between her thighs deepening as she felt Emersyn melting into her with need. Her hands slid over Savannah's waist, tracing lightly up her sides and over her shoulders. As Savannah's fingertips brushed along the hem of Emersyn's shirt, she paused as her pulse pounded in her chest.

"Are you sure you want this?" Savannah asked. "You want to be mine?"

Emersyn nodded breathlessly as a ghost of a smile flashed across her swollen lips. "I've never been more sure of anything."

Savannah captured Emersyn's lips again and swallowed her moan at Emersyn's fingers threading through her hair. She wanted to take her time and enjoy every moment of Emersyn writhing beneath her as she slowly, carefully unraveled her. Emersyn shuddered as Savannah's lips found the spot just behind her ear and then kissed languidly down her neck to her collarbone.

"Savannah," she said breathlessly. "You feel *so* good."

Savannah met her lips and brushed her hand just beneath the hem of Emersyn's shirt. Her skin was soft and heated as she explored higher, over the satiny fabric of her bra, and stroked gently over her nipples. Savannah smiled knowingly against Emersyn's mouth as her nipples peaked and pebbled at her touch over the soft cups.

"I want you to feel good," she said as she nipped gently at Emersyn's neck. "All the time."

Emersyn's back arched against the pillows as she instinctively craned her neck to give Savannah better access. Savannah's mouth and fingertips finally met at Emersyn's breasts, and she helped her slowly wriggle out of her shirt and bra. Savannah swallowed hard as she drank in the sight beneath her, tracing her fingertips across Emersyn's soft skin, over her breasts and teasing her nipples, as heat flooded her core at the sweet half-moan, half-whine that Emersyn made as her touch lingered over her nipples.

As Savannah leaned down, she ran her tongue along her breasts before gently taking Emersyn's nipple into her mouth and teasing it mercilessly. As Emersyn pushed herself further into Savannah's mouth, her expression filled with need, Savannah felt something in her chest tighten.

"You don't have to hold back anymore," she said, her voice quiet but sure. "Not with me."

Emersyn nodded as she threw her head back against the pillow and her eyes closed against Savannah's tongue along her nipples. "God, Savannah," Emersyn said. "I want you. *So* badly."

Savannah brushed kisses along Emersyn's stomach and thighs. "What do you want *so* badly? Tell me."

She could hear Emersyn suck in a deep breath as her gentle kisses teased dangerously close to the space between her thighs. "I want your hands, your lips on me," she said, a slight whine in her voice. "I want to feel you, I want you to…to make me come." She exhaled slowly and squirmed against the pillows, desperate for more, as Savannah's lips languidly explored her inner thighs. "I just want *you*, Savannah. All of you."

Savannah's palms along Emersyn's hips and her fingertips curling into her sides kept Emersyn firmly in place as she gently ran her tongue along the wetness that glistened along her lips. Emersyn groaned as her hips bucked up against Savannah's palms.

"Relax, love," Savannah said. "Surrender to me. Let go."

The pleasurable sigh that she coaxed out of Emersyn sent throbbing jolts through her that tingled and pressed between her thighs. Savannah felt a primal need pulse through her veins to possess Emersyn, to shatter and soften her, and then tenderly put her back together again. She didn't completely understand it yet, but she lost herself in Emersyn's breathy sighs and increasingly urgent moans as her tongue explored around and in-between her folds. She relished the taste of Emersyn as her wetness coated her lips, her mouth, and her chin. Savannah didn't want to ever stop as she gently slid one and then two fingers between her folds as Emersyn's hands wound tighter in her hair. As she gently worked her fingers in and out of Emersyn, she found the ultra-sensitive bud just above with her lips. She could feel Emersyn's legs and thighs tightening as she became more possessive, claiming her as she ran her tongue along and around her clit over and over in endless teasing circles. She knew Emersyn was close and could sense it in the way her body seemed to coil tighter with every stroke of her tongue.

She wanted Emersyn to come apart at her touch and she knew with each trembling sigh of her name from her lips that it wasn't just her body unraveling beneath her; it was her walls, her fears, and her tightly-wound self-defense mechanisms crumbling with each curl of her fingers inside her, each firm, tender stroke of her tongue, and each rapid pulse of Savannah's heart.

Savannah felt the waves of pleasure clenching and rolling through Emersyn on her fingers as her hips arched off the mattress and she cried out Savannah's name over and over again, soaking her fingers and her mouth. Even as the crash of Emersyn's orgasm slowed, Savannah kissed and lapped away her pleasure as Emersyn rode out every last second.

Emersyn reached for her as she caught her breath and Savannah scooted up next to her on the pillows. "I didn't know I could feel like this," Emersyn said, dazed. "I've been waiting for that forever."

Savannah blew out her breath and wordlessly opened her arms. As Emersyn snuggled against her, Savannah kissed the top of her head and traced lazy circles along her bare shoulder blades. "Me too," she said. "You're mine now."

There was something about the way Emersyn had finally yielded to her so easily that seemed to awaken something in her that she didn't fully know yet. As Emersyn tilted her head up for Savannah's lips, the fire deep inside her continued to stoke.

"Haven't you figured it out yet?" Emersyn teased her. "That's all I want."

Savannah grinned as she relished Emersyn's warmth against her. "Careful what you wish for, love," she said. "You might get exactly that."

Emersyn laughed as her hand slid beneath Savannah's sweatshirt. "I'm going to show you exactly how much I want you," she said, her voice lower. "But first…" She tugged playfully at the hem of her sweatshirt. "You need to lose this. Unless you're going to make me beg…"

❖

The early morning sunshine painted the sky in streaks of light pink, soft yellow, and gentle blue from between the trees as Emersyn stirred. She blinked as it dawned on her why she was so warm, comfortable, and relaxed. Savannah's arms were wrapped around her and her head was curled into Savannah's neck. Their bare legs tangled together beneath the comforter and Emersyn realized with a flush that her sweatpants were still wrinkled at the end of the bed alongside Savannah's discarded yoga pants.

Emersyn took a slow, deep breath as she realized she had no desire to move. She closed her eyes as she breathed in the faint traces of Savannah's coconut milk lotion and snuggled closer.

This feels good. This feels right. So, so right.

Savannah shifted against Emersyn and traced her fingertips along her side before dropping a slow, languid kiss to her temple.

"You awake?" she said, sleep still evident in her voice.

Emersyn sighed contentedly but didn't move. "Something like that."

Savannah gently brushed kisses along the side of Emersyn's neck. "Play with me."

Emersyn burst into giggles as she arched an eyebrow at Savannah. "What?" she asked as she slid her leg over Savannah's waist and teasingly straddled her. "Play with you?"

Savannah's expression deepened into a lazy grin as she ran her hands along Emersyn's sides, her fingertips lingering along the waistband of her underwear. "Outside," she said. "Behind the motel. I noticed this old, wrecked hoop out there last night. Catch and shoot?"

"You woke me up to play basketball?" Emersyn said, though her heart pounded in anticipation. "Or, I mean, get your ass kicked playing one-on-one with me?"

Savannah tucked a lock of hair behind Emersyn's ear knowingly. "I think *I* won when we played one-on-one last night."

Emersyn blushed. "You're silly."

Savannah laughed as she kissed Emersyn's lips. "Only for you," she said.

They dressed quickly and slipped out the back door of the motel into the frigid early morning air. Thick, sparkling snow blanketed everything in sight and gathered along the top of the chipped wooden backboard and in a ring along the hoop's rusted rim.

Savannah spun her basketball along the tip of her index finger as she stepped through the snow. "You ready for me?"

Emersyn grinned. "Bring it," she said as she jumped up and down, once, twice, to get the blood flowing through her limbs. "You sure you can handle me so early? You seemed worn out last night."

Savannah tossed the ball to her teasingly. "Catch and shoot. First to ten. I'll even be extra sweet and give you the first shot."

Emersyn shrugged and then pivoted to her right quickly, though she knew it wasn't nearly as graceful or impressive when she was fighting through drifts of snow. She laughed as she dribbled, nearly losing the wet basketball as it slipped through her gloved hands, and she Euro-stepped to the hoop for what would normally be an easy layup.

Savannah was fast as she lunged to block her. Instead, her hands found Emersyn's waist and she pressed her fingertips into her hips just enough to make Emersyn toss up an airball and laugh harder.

"Foul," Emersyn said through her giggles. "*Such* an obvious foul."

"Not in this game," Savannah said, her voice low and teasing as her hands lingered around Emersyn's hips. She leaned in as her lips brushed the shell of Emersyn's ear. "Regular basketball rules don't apply here."

Emersyn turned in her arms and tilted her face up as she pressed a kiss to Savannah's lips. The icy air felt hotter as Emersyn leaned in and deepened the kiss for just a moment, temporarily losing herself in Savannah. She pulled back just as the pressure was beginning to coil between her thighs.

Instead, Emersyn bent down and grabbed the ball before shoving it into Savannah's arms. "First to ten," she said breathlessly. "I guess I don't get to ask a question since I whiffed that layup. Let's see how you do in the snow."

As they played, their casual game became less about basketball and more about teasing each other. They flirted shamelessly as they looked for any reason to touch each other. Emersyn would attempt to slowly back down Savannah near the hoop, enjoying the feeling of her back pressing into Savannah's chest. In turn, Savannah would try to guard by keeping her palm firm along the small of Emersyn's back, her hand lingering there possessively even after Emersyn would put up her shot.

"I forget how competitive you are," Savannah said as Emersyn stole the ball from her dribble and banked it into the hoop with ease.

"And I forget how wildly self-assured you are," Emersyn said, her tone filled with mirth. "Still think you can win by distraction? Just because you *look* at me like that..."

Savannah arched an eyebrow as she stepped closer through the snow. "So far, it's working."

Their laughter echoed across the court as Savannah cupped Emersyn's face in her hand, running her thumb along her lips. Emersyn could sense the desire coiling inside Savannah as she melted into her touch and wrapped her arms around her, pressing herself closer for a kiss.

After a long moment, Emersyn paused as the weight of aching desire and something deeper coursed through her. "*That* was definitely a foul," she said, centimeters from Savannah's lips and nearly giddy with desperation to taste them again. "No question."

Savannah opened her mouth to respond, tangling her fingers in Emersyn's hair, before the sound of a clearing throat near the back door of the motel stilled them both.

"You two going to eat before we get on the bus or are you planning to stay in Superior for the rest of the weekend?" Coach Hanlon's tone was dry and unreadable. "Six thirty sharp, remember?"

Emersyn and Savannah stood frozen on the snowy, cracked basketball court and stared back at Coach Hanlon. She stood casually just outside the back door, a travel mug in her gloved hands, before she walked back into the motel. "Let's get going, ladies."

Savannah bit back a grin as she and Emersyn exchanged knowing glances. "She definitely knows."

"You really think so?" Emersyn said with a hushed giggle.

"By the way, Sanchez, Tanner was right," Coach Hanlon called over her shoulder without turning back around. "That *was* definitely a foul."

Savannah smiled softly as Emersyn leaned into her affectionately. "She's Coach Hanlon," she said. "She always knows."

They fell into step together as they walked through the snow to the back door. Without thinking twice, Emersyn reached down and tangled her fingers around Savannah's. As they reached the door, Savannah's hand tightened around hers. Emersyn glanced down at their joined hands. The gesture seemed to say *we're just getting started.*

Anticipation coursed through Emersyn as she leaned forward and met Savannah's soft lips again. She was done pulling away from what was meant to be—and *who* she was meant to belong to.

PART II

NOW

Chapter One

Emersyn Tanner leaned expectantly over her laptop. With her left hand delicately tracing along the trackpad and her right hand wrapped tightly around a white cardboard cup holding the last few room temperature sips of her caramel latte, she was laser-focused on the movements darting across her screen. The hum of espresso machines, the soft ballads floating from small speakers along the taupe-painted walls, and the bold, rich scents wafting through the cozy corner coffeehouse blended into a familiar backdrop, tucked away in the loud, bustling city of Chicago.

She took a slow sip of the sweet-tinged coffee and savored the bold, velvety espresso and creamy milk as she scrolled through clip after clip of Crestfield Academy's varsity girls' basketball team. Their season had just wrapped and summer break had started only two days before, but Emersyn was already eager to review their season digitally spliced in key highlights and lowlights, quick layups, missed free throws, triumphant buzzer-beaters, and the widely lauded defense that had nearly gotten them to the Illinois state finals.

Emersyn smiled to herself as she paused the footage to track back a few seconds and restart a play that had won them a key game against a division rival. A city bus groaned outside the long, tinted glass window as it braked for a red light at the corner. Emersyn didn't pay the bus or the near-constant stream of eclectic pedestrians power-walking down the wide sidewalks any attention. Her grin deepened as she slowed the clip to watch their point guard apply extra defensive pressure so their small forward could take a quick step behind the three-point line and get an easy basket.

"That's it," she said to herself proudly as she ran a hand through her hair. It was longer than the easy shoulder-length style she'd had in college, and her generous private school salary afforded her monthly appointments at the chic brick-facade salon two blocks away from her spacious condo on the top level of a recently rehabbed three-flat in the heart of Streeterville. "Perfect help defense. We win when we play unselfishly and as a team."

The deep golden late afternoon sunlight pierced through the tinted coffee shop window nearest her. Though her job as head coach of Crestfield Academy's varsity girls' basketball team still required a healthy amount of activewear, at thirty-eight years old, Emersyn had moved on years ago from her northern Wisconsin college uniform of cozy interchangeable hoodies, comfortable track pants, and various pairs of Nikes and Converse low-tops in nearly every color. Her role as head coach at one of Chicago's elite private schools meant anxiously pacing the sideline in tight skinny pants or fashionably baggy belted trousers paired with an array of fitted blazers, satin T-shirts, or high-neck cap sleeve blouses.

As Emersyn clicked the next clip, she took a long sip of her latte and stretched her legs beneath the corner table. She nodded excitedly as she watched the lone sophomore who had made it onto the varsity team this year. Her eyes were focused as she raced up the floor and banked in a wild buzzer-beater right before halftime.

Emersyn shook her head ruefully. "Only Shayla could pull off something like that," she said to herself as she jotted down a quick note on the pad next to her. "*And* have the confidence to even toss that up. That girl has something extra."

Emersyn was referring to the intangible, indescribable "it factor" that so few athletes could confidently claim. Sure, talent was one thing and hard work ethic was another—and those things often led to good, focused players with lofty goals. Still, very few athletes had that extra *something* that set them a little further apart from their peers, whether it was a natural knack for the sport, deep passion colliding with strong commitment, or all of the above.

At the end of the clip, Emersyn noted the disappointed look on the face of the opposing school's assistant coach. *Irina Martlevich.* Emersyn swallowed hard, feeling safe in the relative anonymity of the relaxed coffee shop, as she studied the woman frozen on her screen. They had crossed paths many times before at games, and each time Emersyn had to remind herself to remain focused, keep her eyes on her players, and ignore the little jolt she felt right beneath her skin. Irina's short, dark red hair was a stark contrast to her pale, milky-white skin and her intense deep blue eyes always seemed to burn into Emersyn across the court. She subconsciously adjusted an earbud as she glanced at Irina's mouth for a long moment, her lips turned down in a frown at her team's poor half-court defense, and the way her fingers gripped the edge of the bench.

Just as Emersyn's thoughts began to drift from basketball, a quiet ding on her laptop alerted her to a new text message on her phone. She glanced at the upper-right corner of her screen and blinked at the name: Jared Kaminski. Her neck burned as though she'd been caught doing something illicit and then she glanced at the clock right above the notification: 5:32 p.m.

"Shit," Emersyn muttered as she scraped back the scarred wooden chair and began gathering her things. "I should've been home an hour ago."

As she snapped her laptop shut and gently placed her earbuds in their case, she smiled at the college-aged barista who nodded at her from behind the counter.

"Same time tomorrow, Coach?" she said teasingly. "You know, it *is* summer break now."

Emersyn slung her black leather laptop bag over her shoulder. "I didn't realize how long I was here," she said. "Once I have all my notes organized from this season's film and we have clear goals for training camp in September, *then* maybe I'll think about a summer break."

The barista winked at her. "I hope you get time to enjoy the summer," she said flirtatiously. "But I know I'll miss seeing you here every day. After all, I know how much you love those extra-sweet coffee drinks."

Emersyn flushed as she rolled her eyes and waved once, pushing the heavy door open with her shoulder. She could feel her phone vibrating in her pocket and she sighed. She already knew exactly who it was.

"Hey, Jared," she answered wearily as she slid her black Dolce & Gabbana sunglasses over her nose. She ducked into a throng of fast-moving, well-dressed people streaming from one of the nearby high-rises as the corporate workday ended.

"Baby, there you are!" Jared's jovial voice was loud in her ear. "My gorgeous, ridiculously amazing fiancée. I thought you said you'd be home by four thirty to make that Greek chicken. Let me guess. You got caught up reviewing this season's film." His voice was teasing and held no animosity. "I'm starving. Want me to grab Thai takeout on my way home instead?"

Emersyn veered to her left and ducked into a small market-style corner store. As the door shut behind her, the loud, eclectic soundtrack of the city—the car horns, the occasional siren, the thumping of the El as it passed overhead, the squeaking of brakes from nearby delivery trucks, the conversations of the people around her—immediately faded.

"Thai sounds good," she said distractedly. She remembered that she'd promised Jared she'd grab some Gatorade and the organic frozen burritos he loved to take to the hospital for lunch, and she felt a brief pang of guilt that it hadn't even crossed her mind until he called.

Emersyn wandered slowly down the short aisles, though she was still thinking about basketball. Bits of the clips replayed in her mind's eye as she opened one of the refrigerators and tossed a few bottles of Gatorade into her basket.

"All right, I'll stop by Heart of Bangkok by the condo," Jared said, seemingly oblivious to her distraction. "I tried texting you a few minutes ago too, you know."

Emersyn bit back another sigh. "I *was* in the middle of something, Jared," she said mildly. She reached for the burritos stacked in the freezer. "That's probably why I didn't respond immediately."

Emersyn tried to keep her tone void of annoyance as she grabbed a handful of the individually-wrapped burritos and tossed them into the basket. It wasn't his fault, after all, that her Type A personality meant she had little patience for being distracted out of her flow state.

Jared didn't take the hint. "Yeah, I just left the hospital about ten minutes ago," he said. "How was film review?"

Emersyn shot a quick smile at the cashier as he rung up her items. "It was great, actually," she said. "Excellent. I'm really excited for next season. Shayla Simmons will be doing a Nike training camp in DC this summer, and I think she's going to make an even bigger jump in the fall."

"Cool, that's good to hear, sweetheart," Jared said. Emersyn could tell she was already losing him as a car horn honked somewhere in the background. Though supportive, he tended to tune her out quickly when she said more than a few sentences about basketball or coaching. Sports had never been his cup of tea.

"Thank you," Emersyn said to the cashier as she grabbed the paper bag and headed for the door.

He's a surgeon, of course he isn't interested in basketball. He flew through medical school at the top of his class and he practices with the top orthopedic surgeons at Rush at just forty years old.

"So, Shayla, she's that tall one that transferred over from the prep school in Missouri, right?" Jared said, distracted, as Emersyn heard him step into the corner Thai restaurant. "You want the extra spice on your pad kee mao this time?"

"You're thinking of Danielle Thomas, and she graduated last year and went on to DePaul," Emersyn said lightly. "But yes, she's also phenomenally good and earned a starting role on DePaul's team this year."

"Oh, right," Jared said. "Who's Shayla then? The star of the team?"

Emersyn bit her lip. She knew Jared was happy that she enjoyed her career, but she understood long ago that he didn't exactly grasp the importance of sports. To him, they were fun hobbies while medicine was *real*, tangible, and serious.

Choosing to save her battles, Emersyn smiled tightly as she rounded a corner. "All the girls on the team are important, Jared," she said. "Just like all your patients are."

She paused for a moment, but Jared simply cleared his throat.

"Em? You still there, babe?" he asked after a moment. "Oh man, crab rangoon sounds good."

Emersyn shook her head quickly. "Yes, I'm here," she said. "Anyway, Shayla has been getting a ton of recognition around high school basketball and in the local AAU circuit. She's one of the top twenty college female basketball recruits, according to ESPN. She's only going to be a junior this fall, so that's an amazing accomplishment. And God, Jared, she works so hard. I've never seen a kid with work ethic like hers, not recently anyway," she said, recalling the memory of the halftime buzzer beater. Her mind's eye wandered over the shot banking in as the buzzer sounded and then over Irina on the opposite bench. Her blue eyes had looked stormy and darker than usual and Emersyn had never noticed how slender her fingers were until they curled over the edge of the bench…

"Yes, hi, can I get an order of the pad kee mao, a large order of chicken pad thai, a side of crab rangoon, and two bottles of Fiji?" Jared said, breaking Emersyn out of her reverie. "…No, no extra spice, thanks. Hey, Em?" He turned his attention back to her. "Can I call you back?"

Emersyn was quiet for a moment. "You know what, I'll see you at home. I have a few more clips I want to look at before bed and I know you're in the middle of ordering food." She glanced up as the beige brick three-flat came into view.

"Okay, sweetheart." Jared sounded relieved. "I'll be back soon. With Thai food, no less. Love you, babe."

Emersyn focused on a nearly imperceptible scratch on the brushed nickel doorknob to their shared condo as she turned her key and swung open the door. She breathed in deeply through her nose and hoisted the bulky grocery bag onto the smooth granite breakfast bar. She was practically jumping out of her skin to get into their guest bedroom that doubled as her office and continue where she'd left off with the season's clips. As she was about to hang up, she realized she'd almost forgotten to say something important back to her expectant fiancé.

"Love you too. See you soon."

Chapter Two

Emersyn nearly jumped out of her skin in surprise as she stood before the bathroom mirror, combing out her wet hair, and Jared appeared behind her. He clasped his arms around her waist and bent his tall, muscular frame to drop a kiss onto her bare shoulder.

"I thought you were catching up on some last-minute edits for that abstract!" Emersyn said as she twisted in his arms to face him.

"I had to take a quick call from one of the patient intake managers," he said. "They need to move one of my surgeries next week to next month. Something about the insurance. You were still in the shower, so I didn't want to disturb you." His affable smile turned lascivious. "Speaking of which, you should really lock that door when I'm not around. I could've been a burglar…" he gently kissed her cheek. "Or I could've been one of those giant rats that run around the alleys at night." He placed a finger beneath her chin and tilted her head up. "Or I could've been…" His words hung in the air as he slowly tried to unhook the thick white towel wrapped around her.

Emersyn angled her head away from Jared and wriggled out from where he loomed over her near the sink. He didn't take the hint and continued trying to nuzzle at her neck as his hands frantically tried to work their way beneath the soft towel.

"Jared!" she said, laughing breathlessly. "Jared!"

Finally, his head shot up and he looked at her. A flash of frustration clouded his face as he ran a hand over his short, spiky blond hair.

"Okay, okay," he said as he stepped backward. "Would you rather take this to the bedroom? I suppose you have a point. I didn't spend nearly eight thousand dollars on that bed so we could simply sleep comfortably in it."

Emersyn shook her head as she tightened the towel around her. "Jared, I'm tired," she said with a smile. "I've been so focused on film review all day and now all I can think about is going to bed."

Jared's face fell, dejection written all over his handsome, all-American features. "Well, how about tomorrow night we go for a nice dinner then? Maybe somewhere in Little Italy? And then we can come home, turn down the lights, and I'll give you the best massage of your life," he suggested hopefully.

Emersyn wrinkled her nose. "That's tempting, Jared, but I *have* to finish getting through these clips tomorrow if I want any chance of enjoying a summer break."

Jared sighed and guilt crept up Emersyn's spine.

"What about next week?" she said. "Why don't we go to one of those sweet bed and breakfasts downstate? I've wanted to try one for years and we always seem to plan it and then postpone it."

"I have that surgical conference all next week in Baltimore," Jared said apologetically. "You know this is conference season for me. I leave Tuesday morning. I could've sworn I told you about it. I won't be back until Friday night, and then I'm on call all weekend. Unless…" His face lit up. "Why don't you come to Baltimore too? They booked a gorgeous suite for me, and you could always grab an afternoon flight if you don't want to wake up early with me on Tuesday."

Emersyn considered this, but for some reason the idea of spending the week holed up in a ritzy hotel while Jared was making his rounds at the conference and staying up late for networking dinners sounded unappealing. She could binge something mindless and lie around in a big, comfortable bed by herself without following him to Maryland.

She shook her head as her soft, still-damp hair swung over her shoulders. "It's okay, Jared," she said with a sigh. "I know you'll be busy at the conference. Maybe we can plan something between the work travel you're committed to this summer."

Jared kissed her forehead lightly. "Sounds good, honey."

As Jared quietly left the bathroom, shutting the door gently behind him, Emersyn sat on the edge of the copper claw-footed tub and rested her chin in her hands. Her attraction to Jared had always been lukewarm at best, and she wondered why it was so difficult to feel that sizzling spark that so many other women blushed and whispered about when talking about their men.

She blew out her breath once. "Jared is a good guy," she whispered, though it sounded more like she was trying to convince herself. "We've been together nearly three years. He's successful, intelligent, and treats me like I'm a queen."

Emersyn nodded as she stood again. Her heart sank as her gaze fell to the large diamond and emerald ring waiting patiently on the clean white marble bathroom counter. She recalled Jared's obvious desire to get married soon and his more-frequent-as-of-late mentions of setting a date. She had agreed to a long engagement and was in no hurry to walk down the aisle, despite his eagerness for a future together. *I should be wildly in love with him. The idea of being Jared's wife should feel like a dream come true.*

She blinked back sudden tears, and she wasn't entirely sure if they were out of guilt—after all, Jared had been nothing but good to her—or out of her own stubborn refusal to acknowledge what she had always known deep down. Here it was, rearing its head again, no matter how much she tried to ignore or rationalize it. She had come close, once. Then life happened, and she fell back into the dimly-lit closet where it had always felt much safer. Stable. Expected.

I feel nothing. She swiped away the hot tears. *No butterflies, no pounding heart or excitement when I think about Jared, and no giddiness about the day that most women fantasize about from the time they're children.*

"Most women," Emersyn said as the distant sound of a siren roared down the narrow city street. "God, I wish I didn't feel suffocated by my own fiancé." She stared at the sparkling white tile beneath her bare feet. "I wish I could love him the way he deserves. I wish I felt *something*."

Realizing that she was whispering to nothing except the large bathroom around her and that she was still wrapped in a towel, Emersyn stood quickly and blinked a few times.

As she quietly left the bathroom, she found Jared on a leather stool at the breakfast bar, hunched over his pad thai and scrolling through his phone.

"Hey, I thought you disappeared or something!" He laughed.

Determined to try to feel something, Emersyn padded across the cool maple-colored hardwood and stopped just short of where he sat. Without another thought and swiftly ignoring the thoughts swirling around the sexuality she had ignored for as long as she could remember, Emersyn unhooked her towel and let it fall in a heap onto the spotless floorboards.

Jared paused, a forkful of noodles halfway to his slightly open mouth, and his gaze roaming up her body. He slowly turned in the stool as he dropped the fork with a loud clatter onto the breakfast bar.

Emersyn smiled satisfactorily to herself. Taking a step closer, she didn't fight this time as Jared greedily grabbed her around the waist and pulled her into him.

Internally, she recoiled and squeezed her eyes shut harder as his wet lips, tasting heavily of salt and tamarind, crashed against her own and forced them open to accept his eager tongue. Steeling herself against the disgust she felt rising up inside, Emersyn leaned further into the kiss and wrapped her arms loosely around Jared's neck.

Feel something.

Jared's hands were too rough, too big, and his mouth had no rhythm, no sweetness. He grasped at her and Emersyn fought against every instinct to pull away.

Feel something. Feel something. Anything. Feel something.

❖

Bright early morning sunlight poured through the large living room window overlooking their tree-lined neighborhood street as Emersyn wearily sat hunched over their small, round kitchen table. She tore a piece of buttered toast from the larger slice on her plate, but it was dry and tasteless. Her coffee had long since turned lukewarm, but she gripped the wide latte mug tightly and savored the sweet French vanilla creamer that swirled lazily through the light brown coffee. She curled her fingers tighter around the hand-painted ceramic. She needed something to ground her, soothe her, and help her sort through everything she felt—and didn't feel.

There was a hollowness that had sunken deep in her chest as she tried to focus on Jared's banal chatter near the front door.

"...Should be out of the surgery by six tonight," he said as he clipped his ID tag to his thin leather belt.

Emersyn nodded vaguely as she watched the gentle morning breeze and rustle of bright green leaves in the tree outside their building's front door.

"Oh, by the way," Jared said as he picked up a stack of mail from the edge of the breakfast bar with a squint. "Forgot to tell you there was something for you yesterday. What can I say," he glanced at her knowingly, "you distracted me. Anyway, whatever this fancy-looking envelope is? It's addressed to you."

Jared tossed a thick ivory envelope on the table near her plate. Her name and address were written across the back in sparkling gold script. "I'm off," he said. "Traffic on Lake Shore Drive is going to be a nightmare if I leave any later. Love you."

Emersyn smiled, though she knew it wasn't quite genuine. "Be safe."

She listened as the door shut gently behind him and then turned over the envelope with curiosity. She blinked at the return address. *Northwoods, Wisconsin.*

Her heartbeat quickened as she gently traced the gold sticker seal with her thumb before carefully opening the envelope. The single sheet of thick ivory card stock inside was heavy and tastefully printed with bold script and a single glossy, colorful sheet was clipped to it with an oversized paper clip that had a tiny sparkling heart charm dangling from it.

Katherine "Kay" Hanlon and Diana Miller cordially invite you to join them for their wedding celebration on Saturday, July 16th at Dulces Sueños Resort and Spa, Cabo San Lucas, Mexico.

Emersyn blinked at the words until the bold print blurred before her. Her chest tightened with something she had buried long ago.

"Kay and Diana are finally tying the knot, huh?" she said. She smiled despite herself, the cold coffee and bland toast forgotten. "About time."

She set the invitation down carefully and gazed out the window as the blush pinks and pastel yellows of the early morning gave way to bright, warm summer sunshine. As Emersyn drummed her fingertips against the tabletop, she considered the invitation. She unfolded the glossy sheet that had come with it and glanced over colorful images of a lush, elegant adults-only all-inclusive resort. There were photos of relaxed-looking women on soft massage beds as hands gently kneaded their shoulders. There was a photo of a grinning silver fox with designer sunglasses and brightly colored swim trunks racing through crystal-blue water on a Jet Ski. There were photos of a lush, open-air lobby designed with elegant dark wood and clean marble flooring and there were photos of restaurants and bars, each showing off thoughtfully presented plates of fine dining specialties or beautiful frozen drinks topped with umbrellas and slices of fresh fruit.

Emersyn gently pushed the invitation across the table. She had to hand it to whoever was responsible for marketing at the Dulces Sueños Resort and Spa, it certainly looked enticing.

A destination wedding for someone who I've barely kept in touch with over the last sixteen years. A small part of her thought it sounded adventurous, fun, and way out of her carefully planned routine, but the curl of guilt that twisted in her stomach was more acute as she wondered why Kay and Diana had invited her. It wasn't like she had made many attempts to stay in contact after she'd moved to Chicago. They used to chat regularly and exchange emails, until it became semi-regularly and then a few times each year, and then…

Emersyn bit her lip as she glanced at the open door to her office. As her mind turned to the clips she wanted to finish reviewing today and how long it might take her to summarize her extensive notes into key points on a PowerPoint deck, she twisted her hair up into a loose bun.

With a final glance at the single sheet brochure, she spotted the price per person. The number was steep and, though Emersyn knew she could afford it if she *really* wanted to go, she decided that was precisely why she wouldn't. Spending that kind of money for a vacation she didn't even plan for was out of the question.

And it's not like I really *want to go anyway.* She retrieved her laptop from the office, tucked it in her arm, and moved over to the breakfast bar.

As her laptop flashed to life, another uninvited thought curled into her mind. She ignored the slight tingle that ran down her spine.

If they're inviting the old dream team, Savannah Sanchez might be there too.

Logic told Emersyn that it was impossible for Kay to have invited all the girls she'd coached over the years, but she also knew she'd had a closer bond with their team over their four years together at Northwoods.

She chewed the inside of her cheek in thought as she carefully typed in her password and rested her chin in her hand. Kay and Savannah had developed a tight bond during her season in Wisconsin and Emersyn knew they'd planned to keep in touch after graduation. It wasn't entirely unlikely that she would be there too. Emersyn tried not to think about it, but the thought pressed in anyway and refused to be banished.

With one last glance at the invitation still sitting on the edge of the kitchen table, Emersyn turned her shoulder and focused on the PowerPoint deck on her screen. After a long moment, Emersyn blew out her breath and quickly opened her calendar app. She typed a brief note for the end of the week.

Reminder—Send RSVP card to Kay with decline.

Her fingers hovered over her keyboard as she thought of her former coach and how much she had meant to her. It felt like a lifetime ago, and it probably was. She had always been able to talk to Coach Hanlon. She had always been one of the most unwaveringly supportive adults in her young life and through her high-flying but short-lived basketball career, and Emersyn tried to keep her legacy alive by teaching her girls much of what Coach Hanlon had taught her.

Emersyn took a deep breath and added another line to the note in her calendar app.

Call Kay to congratulate her. Order a gift this weekend to be sent to the resort.

As she clicked out of her calendar app and tried to refocus on her PowerPoint deck, Emersyn glanced down at her hand. She was gripping her coffee mug so hard that her knuckles had turned pale white. The unexpected invitation had been a clear distraction this morning and Emersyn had basketball to focus on. Her mind shifted to Jared's most recent reminder that they needed to set a wedding date, about a week ago during a Sunday afternoon jog along Lake Michigan. An anxious pit formed in her stomach as she remembered the way they had taken a quick breather on a wooden bench and he'd sat close to her as he firmly opened his own calendar app, pointed at different months and dates, and sighed heavily as Emersyn wrinkled her nose and came up with an excuse for each one.

Annoyed that the invitation had seemed to derail her morning and bring back the uncomfortable feelings of suffocation and anxiety around her own engagement, Emersyn finally stood. Taking her laptop with her, she turned on her heel and padded back into the second bedroom office. Though she felt slightly silly since she was the only one home, she gently shut the door behind her as if to shut out the invitation, the thoughts of Jared, and the memories of when she'd *almost* had the courage to set her life on a different, more authentic path.

A pang of something deep and aching settled in her chest like a stone. If Emersyn could go back sixteen years, there was a lot she'd do differently—though she wasn't even entirely sure what. She slid her earbuds into her ears as she blinked at the still-empty PowerPoint on her screen. It was time to focus, rather than get lost in the what-ifs that she hadn't let herself consider in years.

Chapter Three

Later that week, Emersyn sat cross-legged on the sleek suede sofa in the living room. The day had been gray, with low-hanging clouds that threatened rain despite no precipitation, and made it difficult to find the motivation to change from her soft gray jogger sweatpants and white cami. Her laptop was balanced on her knees and she popped a green grape into her mouth from the bowl next to her.

She grinned as her mother's excited face filled the screen. "Emersyn, sweetheart, how are you?"

Emersyn waved. "I'm doing well, Mom," she said warmly. "How's life in Northwoods?" Though she had helped her mother sell their house about ten years ago, her mother had moved into a new condo in an active adult retirement community on the outskirts of Northwoods, preferring to stay in Wisconsin rather than upend and relocate closer to Chicago.

She laughed. "Well, not nearly as exciting as your big city life, I suppose," her mother replied. "Though I hope you're having a chance to relax and get a breather from coaching now that it's summer break."

Her hair had fully faded to a shimmery silver and her oversized red-rimmed glasses made her blue eyes look smaller, but her face was filled with maternal tenderness. "Oh, did I tell you they remodeled the Walmart down on Bradley Street? I couldn't find anything the first few times I went. They've got the produce where the cosmetics were, and the toys where the paint and hardware was…" She sighed and waved a hand. "They even moved the electric scooters to the other side of the doors." She grinned. "Though I'm happy to say I haven't needed an electric scooter in some time, not since Jared and his team fixed me up last. I'm telling you, Emersyn, it's like having a brand-new ankle."

"I'm glad to hear that, Mom."

Jared nodded from where he was watching an action movie on his tablet at the breakfast bar. He swallowed the last of the granola bar in his hand and crinkled the wrapper. "Happy to hear it, Nancy!" His voice boomed across the living room. "We miss you!"

Emersyn watched as Jared's strong, muscular back retreated down the hallway and into the bathroom. That was how they'd met, after all. When her mother needed a minor outpatient tune-up on the ankle that had been giving her trouble since the accident, Jared was the assigned surgeon, and he had pursued Emersyn hard after the procedure was complete.

"He's a keeper, Em," her mother said, hushed. "What a great guy. What do you two have planned this weekend?"

Emersyn shrugged, her gaze lingering on the empty granola bar wrapper that had floated to the floor, forgotten. "Nothing really," she said. "I think Jared has a softball game on Sunday at the lake and then he leaves for Baltimore on Tuesday. I don't have anything on the calendar."

Her mother rolled her eyes. "Goodness, Em," she said. "For someone who never leaves that city, it doesn't sound like you take advantage of nearly anything it has to offer. Why not a museum, a musical…"

Emersyn tuned out her mother's list of weekend tourist activities as her gaze lingered on the bathroom door. Her mind was far away, though she recalled she did have something on her calendar. As her mother went on about the slate of weekend activities lined up at her retirement community, Emersyn remembered the invitation. It still sat untouched on the corner of the kitchen table, where she had left it days before.

"You know, I *did* get an invitation to Coach Hanlon's wedding," Emersyn said. She laughed. "She and Diana are finally tying the knot. At an all-inclusive and ridiculously expensive resort in Cabo, no less. That reminds me, I need to send my RSVP card back and order a gift to ship there."

Her mother placed a hand over her heart. "Mexico?" she asked incredulously. "That sounds amazing. Come to think of it, I did see their announcement in the local paper a few months ago." She squinted at the screen and pushed her glasses up the bridge of her nose. "Wait, you're not going? Why on Earth not?"

Emersyn opened and then closed her mouth, taken aback by her mom's vocal surprise that she wasn't going. "Well, I mean I haven't been the best at keeping in touch with Kay," she said. "And I'm not sure I'll even know anyone besides her and Diana. Maybe they're inviting our old dream team." Emersyn shrugged. "But I'm not sure. Anyway, you know fruity umbrella drinks aren't my thing, Mom."

"Oh, please," she said mildly. "It's a wedding, and you and Coach Hanlon were very close at one point. She mentored you, Emersyn. She and Diana certainly would not have extended the invite if there were bad feelings on their end. I'm sure she wants to reconnect."

Emersyn chewed the inside of her cheek as she thought. "I don't…"

Her mother shot her a knowing look through the screen. "You're on summer break, aren't you?"

"Well, yes, but did you miss the part about it also being outrageously expensive?" Emersyn said. "If I'm going to spend that kind of money on a vacation, I'd at least like it to be one of my choosing."

Her mother sighed. "Emersyn, when *was* the last time you chose to go on a vacation? You're thirty-eight years old, you barely leave the city, and you never travel."

"Thanks, Mom," Emersyn said snippily as she bit into another grape. The sweet juice was cool on her tongue as she shifted the laptop across her legs.

She held up her hands in a conciliatory gesture. "Look, all I'm saying is these are your best years," she said. "You and Kay have always had a strong bond. Would it be so awful to enjoy a little of your summer and reconnect with someone who was once so important to you? Now you can show support to *her* by celebrating their wedding."

Emersyn looked down at her hands. Her mother had a point. "Kay *is* important to me, Mom," she said. "I mean, I guess it couldn't hurt to go. Maybe."

Her mother sat back against her cozy armchair. "*Go*," she said firmly. "Treat yourself for once, Em. Get some new summer dresses, dance, dip your toes in the ocean. Why not do something a little unexpected and celebrate two people who have always cared for you and supported you?"

Unbidden, Emersyn recalled that afternoon practice on the bleachers when she had been benched. She'd told Kay something she'd never admitted to anyone before that. She had been so sure and determined.

I've always known. It scares me. The thought of telling anyone else is terrifying.

She recalled Coach Hanlon's kind smile. *You just did.*

I guess I did, didn't I?

It was a memory she hadn't thought about in a long time. Emersyn wondered what her twenty-two-year-old self would think of her now, but she quickly banished the thought.

As she glanced at her mom on the screen, the light from the living room ceiling fan glinted along the edge of her engagement ring. Reconnecting with Kay seemed like something comforting, something she needed and wanted.

"Fine," Emersyn finally said. "I'll think about it."

A few minutes after they ended the video call, Jared ambled into the living room and sat on the armrest on the other side of the sofa.

"Your mom trying to get you to go to that Mexico wedding?" he asked.

"Trying?" Emersyn said as she shoved her laptop onto the glass coffee table. "She was practically packing my bags for me. According to her, I don't have nearly enough of a life. She has more on her social calendar living in an active adult community than I do here in the city and it concerns her." She sighed as she ran a hand through her hair.

Jared laughed. "Basketball does take up a lot of your time, Em," he said as he absent-mindedly scratched his temple. "You should go. Why not? You haven't taken a real vacation in the almost three years I've known you and you know we can afford the per person price. You never splash out on yourself. Most of that fat private school coaching salary is just sitting in your savings account." He rolled his eyes. "I'll be at that two-week think tank and surgical panel in New York City that I committed to last year. You might as well go enjoy the beach in Cabo for us both."

Emersyn bit her lip as she considered it. The idea of getting away, *really* getting away, was sounding more enticing by the moment. "You think I should?"

Jared shrugged. "Why not? I'll lend my brain to this Rush research grant for a couple weeks and you go sip something tropical and toast to lesbian matrimony or whatever you'll be doing."

Emersyn rolled her eyes. "Once again, fruity umbrella drinks are *not* my thing. But, okay. I'll go."

❖

Later that evening, long after Jared was snoring loudly with his arm draped across a body pillow between them, Emersyn sighed. Sleep wasn't coming easy, and her mind seemed to race with nerves, anticipation, and excitement that swirled through her.

She swung her legs over the side of the bed and padded barefoot to the kitchen table. The invitation still sat on the corner, its flecks of gold glitter in sparkling script dancing beneath the reflection from the street lights outside.

Before she could think better of it, Emersyn grabbed a Sharpie and quickly checked the box on the small card to confirm her attendance. Without another thought, she slid the card into its accompanying envelope, determinedly padded to the front door, gently eased it open, and dropped the response card into their ornate brass mail slot.

As she turned back inside, a wave of comfort washed over her. In the late-night dark, the condo still and quiet save for the muted sounds of the city outside the living room window, she allowed her thoughts to roam.

Emersyn perched on the arm of the sofa as she imagined coming face-to-face with Savannah all over again. She bit her lip. Knowing her love of fashion, she'd probably show up in some sleek black jumpsuit or body-hugging satin dress. Her hair was probably just as silky and dark and her eyes just as knowing beneath her long lashes as they always had been. She always knew exactly what Emersyn wanted and needed. Savannah would probably smile in her usual confident way, already reading what Emersyn was thinking. Would they even acknowledge each other? Or would Savannah hold her gaze just long enough for the tropical air to get thick and warm and for Emersyn to feel the electricity coursing through her?

Emersyn blinked and stood as a shiver ran down her spine. She was aware of the effect that just the unconfirmed *idea* of seeing Savannah again had on her, and she was also aware of the alarm bells somewhere in the back of her mind.

She glanced back at the front door as she realized it was too late and the response card was already at the bottom of their mail slot. Instead, she stepped into the kitchen and opened the refrigerator for a bottle of water. Emersyn blinked at the sudden bright light and tried to ignore the strange wave of longing that began deep in her chest.

"It's been years since we've spoken," she said as she uncapped the water and took a long drink. "It was a lifetime ago. We're different people now."

After graduation, things got messy fast and too much went unsaid. They had been too young to fully understand and process the depths of their feelings, and they had been pulled in different directions. Their lives weren't their own yet, Emersyn realized that now.

She probably won't even be there. Emersyn retreated down the hallway and slipped through the bedroom door. *Where is she now? Back in Phoenix, I think. I'm sure she's way too busy for a destination wedding.*

Feeling somewhat reassured but also strangely disappointed, Emersyn wiggled beneath the comforter and squeezed her eyes shut. *That's the past. This is now, and Mom is right. Now is the time to celebrate Kay and Diana, and to thank Coach for everything she taught me over the years. And perhaps show Coach that I'm a functioning, thriving, successful adult, not the tortured twenty-two-year-old filled with angst, ego, and insecurity.*

CHAPTER FOUR

"Do you even *own* a hoodie anymore?" Jared asked from where he leaned casually against the bedroom doorframe. He took a long swig from his Leinenkugel bottle and raised a thick eyebrow.

Emersyn laughed as she shook her head and picked through the clothes hanging neatly in their shared walk-in closet. "I donated most of those a long time ago," she said. "I don't even have a Crestwood one. Though perhaps if I search hard enough, I'll find an errant flannel."

Jared took another sip and shoved his free hand into his jeans pocket. "Not likely," he said. "Though I guess you won't need rural northern Wisconsin wear for a Cabo vacation."

Emersyn shrugged as she sorted through a stack of folded tops. "It wasn't *that* rural."

"Babe," Jared said pointedly as he took a few steps into the bedroom. "I distinctly remember you telling me about the time a deer wandered into a gas station on the edge of town."

Emersyn rolled her eyes as she gently placed a few pairs of neatly pressed designer linen shorts into her suitcase. "That was one time," she said. "And the deer was very Midwest polite. Left as soon as the cashier shooed it out."

Jared's expression softened as he sat on the edge of the bed and glanced at the beer bottle in his hands. "You seem really happy lately," he said. "Light. Excited, you know? I'm bummed I can't come since I'll be wrapped up at this research think tank all the way on the East Coast."

Emersyn glanced over her shoulder from where she leaned over her suitcase and wedged a pair of heels into a corner near her toiletry bag. "I *am* excited," she said. "It's been…forever since I've talked to Kay, much less spent time with her. She made a huge impact on my life when I was young. I'm excited to be there for her wedding. Your think tank is a big deal." She zipped a smaller cosmetics bag. "It's only the second one you've been invited to, right?"

Jared nodded. "Yeah," he said despondently. "Ten days of roundtables, healthcare policy debates, and listening to smart people argue in polite, passive-aggressive voices."

Emersyn winked. "Basically, your dream two weeks."

Jared laughed. "You're not wrong," he admitted. "But I do wish I could go with you."

Emersyn nodded sympathetically, but the truth deep in her chest was undeniable. *I don't.*

A comfortable silence hung over the bedroom as Emersyn stood and riffled slowly through a few dresses that hung carefully, zipped in protective plastic, at the back of the closet.

"You never talk much about that part of your life," Jared said thoughtfully. He took a sip of his beer and scratched his knee. "Growing up in Northwoods. Being a high school and college basketball star. The team. I feel like we've been together for a long time now and I still only know tiny pieces of the story."

Emersyn rested her hand along a velvet hanger. "That part of my life was…intense," she said slowly. It was the truth. "Basketball was my world."

Jared fixed her with a knowing look. "Not much different from today."

Emersyn smiled in acknowledgement, but she shook her head firmly. "No, it *was* different," she said. "I didn't know who I was outside of basketball and the careful plan I'd laid out for my future. I was young, dealing with a lot, and figuring it all out the hard way. Therapy helped. So did building my own life as an adult. Moving to the city, a brand-new environment, and blending quietly in a sea of millions. Letting go of that part of my life, you know, being the local hoops star who had to say good-bye to what was expected to be a pro career after devastating injury. Finding passion in coaching the next generation and instilling important values and ethics in them so they have a strong foundation, no matter what their futures hold."

She shrugged as she pulled a dark maroon minidress from the closet. With its thin, silver-studded straps and silky-smooth fabric, it had always been one of her favorites. "I had good people, like Coach Kay. Great teammates. A lot of memories that I sat with for a long time over the years and finally got to a place where I can look back with mostly fondness."

Jared nodded thoughtfully. "This trip will be good for you then."

"Yeah," Emersyn said as she bit her lip. "I think it will be too."

Jared stood. "I'll let you get back to packing," he said. He laughed. "Just promise you won't get recruited to go coach somewhere on the beach, never to return to the big city again."

Emersyn ran a hand through her hair. "Please," she said with a dramatic roll of her eyes. "I love coaching at Crestfield. And besides," she added. "I have no idea what the coffee situation is at the resort and that's important information to know."

Jared snickered. "Oh no, what will you do without your frothy, sugar-filled coffee drinks for more than a whole week?"

Emersyn shook her head as Jared gently closed the bedroom door behind him. She pressed her fingertip on the volume button along the back of a sleek black speaker near the nightstand as an upbeat dance song filled the room. Jared was right; she *did* feel happy. Energized. Like this trip was a door opening for *something* deeply anticipated and as yet to be determined, instead of something she had to steel herself against.

As she nodded in time to the beat, a flicker of something else sparked through her chest. *Savannah.* The name had repeated itself in her mind more times than she cared to admit since receiving the invitation. She had no idea what it would feel like to potentially see her again, but over the month since sending her response card the prospect sparked an excitement, a joy, that Emersyn refused to examine too deeply.

It was dangerous once, and we both got burned. Still, she found her mind wandering over Savannah in teasing, undeniable flashes over the last few weeks and in ways that she hadn't let herself even think about in sixteen years. The knowing intensity in her dark eyes and the way she moved with confident command. There had always been something magnetic about her, and it always made Emersyn feel exposed and vulnerable but completely safe—and she suspected Savannah liked that. She recalled the way Savannah could always see right through her stubborn walls to the desperate *want* beneath her composure. Even when Emersyn refused to name what was between them sixteen years ago, she knew that she and Savannah both understood exactly what it was. As she considered it from where she sat over what felt like a lifetime later, it was crystal-clear.

We were madly, deeply in love.

Her pulse quickened as she gazed down at her suitcase. Emersyn tugged the zipper closed with one pull. She was ready.

"Okay," she said to herself as she stood and brushed her hands along the suitcase's hard-shell exterior. "Let's go to Mexico this weekend."

❖

"Hey, Coach Hanl…I mean, Kay," Emersyn said . "Hi, it's, um…"

"Emersyn Tanner!" Kay's voice was warm and familiar. "Of course. How the heck are you, kid?"

Emersyn grinned, unsure whether she was stunned by the fact that Coach Hanlon had so quickly recognized her voice or that she was still calling her "kid" at thirty-eight years old.

"I'm good, thanks," Emersyn said automatically. She glanced at her suitcase and matching carry-on bag arranged neatly by the front door of the condo, ready for early the next morning when the rideshare was scheduled to pick her up and take her to O'Hare Airport. She was filled with nervous energy as she stood from the couch and paced across the living room, the ends of her yoga pants dragging across the gleaming hardwood beneath her feet. There was something about the idea of traveling to a beautiful, tropical resort on the ocean for Kay and Diana's wedding that seemed to cause a jolt in her carefully curated life and it excited her. Thoughts of a warm breeze rustling through palm fronds and falling asleep to the gentle sounds of waves for two weeks had become an intoxicating far cry from the loud, bustling grit of Chicago. "Congratulations on the wedding, by the way. I'm really looking forward to celebrating with you and Diana."

"Thanks, Tanner," Kay said. "Appreciate that a lot. We're looking forward to seeing you too. It's been a damn long time."

A brief pause filled the line and Emersyn took a deep breath. "Tell me," she said lightly. "How did you pop the question? I bet Diana was surprised."

Coach Hanlon chuckled. "I'll say," she said. "We took a trip to Hawaii last summer and it was something I…I really wanted to do. Neither of us had ever thought much about marriage, but we're getting older, you know? Over the last few years, we realized the importance of making it official. Well, in the eyes of the law, at least. It's been official to *me* for decades. When we went to Hawaii, I couldn't wait any longer. I bought a ring and asked her to marry me during our very first night on the Big Island."

"I'm so glad," Emersyn said. The hazy late afternoon sunlight glinted off the oversized diamond that sparkled on her own hand and she swallowed hard. She stuck her hand in the small back pocket of her yoga pants as she began pacing again. "I…I'm sorry for being out of touch for so many years. Especially being here in Chicago…"

"And what is it that you're doing in Chicago?" Coach Hanlon asked with genuine curiosity.

A rush of pride flushed through Emersyn. "Girls' varsity basketball head coach at Crestfield Academy," she said. "It's a private, non-denominational high school on the North Side."

Coach Hanlon let out a low whistle. "Coach Tanner," she said with what Emersyn could swear was a touch of pride in her tone. "That's fantastic. I can't wait to hear more when you get here. You RSVP'ed for just yourself?"

Emersyn laughed. "Just me," she confirmed and then hesitated. "My fiancé, Jared Kaminski, is an orthopedic surgeon. He and I met when his team did one of my mom's most recent outpatient tune-ups a few years ago. She's had some issues with her right ankle ever since that hip was broken. He, um, is committed to a research think tank at NYU for two weeks and he leaves just a couple days after me. He sends his regards."

There was a beat of silence and then Emersyn could hear Kay's warmth through the phone. "Well, that's great, Tanner," she said. "I'm glad you're happy. Tell Dr. Kaminski thank you for his, um, regards. We'll certainly miss meeting him. But I expect to see you at this wedding ready to have a great time or I'm benching you for the first five dances."

"Yes, ma'am," Emersyn said with a roll of her eyes. "Look, I know you'll be swamped with wedding planning and last-minute details, but I'd love to get lunch with you when I get in. It won't be until the afternoon tomorrow, but maybe the day after. I've been dreaming about that ceviche since I saw a photo of it on the resort brochure." She thought of the open-air gourmet restaurant she had seen pictured, all white linen canopies and ocean views across a modern wooden deck. The thought of sitting at one of the white-covered tables, a gentle ocean breeze ruffling her hair, and enjoying lunch with Kay without thinking about coaching next season, her team and her work, Jared's pressure to set a wedding date, and whether or not she'd see Savannah was welcoming. "If you're not too busy for me, we can meet and grab a bite to eat."

"Lunch would be nice," Coach Hanlon said. "We can play it by ear once you get here. Diana has been handling most of the wedding details, but we have a team of planners that's been pushing for fancy while we're just wanting simple. It's nearly at the point now where we're ducking behind potted plants to avoid them every time we walk through the lobby," she said dryly. "And we just got here this morning."

"Oh," Emersyn said, unsure what to say. "Well, I'm sure they just want to make your wedding memorable."

"Why don't you plan to come by the suite and we'll order room service in, including that ceviche you mentioned?" Coach Hanlon said. "I know Diana would love to see you too. We can have a casual lunch out on the balcony."

"You got it," Emersyn said as she ran her fingertips along the back of the plush suede couch. "Tell Diana I said hello and congratulations. Talk soon."

As they hung up, Emersyn collapsed onto the soft couch as a smile tugged at her lips. Coach Hanlon had been so important to her when she was younger and it was nice to reconnect as an adult. There was something easy, natural even, in the way that their conversation had flowed as though no time had passed at all. For the first time since she had opened the wedding invitation, Emersyn realized that maybe, just maybe, she was truly looking forward to the trip.

Who am I kidding? I always knew I was going to go. Just to celebrate Kay and Diana, of course.

Chapter Five

The bright morning sun was barely at its peak in the cloudless crystal-blue sky as Savannah Sanchez stepped carefully out of the black Mercedes S-Class at the wide, semicircular entrance to Dulces Sueños. She pushed her brown Prada sunglasses back into her hair, down in loose waves around her shoulders, and closed her eyes for a moment against the soft breeze. It was tinged with the scents of the beach, hibiscus, and a hint of coconut, and she paused as warmth settled into her.

"Señorita Sanchez?" the young, uniformed bellhop asked with a polite smile as he gestured toward the luggage that her driver had neatly set along the curb of the main entrance to the sprawling, expansive resort.

"Hola," Savannah said as she nodded and smoothed her light gray sleeveless satin blouse. "Bueno, gracias."

The bellhop began loading her luggage onto a wheeled cart as Savannah drank in the lush, tropical landscape. Vibrant bougainvillea spilled over the white stucco walls and onto smooth stones around the entrance's wide, automatic double doors that quietly whooshed open as guests wandered in and out of the resort.

Being here felt like a dream and a slow, grounding relief washed through Savannah as she followed the bellhop into the open-air lobby. She was finally here and, as she gazed out the open wall on the other side of the lobby to a colorful bird gliding just beneath the sun, she realized this was the pause she desperately needed.

As she checked in, tapping one of her white heels against the sleek marble flooring as she handed over her credit card and driver's license, the scent of grilled pineapple drifted in the warm sea air. Savannah's stomach growled as she realized too late that she hadn't eaten since a quick cup of yogurt before getting onto her early morning flight from Phoenix.

"I will take your luggage to your room," the bellhop said as he gestured to the cart.

"Sí, gracias," Savannah said as she turned from the long dark wood counter of check-in stations. She pulled a neatly folded wad of bills from the pocket of her navy blue bootcut jeans and pressed them into his palm. "I'll be up shortly."

The bellhop's face lit up as he nodded and pushed the cart toward an elevator bank opposite the check-in counter. "Gracias, señorita," he said.

Savannah walked to the open wall looking out at the white sand beach and expanse of bright blue water beyond. It was a far cry from the desert, but there was something about the ocean that was calming. It made her feel both insignificant and invincible, and she smiled as she felt herself relax. She had earned this break from her gym business and intended to make the most of it before preparing for another strategic expansion in the Phoenix area.

"Sanchez!" A familiar voice echoed across the lobby. Savannah turned expectantly.

Kay strode toward her, hands in the pockets of her khaki Bermuda shorts and a matching panama hat shading her face, and Diana waved excitedly. Savannah closed the distance across the lobby quickly as she embraced them both.

"Look who finally made it!" Diana said as she hugged her. "We're so excited to see you."

"How is it that you two haven't aged a day?" Savannah said with a grin. She slipped her sunglasses from her head into the neckline of her blouse. "Do destination weddings come with a magical anti-aging serum or is just a couple days with the sea breeze?"

Kay rolled her eyes, though they crinkled at the corners. "Flattery won't get you a free tequila shot."

"It might," Diana said as she nudged Kay playfully. "But seriously, don't listen to her. You can continue complimenting me all you want."

Savannah laughed as she followed them into a casual sit-down restaurant adjacent to the lobby, where they had brunch reservations. Long, thin dark wood columns lined up to hold the flat roof, designed with a thick white canopy woven through sleek dark wood beams. The restaurant was lined with community-style tables and benches through the middle and plush private booths along the open-air side walls.

Savannah slid into one of the cushioned booths. She hadn't realized just how much she'd missed Kay and Diana until that moment, as they fell back into comfortable, easy conversation. She had missed *all* of this—the sense of unwavering support, the safety to set aside her corporate persona and just *be*, the belonging and grounding that could only come with spending quality time with two people who had known her for years.

Diana reached across the table and squeezed her hand as a waiter in a crisp white button-up shirt filled their glasses with ice water. "We're so happy you're here, Savannah," she said warmly. "I know it must not have been easy to get away from your company for a full two weeks. How are the gyms doing?"

Savannah gazed out at another stretch of the private beach just beyond the restaurant. She felt good. Steady. Rooted and sure.

"Really well, thanks," she said. She nodded in thanks as the waiter placed a wicker bread basket at the center of the table. "The four Vault locations we currently have in Phoenix are doing great. I have a few investors who have been pushing for an expansion over the last few months, and it sounds like we're going to go for it." She took a deep breath and smiled. "It'll be a lot of strategic ramp-up. Budget planning, location scouting, kick-off meetings with our construction crews and interior design team, and then we'll hit the ground running. I'm glad to take this break first." She looked around. "Quiet mornings waking up to the ocean. Sitting on the sand and watching the sun set. Disconnecting as much as I can from my phone and laptop."

"You're getting soft on us," Kay said as she raised an eyebrow knowingly.

"Maybe," Savannah said. "Either way, I finally have bandwidth to breathe. Five straight years overseas playing pro ball, coming back to Arizona and getting my doctorate in physical therapy, getting my personal training licensing, opening the gyms and learning the business side of the industry." She shook her head. "I've been running them nonstop for four years. I finally feel like I have the best management team in place. Now they're running themselves even better than I expected. When I got your invitation to the wedding, it was easy. *And* the perfect excuse to take a pause and enjoy all the work I've put in to the Vault."

Kay leaned back as she rested an arm around Diana's shoulders. "You've really built something, Sanchez."

Savannah nodded as a flicker of pride warmed her face. "It started when I came back from Germany," she said. "I fell in love with the rehab side of things. After getting my doctorate, I started working with injured athletes and it just took off. The natural next step was to focus on the whole body, and that includes the well body too. And now I'm here, celebrating two of the best people to ever get married."

Diana lifted her water glass, condensation already trickling down the sides. "I'll drink to that," she said with a nod. "Well, water anyway. Here's to being in the right place at the right time and getting that special team all back together. *And* to marrying this amazing woman next to me."

Savannah clinked her glass against theirs. "And to not tripping in the sand on heels."

She and Diana burst into laughter as Kay shook her head in amusement. As the conversation drifted to their wedding plans and the floral arrangements that Diana had designed herself, something else stirred inside Savannah.

Did she say getting the team back together for the wedding?

Savannah bit her lip as the waiter returned to take their orders. Her mind flitted over all the friends she'd made during her short time in Northwoods. Erica, Mia, Arissa, the list went on.

And then there was *her*. Savannah could picture her face as though twenty-two was only a few years ago. Just the thought of Emersyn Tanner was enough to feel a faint flutter of anticipation in her chest stir to life and an unexpected pressure deepen between her thighs.

She took a grounding sip of her ice water and glanced across the table as Diana smiled at her. "So, what do you have planned this afternoon?"

Savannah shook her head. "Nothing today, except getting settled into my suite," she shrugged. "Maybe connecting with Arissa Johnson once she gets in later. She and I found each other on social media a few years ago and have exchanged a few messages since."

"That sounds great," Diana said. "Say, would you be able to do me a favor?" She frowned as she glanced at her phone. "All these last-minute wedding details keep coming up and I can barely keep track of them all. I just got *another* notification."

"You know I can—" Kay started, but Diana tutted.

"No, no, I want you to relax," she said before glancing at Savannah knowingly. "After all these years, I'm still not certain Kay knows how to relax."

Savannah laughed. "Sounds about right. Is there something I can help with?"

Diana shot her a grateful look. "I have so much scheduled for tomorrow," she said as she scrolled through her phone and read from an email. "Apparently, the resort's director of events wants us to choose a layout for the wedding reception in the banquet room as soon as possible. They have a few options, but I can't seem to get them via email. Something about the file sizes for the mockups being too large, I think. Could you run by his office tomorrow and grab those printouts for us? I would, but I don't even know when I'd be able to do it. I'd be so grateful."

Savannah nodded. That was easy enough. She had spied a quiet darkened hallway toward the front entrance that appeared to hold the private offices for resort management. "Sure, I can do that," she said. "After lunch, maybe around two? I was going to run over to the boutique mall and do some shopping in the morning, but my afternoon is wide open." She smiled. "I figured it would be easier to get some clothes while I'm here rather than pack a small army of suitcases."

"You've always loved your fashion, Savannah," Kay said. "I'll give you that. We appreciate the favor."

Diana pulled a folded sheet of paper from her purse. "Before I forget, since we're on the subject of the wedding," she said. "We've gotten all the confirmed guest reservations back." She unfolded a pair of reading glasses and balanced them on the tip of her nose. "Mostly family, but Kay was adamant about inviting all the former players on that special team you guys had. I mean, all the teams have been special, but there was just something about the synergy with you girls and all you accomplished during your time together."

Savannah smiled politely. "You're giving me too much credit," she said. "I was only there for our senior season. I think the team achieved more before I was ever there."

Kay fixed her with a look as she took a sip of her water. "Savannah, you were just as much a part of that team as anyone," she said. "Regardless of how many seasons you spent in Northwoods."

Diana ran her finger down the list and paused by a name. "Speaking of the team, did you mention yesterday you spoke to Emersyn Tanner?" Diana glanced at Kay expectantly as Savannah blinked.

Hearing the name said out loud after she had just allowed herself to think of her for the first time in years was jarring. Her hands tightened slightly around her sweating water glass as she tried to bury the memory of Emersyn gazing back at her like Savannah was a threat and a promise all at once. She crossed her legs beneath the table as she recalled the way Emersyn had finally let her in and allowed Savannah to claim her, to unravel her, and then put her back together again.

Kay nodded once as she absent-mindedly rapped her knuckles on the tabletop. "I did, finally," she said. "We had a brief conversation yesterday afternoon while you were with the wedding planner. Confirmed the reservation and the RSVP card is just for her. Sounds like she's made a good life for herself."

Savannah exhaled slowly and deliberately as she lifted her chin. "That's great," she said smoothly. "Haven't heard that name in years, wow."

She knew Kay didn't miss the ultra-casual tone she'd injected into her voice or the beat of silence that followed, but she didn't say anything. Instead, Kay smiled as she glanced at the ocean just beyond the restaurant.

"Surprised even me that she decided to attend," she said. "She was pretty adamant about leaving Northwoods and not looking back. We kept in touch here and there, but she needed to learn how to spread her wings again. I get the feeling she's in a good place. Seems to be doing really well for herself. Coaching varsity at Crestfield Academy in downtown Chicago."

"Good for her," Savannah said, grateful for the distraction as the waiter arrived with a round silver tray filled with plates of food. "She always had the ability to lead."

But deep down she always wanted to let go and submit. The tantalizing thought crossed Savannah's mind before she could stop it. Her neck flushed beneath the hot tropical sun.

Kay turned to Diana as she picked up her fork. "By the way, I invited her to the suite for lunch tomorrow. I'm looking forward to it."

Diana nodded. "That sounds lovely," she said. She carefully cut into her Belgian waffles and glanced at Savannah. "You two never kept in touch?"

Savannah forced a smile that felt practiced but not quite authentic. "No," she said. "Different lives. Different careers. Different countries for a while, then different states. We haven't spoken since shortly after graduation."

Diana nodded again and the conversation slowed to a lull as they focused on the nearly overflowing plates of food before them. As Savannah speared a piece of cantaloupe with her fork, the faint ache seemed to intensify into something that pulsed and burned deep in her core. She knew this time the sudden flicker of heat had nothing to do with the tropical sunshine or humid ocean air.

"Oh, you got the shrimp ceviche!" Diana exclaimed as she pointed at Savannah's plate with her fork. "I thought about that. It looks delicious."

Savannah bit into a chunk of cool, sweet melon from a small side bowl. "I've been dreaming about a good ceviche since I booked the plane ticket to Cabo."

Kay's head seemed to snap up as an unreadable look of—was that recognition?—flashed across her face. It disappeared so quickly that Savannah was sure she had imagined it.

As the conversation turned to Kay and Diana's planned honeymoon cruise through Europe, Savannah wondered if Emersyn was still much the same. She knew *she* wasn't. Savannah knew who she was, what she wanted, and how she wanted it, but had never been able to quite find it in the years since college. Or maybe it was that no one had captivated her and brought out her dominant instincts as completely as…

What if you see Emersyn and there's still something there? The thought was dangerous and spiked the warmth in her core. *Kay said it would just be her, didn't she?*

Savannah nodded along as Diana laughed about the last time they had visited Italy and how she'd nearly twisted an ankle on the cobblestone streets after a few too many glasses of red wine, but her mind was lingering somewhere else. She remembered for the first time in years how her heart felt as though it broke into a thousand pieces when she'd signed the contract from her former manager to play in Germany. How Emersyn had cried, wriggling out of her arms when she tried to hold her tighter, and then slammed the front door of Savannah's half-packed on-campus apartment behind her so loudly that the thin walls shook.

We were too young. Savannah watched a lone western gull circle over the beach. *I had no idea the trust and vulnerability she gave to me when she finally let me in.*

Savannah swallowed hard as she took a long sip of her ice water and forced herself to refocus on brunch with Kay and Diana. As she gazed at the sparkling horizon, she had no idea what the next two weeks would bring, but for the first time in a long time, she realized she was exactly where she needed to be.

Chapter Six

Emersyn pressed her forehead to the tinted window of her taxi as it pulled gently to the entrance of Dulces Sueños. The sun was sinking deep into the horizon just beyond the large resort. The sky was painted with splashes of bold red, deep gold, and an encroaching navy blue along the blurred edges where sky met water. A layover in Dallas and a two-hour delay for her connecting flight had made Emersyn's arrival in Cabo San Lucas even later in the day than anticipated, and it was rapidly waning around her.

Thick humidity hugged her as she stepped out of the taxi and a soft ocean breeze tousled her casual ponytail. As she strode into the lobby, wheeling her oversized suitcase behind her, she took in the natural luxury of the resort. As beautiful as the glossy photos on the brochure were, they didn't quite do justice to the flowing white curtains pulled over the open-air walls to keep the cooler evening breeze out or the gentle Spanish guitar strumming somewhere from the small, elegant lobby bar.

The ocean lapped gently at the white sand beach, only a few lingering guests left lounging in cushioned bamboo chaises, and the scent of tropical flowers, hibiscus, and coconut floated on the breeze. Emersyn stilled as her body reacted to the light scent of coconut before her brain, frayed from hours of travel, caught up.

Something about that milky coconut scent...

"Welcome, Ms. Tanner!" An exuberant hostess approached Emersyn and smiled. Emersyn had called the resort during her layover to let them know her check-in would be later than anticipated, but she hadn't expected a personal welcome. The hostess's sleek navy blue skirt and blazer were smooth along her ample curves and her hair was pulled into a neat bun. She handed Emersyn a flute of champagne. "We greet our evening check-ins with fresh champagne," she said with a wink. "Let's get you checked in. You're part of the Hanlon-Miller wedding party, sí?"

Emersyn blinked, momentarily stunned, as she accepted the flute. "Thank you," she said as she took in the dark wood accents and flowing tropical greenery at every turn. "This is…wow."

As the hostess pecked at her tablet and began checking her in, Emersyn was all too aware of her wrinkled black linen pants and rumpled gray tank top. She felt wildly underdressed, despite standing only in the lobby, and desperately craved a hot shower. Still, she couldn't help but feel like she'd tumbled out of a cramped airplane into the middle of a *Vogue* editorial.

Maybe Jared was right and I should've booked the business class seat. Emersyn fiddled with the black Wayfarer sunglasses hanging from her carry-on. *Though I can see now why this resort was so pricy.*

"Come." The hostess gestured. "We'll take a quick tour of the grounds and then you can get settled into your suite."

Emersyn nodded as she fell into step with her and glanced out the open-air hallway toward the sparkling infinity pool. Hummingbirds darted in and out of thick greenery and golden lights beneath the water gave the pool an almost sensuous glow in the evening hours. There were still several people lounging in the oversized private cabanas as they sipped frosty cocktails.

"Since you're part of the Hanlon-Miller wedding party, you'll be in one of our ocean-view suites with a private balcony," the hostess said matter-of-factly. She handed Emersyn a large envelope with a gold foil Dulces Sueños logo across it. "You're all set for early access to the spa, our private poolside cabanas, and any resort group activities." The hostess pointed down a shorter tiled hallway. "The fitness center is world-class and will be on your left side down that hallway. Locker rooms are at the end of the hall." She nodded once. "The last door on the left is a full-sized pickleball and tennis court. The first two doors on the right open up to a half-sized basketball court."

Despite the jet lag weighing heavily along her shoulders and arms, Emersyn's ears perked up and she filed it away in her mind for later. A small glass window looked in at the empty half-court and Emersyn stole a quick glance, impressed by the gleaming hardwood and pristine backboard. She couldn't help but think it looked rarely used, though that didn't surprise her given the resort's location and impressive other amenities.

The hostess quickly turned a corner down another hallway and they arrived at a smaller elevator bank. "The Mrs. and Mrs.-to-be have arranged a few pre-wedding events, including an upcoming cocktail party, as well as the standard wedding activities. Rehearsal dinner, ceremony, and reception. You'll find a full schedule inside as well as a detailed map of the resort."

Emersyn turned the envelope over in her hands and exhaled. She hadn't realized she'd been holding her breath. The chaotic, dense bustle of Chicago where she had woken up that morning already felt like a lifetime away.

As the hostess led them out of the elevator onto the sixth floor, the hallway was silent. She paused outside a cherry wood door and turned to Emersyn. "And here," she said as she handed Emersyn a small square keycard, "is your room, Ms. Tanner. Is there anything else I can do for you right now?"

"No." Emersyn shook her head. "Thank you. This is wonderful."

As she dug around her pocket and slipped the hostess the last of her wrinkled cash, Emersyn's heart thudded as a small voice somewhere at the back of her mind reminded her that Savannah might be somewhere in this large, sprawling resort right now too. The thought was threaded with something else; something anticipatory and electric that Emersyn hadn't felt that intensely in years. Despite her desire to shower and then fall into bed, there was something creeping around the edges of her consciousness and sinking deep into her veins: the intoxicating feeling of being *alive*.

❖

Midday sun streamed through the large sliding glass door leading to a curved balcony overlooking the ocean. The sun cast warm light across the dark hardwood floors. Emersyn had slept better than she had in years in the comfortable king-sized bed, the last few minutes between stepping out of the glass-walled shower and into her gray yoga shorts and oversized white T-shirt an exhausted blur, and she awoke feeling lighter than she had in weeks. She had opened the sliding glass doors and ordered room service for breakfast, indulging in the skin-hugging humidity and salty breeze that blew through the room.

Her room wasn't large, but the space had been designed thoughtfully. The king-sized bed took up most of the room, with a dark hardwood dresser and a small desk opposite the foot of the bed. A large television set hung from the wall over the dresser and an oversized ceiling fan spun lazily above. On one side of the bed, a small closet with white wooden slats was built into the wall. On the other side, a small granite-topped table and cushioned chair sat before the sweeping sliding glass doors that led to the balcony.

Even the small bathroom, with its slate-colored tile walls, glass shower, and granite-topped vanity, seemed designed for elegant relaxation. Emersyn glanced in the mirror as she carefully changed her clothes, pushed a pair of thin silver hoops through her ears, and ran a brush through her hair, leaving it down over her shoulders. She was used to moving quickly and precisely, each step carefully coordinated, and her days broken down into hours and even minutes. Here, she already seemed to move slower and more languidly as she gently swept a coat of mascara over her lashes. Something about the faint rushing of the waves in the background felt as though it softened the defensive edges that Emersyn hadn't even realized she'd been clinging to so tightly. The light scent of coconut smoothed out her thoughts and teased an intoxicating state of surrender that she hadn't felt in years.

As she stepped into the quiet hallway and adjusted the strap of her casual, sleeveless navy blue-and-white-striped sun dress, enjoying the way the thin fabric hugged the curve of her breasts, Emersyn couldn't help but smile. Today felt easy, unforced, and natural. Distant laugher echoed from a nearby room as she approached the elevator bank and glanced down at the resort map in her hands.

Tenth floor. Room 1020. Emersyn thought as she traced a line on the colorful map with her fingertip. She looked forward to lunch with Kay and Diana and, as the elevator softly dinged with its arrival, Emersyn couldn't shake the feeling that she made the right decision by accepting the invitation and that she had somehow ended up exactly where she needed to be.

CHAPTER SEVEN

The door to Kay and Diana's honeymoon suite swung open before Emersyn could knock, and she couldn't help but notice how happy and comfortable Kay and Diana appeared as they greeted her with a big hug. Emersyn felt familiarity flood her veins as the long embrace seemed to pull all the years and distance away.

"Still hate texting, huh?" Emersyn said as Kay ushered her into the suite. "I sent you a message when I was about to leave my room. I thought you forgot about me."

"Of course not," Kay said with a hearty laugh. "It's not that I hate texting. It's just so much easier to pick up the phone and call."

Emersyn rolled her eyes. "You know, there's a lot you can do with smartphones these days. There are even apps that will deliver groceries right to your front door."

Kay scoffed and shook her head. "And trust some Northwoods College kid to pick the bananas that aren't bruised and look like they've been tossed out of a car window? Not a chance. I'll get my own eggs and milk, thank you very much."

Diana led Emersyn through the room and to their wide balcony. "She'll never give up her flip phone," she said. "I've been trying for years."

The time between them seemed to melt away as Emersyn slid into a wicker chair at the round glass-topped table on their balcony. "It's *so* good to see you," she said. "I can't believe it's been so long. You look exactly the same."

Emersyn meant it too. Aside from some deeper lines across Kay's forehead and her short blond hair having faded into a silver much like her mother's, she looked largely the same.

Even age isn't going to slow her down.

"You're kind," Kay said warmly. She settled into a wicker chair opposite Emersyn. The table had already been set with cold sandwiches, fresh fruit salad, colorful shrimp ceviche, and lemonade in a tall glass pitcher. Cool drops of condensation snaked down the sides of the pitcher as streams of afternoon sunlight bounced off the sparkling ocean below the balcony and bathed it in bright white light. "I wish I could say the same for you, but you went and became a grown-up on us. Adulthood suits you, Tanner. Or should I say, *Coach* Tanner."

Emersyn blushed. "Thanks, Coach…"

Kay held up a hand. "Please, call me Kay," she said as she leaned back in her chair. "We're all adults. Besides, I haven't been your coach in about sixteen years now, isn't that right?"

Emersyn nodded. "This looks amazing, thank you for ordering lunch," she gestured to the spread on the table. Her gaze landed on the shrimp ceviche in a white bowl. Bright green cilantro leaves and chunks of avocado blended seamlessly with the poached shrimp and juicy, deep-red tomatoes. "Oh my *God*, thank you for remembering the ceviche too! I've been dying to try it since I got in last night."

Emersyn could practically taste the zesty lime that had been squeezed over the dish as she caught Kay glancing at her in her peripheral.

"It seems to be popular," she said dryly, though Emersyn could've sworn it sounded like she was refraining from saying more.

"I'll let you both catch up," Diana said as she leaned down with a soft kiss for Kay's cheek. "I've got to meet with the wedding planner. Last-minute cake drama. We asked for a simple vanilla buttercream, but they're *insisting* we add a touch of lavender and honey." She rolled her eyes. "Now, isn't lavender a flower? Why on Earth would we want that in our cake? Besides, I told them we met decades ago at a charity volleyball game for the northern Wisconsin Boys and Girls Club, for God's sake. We aren't lavender cake people, *despite* splashing out some of our hard-earned savings for this wedding."

Kay smiled. "Tell them how you really feel, Dee."

Diana shook her head and patted Emersyn's shoulder on her way back into the suite. "She's all yours."

The gentle breeze rustling through the palm trees was a relaxing soundtrack as Emersyn poured herself a glass of lemonade. "This resort is beautiful," she said. "If you're going to have a destination wedding, I suppose you might as well do it big and go all out." She glanced at Kay across the table. "Besides, this would be a lovely place to visit regularly when you retire."

Kay glanced down at her sandwich. "That's the idea, yeah," she said carefully. "Diana has been begging me to retire for the last five years, but I just haven't been able to give coaching up. I always told her I'd know when it was time. She's been patient so far, but I have to admit that the seasonal grind is getting tiresome."

Emersyn noted the soft speculation in Kay's voice. "You may enjoy it more than you think," she said. "Besides, you deserve to take some time to enjoy what all your hard work over the decades has provided for you both."

Kay nodded. "I agree, Em." She sighed as she squinted toward the sun. "God, I haven't even mentioned this to Diana yet, we've been so focused on wedding planning. But I think my time is coming sooner than later, kid. I always said I'd retire when I knew it was time and, well, I think my body is finally telling me it's time. The last couple of seasons have been tough, maintaining the energy to coach through March. I started to realize I was slowing the team down instead of doing my *job*. It was a hard pill to swallow, but just like any teammate who realizes they're hindering instead of helping the team, I decided next season will be my last. I've been helping Coach Connor prepare to take over. She and her fiancée will be here too, actually. They get in this weekend."

"Oh, Kay, I'm sorry," Emersyn said. She knew how much Kay loved coaching and recalled the strange, unwelcome feeling of realizing that she had to build a life outside of basketball so many years ago. "I can't imagine you *not* being part of Northwoods College, but I can't help but agree with Diana. Maybe it's time to step back and enjoy these years."

"It's tough, Tanner," Kay admitted as she took a long sip of lemonade. "When you're young, you never really picture yourself as an old person. It always seems eons away. Suddenly, you wake up one morning and you're pushing seventy and your body just isn't working the way it used to. But that's just it. I was feeling down and sorry for myself as I fought with the idea of retirement, but then I realized something. Why *wouldn't* I retire?"

Emersyn nodded as Kay leaned forward in her chair. "I've had a damn good career, Tanner," she said. "Three-time Midwest Conference Women's Basketball Coaching Staff of the Year, ten-time Divisional Champions, a handful of Sunday Selections, countless girls have gone on to play professionally. But more important than all that resume crap is that

I've *loved* my career. I've loved coming to school every day, coaching you girls, and sharing my passion for basketball. If the only thing standing between me and retirement is my own pride, well, then that's pretty selfish, isn't it?"

"I get it," Emersyn said. She bit into a citrusy-sweet forkful of the ceviche and closed her eyes for a moment as the flavors exploded on her tongue. "As a coach, I really do. And as a woman. Diana has been waiting patiently for a long time to finally have you all to herself."

Kay cracked a grin. "You better believe it," she said. "I still have a lot of living to do with that woman." Her sharp gaze swept over Emersyn. "It's good to see you, Em. And I don't just mean *here*, in Cabo. You look settled. Confident. I like it."

Emersyn smiled as she crossed one leg over the other and brushed an invisible crumb off her dress. "I appreciate that," she said. "I *feel* good. Coaching has been surprisingly right for me."

Kay nodded thoughtfully. "You've got the mind and the IQ for it. And the heart."

She nodded down at the oversized diamond ring on Emersyn's slender ring finger. "Speaking of hearts, I need to congratulate you too. We've been going on about me, but we should be celebrating your engagement. That's some rock you've got there. I'm so happy to hear you've found happiness, Tanner."

Emersyn swallowed hard, unsure why her stomach sank. Before the beat could stretch on, she forced a smile. "Thank you," she said, hoping her tone sounded more enthusiastic than she felt. "Jared is a great guy. Really, he's very good to me."

Kay nodded as a brief question flashed across her face and then disappeared as quickly as it had flickered by. She glanced down at her phone on the edge of the table as she bit into the corner of a cold-cut sandwich and blinked as though she had just remembered something. "Shoot, I can't believe it's already ten to two," she said. She shot Emersyn a friendly smile. "Time flies when you're in good company, I suppose. On that note, though, I don't want to keep you all afternoon. I know you're probably eager to check out the rest of the resort."

Emersyn paused, her glass of lemonade halfway to her lips. *Is Kay trying to politely shuffle me out? No, that can't be.*

She shrugged. "That's all right," she said. "I have a facial scheduled at the spa, but not until three. I don't mind keeping you company until Diana gets back, unless you had plans."

Kay looked downright flustered—something Emersyn had never witnessed before—as she rubbed her thumb along the smooth glass edge of the table and nodded quickly. "I did have a last minute—" She was cut off by a single knock echoing through the suite and floating onto the balcony.

Emersyn stood and placed her white linen napkin next to her half-eaten plate. "I'm sorry, I didn't realize you had last-minute wedding plans to attend to," she said. *Of course. The wedding is coming up fast.* "I don't want to take up your whole afternoon. I'll get out of your hair and we'll chat again soon."

Kay stood hastily as she followed Emersyn through the suite. She turned. "I'll give you a call soon?" Emersyn asked and then smiled. "*Call*, not text. I promise. Reach out if you or Diana need any help in the meantime…"

Kay opened her mouth to reply as Emersyn swung open the door and froze.

Time seemed to stand perfectly still as the light-filled suite and the sounds of the spinning ceiling fan above faded to nothing. The suite felt impossibly cramped and it was as though all the oxygen in the narrow foyer had been sucked out. Try as Emersyn might, the only person she could focus on was standing equally still in the silent hallway wearing a tight white and tan ombre halter dress. Without warning, a familiar magnetic pull hit Emersyn like a slow-rolling wave.

Savannah smiled knowingly, as cool and poised as always. "Hey, Kay," she said smoothly. Gold earrings dangled beneath her long, dark hair and caught just enough of the light to illuminate her profile in a dancing glow. Her gaze swept over to Emersyn and their eyes locked for a long moment. The thick, humid tropical air felt hot and stifling, but everything else remained a blur. "Hey, Emersyn."

Chapter Eight

Savannah," Emersyn replied evenly. She was relieved that her voice was steady despite her pounding heart. It echoed loudly in her ears as she registered Kay warmly greeting Savannah and the woman who stood next to her.

God, she's gorgeous. Her lips were still lush and full and her brown eyes were as knowing and intense as Emersyn remembered. She noticed that Savannah wore less makeup than she did in college. Her long, dark eyelashes were simply swept with a coat of mascara while a light dusting of bronzer and powder highlighted the natural angles of her face and the gentle slope of her cheekbones. As Emersyn took her in, her gaze fell to Savannah's lips again. They looked as soft as she remembered, even without the sticky, shiny gloss she used to wear.

Emersyn flushed at the thought, unnerved by her reaction to Savannah so many years and a fiancé later. The air between them seemed to sizzle with anticipation, memories, and a strange, heated tension as Savannah turned her attention back to Emersyn.

"You look good," she said, her voice tinged with a softness that Emersyn immediately recognized. It coiled inside her, pulling tight, as she tried not to remember the way Savannah used to hold her close, lips brushing her temple, and speak to her with that exact softness. "Didn't expect to run into you so soon."

Emersyn nodded politely, though her fingertips curled slightly against her thigh. "Thank you," she said. "You look great." She tried not to blush and quickly glanced at the woman standing next to Savannah instead. "Oh my *God*, Arissa Johnson!"

Arissa laughed and opened her arms for a hug. Her smooth dark brown skin and tight black curls glowed under the stream of sunlight that danced across the foyer and into the hallway. "Live and in person," she said. "This resort is gorgeous. Thank God my team of Realtors was able to cover during our busy season so I could stay for the wedding." She glanced around. "I would've been *pissed* if I missed this. Anyway, I got in yesterday and Savannah already kidnapped me for a shopping trip this morning. How fun is that?"

Emersyn glanced between them and arched an eyebrow. "Are you both staying the full two weeks?"

Savannah laughed. "That's the idea," she said. "I haven't taken off two weeks in as long as I can remember. I've been so busy with the Vault and running these gyms, and I haven't really gotten out of Phoenix since…" She glanced down to the crisp folder in her hands and lingered for a beat too long. "Since I got back from Germany."

Kay clapped her hands together and ran a hand through her short hair. "Well, come on in, Savannah, Arissa," she said, a little too loudly. "Let's see those mockups for the wedding reception that you were kind enough to grab for Diana and I. Em, why don't you hang out until your facial? I know we barely finished lunch."

Emersyn blinked as her mind scrambled to keep up with the throbbing heat in her veins and the ache in her chest. Suddenly, she could recall with perfect clarity how Savannah's hands felt on her skin, tracing each curve, and how soft her lips were.

This is ridiculous. All she has to do is stand there and I'm melting? I have a fiancé. A smart, kind fiancé who has been nothing but loving to me. It's just unresolved tension, that's all. Residual angsty twenty-something energy. Obviously.

She straightened and then shook her head politely. "No, you're right," she said. "I wanted to check out the rest of the resort and scope out the best cabana spot for when I eventually make it to the pool."

Emersyn could feel Savannah's deliberate gaze on her as Kay nodded. "No problem, Tanner," she said. "We'll talk soon."

Emersyn tried not to look at Savannah's mouth again. "Right," she said as she paused in the doorway and glanced at Savannah. "Good luck with your gym empire."

As she gently shut the door to the suite behind her, Emersyn stopped in the hallway for a moment longer than necessary and took a deep breath at the way her heart raced against her ribcage. The faint scent of coconut milk lingered outside the doorway as a rush of heat curled deep in Emersyn's stomach.

Of course, that's where I recognize that scent. She pressed the elevator button and took a deep breath. *I need to steer clear of Savannah and the smell of coconut if I want to make it through Kay's wedding without...*

Emersyn stepped into the elevator. As the doors slowly closed, Emersyn shook her head once. *Without what? Losing my mind? That's what we'll call it. Because it definitely isn't anything else.*

Satisfied, Emersyn stepped confidently into the lobby as the elevator doors opened softly. Of course it would be awkward and strange to see each other again after so many years. But now that they had gotten the initial reintroduction over with—despite Emersyn being caught off-guard—it would be fine. It had to be.

Emersyn blinked away the memory of Savannah standing so near in the doorway, suddenly grateful for her splurge on a facial at the spa. A darkened room, a soft table, maybe some gentle instrumental music in the background as the esthetician pampered her sounded especially enticing right now. A little grounding and zen to snap her out of whatever off balance energy was swirling through her after coming face-to-face with Savannah Sanchez all over again.

Emersyn made a beeline toward the frosted glass door of the luxury spa. She was way too early, but she didn't mind waiting.

"Maybe I should do sixty minutes instead of thirty," she said to herself. She already knew she would, as she dug into her small purse for her credit card. "You know, just to make sure."

❖

Savannah stood frozen next to the white loveseat in the living area of Kay and Diana's suite. She tossed the folder she had been gripping onto a cushion. Kay gestured for her to sit as Arissa sank comfortably onto one side of the loveseat, but Savannah preferred to stand. She hadn't expected to walk into a storm of intensity that seemed to peak as Emersyn's gaze collided with her own.

She took a deep breath as Arissa congratulated Kay and asked polite questions about the wedding plans. *Okay, so the intensity was really only radiating from one person—Emersyn Tanner.* It rolled off her in massive, scorching waves that Savannah immediately recognized, and it spiked a familiar longing that panged through her chest stronger than expected. For some reason, memories of a worn pink-and-green-flowered quilt and a dated Super 8 motel room in Superior, Wisconsin, rushed back to her, and her face burned at the sweet intimacy and slow, heated kisses.

"I'm going to grab the pitcher of lemonade from the balcony," Kay said. "I'll get you both a glass before we look at those reception mockups. I'd love your thoughts on them. Diana should be back any minute."

Savannah nodded and ignored the look of confusion Arissa shot her from where she'd crossed her legs politely at the end of the couch.

"Are you going to sit or just tower over us?" Arissa asked as she raised an eyebrow.

Savannah shook her head. "I'm going to stand for a minute."

Arissa looked at her a moment longer. "That was…weird," she ventured hesitantly. "I don't think Emersyn was expecting to see you, at least until the wedding."

Savannah sighed as she ran a hand through her hair. "I was caught off-guard, that's all," she said, hoping her voice sounded nonchalant. "I wasn't exactly expecting for Emersyn to swing open the front door to Kay and Diana's suite either."

Arissa fixed her with a look that told Savannah she didn't quite believe her. "It's been a long time, hasn't it?"

Savannah glanced down at the glass coffee table as Diana swung open the front door and greeted them with an enthusiastic hello. "Shit," she said as she looked around. "Where is the folder with the mockups? I don't see it here and I know I just had it…"

Arissa carefully grabbed the thick folder Savannah had dropped onto the empty loveseat cushion moments before. She held it out to her silently.

Savannah flushed. This wasn't like her to feel so put off after a chance encounter. "Thanks." She gestured awkwardly at the folder in her hands. "Got it."

Arissa stared back at her and nodded. "Yup," she said as she scanned her face dubiously. "You got it."

Just then, Kay returned from the balcony balancing a small silver serving tray with three glasses of bright yellow lemonade. The square ice cubes clinked against the glass as she handed one to Savannah. "You look like you could use a drink," Kay said, bemused but otherwise unreadable.

"I think there's a few tiny bottles of Grey Goose in the minibar, if you want a shot of something stronger than sugar in that lemonade."

Savannah glanced at Kay, but her focus was already on the three mockup options for the reception layout as she pointed at one and mentioned something about awkward placement of the cake table. She brought the glass to her lips and enjoyed the icy tartness dancing along her tongue.

She's not wrong. She tried to focus on the layout options on the coffee table. *What is it I've been saying since I was twenty-two years old? Oh, yeah. Coach Hanlon always knows.*

Chapter Nine

That evening, Emersyn felt restless in her suite despite the afternoon in the quiet, low-lit stillness of the spa. Though the afternoon had helped calm her racing thoughts, it didn't help alleviate the tingle she felt as she remembered the way Savannah's gaze had lingered on her earlier.

Emersyn sighed as she perched at the foot of the bed and flipped blankly through television channels. The sun was beginning its descent into the expansive horizon as the shades in the sky started to gradually darken. As Emersyn tore her eyes from the breathtaking tropical sunset, she chewed the inside of her cheek in thought. Savannah had gazed at her like she already knew exactly how Emersyn's body would respond, like she hadn't forgotten anything. Emersyn was frustrated that she hadn't either and that it had taken so little—an invitation to a destination wedding, hearing Savannah's name, coming face-to-face with her after all these years—to put her so off balance.

As she glanced at her suitcase and pondered the time, the growth, and the lives they had built for themselves at opposite corners of the country, a news report from the local Mexican TV station droned in the background. The rapid-fire Spanish was far too fast for Emersyn to understand a word they were reporting. With a start, Emersyn realized her phone was buzzing on the nightstand insistently. Emersyn's heart sank as a photo of Jared, his blue eyes sparkling and his easy grin lighting his face as he posed in front of Buckingham Fountain, flashed across the screen. She had been so distracted by running into Savannah earlier that she hadn't even thought to call or text him today.

With a deep breath, Emersyn answered. "Hey, Jared."

"Hey, you," he said amiably. "Just checking in. I'm getting settled here in the Big Apple. How was your first full day in Cabo?"

"It's been nice," Emersyn hedged as she fingered a tiny thread along the hem of her dress. "I had lunch with Kay earlier and got in some time at the resort spa."

"That's cool," Jared said. "So far, this think tank appears to be as dry as expected. Even if you came to New York instead, you would have been bored out of your mind with me wrapped up in all this clinical stuff. How's your old coach doing?"

"Happy," Emersyn said honestly. "Relaxed. Readying herself for retirement."

"That's the dream," Jared laughed. "Wish I could be there with you."

Emersyn stared out the sliding glass door past the balcony as the sun sank lower into the ocean. The bright yellows and soft blues that had streaked across the sky minutes before had darkened into deep orange and dark navy. "Me too," she lied as a beat of guilt flared in her chest.

Jared was silent for a moment. "You sound quiet. Is everything okay?"

"Yeah, I'm just really relaxed after the afternoon at the spa," Emersyn said. *Another lie.* "What's tomorrow's roundtable about?" She wasn't sure how interested she was in ultrasound-guided nerve blocks and pain management technology or new lymphatic drainage techniques in carpal tunnel management, but she was eager to change the topic so she didn't have to keep hedging and offering half-truths.

"Mostly focused on the tendons in the knee," Jared said before he took a bite of something. "Mmm, sorry, I'm famished. I haven't had a chance to eat since I landed. I'm about to dig into the best-looking lobster at the hotel restaurant."

"God, lobster sounds amazing," Emersyn replied wistfully. Her gaze landed on the black body-sculpt workout leggings and matching cropped halter in her half-open suitcase, slung onto the desk chair. She had brought a set of activewear in anticipation of getting a few workouts in during downtime at the resort, but she remembered the basketball court down that same hallway. "I might try to duck out of the room and shoot some hoops. I actually don't think I have since Crestwood's season wrapped."

"Hey, Dr. Paulson!" Jared's jovial voice greeted someone at the restaurant. "Good to see you too, man. Yeah, I'm just checking in with the fiancée. Want to join me for dinner?"

Emersyn sighed as she curled a lock of hair behind her ear. "I'll let you go, Jared. I know you're busy."

Jared's voice came back on the line. "All right, we'll talk soon. What are you up to now?"

A flash of annoyance rose in Emersyn's chest but she shook her head. "Nothing," she said after a moment. "We'll talk soon."

As they hung up, a mixture of guilt and frustration settled in her stomach like a stone. Emersyn glanced at her suitcase again. She needed *something* to distract her and clear the restless swirl of contradicting emotions she felt. She knew exactly what to do as she wriggled out of her sun dress. It was the same thing that had always helped for as long as she could remember.

As she tied her white Nike low-tops, Emersyn's mind was already on the gleaming hardwood and rack of brand-new basketballs waiting to play in the half-court downstairs. She was ready to clear her mind and maybe remember exactly who she was beneath all the tugging feelings and strange emotions running through her.

❖

Emersyn wondered if she should have grabbed a zip-up sweatshirt to wear over her sports halter as she opened the door to the half-court and shivered at the blast of air conditioning. Still, she knew as soon as she started moving and her blood was pumping, the high-cranked air conditioning would feel refreshing.

This is silly. You're thirty-eight years old. You're choosing to shoot hoops over taking an evening swim in that gorgeous infinity pool?

She bit her lip as she grabbed a ball from the end of the rack in the corner and bounced it from her right hand twice. The familiar thud against hardwood had provided a soundtrack for most of her younger life and drowned out that inner voice. The temptation was too great.

Infinity pool forgotten, Emersyn stepped confidently farther onto the court and dribbled the ball until she lulled herself into a muscle-memory rhythm. She grinned and stretched her arms overhead for a moment so she didn't strain a shoulder. Basketball at thirty-eight years old was a lot different than basketball at twenty-two years old.

Emersyn bounced the ball hard onto the hardwood, then elevated and watched it sail straight through the bright white net without so much as a whisper. She gathered the ball and backed up, positioning herself just outside the white arc, and noticed a flash of movement around the small window. *Just my imagination. Probably one of the thousands of guests looking for the fitness center.*

She dribbled around her left leg and then shot the ball from left-center of the three-point line. She grinned as the ball clanged through the hoop, the echo bouncing loudly off the walls of the court. She jogged to a corner behind the hoop and plucked the ball from where it had rolled to a gentle stop.

Emersyn was in rhythm now. She strode back to mid-court, turned, and shot a quick one-legged fadeaway as she focused on the motion of her wrists. Still, her thoughts didn't stay still. Savannah, tall and just as devastatingly gorgeous as ever, lingered in her mind as a tantalizing heat that didn't seem to subside rose low in her stomach.

Focus. That's why you're here instead of lounging with a cocktail in one of those cabanas.

She turned as she flexed her wrist and then froze.

Savannah leaned casually against the doorframe, impossibly cool in the casual white and tan ombre halter dress she was wearing earlier. Her hair was still long and loose over her shoulders and she smiled slowly. Her dark eyes held a combination of intrigue, amusement, and something else that made Emersyn feel inexplicably warm all over. She tried to ignore how the heat that had pulsed low in her stomach before seemed to ignite.

"So..." Savannah stretched the word as she held Emersyn's gaze. Her casual dominance radiated from her as she unfolded her arms and took a step forward. The air felt thick around Emersyn as her heartbeat quickened. "Are you going to invite me to play or not?"

Chapter Ten

Savannah bit back a smile as Emersyn lifted her chin in defiance.

"You want to play?" Her voice was quiet, but there was an electricity in her hazel eyes that Savannah recognized immediately.

"I want a lot of things," she said as she closed the gap between her and center court. "Besides, *someone* needs to remind you how it's done."

A faint smile flickered across Emersyn's face as she raised an eyebrow. "I may be a little rusty, but that's only because I haven't had a chance to get onto a court since Crestwood's season wrapped."

Savannah kicked off her tan pumps and walked barefoot over to the corner rack as she ran her hand over one of the basketballs. "That surprises me," she said carefully. "You couldn't go twenty-four hours without getting on the court before."

"Here, we can share," Emersyn said as she zinged her basketball to Savannah. She caught it easily. "Anyway, that was a long time ago. My focus is on coaching my girls now. They're amazing." She looked Savannah up and down. "You're going to play in a dress?"

Savannah dribbled the ball with ease and arched into a quick layup before fixing Emersyn with a look. "I think I can manage," she said. "I had to take a couple of work calls in the conference center and was headed back up." She smiled. "I knew it was you as soon as I saw someone in here. Do you remember our old catch-and-shoot game?"

She didn't miss the brief flash in Emersyn's expression as she rose into a casual jumper. It air-balled to the left of the backboard.

"You mean that old game where if you made a shot, you'd get to ask the other person a question they had to answer honestly?" Emersyn shook her head as she retrieved the ball. "That was just silly kid stuff, wasn't it?" She tossed her the basketball.

Savannah glanced at Emersyn pointedly before shooting a quick midrange jumper. It sailed through the net without so much as touching the iron. "I don't know, was it?"

Emersyn grabbed the ball and bounced it a few times before considering her response. "No," she said. "I guess it wasn't. It was fun when we played."

Emersyn raced toward the hoop and then stopped on a dime to lean into her shot, watching with satisfaction as the ball swished through the net. She glanced back at Savannah and rolled her eyes as she remembered something from earlier. "A shopping trip on your first full day here, Savannah, really?"

Savannah smiled as Emersyn bounced the ball to her. "I've worked hard," she said simply. "After I returned from overseas and my pro career was over, I pursued my doctorate in physical therapy and got licensed as a personal trainer." She turned the ball in her hands. "I worked in a lot of gyms and I loved it. I started studying the business side of the gym and fitness industry, and eventually opened a handful of gyms in the Phoenix area. They've been doing really well and they're at a point where I can step back a little and trust the management in place to run the day-to-day operations. Though that's after a lot of years with long hours and giving up things socially. Romantically. Whatever. Besides, fashion is a form of self-expression." She winked. "There's a Mercedes in my garage at home too. Maybe I'll show you that one day and you can tease me about it too."

Emersyn hesitated as a flare of tension seemed to coil between them. "Your turn," she finally said, her voice soft.

Savannah turned and swished an easy hook shot from the right side. "Your ring," she said after a moment. She nodded down at an obnoxiously large diamond on Emersyn's hand that sparkled beneath the bright industrial lights above the court. "You're engaged."

A trace of a smile ghosted over Emersyn's lips. "Was that a question?"

Savannah blinked and then bulleted the basketball to Emersyn, a little faster than intended. "When's the wedding?"

Emersyn paused for a moment. "We got engaged a while ago," she said evasively.

"That wasn't the question," Savannah replied as she scrunched her nose. "But how long is a while?"

A flush bloomed across Emersyn's chest around the tight activewear top that hugged the curve of her breasts. "Um," she said. "Like, a year."

Savannah arched an eyebrow and tried to wipe the mild disbelief she knew was all over her face.

Emersyn sighed. "Or a year and a half," she said slowly. "We don't have a date set yet or anything."

For some reason, Savannah felt a flood of warmth deep in her core at this information. "I've got to be honest, Em," she said. "If you two have been engaged eighteen months and she still hasn't set a date yet, that's a red flag."

Emersyn's flush deepened as she averted her gaze. "It's me who hasn't set the date yet," she said. "If it were up to *Jared*, we would've been married already."

Savannah couldn't hide her knowing smile as she glanced down at the ball. Now it seemed to make more sense, and she had a sneaking suspicion she knew exactly why Emersyn hadn't set a date yet. She took a deep breath as she dribbled the ball and then bounced it to Emersyn.

"Okay," she said with a confident air of finality. "Your turn."

Emersyn caught the ball easily and raised into a jump shot as soon as it hit her hands. She smiled with smug satisfaction as it bounced off the backboard and through the net. "What about you? I find it hard to believe nobody is madly in love with you at the moment."

Emersyn stilled as soon as the words escaped her lips. She looked horrified that she had said that out loud. "Sorry," she corrected herself quickly. "You don't have to answer that. It's not my business to inquire about your personal life. I'll think of something else."

"No," Savannah interjected quickly as her gaze fell to the hardwood between them. "That's the game."

Emersyn nodded once. "Fine. No big love right now?"

Savannah shook her head. "No," she answered honestly. "I've been so focused on my career and then the gyms that this is the first time I've really been able to step back. I've had relationships here and there, but nothing that's turned into long-lasting love. No, um, love at first sight or anything like that." Her voice softened as she met Emersyn's eyes.

She tossed the ball at Emersyn, who threw a bullet pass back to her. Savannah caught it and laid it into the basket from her spot beneath the hoop. "How did you and that guy meet?"

Emersyn wrinkled her nose as she tightened her blond ponytail. "Jared?"

Savannah rolled her eyes. "Whatever," she said. "You two have been together a long time?"

Emersyn laughed, the same genuine one that Savannah remembered. She tried to blink away the sudden image that flooded her mind of her trailing kisses along the soft heat down Emersyn's neck.

"I think you only get one question per make, Savannah," she said. Savannah felt the warmth in her core deepen at hearing Emersyn say her name. She knew her name hadn't been on her lips in years and there was something about it that sounded...*good.* "But I'll play nice. Jared and I have been together for almost three years. His team did an outpatient tune-up on my mom's ankle that she's had on and off issues with since the accident and all the stuff with her hip. He asked me out to an Argentinian place for dinner and then we went to a blues concert at one of the nearby pubs."

Emersyn appeared momentarily surprised by the unintentional strength with which the basketball was bulleted over to her from a quiet, contemplative Savannah. Emersyn set her feet just inside the arc and watched as the ball bounced once, then twice, and finally rolled into the hoop.

"What was your favorite thing about your year at Northwoods College?" Emersyn said breathlessly as she ran after the ball and tossed it to Savannah.

Savannah bit her lip as she considered this. "The warm cherry pie in the student union on Fridays?" She laughed. "It's tough to think of something about Northwoods specifically. I was only there for our senior season, so I don't have the history that you or even the other girls on the team do."

Emersyn nodded. "Understandable."

Savannah wanted to say more, to tell Emersyn the truthful answer. As the air conditioner rattled to life somewhere in the ceiling, she opened and then closed her mouth. *I didn't tell her how I felt sixteen years ago. I was young. Playing pro overseas was too good to ignore. And now we're all grown up and she's engaged.*

After a moment, Savannah straightened her shoulders. She could feel the way Emersyn's gaze lingered a moment too long while they played, she knew the look in her eyes well—half-defiant, half-undone—and she recognized the slow tension and jolts of electricity that crackled between them as soon as the door to Kay and Diana's suite swung open. She wondered if Emersyn even knew she had that look in her eyes or if she was the only one who could recognize it.

Emersyn was all mine once. And I've always been honest with her. Well, except that one time when it really *mattered and I didn't tell her how deeply I felt for her.*

"Honestly? If I had to choose my favorite thing about Northwoods, the answer is simple. It was you."

Emersyn was still for a long moment and then she averted her eyes before she took a deep breath. "Even though you decided to go overseas?"

Their gazes locked across the court and Savannah watched as a few pieces of Emersyn's hair escaped her ponytail and swept around her face as a gust of air conditioning floated over them. She nearly gasped as she caught the ball that Emersyn unexpectedly heaved at her.

"It's your turn," she said.

Savannah didn't break her gaze. "Shoot it and ask me again."

Emersyn smiled and lobbed the basketball to the right of the backboard, catching it as it bounced back to her, and then laid it in the hoop.

"Oh, you're showing off now, is that right?" Savannah teased her.

Emersyn laughed. "It's been forever since I've really played," she said. "Not just running through drills with the girls I coach. I'm surprised I didn't end up falling or air-balling that layup, honestly."

Savannah took a step closer across the court. "To answer your question, yes. You were my favorite part of Northwoods, even though I pursued a pro career overseas." She felt a trace of a smile. "I was heartsick my entire first year in Germany."

Emersyn was quiet for a moment as she thoughtfully dribbled the ball around her ankles. "It was the right decision," she finally said. "I was heartbroken when you left, but I think even then I knew it was the right choice for you. I wouldn't have wanted you to give up that offer and it wouldn't have made sense for me to tag along. I wanted to be mad at you for leaving, but I…I couldn't. Honestly. I was happy for you, Savannah. I still *am* happy for you, especially with your gyms and how hard you've worked to make them a success."

Savannah took another step closer and poked the ball away from Emersyn before nailing a quick jumper from the free throw line. "It didn't make sense to tag along, or you weren't ready to come out to your mom?" She sighed and realized she had said too much. *She's engaged. And presumably happy with whoever that guy is. Her life isn't my business to dig into anymore.*

"Never mind," Savannah said quickly, before Emersyn could respond. "I…I guess I want to know why you never tried to keep in touch." She grabbed the ball and jogged back in her bare feet. "Now, with social media and everything? It would've been easy to find me. Arissa and I found each other recently and have gotten back in touch. I guess I'd hoped, in some small way, that we'd keep in touch too and maybe eventually…" Savannah felt an uncharacteristic flush bloom across her neck. *Wait, what? Stop. Talking.*

"A lot of it was pride," Emersyn said. Savannah was relieved she didn't look to her to finish that sentence. "Even though I know you did the right thing, I was hurt. I was twenty-two and just wanted to get over you, you know? Maybe it wasn't mature of me to disappear and stay out of touch until our lives eventually faded into different places anyway, but I was young. I had no idea how to handle *anything.*" She took a deep breath. "Besides, it would've hurt more to stay in touch and be platonic. You know, be the supportive friend who watches from afar as you date other women, fall in and out of love…"

"I've only been in love once," Savannah countered. Her words hung in the thick air and she swallowed hard. "I mean, I've lusted after women I've dated over the years. But looking back from where I am now, I'm confident that it's just been once when I knew without a doubt that it was love."

Emersyn reached in and stole the ball from Savannah mid-dribble. She easily sank a quick jumper before turning back to her. "How come you went back to Arizona after five years overseas? You could've pursued the WNBA if you really wanted to, Savannah."

The questions and answers were tumbling out of them now and Savannah was lost in the game, laser-focused on Emersyn and trying to make sense of the magnetic pull that was always there when Emersyn was near. It was the same strong pull that always made her want to unravel and claim her.

"I just didn't love pro ball the way I thought I would." Savannah shrugged. "I left it as the offers were starting to fade anyway. I wanted to pursue the physical therapy doctorate ever since I finished undergrad at Northwoods with my health science degree. Then *that* became exciting and a passion I didn't even know I had." She turned, dribbling the ball just out of the way of Emersyn's hand as she guarded her. "I still love basketball, but it was an easy decision."

❖

The game was becoming more charged with an electric energy in the air as Emersyn grabbed the ball after Savannah's last shot. She dribbled around her right leg and tried to turn to her left, but the taller Savannah was defending her closely and it had been too long since Emersyn had played a pickup game.

They were both breathing hard as Emersyn backed her down closer to the rim. Strands of Savannah's hair tickled her neck and Emersyn felt the heat of her body against her back. For a fleeting moment, she considered purposely continuing to struggle with her shot just to lose herself in Savannah's nearness and the sweet warmth that radiated from her. It was completely against her natural competitive instincts, and a jolt of guilt, weaker than the ones before, flashed through her.

What am I doing? Emersyn pulled forward and drove to her right. She felt herself internally groaning at the loss of Savannah's warmth at the same time that she tried to tell herself that she was just feeling good, playing loose and free, and it gave her a rush of happiness that she was mistakenly attributing to Savannah instead.

Emersyn turned and elevated quickly before switching to her left hand as she wildly laid the ball in. The basketball bounced across the hardwood as both of them stopped to catch their breath. Emersyn glanced up from where she had leaned on her knees and threw Savannah a teasing look.

"Can't guard me," she laughed breathlessly.

"It was supposed to be my shot," Savannah shot back, her dark eyes twinkling. "Brat."

Emersyn bounced the ball to Savannah. "You're right," she said reluctantly. "Rules are rules. Your shot."

Savannah grinned. "No, you made a really tough bucket," she said. "It's fine. You deserve to ask another question after that one."

"Okay," Emersyn thought for a moment. "Why physical therapy and personal training? What made you so passionate about it?"

Savannah's face was serious for a moment as she bounced the ball against the shining floor. "I don't know if we should go there…"

Emersyn raised an eyebrow. "That's the game," she said. "Fine. I'll think of another then."

Savannah finally sighed. “You were what inspired me to get into physical therapy, Em,” she blurted out.

Emersyn stilled and met Savannah’s eyes. “Me?”

“Yes, you,” Savannah said. “Your story. Everything you went through with your injury, missing a huge chunk of college ball, you know? I saw up close and personal the effect that accident had on you. Everyone saw it. I just…I thought it was so unfair to you.” Savannah blew out her breath. “I thought that if I could help by providing innovative, evidence-based therapies, exercises, body wellness, and elite training to other athletes and kids especially, then that’s something I’d wake up and love doing. I’ve gotten away from the hands-on work over the last few years as I focused on the business side of the industry and bringing the Vault’s brand to life, but we still employ some of the best athletic trainers and physical therapists in Phoenix.”

Emersyn was stunned into silence as the quiet lingered between them. She couldn’t help but feel a tug of something unspoken that began pulling at her more insistently. “I…I don’t really know what to say,” she said. Her words were drowned out by the large air conditioner heaving to life once more and shuddering with a blast of frigid air. It seemed to cut right through her as the beads of sweat along her collarbone turned cold against her skin with the pause in basketball play. Emersyn shivered as she wrapped her arms around herself. A thought flashed through her mind as she wondered how much of that could be attributed to the air conditioning and how much could be attributed to…*what*? *Savannah? No way.*

“Oh, you’re freezing!” Savannah said. Goose bumps rose along her bare arms and shoulders. “We’ve been shooting hoops here forever. I know you must be tired.” She rolled her eyes as she slipped back into her long-discarded heels. “I’ll walk you back to your room.”

Emersyn didn’t argue as she followed Savannah out of the basketball court, down the winding hallways, and into the open-air lobby. The sky had darkened into a velvety-soft black as an array of tiny stars twinkled over the resort. The gentle sounds of the ocean lapping at the sand and the dimly-lit, hand-carved dark brown and gold sconces along the lobby walls provided a relaxing evening atmosphere that settled into Emersyn’s bones.

The air was thick with humidity and the same unspoken something that Emersyn had felt on the basketball court. Savannah walked beside her, relaxed and confident, as the sway of palm fronds rustled just outside the open-air hallway.

"You still talk a big game, but your defense has gotten soft," Savannah said as she glanced at Emersyn.

Emersyn rolled her eyes and grinned. "I don't know what you're talking about," she said. "You couldn't guard me. Those few airballs I threw up was just me being generous."

"Oh, you're into charity, is that it?" Savannah teased her back. "How kind of you. I'm touched."

"You should be," Emersyn shot back and then felt her cheeks warm. She glanced away, focusing on the manicured hedges lining the other side of the open-air wall. They paused in front of the elevators and Emersyn could still feel Savannah's gaze lingering on her face.

"You always get flustered when your shots aren't falling," she said. "Or your shots aren't falling because you get flustered. It could go either way."

"Flustered?" Emersyn laughed. The goose bumps across her arms returned under Savannah's gaze. "*Please*."

Emersyn swallowed as they stepped into the elevator. She *was* flustered and she couldn't deny it. She was all too aware of the close quarters she found herself in with Savannah as the elevator doors shut. As Savannah gently pressed the buttons for their floors, her arm brushed against Emersyn's and sent a flicker of electricity through her.

Savannah turned as the elevator smoothly ascended to the sixth floor. "Do you get back to Northwoods often?"

Emersyn shook her head. "Not as much as I should," she said honestly. "We sold the house about ten years ago and moved my mom into a condo in an active adult retirement community on the outskirts of town. She loves it. Just enough space, zero maintenance or yard work, tons of friends, and a calendar of weekly activities."

"That's good," Savannah said. "You know what I miss? Min's Kitchen. They still have the best Chinese takeout of any place I've ever lived."

Emersyn laughed as they stepped out of the elevator onto her floor. "Oh my God, tell me about it! They have the best chicken and pineapple fried rice. Would you believe I haven't found a single Chinese takeout in Chicago that carries chicken *and* pineapple fried rice? They all have chicken fried rice or orange chicken, but Min's is the only place that combined it into kind of the same dish. There's nothing else like it."

Emersyn realized too late that she might be babbling, but Savannah eagerly nodded her agreement. "Personally, the spicy shrimp lo mein was my go-to," she said. "I had that exact thought when I first moved back to Arizona. I could never find another shrimp lo mein that had that perfect slow-building fieriness. Now I'm going to get back to my room and see if I can find something similar to order for dinner."

Emersyn nodded her agreement and then blinked. "Wait, you haven't eaten?" she asked, realization dawning on her. "You must be starving!"

For just a second, Emersyn wondered if that was a faint blush creeping up Savannah's smooth neck. She glanced down as they paused in front of Emersyn's suite, her long, dark eyelashes illuminated along the side of her profile by the glow of an amber wall sconce. "I'm used to long days from getting the gyms off the ground," she said off-handedly. "It was my fault for squeezing in some business calls when I'm supposed to be mostly offline these next couple of weeks." She finally turned and threw Emersyn a teasing glance. "Besides, if I had the choice between a quick room service dinner or playing catch-and-shoot with the infamous Emersyn Tanner again, I'd pick basketball every time. *Even* in a dress and no shoes."

Savannah's words lingered along Emersyn's skin longer than they should have. She swallowed hard as she dug her key card from a side pocket of her leggings. "Thank you," she said as she held the small piece of plastic to the automated lock. "For the game. I…I really enjoyed it."

Emersyn recalled how she pretended to struggle with her shot longer than necessary when Savannah was guarding her because her nearness, the light scent of the coconut milk lotion she still wore, and the soft warmth of her skin felt *so* intoxicatingly right.

Wait. I really *shouldn't be thinking about Savannah like that. For a million reasons.*

Savannah smiled. The dim light in the hallway shadowed her profile with an almost sensual, mysterious glow. "See you around, Emersyn."

Chapter Eleven

Emersyn leaned back in the plush white leather chair as warm water hummed and bubbled around her bare feet and calves. The boutique nail area of the resort spa was trendy and designed for aesthetic interest, with its white-washed shiplap walls and brightly colored flowers lining the wall adjacent to the reception desk beneath a large neon sign that spelled out the words *Hola, Bonita* in flowing script.

Emersyn closed her eyes against the gentle lavender and bergamot scents puffing gently from a diffuser near her chair. With her casual white jeans pulled up past her knees and a soft pink towel draped over her legs, the pedicure had been a relaxing after-breakfast decision. She relished the tension melting from her shoulders as she shifted against the cushioned chair. Ever since she had firmly warned herself last night that she shouldn't be letting herself think of Savannah the way she had while they were playing basketball, a smaller, louder voice continued to pipe up in the back of her mind questioning why it felt so right then. Emersyn wasn't sure if she was ready to examine that too deeply.

As the nail technician stood to grab three different purples—Emersyn's color of choice—from a long, clear plastic rack, Emersyn's phone buzzed loudly in her pocket. She wrinkled her nose as she glanced down at the group text she had been added to with a handful of phone numbers she didn't recognize.

The first message was filled with fire emojis. *Your girl E is officially in Cabo, y'all! Kay shared your numbers with me, so I'm getting a group text started. My wife Kayla and I would love to invite you all to an unofficial team reunion tonight. There's a cool dive bar about a mile down the road from the resort. El Gato Azul, 8 PM?*

Emersyn smiled. Erica Owen. *Of course.* Her fingertips hovered over her phone as she hesitated for just a beat.

Another phone number buzzed in the group text. *New York is in the house! I'm in.*

Emersyn's smile gave way to a grin. That could only be Mia DiCorro. *Still as extra as always.* She stretched her left foot languidly in the warm water.

As she poised to respond, another response illuminated her screen. One that Emersyn recognized as having a Phoenix area code.

Wouldn't miss it.

It was just three words, but they landed like a live wire beneath Emersyn's skin and sent jolts of electricity sizzling through her veins. A thrill of anticipation bloomed in her chest before she could stop it, and then the nail technician was back. She stood expectantly before Emersyn and gestured to the three different purple options in her gloved hand.

"Do you like any of these?" she asked kindly. "I have a few other shades too."

Emersyn glanced at the small glass bottles and quickly selected the dark maroon shade that perfectly matched the dark maroon minidress she'd packed days earlier. She knew exactly what she was going to wear tonight.

She bit her lip. Before she could think better of it, her fingertips flew over her phone.

See you then.—Em

With a deep, grounding breath, Emersyn quickly pocketed her phone and glanced at the nail technician as she settled back onto the small cushioned stool in front of the bubbling foot soak.

"Exciting plans today?" she asked. She turned off the bubbles and pumped a few quick squirts of lotion into her hands. "That smile looks like something fun is in the works."

Emersyn laughed. *God, am I that obvious?*

"Something like that," she said as a devious, anticipatory thrill curled through her at the prospect of seeing Savannah again so soon.

Careful. It's just a fun night out with the old team, for laughs and nostalgia. There's no reason to be that *excited just to see Savannah.*

As Emersyn's mind flitted over her and Savannah's catch-and-shoot game the night before and the confident intensity in her dark eyes, she took a breath and told herself that she was just excited at seeing her old teammates after so many years. She'd focus on catching up with all of them and try her best to politely steer clear of Savannah tonight, just until she could get the last of this residual attraction out of her system. It wouldn't be difficult in a crowded, tourist-centric dive bar and then she could show herself that everything she was feeling was nothing more than the lingering effects of a long-ago college love that she had firmly put behind her.

❖

As Emersyn stepped out of the taxi outside El Gato Azul, she shook her head. It was just like Erica to choose the silliest, most tourist-y place around for their team reunion. The bar was tucked between a small surf shop and a street taco stand, and it was decorated with sun-bleached murals of mermaids and sea turtles behind ratty fishing nets and Day of the Dead skeletons across the outer wall of its stucco main entrance.

She could already hear the music and raucous laughter spilling out from the open windows. As a burly security guard in a black polo shirt glanced down at her ID before waving her in, Emersyn caught a scarred wooden sign on the door behind him that read *Bienvenido! Cerveza, Musica, y Problemas.* She gave herself one last quick glance in a long mirror on the opposite wall. She had dressed deliberately that evening, though she wasn't entirely sure why. Maybe some twisted part of her tonight wanted Savannah's attention, wanted her gaze traveling over every inch of her body so she could burn with the same pulling energy that Emersyn hadn't been able to settle since they laid eyes on each other the day before.

A shout inside the bar brought Emersyn out of her Savannah-focused reverie. El Gato Azul was loud, chaotic, and exactly what she needed to show herself she was simply overreacting after years of unresolved tension. She made her way through the bar, noting a neon jukebox in the corner and dark walls covered in years of old concert posters, colorful mismatched string lights, signed pesos, and even a few dusty bras. The dark wood bar was long and wrapped into a gentle U-shaped curve that faced rows of scarred tables and booths centered around a few billiards tables. Bathrooms appeared to be down a short, sticky hallway in the opposite corner, past a karaoke table and walled-off kitchen.

The air was thick with heat and laughter and someone was belting out a bad rendition of a popular Bon Jovi song at the karaoke table, but Emersyn's gaze locked onto a familiar group at a long back table. She barely registered the throngs of frat guys that openly ogled her from where they leaned against the bar or the subtle heads of a few middle-aged couples that turned from one of the billiards tables.

Erica Owen glanced in her direction, raised an eyebrow, and let out a loud whistle.

"*Damn*, Emersyn! Okay, I see you," she greeted her with a laugh. "But no, really, it's so good to see you!"

Emersyn grinned as she embraced her former teammate. "I missed you, Erica," she said over the loud music. "It's so good to see you too. Thanks for getting us all together tonight."

"I'm just glad we all made it," Erica said warmly. She tipped her Bud Light bottle toward the bar. "Kayla is ordering a drink. You remember her, right? I'll reintroduce you when she gets back to the table." Erica glanced at Arissa. "I heard you already ran into Arissa, who went and became the hottest Realtor in Atlanta on us."

Emersyn laughed as she quickly embraced Arissa once more. "Couldn't miss her."

"And I think Mia went to the bathroom," Erica said.

Mia's distinct voice chimed in behind Emersyn. "Mia's back!" Mia laughed. She hugged Emersyn. "Good to see you, Em."

"Good to see you too," Emersyn said. "And congratulations on the wedding. I saw through the social media grapevine that you and your husband tied the knot in Paris, how romantic."

Mia snorted as she took a sip of her rum and Coke. "Thanks, Em," she laughed. "I filed divorce paperwork last month. Hopefully, it'll be over as quickly as it started."

Emersyn's mouth fell open as she smoothed her dark maroon minidress and gently adjusted its thin straps. "Oh, I'm sorry…" she said.

Mia grinned. "Don't be." She waved her hand. "You'd think the third time would be the charm, but no. So, Danny's out of the picture. Just like Randall before him and Nick before *him*." She rolled her eyes. "One day I'll find a good one, but I might have to go through all the men in New York City first. And I'm not opposed to a Jersey boy either."

Emersyn laughed, feeling at ease with her former teammates, as she ran a hand through her hair. It fell down her back in loose curls and her black open-toed heels showed off the gorgeous pedicure she'd gotten that morning. Emersyn felt good. Confident. Ready to enjoy the night with her old teammates.

She glanced around the table as Mia loudly lamented the horrors of using apps to date. *It's remarkable. It really is like no time has passed at all.*

The thought faded as her gaze immediately found Savannah. She was seated at the end of the table, all cool confidence, with one leg neatly crossed over the other in her chair. Her dark hair had been pulled into a casual ponytail and she wore a fitted green blazer over a white cami, light gray skinny jeans, and a pair of black heeled ankle boots. As she looked across the long table, Emersyn was sure Savannah's poise faltered for just a brief moment as her dark eyes swept over her slowly. She didn't even bother to hide it as she arched an eyebrow and met Emersyn's gaze again.

For some reason, Emersyn was immensely satisfied. Low heat coiled inside her as the loud bar music and conversation around the table faded into oblivion. Savannah didn't get up and she didn't say a word. Too late, Emersyn realized she was staring at her. Every part of her was screaming to walk around the table, go to Savannah, say hello, and give her a polite hug so she could deftly avoid her the rest of the night and prove to herself that this was fine and under control.

Instead, Emersyn turned abruptly. "I need a drink," she announced to Arissa, who stood next to her. "Is Jäegermeister and Red Bull still your go-to?"

A sickly green shadow flashed over Arissa's face at the memories. "Not a snowball's chance in hell," she said over the music. "If I tried to drink that tonight, it'd take me until the wedding to recover." She nodded at the bar. "Surprisingly, they have a decent wine selection here. My Pinot Grigio isn't horrible. Though I *am* intrigued by whatever a Tequila Thunder is."

They watched for a moment as a scantily-clad young bartender unleashed a healthy serving of Patron through a funnel, down a stretchy plastic tube, and into the mouth of a muscular tourist wearing a backward baseball cap. His friends shouted and cheered as he stumbled away from the bar and raised his arms in celebration.

Emersyn flashed Arissa a cheeky glance as she headed for the bar. "Pinot sounds perfect."

Chapter Twelve

Savannah leaned back casually in her chair as she sipped her Malibu and pineapple juice and pretended to follow along with the chatter and inside jokes from her former teammates. Still, she couldn't seem to tear her focus away from Emersyn. Every time their gazes locked across the table, it felt like the oxygen in her lungs got heavier and every nerve coiled tightly beneath her poised expression. She couldn't help it; Emersyn was an absolute knockout, her hips swaying beneath her dress, as she strode to the bar and back again with a glass of white wine in her hand. The creamy flash of collarbone and the soft skin of her neck, as if begging for Savannah's lips, caught her gaze like a wolf circling her prey.

Stop it. Well, okay, maybe you can look. It's been years, after all. But that's it.

When Emersyn was making her rounds across the table, she stopped short when she landed at Savannah. Instead of acknowledging her, Emersyn turned and headed to the bar after a brief conversation with Arissa.

Savannah watched her for a moment as Erica reintroduced Emersyn to her wife and they shared a quick embrace. Still, Emersyn didn't so much as glance her way again. Savannah smiled as she tried to push away the same flash of something hot and possessive deep in her chest that she always felt whenever Emersyn was around.

Game on.

Savannah knew Emersyn well enough to know she was trying to play it cool, but she could see the cracks in her walls—the same walls Savannah had always seen right through. She could sense it before, when Emersyn's gaze had collided with hers and she had shot Savannah the genuine, unguarded smile tinged with that teasing, knowing gleam she knew too well. She could sense it now, with the way Emersyn's fingertips gently toyed with the stem of her wine glass and she giggled a little too hard at whatever story Kayla was loudly regaling her with about Erica.

She's trying too hard to stay guarded. Perhaps it was the rum working its way through her bloodstream, but this time Savannah didn't try to ignore the flush of warmth that flooded her as she watched Emersyn for a moment longer. *Fine. She'll come to me eventually.*

❖

Nearly an hour later, Emersyn was mildly frustrated and she couldn't pinpoint exactly why. She nursed her second glass of wine, though it was rapidly growing stale in her glass, and sighed. Erica and Mia were howling their way through a Spice Girls song at the karaoke table and, shockingly to Emersyn, most of the bar was laughing, dancing, and singing along to their off-key screeches and silly poses. Kayla was practically doubled over with laughter as she recorded their over-the-top performance on her phone. Arissa had made friends with a few tourists at the bar and they had split into teams, embroiled in a serious billiards competition. Everyone was letting loose and appeared to be having a great time, comfortable, relaxed, and enjoying the impromptu reunion.

Still, Emersyn felt like something was missing. Too late, she realized her gaze kept drifting back to the semicircular corner booth that their group had spread into once there wasn't any more room at the rectangular table they'd met at earlier. Savannah sat casually at the booth, watching Erica and Mia, and running a fingertip along the condensation trickling down her glass. It was only her second Malibu and pineapple juice, and Savannah appeared to be sipping her drinks just as slowly as Emersyn was nursing hers. With a sigh, Emersyn reminded herself that it wasn't entirely fair to be annoyed that Savannah hadn't acknowledged or approached her all night when she hadn't bothered to say hello either.

She watched as Savannah glanced at the billiards tables and watched Arissa play for a moment with the same quiet confidence she always seemed to have. Her lips curved into a faint, sweet smile and then her gaze drifted to Emersyn.

As their eyes locked across the bar, this time Emersyn didn't turn away. Though Emersyn rationalized the sudden fluttering in her chest as the wine making her emotions a bit sharper and more pointed, it was too great to ignore. She didn't think; instead, she stepped around the table and slipped into the cracked leather booth next to Savannah. Low lights bathed the booth in shadows as Emersyn realized she had not just sat next to Savannah, she had practically perched herself on her lap. Her bare leg brushed against the smooth denim of Savannah's tight jeans, but Emersyn didn't pull back or scoot away. Her heartbeat pulsed a little faster when she realized Savannah hadn't either.

Emersyn turned and smiled at her, holding her gaze for a moment longer than she meant. "Hi," she said, announcing herself over the loud karaoke.

"Hi," Savannah echoed teasingly. "Are you always going to be this good at avoiding me?"

Emersyn bit her lip but couldn't tear her eyes from Savannah. The booth felt smaller and charged with the same low current that Emersyn felt ever since seeing Savannah at Kay and Diana's suite. "No," she said, her reply quieter and more vulnerable than she intended.

Savannah tilted her head and then glanced across the bar for a thoughtful moment. "Good," she said softly. After a beat, she nodded at Erica and Mia. "It's great that they're so amazing at basketball, because they definitely did not get the vocal talents to propel them to fame and glamour."

Emersyn laughed, her loose curls brushing Savannah's shoulder as she turned just in time to see Erica and Mia clasp sweaty hands and take a dramatic bow. "Good thing," she said. She watched as the DJ poured them both a shot of Jack Daniels in celebration and they raised their glasses to the ceiling before tipping them back. "Oh, they'll be regretting that in the morning."

Savannah snickered in agreement as she glanced at Arissa, who had been spun into an upbeat dance near the billiards table by a bearded college-aged guy in jeans and an old Nirvana T-shirt. "It's good to see everyone here together again," she said. "You know, having fun. Living it up. Smiling and celebrating."

Despite the rush of activity, laughter, and alcohol-fueled excitement around them, Emersyn couldn't help but feel that she and Savannah had somehow cocooned themselves at the shadowy booth. It felt slower, more tender, and private here and Emersyn kind of liked it. In fact, she preferred it. Selfishly, she felt inexplicably happy that their friends were all tipsy after hours of flowing drinks, their focus instead on the fun, celebratory night around them.

As Emersyn opened her mouth to respond, an all-too-familiar beat flooded the bar. She swung around and squealed with surprised delight as Erica and Mia danced around the karaoke table, microphones in hand.

Mia's off-key voice began crooning the first lyrics to Whitney Houston's "How Will I Know" as the rest of the bar erupted into cheers and whistles. Soon, Erica joined in the song, holding out her hand so Mia could take it and twirl, as Emersyn clapped along loudly.

Arissa and several other vacationers at the bar were all dancing around the billiards tables as Emersyn caught even Savannah taking it all in, unable to hide her surprise.

"Oh my God, they're doing Whitney!" Emersyn exclaimed. She turned and grabbed Savannah's forearm in excitement. "Well, not *doing* Whitney. You know what I mean. I can't believe them."

They continued singing and screeching enthusiastically as Emersyn cupped a hand around her mouth. "Go, Mia, go, Erica!" she called before turning back to the table.

"They're totally doing Whitney," Savannah said. "The Jack Daniels definitely told them they should do Whitney."

Emersyn wasn't sure what exactly it was, but it felt good to be there in that moment with friends who had known her—and loved her—throughout what felt like an entire lifetime ago. She glanced at Savannah and felt something stir in her chest that she tried to blink away. Instead, Emersyn took a deep breath as she steered herself into polite, neutral territory. *Small talk.*

"Your parents are still in Phoenix, I take it?" she asked.

Savannah nodded. "They are," she said. "They're living their weirdest and best lives over in Scottsdale. They travel a lot. They refuse to age. Father Time's got nothing on them. My mom teaches yoga part-time at a studio near their house. It gives her something that's her own to do, I guess. My dad still follows MLB religiously." She shrugged. "What can I say? They're happy."

"They always have been," Emersyn said warmly. "That's great."

She nodded toward the bar as her gaze fell on Erica and Kayla laughing as they danced slowly together. "You know, I'd heard a long time ago that Erica got married," she said thoughtfully. "I always wondered if Erica and Kayla would ever feel like they missed out by tying the knot so young. I mean, they were only twenty-four. That's wild to me. But seeing them now? They look so in love."

Savannah looked at her for a long moment, her expression unreadable. "They *are* in love," she finally said. "Besides, I think it depends on the couple. If you think it's going to fail, then eventually it will. But not all young couples fail, not if they recognize they really love each other. I think Erica and Kayla were just lucky." Savannah glanced at them, though Emersyn wondered if that was a tinge of wistfulness she spotted in her gaze. "They found their person early and had the guts to hold on tight. Young love can be real."

In the relative shadowy privacy of the booth, Emersyn wondered if she and Savannah would have stayed together if Savannah had declined going overseas. *Or if I had the guts to find her later, after she returned. Instead of putting Northwoods firmly in the rearview mirror and disappearing into Chicago.* It was the first time she had let herself truly consider the what-if, and something about it made her heart unexpectedly ache.

"My parents were young when they had me," Savannah said as she took another sip of her fruity drink. "My mom was twenty-four and my dad was twenty-five, right in the prime of his baseball career. It was definitely challenging for them in the early days, especially with my mom being young herself and caring for a baby while my dad was always on the road during the spring and summer seasons. I remember being about six when my parents finally realized how much they truly loved each other and how unbreakable their bond was. Since then, they've been one of the happiest couples I've known. I can't imagine them *not* together."

Emersyn watched Savannah's dreamy, faraway expression. "Your parents are wonderful," she said. "They've always been one of my favorite couples. Right up there with Kay and Diana."

Savannah blushed as she glanced down at the table. "You don't always have to have it all figured out to be in love," she finally said. "Love just *is*. It might hit you at sixty-two or twenty-two." Her face flushed again. "I mean, or any age in between. Anyway, listen to me," Savannah's voice quickly returned to her confident, teasing tone. "Who knew I'd grow up to be so soft? Even Kay told me I was."

Emersyn glanced at her playfully for a moment. "I kind of like it," she teased. "But you didn't *grow up* to be soft, Savannah. I always knew you were sweet." The words were out of her mouth before she could stop them, but luckily for her Arissa sat down heavily at the booth.

"I need more pesos for the pool table," she said breathlessly. "I think I hid my bag somewhere over…"

As Arissa groped around the seat for her purse, Emersyn scooted over and realized too late that she had pressed up closer against Savannah as their shoulders brushed. She busied herself with helping Arissa find her oversized purse as Erica approached the table and grinned. She placed a small tray with several neon-colored shot glasses before them.

Emersyn finally held up a black leather tote. "This one is yours, no?"

Recognition flashed across Arissa's face as she nodded. "That's it, thanks, Em," she said as she fished out a few more pesos.

"Team reunion shots, ladies!" Erica announced. "Come on, everyone has to do at least one. I may have already done two."

Arissa laughed. "No chance, Erica." She shook her head before glancing at Emersyn and Savannah. "Come over to the tables if you two want to play. We're doing a best of five, me and Nikki versus Kayla and Drew."

Emersyn wrinkled her nose. "Wait, who are Nikki and Drew?"

Arissa shrugged as she straightened, looking a bit unsteady on her heels. "What can I say, we're making friends. See you over there," she called over her shoulder.

As Arissa's lithe form blended back into the crowd, Emersyn registered that she was still sitting practically on Savannah's lap, but neither of them moved to put any distance between them.

Erica looked between Emersyn and Savannah expectantly. "Em? Savannah?"

Savannah shook her head quickly. "I'm on Team Arissa for this one," she said. "No way."

Erica shot Emersyn a wounded look. "Em?" she asked. "Come on. Take one for the team. Literally. Since I guess Arissa and Savannah went and got old on us, right?" She laughed as Savannah rolled her eyes.

Emersyn wrinkled her nose as she regarded the neon shot glasses suspiciously. "What even are these?"

Erica clapped her hands. "Bartender's special." She shrugged. "Something called *gatos del diablo*?"

Savannah burst into laughter as they looked at her expectantly.

Emersyn narrowed her eyes. "What does that mean?"

Savannah shook her head and gestured at the tray. "Devil cats," she said. "It doesn't sound promising."

"Please?" Erica wheedled her. "Come on, one for old time's sake."

"Fine," Emersyn finally said. "One and done for me though."

Erica grinned as she handed Emersyn a neon pink shot glass and took a neon green one for herself. "Deal," she said as they gently clinked their glasses together. "Cheers!"

Emersyn swallowed the shot as she wrinkled her nose again and let the empty glass clatter back onto the tray. "Erica, whatever that was, it was horrible," she said after a moment. The fruity spirits minimized some of the liquor's burn, but not how strong it was.

As Erica was pulled away by Kayla to dance, Emersyn noticed Savannah's teasing gaze on her. "Now *you're* going to be regretting that in the morning," she laughed.

"Probably," Emersyn said. "I never drink like this. I can't even remember the last time I had more than an occasional glass of wine with dinner." She could already feel a slight glow warming her cheeks as Mia and a random tourist launched into a barely-recognizable version of Prince's "Little Red Corvette" to loud cheers from the bar.

"I get it," Savannah said. "Work has kept me so busy for so many years that I never really had time for the club or bar scene." She shrugged as she swirled the small paper straw in her drink and then nodded at the billiards tables. "Want to get in on those pool games? Someone has to keep Arissa's ego in check." She grinned. "I think she's won all three games so far."

Emersyn nodded. Her body felt warm and soft as the liquor from the mystery shot settled into her veins. She blinked slowly as Savannah stood and gazed at her, holding out her hand to help her up.

Emersyn opened her mouth to argue, to swear up and down that she wasn't *that* much of a lightweight, but the truth was that after two glasses of wine and a shot, she *was* feeling herself relax and loosen. As she grabbed Savannah's hand, her fingers naturally interlocking with hers, Emersyn was taken by the sizzling jolt that quickened her heartbeat as they held hands over to the billiards table. Even as they stood there, pausing as they watched Arissa sink another striped ball, Emersyn didn't want to let go. Savannah's fingertips curled around her own like they belonged there and for a brief, brave moment, Emersyn wondered if they did. Warm, slow heat coursed through her at the thought.

Before she had a chance to process it, Arissa was dragging her to the pool table and handing her a freshly-chalked cue. She felt something akin to disappointment and realized somewhere in the back of her mind that she already missed Savannah's hand in hers.

Chapter Thirteen

Savannah watched with amusement as Emersyn lined up her turn with intense, tipsy focus. "Okay, if I make this one, you have to admit I'm better at pool than you," she teased Arissa.

Arissa rolled her eyes. "One good game definitely doesn't negate the three I won before you decided to leave that dark booth and join us," she said. "Anyway, you're just lucky I scratched twice."

Emersyn stuck her tongue out at her and tapped the cue ball. It ricocheted off the worn felt side of the table and missed everything. She let out a dramatic groan and laughed. "Okay, fine," she said. "I'm a little drunk."

Savannah stepped closer and rested the cue against the table as she instinctively placed a hand on the small of Emersyn's back. "All right, Cabo pool champion," she said. "Time to get you back to the resort. I'll rideshare with you."

Emersyn tilted her head at Savannah as she gazed at her with mirth. "Are you always this bossy?"

Savannah grinned at her. *You know I am* is what she wanted to say, but she bit her tongue. "Only when necessary," she said instead. She glanced at her phone. "The car will be here in five. You ready?"

Emersyn fixed her with a smile. "I was *born* ready."

As they said a quick round of goodbyes to the group and then headed into the salt-tinged night air, the sounds of the ocean in the distance and the bar behind them faded into a comfortable hum. The rideshare arrived and Savannah opened the back door for Emersyn. She slid into the darkened vehicle and leaned back against the headrest as Savannah sat next to her.

She took a deep, cleansing breath as she tilted her head to the inky black sky. Tiny stars glinted in a brilliant, wide tapestry that stretched beyond the busy street and the blur of karaoke, laughter, and the scent of stale alcohol outside the car.

Savannah blinked up at the stars once more and then turned to Emersyn. "I can't believe you didn't sing," she said. "Weren't you wildly obsessed with Tegan and Sara?"

Emersyn groaned as the car swiftly pulled into the street. "I'd argue that wildly obsessed is an exaggeration," she said playfully. "But who can argue that they have some of the most underrated albums of, like, all time? Besides, we all know I was angsty then. Kay's maddening practice drills and way too many servings of fried cheese curds from the student union."

"Peak angst conditions," Savannah agreed.

Emersyn shook her head as large resorts and brightly lit nightclubs streaked past them outside the tinted car windows. "Besides, how could I ever forget your obsession with those sad Spanish ballads?" she teased her. "I may not have known exactly what they were saying, but I remember they were intense. *And* I distinctly recall you singing along to them every time you were in the shower."

Savannah grinned. "I *crushed* those sad Spanish ballads," she said confidently. "Bathroom acoustics are the best. Anyway, I was feeling every syllable at the time."

As Emersyn met her eyes across the darkened back seat, Savannah felt the air between them shift as their easy playfulness gave way to something quieter and warmer. Her soft gaze danced over Savannah's face, as if trying to decide whether to say more, and then Emersyn was looking at the scenery blurring past the window. Her shoulders were relaxed and her lips were slightly parted in awe as she took in the expanse of surrounding resorts as they slowed at a stoplight.

Savannah didn't say anything. The last few minutes of the ride were mostly quiet as she realized she was equally content to watch Emersyn, her defenses lowered and her hazel eyes bright with life, though warning bells began ringing in the back of her mind.

As the rideshare paused in front of the resort, Savannah slid out of the back seat first and then held her hand out for Emersyn. She climbed out of the back seat a bit clumsily and grinned as Savannah's fingers tangled with her own.

"You sure you're okay?" she asked in amusement as she stole a sidelong glance at her.

Emersyn exhaled and closed her eyes for a moment as they stepped into the lobby. It was quiet at this hour. "I'm amazing," she said after a moment. She took a deep breath. "Also, you *smell* amazing."

Savannah arched an eyebrow. "That's definitely the gatos del diablos talking."

Emersyn shrugged. "Maybe," she said. "But it's still true." She blinked as she gazed around the lobby. "I think I need some air. Can we… Do you mind if we walk down to the beach? Just for a few minutes. I haven't even properly enjoyed it yet."

Savannah nodded. "Sure," she replied. "Come on."

She led them through the other side of the lobby and down a stone path surrounded by manicured greenery. It wound through a crop of tall, swaying palm trees and colorful bougainvillea before ending where the warm white sand began.

Emersyn slipped off her heels and held them by their thin straps as she gazed at the inky dark water. "I can't believe this is real," she murmured, taking in the gentle ocean waves tugging at the shore. "It's so different from Chicago. My mom was right; I've rarely left the city in years. And I don't know why, because everything here feels slower and softer." She turned to Savannah and smiled, a genuine one that made Savannah's chest ache just a little bit. "It's nice."

"I know the feeling," Savannah said as they sat comfortably in the sand. "I didn't even realize how much I needed this trip."

"Do you…" Emersyn paused, her voice thoughtful. "I feel like everything's louder here, without the crush and chaos of the city to mute everything."

Savannah leaned back on her arms, her hands sinking into the soft sand. "Louder how?"

"I don't know," Emersyn said after a moment. "Just inside, I guess. My thoughts. My feelings. It's like they've been muted for so long and I've functioned just fine like that, but now that I'm here where it's quieter, slower, softer? I feel like the volume got turned *all* the way up and I can't shake it."

Savannah opened her mouth, but Emersyn continued. "You know, I never came out to my mom." Her voice was soft now as Emersyn tilted her face to the night sky and closed her eyes for a beat. A gentle breeze threaded through her loose curls, ruffling a few over her bare shoulders. "I don't know why."

Savannah gazed at her for a moment. "You think your mom knows? She seemed like she would be supportive."

Emersyn shrugged one shoulder. "I always thought she did," she said. She sifted a handful of sand through her fingertips. "But we never talked about it. I tried to date a few women after college, but nothing really stuck. Nothing that made coming out an inevitability, at least. So." She took a deep breath. "I just kept pushing it to the back of my mind. It was easier not to say it out loud. To her *or* to myself again, I guess. And then later I met Jared. He's so kind. Smart. Safe. My mom really likes him, so I feel like I'd be breaking her heart all over again in a weird way. He and I just sort of fell into a rhythm, you know?"

Savannah's gaze darkened as she contemplated the endless shoreline. "Sexy," she said dryly and then sighed. "But no, I *don't* know, Em," she went on, softer this time. "I mean, I've been out to my parents since I was eighteen. Sexuality is fluid for a lot of people though and bisexuality exists too…"

Emersyn shook her head. "I know it does, but deep down I…I've always known who I am, Savannah." Her voice was bolder now. "I don't know if I ever really chose Jared or if I just kept going with what seemed to be safe and what makes my mom so happy. He's a great guy. If there was any ounce of me that…" She blew out her breath in frustration. "Well, we would've been married with little blond babies already. I should feel lucky to have this future with him, but I know I'm pushing too many things down. And that scares me, knowing I've never looked at Jared, or any man, and wanted him the way I…" She dug her toes into the sand. "Am I crazy?"

Savannah gently brushed her hand with her thumb, hoping to ground her from her spinning thoughts and anchor her back into the moment. "You're not crazy," she said. "I get it. Sometimes it feels easier to live the life that everyone expects of you."

"I do like my life," Emersyn said thoughtfully. "I love coaching. The city *has* been good to me. I've found success and peace beyond the future I was so sure I'd have for myself when I was in high school and college. I just… I've never said this out loud before, but I just wonder if I chose Jared because I was scared to choose myself. Or scared to truly imagine a life with something, someone, more complicated."

Savannah felt herself shift in the dark, though her gaze on Emersyn was soft. "Complicated, huh? Is that what I was?"

Emersyn arched an eyebrow and leaned her head playfully on Savannah's shoulder for a moment. "Not you. But between us?" She giggled. "It was *so* complicated."

A curl of warmth pulsed through Savannah. "You still liked it."

Don't even think about it. She warned herself as Emersyn's hair tickled her shoulder. *Definitely don't think about how much you want to tangle your fingers in the ends of her hair.*

"I never said I didn't," Emersyn teased. She lifted her head for a moment and met Savannah's eyes as her words hung between them. There was a vulnerability laid bare in her gaze that Savannah felt deep in her core.

Emersyn stood abruptly and held her arm out for balance as she stumbled a bit over the sand. "I should get to bed." Her voice was guarded again. "It's been a long night."

Savannah stood too, brushing off her jeans, and nodded. "I'll walk you to your room."

As they stepped through the thick sand before reaching the stone path, their fingers brushed and lingered. Each time they did, Savannah felt the slow-burning heat she couldn't seem to tamp down. As she stole a glance at Emersyn, she couldn't help but fight the urge to brush a windswept lock of hair behind her ear.

Uh-oh.

Chapter Fourteen

As Emersyn reached the door to her suite, she faced Savannah and crossed her arms. The alcohol was wearing off quickly and leaving her instead with an exhausted, drawn feeling that made her want to pull off her dress and crawl into bed.

"Thanks for taking care of me," she said. "I'm sorry I talked your ear off all night."

Savannah smiled. "Anytime," she said. "I see you, Em. You don't have to figure it all out tonight. Sometimes it just feels good to talk to someone."

As Emersyn watched Savannah retreat down the hallway for a moment, she took a deep breath. She closed the door behind her and then closed her eyes and leaned against the wall. Whether it had been the darker confines of the booth at the bar, the comfortable familiarity of being with so many longtime friends, or the steady grounding she always felt with Savannah no matter how many years went by, she knew deep in places she hadn't acknowledged in years that the love they had shared was real and not some passing college fling fueled by hormones and drama.

Maybe it would have worked out. She lazily unzipped her dress and pulled on a T-shirt and sweatpants. *Somehow.*

As she tumbled into bed, an unfamiliar longing tugged at her and melted into the anticipation of the present. It seemed sharper, aching, as though the alcohol had blurred the walls of her cautious defenses and was pulling something dormant, something real and truthful, dangerously close to the surface.

Emersyn closed her eyes and drifted into sleep almost immediately. As everything faded to black, she realized somewhere in the back of her mind that she hadn't thought of Jared once.

❖

Late the next morning, Savannah crossed her legs as she opened her laptop at a bleached wood desk in the resort's business center. The spacious room was calming and sophisticated, with floor-to-ceiling windows that let soft, natural morning light bounce through the palm trees and across the cool marble floor.

As she logged in to her computer, Savannah glanced up as Arissa walked into the room. Her own sleek laptop was tucked in her arm and a pair of black oversized sunglasses were perched atop the dark curls gathered into an effortless bun on top of her head.

"You're alive after last night!" Savannah said teasingly.

Arissa laughed as she eased herself into an ergonomic office chair at a desk near a large succulent potted in a hand-thrown clay pot. "Never doubt me," she said. "My team has six closings in the next two days, and I need to make sure there's no final walk-through drama with any of them." Her laptop pinged to life. "But enough about me. How's Emersyn doing? She seemed pretty tipsy when you two left. Who knew we'd all become such lightweights?"

"She's good," Savannah replied easily. *I think.*

She had sent a quick just-checking-on-you text to Emersyn that morning but hadn't yet received a response. Her chest tightened as she wondered if Emersyn was horrified at spilling her soul to her on the beach. She hadn't been overly drunk but had certainly been tipsy enough to let go and allow the alcohol to loosen her defenses.

As Savannah scanned an email from her director of acquisitions and real estate, her phone buzzed loudly on the desk. She smiled as Emersyn's name flashed across the screen.

Sorry, I just woke up. Thanks again for everything last night.

The text was short, but Savannah was relieved that Emersyn was okay. She set her phone on the desk and, as she reached for her half-full iced coffee, realized Arissa had narrowed her eyes at her.

"What's that smile about?" Arissa asked.

"What smile?" Savannah said innocently. *Shit.*

"Oh, don't give me that." Arissa rolled her eyes. "That was definitely an I-got-a-message-from-a-woman-I-like smile."

Savannah rolled her eyes as she turned her attention back to her email. "I think you're reading way too much into a simple smile."

Arissa shrugged. "If you say so… Apparently, Mia helped me download one of those dating apps and set up a quick profile before we left the bar last night. I woke up and went to delete it, but I had a message from a really interesting woman. And *hot*. So, yes, Savannah, I definitely know that look." She shook her head. "Hey, you were going to the beach yoga session that Kay and Diana planned for the group this afternoon, right?"

Savannah groaned inwardly. "I don't know," she said. "You're forgetting my mother is Lisa Sanchez. I've done enough yoga in my life to last for three lifetimes. I was going to finish up checking in here and…" Savannah waved her hand, realizing she couldn't come up with an excuse fast enough.

Sit in my room so I don't run into Emersyn again? Avoid her because… what? She's beautiful? Being close to her clearly isn't a good idea, because you suddenly want to crush your lips against hers all over again?

Arissa blinked at her. "And what?" she said. "Kay and Diana planned the event for our whole group, so we should go. Also, I selfishly don't want to go alone." She winked. "So, I'll go with you, our resident yoga expert."

Savannah leaned back in her chair and fixed Arissa with a look. "Fine," she said. "I'll do the beach yoga. But only because I want to hear about this mystery woman who messaged you *and* I don't want to miss it if you fall on that glorious butt in the sand."

Arissa laughed. "Fair," she said. She took a sip from her water bottle. "Good." She paused. "My butt *is* pretty glorious, isn't it?"

Savannah laughed so hard in the quiet conference space that she nearly spit her sip of icy, sweet coffee across her keyboard. Despite the inexplicable pull toward Emersyn that tugged at something buried deep in her chest, Savannah felt good as the morning sunshine splashed across the room. It was good to be here.

As for a certain short, feisty blonde? Savannah wouldn't let her mind wander over that just yet.

❖

Midafternoon sun streamed hot and bright through gauzy white curtains that swayed languidly in the breeze as most of the group gathered on a long wooden platform on a quiet area of the beach. Thick, oversized linen canopies hung from beams at each corner of the platform, providing soft shade from the white-hot tropical sun. A line of dark, low-hanging clouds hung at the horizon, hinting at a quick thunderstorm later.

As Emersyn strode onto the platform, her hair in a low ponytail and sunglasses pushed up her nose, she blinked at the ocean glittering just beyond the platform. The bright light pressed against her temples, leaving a gentle ache behind her eyes, though she felt a lot better after a lazy morning and room service breakfast. She grabbed a rolled yoga mat from a stack near the back of the platform and gently knelt to unroll hers in an uneven row between Diana and Mia. She sat and crossed her legs, closing her eyes and taking a deep breath, as Erica and Kayla trickled in with excited chatter and brightly colored beachwear.

I can't believe how much I told Savannah last night. Emersyn tried not to flush as she recalled how she'd told Savannah how good she smelled and that she had no idea why she agreed to marry Jared. *Now that it's out there, I can't exactly take it back.*

Easy laughter and breezy, light energy filled the platform as more of the wedding group arrived for the yoga session. *And I can't bury it anymore either.*

Suddenly, the idea of setting a date and walking down the aisle with Jared seemed like an impossibility, something that Emersyn desperately knew wasn't right for her. Urgency set in low in her stomach as she thought of the ramifications—breaking Jared's heart when he had been nothing but good to her, starting all over again, explaining to her mother why she had turned away what she was convinced was the perfect man, navigating things like sexuality and coming out at thirty-eight years old instead of in her early twenties. Was she ready for that? Could she embrace herself and her truth once and for all? She knew there would be no going back once it was out there. It was practically overwhelming, and Emersyn's heart raced in her chest. She tried to pay attention as the resort's yoga instructor, a tanned, slender woman with dozens of beaded bracelets on each wrist, stood at the front of the group and welcomed everyone.

"Good afternoon, friends," she said as she pressed her hands together at her chest. "I am so glad we could all be here to share in an hour of practice together. No matter what level of yoga you're at, whether you just did yoga last week or it's been ten years, the important thing to remember is to do this at your own pace. I'll occasionally walk around and adjust your pose if needed, but I want this to be an hour of self-reflection and gratitude for us all." She glanced over her shoulder at the horizon. "We should have just enough time before those clouds reach us, but if they start moving faster then I'll wrap us up early. Sound good?"

Just as Emersyn wondered if she was truly ready for an hour of self-reflection, her spiraling thoughts compounded by the slight hangover that pulsed at her temples, Savannah arrived.

Emersyn was breathless as her gaze followed Savannah and Arissa next to her. Her long, dark hair had been pulled back into a loose braid and her golden-tan skin practically glowed under the sun. Her dark gray yoga shorts and a loose, burnt-orange racerback tank top hugged her curves. She looked impossibly calm, grounded, and at ease.

Savannah nodded in greeting at Diana, glancing at Emersyn with a flicker of something unspoken in her dark eyes, before quietly unrolling her mat next to Arissa a few rows down and behind them. Emersyn was almost certain there had been a flash of longing before Savannah quickly averted her gaze. That brief moment was enough to sustain and ease Emersyn, spiking her pulse and filling her veins with a slow-simmering warmth.

As the class began, Emersyn was easily distracted as the instructor patiently led them through breathing exercises, light stretching, and sun salutations. There were occasional chuckles when someone wobbled or stumbled into their pose, but all Emersyn could think about was Savannah and why she had a panging ache in her chest that hadn't been there before she'd walked confidently through the sand and onto the wooden platform.

"You can hold warrior one here," the instructor said softly. "Let's move that heel so it should now be parallel to the back of your mat. Make sure those hips are facing forward. When you're ready, open those arms and hold them at your sides. Lean into that front knee and let your torso lengthen as you stretch your fingers over your bent knee." She walked slowly through the group and gently adjusted Kayla's arms and then the angle of Mia's hips. "Good, good. This is warrior two, nicely done."

Emersyn finally risked a glance over her shoulder at Savannah and gazed at her in profile. She was strong, controlled, and elegant as she easily held warrior two, her spine straight and her shoulders relaxed. As Emersyn leaned further into her knee, she nearly buckled and lost her balance.

"You okay?" Diana whispered from her left.

"Yes," Emersyn replied as she blushed. "I, um, forgot that yoga is like a whole different species of discipline." She shook a lock of hair that had fallen from her ponytail off her face. "It's been a while, can you tell?"

"We thought this would be a good group exercise for everyone," Diana said kindly. "We all get so busy in our daily lives, we rarely think about releasing those distractions. It's hard to remember to tune in to our heart-center."

Emersyn nodded as she stole another glance at Savannah. *Easy for Diana to say. My distraction is tall, smoldering, and barefoot ten feet away from me. And for some reason, my heart-center or whatever it's called, keeps wanting me to look over there.*

As Emersyn tried to focus back on the instructor, she noticed Diana glance at her knowingly before she, too, refocused on the instructor. *What was that about?*

Emersyn didn't have time to ponder it, as a loud rumble of thunder shook the platform in ominous warning. The instructor glanced over her shoulder again and smiled. "I think we're about to receive a beautiful blessing from Mother Nature," she said. "There's only five minutes left in our session, so let's wrap up now. These storms tend to come through fast and furious."

As she guided them through a final stretch and then down into child's pose, Emersyn exhaled softly. The wind had picked up and brought with it the damp, refreshing scent of rain. Her gaze wandered to Savannah again, and she blinked as she realized Savannah was looking back at her. Another clap of thunder, louder this time, shook the platform again.

Shrieks and laughter echoed across the beach as a torrential rain whipped down, streaming over the platform and soaking the canopies. As the group scrambled to grab their sandals, towels, and water bottles, the wind sent the rain zigzagging across the wooden platform while everyone took off in different directions and tried unsuccessfully to cover themselves with their towels.

Emersyn laughed as she hurried down the beach toward the resort, trying in vain to cover her head but realizing it was to no avail as the rain slashed across her with each strong gust of wind. Palm fronds whipped and bent beneath the sudden afternoon storm as Emersyn heard Mia squealing behind her as she splashed through a puddle.

"Emersyn!" Savannah called breathlessly. She was jogging behind her, her thin tank top already soaked through and clinging to her torso.

Emersyn turned, blinking at the raindrops that streaked from her hair down her face, and laughed at the absurdity of it all. "This sudden sprint counts as a workout too, right?"

"It definitely does," Savannah said as she grabbed her hand. "Come on, there's a cabana over here."

Emersyn followed, her hand in Savannah's, as they ducked into one of the white linen tents between the beach and the pool. The front panel billowed in the wind as Emersyn sat on the edge of a white chaise and shook her head. She held her arms in front of her and shook her head at the rain droplets snaking down her wrists.

"Well, that escalated quickly," she said. "Who knew torrential downpours could start that fast?"

Savannah laughed. She stood, leaning against a corner column, and folded her arms. Her cheeks were flushed and her braid was dripping down her back. "Welcome to Cabo in July."

"I don't think I packed for tropical storms," she said as she leaned back in the chaise for a moment. Savannah's face softened as her gaze danced from Emersyn's soaked T-shirt down her bare legs and then back up. Something about Savannah looking at her gave Emersyn a thrill of anticipation deep in her core.

"You can't prepare for everything," Savannah said. "Sometimes a little unexpected storm to break you out of your comfort zone isn't all bad. Besides, you look good soaked."

Emersyn stilled as she realized how unguarded she looked as she stretched along the chaise. Heavy rain beat loudly against the wooden cabana roof. "Do I?"

"Yeah," Savannah said, her voice low. "You do. You look…free. Exhilarated. It looks good on you, Em."

Emersyn swallowed hard, sensing something deeper beneath the teasing and humor, and opened her mouth just as Kay and Diana rushed into the cabana. They chuckled loudly as they tried to shield themselves with oversized pool towels, but their hair clung to them and water dripped down their faces.

"This is cozy," Kay said and then glanced between Savannah, leaning casually against the beam, and Emersyn, wet and stretched languidly along the chaise. "Whoops, didn't realize this one was taken."

"We'll find another," Diana said quickly as she grabbed Kay's hand and tugged her toward the entrance. "I think only half the group made it back into the resort. The rest of us are ducking into shelter where we can."

Emersyn sat up quickly. "No, you don't have to—"

Kay was already waving as she and Diana backed through the front curtain. "Ready to run again?" she asked Diana.

Savannah opened her mouth and then shut it, looking like she was caught somewhere between amused and mortified. "No, really, you—"

Kay and Diana had already disappeared out of the cabana as Emersyn groaned softly and flopped back onto the chaise. "That was weird," she said. "And I'm still soaked."

The rain fell steadily against the roof of the cabana as Savannah peered out the front curtain. All Emersyn could see were thick gray sheets of rain that soaked the sand and blurred the horizon. She turned back and glanced at Emersyn apologetically. "Looks like we're stuck at least another fifteen minutes or so."

"Good thing we like each other," Emersyn said, realizing too late how charged her words sounded in the small cabana.

Savannah smiled but didn't say anything as she grabbed a white towel that had been hanging neatly on a bamboo hook. "Here," she said as she tossed the towel to Emersyn. "Dry off."

Emersyn glanced up at Savannah. "There's only one?"

Savannah nodded. "I'll live," she replied. "It's just water."

Emersyn scooted over on the chaise as she opened up the towel. "I'm not going to leave you hanging and soaked while I enjoy this amazingly dry towel," she said. "Here, we can share."

Savannah sat next to Emersyn on the chaise cautiously. "Thanks," she said, her voice uncharacteristically quiet. "Appreciate you sharing, city girl."

Emersyn instinctively moved closer and opened the towel so Savannah could wrap herself in the other half. Savannah's arm brushed against Emersyn as she pulled a corner of the towel over her shoulder. Her wet tank top was a shock of cold against Emersyn's skin that warmed into something flushed and heated, as though she had been branded by the touch.

The towel was barely big enough for one person and Emersyn realized the proximity was unavoidable as her thigh pressed against Savannah's. She closed her eyes for a moment, relishing her nearness and her soft skin against hers, as their breathless laughter faded.

Emersyn sensed a shift in their energy as she opened her eyes and stole a glance at Savannah, just centimeters from her. A droplet of rain snaked from her hair and down her cheek. Without thinking, Emersyn carefully brushed it away with her thumb.

Savannah stilled and then glanced at Emersyn, holding her gaze. "You always look at me like that," she murmured.

Emersyn's heart pounded as she searched Savannah's face. "Like what?"

Savannah arched an eyebrow. "Like you're daring me to do something."

The rain pattered against the cabana roof, slower now, as time seemed to stop. A corner of the towel slipped from Emersyn's shoulder as Savannah caught it, her other hand landing on Emersyn's waist, and gently pulled it back to her shoulder. Savannah's fingertips lingered along her neck and collarbone, and Emersyn felt a slow-rolling wave of warmth as the air around them sparked with electricity.

"Maybe I want you to do something," Emersyn said. She was unsure where her sudden nerve was coming from, but her desire for Savannah seemed to only blossom since the night before. It bloomed through her core and easily outweighed all the logic and rationalization she had so far tried to hide behind.

Savannah's gaze fell to her lips and she leaned in slowly, tentatively, as she closed her eyes. "Be careful what you wish for," she said.

As Emersyn leaned in, her lips hovering millimeters from Savannah's, she felt warmth radiating from her body. Her senses and nerves were alight with delicious anticipation as she acknowledged there wasn't a single ounce of her that *didn't* want this.

Just as Emersyn was sure Savannah was going to close the short distance and capture her lips with her own, a loud gust of wind rustled the front of the cabana. The panel swayed open and a cloud of sand floated in. Outside had already brightened, with fluffy white clouds replacing the menacing, low-hanging dark ones, and rays of sun pierced through the sky. The only evidence of the fast-moving storm was the wet sand and a few scattered palm fronds along the frothy tide.

Emersyn wasn't even sure what she was doing as she reached over, interlocking her fingers in Savannah's and squeezing once, slowly. She just knew it felt *right*. Savannah gazed back at her for a moment and then glanced down at their joined hands resting on her thigh.

"Do you know what you do to me?" she said quietly. "Still?"

CHAPTER FIFTEEN

Savannah's breath caught as the words, rhetorical but thoughtful, escaped her. Emersyn shifted closer beneath the towel and their legs brushed as an unmistakable warmth rose between their damp bodies. Savannah pulled a corner of the thick terrycloth tighter in her fingertips and took a deep breath. She was all too aware of the faint cherry-almond scent of Emersyn's shampoo and the way the breeze had brushed a loose lock of hair over her cheek. The cabana was filled with the mingling scents of sunscreen, rain, and something sweetly and inherently *her*.

Savannah lifted her fingers almost without thinking as she gently brushed the soft lock of hair from Emersyn's face. Her gaze traveled slowly to Emersyn's lips, full and pink, and she was nearly overcome with the desire to pull her close and kiss away the rest of her clear gloss until her lush mouth was swollen and begging for more.

"Show me," Emersyn said. "Show me what I do to you, Savannah."

Warmth surged through her as she recognized that same vulnerability that had been laid bare in Emersyn's gaze the night before. The ache in Savannah's chest deepened. It was the same vulnerability that had been there sixteen years ago, in a tiny hotel room during a late winter blizzard, and behind it stood desire. Aching. Longing. All at once, Savannah understood exactly what she wanted: Emersyn all over again, as the magnetic, pulsing desire that was equal parts unshakable and terrifying crashed through her while the realization settled.

Emersyn caught Savannah's fingertips in her own and squeezed gently, her eyes never leaving Savannah's face. Her hand gently fell from Emersyn's waist and brushed along her warm thigh beneath the towel.

Just as Savannah was about to close the short distance between their lips, Erica's voice was loud right outside the cabana.

Savannah felt Emersyn shift quickly as she pulled her half of the towel around her tighter. Savannah stood quickly and nearly knocked over her water bottle as she sidestepped away from the chaise. She shook her head as if to clear away the coil of electricity simmering deep inside her, before she did something crazy like kiss Emersyn Tanner in a beach cabana in Cabo San Lucas. Emersyn Tanner, who was definitely engaged to her fiancé. The *safe* choice, as she'd insinuated the night before.

"Hey, there you two are!" Erica said. She poked her head through the front panel, one arm slung around Kayla, as they padded through the wet sand. "We didn't make it that far either. Talk about getting drenched." Erica opened her arm and gestured at her soaked clothes.

"We thought you two got swept away in the storm," Kayla teased her. "I think Mia and Arissa made it into the resort."

"We were just drying off." Emersyn's voice sounded breathy and high-pitched. She gestured lamely at the towel slung over her shoulders. "We, um, found an extra towel."

Savannah watched Erica shoot Emersyn a confused glance. "Since the storm passed through, Kayla and I wanted to see if anyone wanted to play beach volleyball." Erica pointed down the beach. "We found a couple nets over there. What do you say? Two on two?"

Savannah grabbed her sandals and water bottle as she avoided their expectant gazes. "I should head back," she said quickly and then flashed a smile. "I desperately need a shower after the impromptu one I got a half-hour ago."

She didn't wait for anyone to question her or try to cajole her into a game. Instead, her legs moved on instinct as she slipped out of the cabana. Her toes sank in the wet sand and the humid post-storm air clung like a heavy blanket on her damp skin.

"Savannah?" Emersyn's voice was hesitant as she blinked, the sweet vulnerability in her hazel eyes almost too much to bear.

"I'll see you guys later." Savannah turned and hurried across the sand. "Have fun!" she called over her shoulder.

Savannah's heart pounded like she'd sprinted a mile and her breath was tight in her chest as she pushed open the lobby door and shivered beneath the blast of air conditioning that greeted her.

As she waited impatiently for the next elevator, Savannah stared at her distorted reflection in the polished doors. "What am I doing?" she said to herself. "Emersyn and I already did this once. Wasn't that enough?"

Still, as the elevator doors slid open and Savannah quickly jabbed at the button for her floor, the piercing longing in her chest remained strong. Emersyn had a look that said *I want you too* as her gaze slid over each millimeter of Savannah's lips.

She stepped into her room and sat heavily on the edge of the bed. Savannah knew she was supposed to be better than this, smarter, and in control of her feelings. Emersyn was engaged, after all, with an obnoxiously ostentatious ring on her finger even if she had admitted that she wasn't in love with her fiancé. It was messy, but she couldn't deny the way her heart skipped each time Emersyn looked at her like she wanted desperately to hold onto her, like she wanted to yield to Savannah, and give herself to her all over again.

Savannah shivered as she recalled how their bodies had fit perfectly together so many years ago, the way Emersyn had let go in her arms and allowed Savannah to unravel and claim her. Just the thought was nearly enough to make her body light with desire the same way it had minutes ago when they were dangerously close to kissing in the private proximity of the cabana.

"This is ridiculous," Savannah said as she slipped her earbuds on and decided that a workout in the fitness center would be exactly what would take her mind off the curling heat that slid through her veins. "I can't want her like this. That's it."

Still, Savannah knew the truth as she stripped off her wet clothes and dug out a clean pair of dusty rose-pink exercise leggings and a matching pale pink sports bra. She *did* want Emersyn all over again and it was driving her crazy. The pull between them was always there; it had never gone away.

The best thing is to avoid Emersyn for the rest of this trip. Savannah tucked her phone and key card into a small pocket in her leggings. *That's what a responsible adult does in this situation.*

As she set off for the fitness center, Savannah also knew deep down that she wouldn't be able to walk away from Emersyn a second time.

❖

It was nearly dinner time and three hard-fought beach volleyball games later when Emersyn returned to her suite. She peeled off her yoga shorts and tank top before tugging out the band holding her ponytail. As her hair cascaded down her back, she turned to crank the faucet in the glass walk-in shower to its hottest setting.

As thin tendrils of steam began to curl through the small bathroom, Emersyn looked at herself in the mirror as it slowly fogged over. Her eyes looked brighter, more alert. There was an exhilaration in her gaze that flushed her cheeks and pursed her lips into a teasing, knowing smile as she thought about how close she had come to kissing Savannah in the cabana earlier.

Am I glowing?

Shaking the thought away, she stepped into the shower and took a deep breath as she rolled her shoulders beneath the hot spray. Rivulets of warm water ran through her hair, snaking down her back, and gently massaged her muscles and relaxed the tangle of emotions that sat low in her stomach.

Savannah almost kissed me. Emersyn picked up a small loofah and drizzled a generous amount of body wash from a resort-branded bottle on a nearby shelf. *And I almost let her.*

As she caressed the soapy loofah down her chest and across her stomach, a low burn pulsed through her. She took a deep breath as she tilted her head further beneath the spray.

I would have let her.

The realization was simple and clear as Savannah's face flashed behind her closed eyes. A familiar ache rolled slowly through her as she recalled Savannah's teasing smile, the weight behind her gaze, and the way she looked at her as though she could see through everything else and directly into Emersyn.

She always saw me. Slowly, she moved her free hand lower as she gently rubbed the loofah over her breasts and paused as it caressed her nipples. As she reached between her wet thighs, she pictured Savannah there with her, naked, in the shower, and brushing kisses along every inch of skin the loofah was massaging. She thought of what it would have been like if they had kissed, before Erica and Kayla stumbled upon their cabana, and what would have happened next.

Emersyn thrust one finger inside herself and then another as she imagined Savannah's wet body against hers and her lips right *there*…

Emersyn stilled as she brushed the tip of her clit with her thumb. She blinked and swallowed hard as she quickly brought her fingers out of her and rinsed them under the shower.

"Am I really doing this?" she said as the weight of it all hit her. "Fantasizing about Savannah making love to me while I touch myself in the shower?"

Guilt crept through Emersyn as she quickly washed and conditioned her hair, and then stepped out of the shower and wrapped a thick towel around herself. Still, the guilt was no match for the deep ache that sliced right through her.

As Emersyn reached blindly onto the granite-topped bathroom counter for her comb, her fingers brushed the ring that sat patiently near the soap dish—her engagement ring from Jared, with nearly ten thousand dollars of deep-green emeralds surrounding a large, sparkling diamond. She had thought it a bit ostentatious and flashy at first, but Jared had insisted on sparing no expense.

I should talk to him. She needed something safe, something solid. Jared would know how to ease the swirling guilt and deep desire that flooded her. Maybe he would even talk some sense into her and they would laugh about how something in the tropical Mexican air seemed to enliven and free her.

With her mind made up, Emersyn pulled on a pair of baggy gray sweatpants and a thin black cami before padding to the bed. She crossed her legs beneath her as she twisted her wet hair up into a clip before picking up her phone. She tapped Jared's name and waited impatiently for him to answer.

She anxiously drummed her fingers against the buttery-soft fabric of her loose sweats. Jared finally picked up on the third ring. Laughter and music echoed in the background as Emersyn wrinkled her nose at the loud sounds in her ear. "Hey, Em!" Jared's voice was carefree and breathless. "How are you, gorgeous? Everything good?"

"Yeah," she said hesitantly. "I, um, just wanted to check in, but I forgot you're a few hours ahead. How's the work stuff going?"

"It's great!" Jared had to yell over the bar noise. "Our panel tomorrow doesn't start until ten, so some of us went to the hotel bar after dinner to let loose a little. Nothing too crazy," he went on quickly, though Emersyn recognized the slight slur in his words.

She smiled down at her lap. "Sounds like you're having fun," she said. "You deserve it, Jared." She swallowed as she wondered if he'd still be having a good time if he'd known that she'd almost kissed Savannah earlier or if he could've telegraphed her thoughts in the shower.

"Thanks, babe," Jared said. A shriek of laughter exploded somewhere nearby. "It's been good. I wish you were here. You'd probably hate the geeky clinical talk but love the wine list."

Emersyn laughed despite herself. "You're probably right," she admitted. "Maybe another time."

There was a long pause as Jared spoke to someone in the background before returning to the call. "Definitely," he said distractedly. "Sorry, Dr. Yang, remember him from St. Louis? He just challenged me to darts at the bar next door. He doesn't know it yet, but he's about to loose. Lose, I mean. I'll call you tomorrow?"

"Sure." Disappointment flared in Emersyn's stomach. "Be safe and have fun."

"You too," Jared said. "Talk soon, babe."

Emersyn hung up and tossed her phone onto the nightstand before collapsing back into the soft comforter. She blinked at the ceiling for a long moment as the sudden, deafening silence of the room surrounded her. She thought of cracking open the balcony door, just enough so the soothing lull of the ocean waves could dispel some of the sadness she felt after speaking to Jared. She couldn't help but feel deep in her bones that it was all wrong, everything about her relationship with Jared—and she understood that it wasn't Jared who was the problem; it was her.

For the first time in years, Emersyn allowed herself to reflect on how she struggled to feel something, anything, for Jared and yet just the thought of *almost* kissing Savannah was enough to practically bring her to her knees, bathed in golden late afternoon sunlight dancing through the sliding glass door. Alone in the suite, Emersyn was surprised as she felt a trickle of something wet and hot snake down her cheek. She wiped it away with her fingertip, but another trickle followed, and then another.

Before Emersyn knew it, her body was wracked with sobs. Somewhere in the back of her mind, she knew this was cathartic, that it was too late to put the magic back into the bottle and rationalize everything away. She understood then that she would never marry Jared or have his children and that she would never fully learn to live if she didn't embrace who she was—all of who she was. She had come so close in her early twenties, and she wondered through her tears how different things would have been if she'd had the courage to fully come out then. Realistically, she knew the likelihood of it working out with Savannah then would still have been small, and maybe that was for the best. Sixteen years was a lot of time to grow and settle into a comfortable adult life, find stability in careers they were passionate about, and discover who they really were.

As Emersyn strode to the sliding glass door, wiping her hot tears on the heels of her palms, she gazed at the ocean six floors below. Bright, rolling turquoise gave way to deeper pockets of navy and then finally to inky midnight blue closer to the horizon. She recalled for what felt like the millionth time that evening the near-kiss in the cabana and how she would have kissed Savannah back without hesitation.

Show me Emersyn had said. *Show me what I do to you.* And, God, Emersyn had wanted Savannah to take her face in her hands and show her.

It was maddening how attracted and drawn she was to Savannah. Emersyn understood now that there was nothing sweetly nostalgic or firmly forgotten when it came to them, no matter how hard she tried to dismiss it. The pull between them was *always* there.

Chapter Sixteen

The scents of bold espresso and sweet caramel drifted up from the wide latte mug in front of Savannah as she tipped her face toward the sun and enjoyed the early morning warmth tickling her skin. There had been a full day between the near-kiss with Emersyn in the cabana and this morning's early breakfast at the same casual resort restaurant where Savannah had met Kay and Diana for brunch before.

She stared out at the hazy line where the shimmering ocean met the pale blue morning sky and speared a piece of pineapple on her plate as she chewed absent-mindedly. Despite doing her best to avoid Emersyn, Savannah hadn't stopped thinking about her. There had always been something deep and magnetic between them, something that felt a lot like…

Stop it Savannah warned herself as she breathed deeply, inhaling the scent of hibiscus and night blooming cereus. She had chosen a small table near the edge of the outdoor eating area in hopes of a quiet, relaxing start to the day. The longer her thoughts tangled in the memory of Emersyn sitting so close to her that their thighs had pressed together and the more often she recalled the melodic tease in her voice when they spoke, the less anchored she felt. Savannah desperately wanted to get herself back under careful control, no matter how soft Emersyn's skin was beneath her fingertips or how silky her hair had been when she curled a loose lock behind her ear.

Savannah subconsciously pressed her thighs tighter together as she brushed off her short light denim cut-offs. *Let it go. You can want her all you want, but that doesn't change the fact that Emersyn is engaged. You're thirty-eight years old and you have a brand to expand soon. Be smart and strong.*

"Savannah!" A familiar voice rang out over the rustle of nearby palm trees in the morning breeze.

Savannah glanced up as she spotted Kay and Diana strolling toward her. "Good morning," she said warmly. "Great to see you both."

"Look who's here bright and early." Kay grinned. "You're up with the rest of us old folks today."

Savannah laughed as she set down her fork. "Hardly," she said. "I've seen how the mimosa line gets at this place anytime after nine. I'm just trying to beat the rest of the turistas."

"Mind if we join you for a minute?" Diana asked, her hands already resting on the back of the chair across from Savannah. "How nice to run into you here."

Savannah hesitated for a beat and then gestured at the small square table. "Of course," she said. "I'm getting a quick breakfast in before I go camp in the business center all morning."

Kay leaned her elbows on the table as she slid a pair of black wraparound sunglasses over her face. "Someone hasn't left executive mode behind," she observed wryly. "Weren't you supposed to be unplugged?"

Savannah gave a little shrug as she blew once on her hot coffee. "Old habits, I guess," she said. She didn't mention that it had been the only thing to provide momentary distraction from Emersyn. "Besides, we're gearing up for that expansion, and my senior leadership team is starting to narrow down strategic locations around Phoenix for consideration."

"Sanchez, that's great," Kay said. She crossed her arms. "I'm proud of you. You've built something really special with the Vault. I can't wait to see where you take it next."

"Thank you." She sipped her coffee. "What are you two up to this morning? Let me guess. Final wedding war room meeting over breakfast, featuring lots of caffeine?"

Kay chuckled. "Something like that. Though most things are pretty set now. Dare I say we're at the finish line."

Diana nodded. "Well, except for the signature cocktail that the wedding planner is insisting we need." She waved a hand. "What the hell is that? Do people do that for weddings these days?"

Savannah laughed. "As long as there's wine, we'll survive."

As their banter turned to the other wedding plans that had been finalized, Kay leaned back in her chair as she regarded Savannah thoughtfully. "I know you only have a few minutes and we won't keep you," she said after a moment. "We have our own reservation for breakfast anyway. You'll be at the pre-wedding cocktail party we're hosting in the banquet room tomorrow night, right?"

Savannah nodded. "Of course." She thought for a moment. "Arissa mentioned that she met some woman staying at the resort on one of the dating apps Mia was talking about earlier this week. I think she was going to bring her."

"Good, good." Kay nodded. "This will be a more formal event to kick things off. Cocktail attire, suits, that kind of thing."

Savannah nodded again, less sure of herself this time. *Where is Kay going with this?* "Got it. I'm sure I have something I can wear."

Amusement was all over Kay's face. "I'm sure."

"There will be dancing," Diana volunteered . She exchanged the briefest of glances with Kay. "And I think most people are bringing a plus-one. Just something to think about."

Savannah's stomach sank as she took a quick sip of her coffee to mask her frozen expression. "I...I don't have one," she said as she looked between them. She could feel the sun warm against her bare arms as she shifted uncomfortably.

Kay raised an eyebrow. "You know," she said thoughtfully. "I don't think Emersyn does either."

A beat of silence stretched across the small table before Savannah firmly set her jaw. "Yes, she does." Her voice sounded snarkier than she intended. "She has a fiancé."

Diana jumped in. "Sure, but he's not accompanying her in Cabo." She shrugged before glancing across the patio in thought. "I wonder if she may feel a little out of place without a plus-one tomorrow night too."

Kay met Diana's eyes for the briefest of seconds. "You know, that's a great thought, Dee," she said. Savannah wondered why it sounded like Kay had already thought of this before they even strolled to her table. "You two are friends, aren't you? Why don't you reach out to Emersyn and you two can come together tomorrow? I was going to get in touch with you today and suggest it, but since you're here that saves me a call."

"Oh, that's a lovely idea!" Diana said. "You're here alone, she's here alone, that's perfect. Certainly nothing wrong with two friends coming to the cocktail party together. I wouldn't want any of our guests to feel out of place just because they don't have a plus-one."

Savannah shook her head vehemently as her hair fell around her shoulders. "No way," she said as she crossed her arms stubbornly over her navy blue satin T-shirt. "We're all adults. Surely the cocktail party isn't *that* formal."

She looked between Kay and Diana again, but they blinked back at her. Diana glanced down to pour herself a glass of ice water from the pitcher on the table.

Finally, Kay shrugged. "I'm just throwing it out there, Sanchez," she said easily. "No harm in asking Emersyn to join you tomorrow night since most everyone else will be there with a date. You two can go together platonically and keep each other company."

Savannah chewed the inside of her cheek as her mind screamed at her all the reasons why this was a bad idea. "What about Mia?" she blurted out as she tightened her fingers around her ceramic latte mug. "She's single. After all, she announced her latest divorce to the entire bar the other night. Can't she get in touch with Emersyn and ask her to go together?"

Diana grimaced. "Mia let us know this morning that she won't make it tomorrow night. She isn't feeling well and suspects food poisoning." She glanced at Kay. "Did I get that right?"

Kay nodded. "Mia is staying in her room today and tomorrow," she said with a shrug. "Nothing serious, but she's planning to lay low the next couple days and let it run its course."

Savannah wrinkled her nose as she took another sip of her coffee. "Ouch. I hope she feels better soon."

Diana placed a gentle hand on Savannah's arm. "Look, it's just a silly pre-wedding cocktail party, right?" She said. "A reason to get dressed up and pretend to be fancy. If you really feel more comfortable stopping by alone, we'll be excited to see you either way."

Savannah stared down at her latte mug silently. Even though her mind was still filing through the long list of reasons why this was a bad idea, the piercing longing deep in her core was saying something entirely different. The tug of want pulled in her chest as it gave way to the same smoldering fire that always flooded her at the thought of Emersyn. Deep down, she knew she wanted Emersyn beside her—and only her—tomorrow night.

"Fine," she practically spat the word and then sighed grudgingly. "I'll ask her." She met Kay's eyes and smiled.

Kay grinned back at her. Savannah couldn't help but notice with annoyance that it appeared she was trying to tamp down her pleasure. "Sounds good, Sanchez," she replied breezily. "That's all I wanted to hear."

As Savannah rolled her eyes, Diana stood. "On that note, it looks like our table is ready," she said. "We'll see you both tomorrow night."

Savannah waved her hand in acknowledgement as Kay and Diana followed a uniformed server to a shaded table beneath an awning facing the beach. Her latte mug was warm in her hand as a gentle, salty breeze ruffled through her hair. Despite her best efforts to ignore it, Savannah felt a flicker of anticipation curling through her at the following evening.

❖

The white-hot afternoon sun glinted off the deep turquoise water that filled the infinity pool as blurs of heat radiated off patterned blue and white tiles along the pool's narrow edge. A clear glass fence lined the pool just beyond, maintaining a safe barrier between the edge of the infinity pool, where the water rippled and spilled over, and a steep drop to the white sand beach below.

Rows of short palm trees were planted in concrete squares dotted along the other side of the pool, providing shade and a semblance of privacy between long white outdoor chaises that stood in the shallow side of the water. An expansive concrete deck lay just beyond, filled with precisely spaced chaises and smaller private cabanas where guests sipped from frosty umbrella-topped drinks.

Emersyn reclined back in one of the chaises along the shallow end of the water, her legs crossed and her black Wayfarer sunglasses pushed to the top of her head, and watched Erica and Kayla take a silly selfie along the infinity edge of the pool. She could feel the warm flush in her cheeks, though she couldn't be sure if it was from the afternoon sun or the poolside margarita that she carefully nursed. Her black bikini was hot to the touch beneath the sun, its halter neckline embellished by tiny silver beads that shimmered in the light, and she carefully pulled her oversized white crochet cover-up tighter over her.

"Hey, Em!" Erica called from the pool. "Toss me an alley-oop! Let's see if I still got it."

Emersyn laughed as Erica easily threw her a miniature rubber basketball before nodding at a small poolside hoop in a far corner. "I know you still got it," she said. "But I don't know if my handles will translate to a tiny rubber ball."

All day, Emersyn tried to ignore the tingles she felt each time her mind wandered to Savannah. She could almost feel her low, teasing voice against her ear. As Emersyn imagined giving in and letting go all over again, desire began to take root and bloom. She was relieved when Erica had asked her to meet them by the pool. Getting out of her suite and enjoying the resort was exactly what she needed to prevent herself from nearly getting carried away again by the intoxicating idea of letting herself be wanted the way Savannah had always wanted her, shattering her and putting her back together again and again.

"Give it your best shot, Em!" Kayla called back as she hoisted herself along the edge of the pool. "Erica doesn't have those hops anymore!"

Erica fixed her wife with a look. "Don't test me, Kayla," she said with mock warning. "Come on, Em, show my wife how wrong she is!"

Emersyn laughed and sat up, her cover-up slipping from her right shoulder, as she squinted at Erica and the four-foot-tall hoop in the corner. The sun was too bright in her eyes and, though Emersyn gave it her best shot and Erica valiantly tried to catch it, the ball sailed over the hoop. Erica landed in the water and recovered as she shook her head and chuckled.

"Oh, I like this song!" Kayla said. She leaned over to the small portable speaker behind Emersyn's chaise and pressed the volume button. "This is a good playlist."

Emersyn nodded along and gently rolled her hips in time to the music as she lounged in the chaise while Kayla swayed along the edge of the pool.

Yup. She took another sip from her rapidly-warming margarita. *This is exactly what I needed to get my mind off—*

"Hey, Savannah!" Erica called. Emersyn froze as that familiar heat swarmed low in her stomach all over again. "You know, you probably need a bathing suit if you're swimming."

❖

Savannah held a hand over her eyes as she smiled at Erica. "Not swimming today," she called back. "I was actually looking all over for Emersyn." Despite her better judgment, she glanced at her, all sun-kissed skin and flushed cheeks as she stretched out across a chaise and lazily dragged her hand through the shallow water lapping at its legs. It was completely unfair.

She was mildly frustrated after having spent nearly forty-five minutes walking purposefully through the resort searching for Emersyn as she tried to shake the tangle of emotions clinging to her, unable to stop thinking about how her eyes had searched hers in the privacy of the cabana and how devastatingly close they had been to kissing. Savannah had texted her twice with no response, though she realized now Emersyn's phone was probably stashed in the pool's locker room.

Of all places at the resort, the pool was the last that Savannah thought to check, yet here she was. Emersyn's hair was down and wavy with humidity, and her bikini teased smooth cleavage that Savannah tried very hard to not look at. Emersyn appeared to be having a completely carefree afternoon, chatting casually and shimmying to music while lying on the chaise, with a half-empty frozen margarita melting languidly next to her.

She could feel Emersyn's gaze on her from beneath the hand that shaded her eyes and, for a long moment, no one said anything. Savannah exhaled loudly and crossed her arms as she leaned against the rough trunk of a palm tree.

"Emersyn, can I talk to you for a second?" Savannah tried again, pointedly this time. "Or are you going to make me walk into the pool to speak with you?" The teasing undertone betrayed the coolness in her voice as she steadily regarded Emersyn, who rolled her eyes as she pulled herself from the chaise.

"Whoops, sorry, I'll turn this down." Kayla quickly jabbed at the portable speaker. "I guess we were getting carried away with the music."

"I'll be right back," Emersyn said over her shoulder to Erica and Kayla as she approached Savannah. She stopped short, just in front of the palm tree, and crossed her arms. Savannah watched as Emersyn bit her lip as though warring with herself.

"I'm sorry, was I interrupting your afternoon?" Savannah asked as her gaze swept over the infinity pool. She couldn't help it. Annoyance prickled beneath her skin at the thought of Emersyn being so nonplussed and evidently unbothered by their near-kiss, as she enjoyed the unofficial pool party instead.

"Oh, um, not at all," Emersyn said. She flashed Savannah a smile. "Didn't expect you to find us out here."

"I tend to find what I'm looking for," Savannah said coolly. She stayed rooted firmly to her spot against the thick trunk of the palm tree. "Anyway, I needed to talk to you about tomorrow night's cocktail party."

Emersyn blinked in surprise. "Well, this is the most dramatic lead-in for a conversation I've had today," she said. "What's up that you had to track me down all the way at the pool?"

Savannah felt herself soften, just a little bit. "I ran into Kay and Diana at breakfast this morning," she said. Emersyn's nearness and her sleek bikini was all Savannah could think about. "And they emphasized *very* strongly that the cocktail party will be a formal event. Everyone is bringing a plus-one."

Emersyn gazed back at Savannah, appearing unsure what she was alluding to. "Oh," she said after a moment. "Okay."

Savannah felt very close to stomping her feet in her white leather wedge sandals as she looked anywhere but at Emersyn's bare shoulders or the way her bikini top hugged her breasts. "I don't have a plus-one," she said. "And Kay said you didn't either."

Emersyn tilted her head. "So you want to go together?" she asked as she turned to retrieve her margarita. Savannah realized Emersyn could see that her gaze had drifted to her bare legs when she bent to grab her drink.

Savannah swallowed hard, not used to feeling so off balance. "I'm asking if you want to come *with* me," she clarified quickly. "You know, as a favor to Kay and Diana since they emphasized that this will be a plus-one-type of event." She shifted and ran a hand through her hair. "I mean, just so we're not both standing awkwardly around the bar all night and third-wheeling on everyone else's dates."

The thick tropical air felt warm between them, the coiling tension and unresolved energy lingering, as their eyes locked. "Is this a request or a demand?" Emersyn said as she crossed her arms again.

Savannah arched an eyebrow. "Which do you want it to be?" She felt electricity sizzling through her and then shook her hair off her shoulders. "Look, we don't have to go together, I—"

"Of course," Emersyn cut her off, an easy smile curving her lips. "I'd love to go with you."

Savannah stilled and then nodded quickly. "Cool," she said. "Okay, I'll get you from your suite tomorrow at six." She turned a little too quickly, calling out a quick goodbye to Erica and Kayla as she strode off stiffly.

The last thing she heard as she stepped through the short white pool gate and back onto the smooth stone path to the resort was Emersyn's teasing voice behind her. "See you then, Miss Thing."

CHAPTER SEVENTEEN

As Emersyn turned back to her chaise, she stopped short at the sight of Erica in the pool. Her elbows were resting along the tiled ledge and she shot Emersyn a confused glance.

"What's up with her?" Erica asked as she nodded toward where Savannah had left. "She seemed…stressed."

Emersyn was still stunned that her daydream had seemed to manifest itself with startling accuracy right there on the pool deck and wondered why Savannah had shown up like there was something under her skin. "Maybe work is getting to her." She shrugged lamely.

As she settled back onto the chaise, Emersyn's shoulders felt looser and more relaxed and she fought to contain her smile. Still, her thoughts were anything but calm.

She glanced up as Erica attempted a reverse windmill dunk in the poolside basketball hoop and caught Kayla's knowing look. As Emersyn twisted her hair back into a low ponytail, she blinked back at her.

"What?" she finally asked, amused.

Kayla raised an eyebrow as she floated closer to Emersyn's chaise. "You're definitely not hiding that smile very well."

Emersyn rolled her eyes, though the image of Savannah leaning casually against the tree burned into her. Her arms were tanned and toned beneath her fitted satin T-shirt, and a delicate white-gold watch had glinted along her wrist. Her short denim cut-offs hugged her thighs and her wedge sandals added a couple extra inches to her height. Her hair had been loose down her back, and Emersyn was positive she had never seen anyone so gorgeous before in her life.

She quickly pressed the volume button on the speaker again. "I don't know what you're talking about," Emersyn called over the music, though her smile didn't waver.

Erica paddled over. "Who's smiling?" she asked as she looked between them, clearly not putting it together. She squinted up at Emersyn. "What did Savannah need you for, anyway?"

Kayla laughed as she grabbed Erica's arm and led her back to the ledge of the infinity pool. "Too many questions, wife," she said. "Come on, I want to get a few more photos with this gorgeous view."

Erica nodded, Savannah's sudden visit forgotten, and Emersyn was grateful for Kayla. She couldn't shake the jolt of heated anticipation as she dipped her toes over the edge of the chaise and into the cool turquoise water. It wasn't just the way Savannah had looked at her, though she appeared to be trying not to. It was that cool confidence, the command in her tone and her posture, and that dizzying attraction that simmered and smoldered between them. Beyond that, it had always been grounded by a deep understanding and tenderness that Emersyn hadn't ever experienced with anyone else.

Though her gaze was on the hazy horizon, Emersyn's mind was elsewhere entirely. Memories from years ago flooded her uninvited but not, she understood, unwelcome. Savannah's fingers gently gliding through her smooth wetness as she kissed her passionately. Her slow, confident tongue teasing her clit as her free hand held her firmly in place, despite the sensations and rockets of pleasure practically arching her hips right off the mattress. The way she unraveled and claimed her, and Emersyn had felt completely safe in her arms.

After a moment, Kayla swam up to her again. "You're still glowing, babe," she remarked knowingly.

Emersyn shook her head. "I..."

Kayla held up a wet hand and nodded toward the pool bar. "Don't worry, Erica is going to re-up on her margarita," she said quietly. "I'm not going to say anything other than it's good to see you smiling like that, Em. *Whatever* may have caused it." Kayla rolled her eyes. "That's all."

Emersyn blew out her breath and laughed lightly. How long could she deny the obvious? "Don't get ahead of yourself," she said neutrally instead. "Savannah just wanted us to go to that pre-wedding cocktail thing tomorrow night together, though I'm almost positive Kay and Diana put her up to it." She tried her best to keep her face expressionless. "It's just a party."

Kayla shot her a look that said *yeah, right* but nodded and swam off, kicking her legs beneath the water to propel her to the other side of the pool. Inside, Emersyn knew Kayla was right. It wasn't just a party, not anymore. As she stirred the last of her slushy margarita with her long neon-colored straw, Emersyn felt the sun catch the edge of her profile. Something hopeful, terrifying, and completely undeniable bloomed inside her chest. Tomorrow night couldn't arrive fast enough.

❖

The following evening, Savannah stood outside the door to Emersyn's suite as she bit her lip and debated if she should wait patiently in the hallway or go into her room if invited.

As she brushed a speck of lint from her navy blue silk cocktail dress, Savannah shifted in her silver open-toe heels but remained firmly in place. Her mind wandered to the memory of Emersyn lounging on the poolside chaise yesterday, her skin flushed and her bare legs practically begging for Savannah to slowly peel off her bikini bottom and cover her inner thighs with soft kisses. She had felt Emersyn's bright gaze following her as she quickly left, eager to leave the pool deck before her restraint frayed and she did something crazy like pull Emersyn into her arms and capture those pouted lips with her own in front of everyone at the pool.

Savannah closed her eyes for a brief moment as she knocked once on the door as the hallway air conditioning brushed through her loose curls. When she opened her eyes, she was sure her heart had stopped completely. Emersyn opened the door, her face lit up with excitement. Savannah melted just a little bit at the heat that coursed through her as she realized that Emersyn's excitement was directed at her.

It's not like this is a real date. We're friends.

"Hey," Emersyn said, her voice low and laced with something that made Savannah's chest tighten.

"Hey yourself," she murmured, unable to stop smiling.

"I need to grab my phone from the charger," Emersyn called over her shoulder as she turned and unplugged her phone from a small desk. There was a quiet self-assurance in the way she moved, a confidence and poise that only growing up and settling into your maturity could bring, and there was a trusted openness emanating from her that Savannah recognized.

She's so beautiful. The thought came from somewhere deep in her chest and extinguished the logical inner voice reminding her that this wasn't a real date. Emersyn's black one-shoulder dress clung to her toned limbs and gentle curves, and her black heels teased sharp stiletto spikes that made Savannah's mouth run dry. Dangly silver earrings glinted beneath the straight blond hair that fell over her shoulders and spilled down her back as Savannah's hand tightened around her navy blue clutch.

She turned, falling into step with Emersyn, as they headed to the elevator. As the thought of threading her fist into Emersyn's hair to gently pull her head back and nip at her neck fired through her mind, Savannah instead looked straight ahead as they paused in front of the sixth floor elevator bank.

Just don't look at her. The entire night. Look anywhere but at her.

"Thanks for going together," Emersyn said as they stepped into the elevator. She opened a small compact mirror and gently dotted a soft nude lipstick over her mouth. She rolled her eyes. "I appreciate not being forced to feel awkward and alone while everyone else feeds their dates hors d'oeuvres or whatever you do at a formal cocktail party." She shook her head ruefully. "Who knew Kay and Diana were so fancy? At least they stopped at lavender cake."

Savannah couldn't help it; she glanced at her and was overcome by Emersyn's disarming warmth in the close confines of the quiet elevator. Gentle highlighter emphasized the softness of her features and her delicate cheekbones while natural, earthy shades around her eyes illuminated their bright hazel color.

"Of course," Savannah said. "*And* I'm pretty sure they gave a resounding no to the signature cocktail."

As the elevator doors opened into the lobby, Savannah's phone vibrated in her clutch. She slowed as they stepped out of the elevator and dug it out.

Emersyn laughed. "Well, I appreciate us going together nonetheless," she said. Her voice softened barely an octave. "I missed you, Savannah."

Savannah's fingers stilled on her phone, but she didn't dare meet Emersyn's gaze. Instead, she kept her focus firmly on the lobby before them. The open-air space teemed with life as guests wandered excitedly in various directions. "I missed you too, Em," she said, hoping her voice sounded light. "Besides, any excuse to hang out with Emersyn Tanner again."

As Emersyn waved in greeting to one of the uniformed resort staff across the lobby, Savannah glanced down at the text message from Diana.

Stop thinking so much and get over here! The night is young and the party has just begun.

Savannah smiled as she shoved her phone back into her clutch, though she wondered what the beginning of Diana's text had meant. Maybe she *did* need to stop thinking so much and enjoy the moment for what it was instead.

Savannah stole a glance at Emersyn and then quickly looked away. The air between them was humming with a familiar undercurrent as they approached the reserved banquet hall at the far end of the resort. *Why shouldn't I enjoy this evening and the way Emersyn keeps looking at me? This is the real, genuine Emersyn all over again without all those walls. The Emersyn I've always seen.* Somehow, the idea of avoiding her at all costs now seemed silly. If Savannah was being honest with herself, it was the last thing she wanted to do.

Her anticipation for the evening sharpened and spiked with a rapid pulse that matched her own as she politely held the arched wooden door to the banquet hall for Emersyn. *Go with it. This is a celebration, after all.*

CHAPTER EIGHTEEN

Emersyn glanced around as she took in the smallest of the four banquet rooms at Dulce Sueños. Tall floor-to-ceiling windows offered sweeping views of the bright red sun beginning its descent into the turquoise ocean. A combination of exposed white-washed ceiling beams, polished stone flooring, and round linen-covered cocktail tables with tropical centerpieces all provided a luxurious island-themed ambiance. Delicate frosted glass pendant lanterns gave the large room a more intimate, soft glow and colorful, untamed bouquets of white orchids, coral-pink hibiscus, and monstera leaves spilled from clear vases at the center of the high-top tables and mingled with the scent of sea air and something garlicky that was being passed around on silver trays by crisply uniformed staff in white button-up shirts.

An empty wooden dance floor was set up where a norteño band was organizing their accordion, drum kit, and bajo sexto. On the other side of the room, a bar stood near the floor-to-ceiling windows, where a handful of bartenders in polo shirts monogrammed with the Dulces Sueños logo deftly made cocktails and poured from wine bottles.

"Sanchez, Tanner," a familiar voice called out. Emersyn turned and smiled at Kay, who was standing near the bar with Diana. She looked effortlessly handsome in her tailored black tuxedo, with a pair of white-gold studs glinting on her ears. "Glad you two could make it."

"My goodness, Coach Hanlon," Emersyn said as she embraced Kay. "Look at you!"

Emersyn was sure she caught a faint flush across Kay's cheeks before she took a sip of her whiskey and shook her head ruefully. "A lot less comfortable than basketball sweats and a T-shirt," she said. "But you're one to talk, Tanner." She gestured at them. "You and Sanchez clean up nice."

As they greeted Diana, Emersyn spotted Erica and Kayla a few yards away as they turned from the bar with full glasses of Merlot. Erica nodded at her as they strolled over.

"Well, well," Erica said as she gave Emersyn a quick hug and then smoothed her pressed gray suit. "Look who showed up looking like a damn movie star." She grinned at Savannah. "And you look like you stepped straight off the set of a telenovela."

Savannah laughed as she greeted them. "Would it be a lot to ask for you to follow me around every day and inflate my ego with compliments? Besides, look at *you* in that light gray! I didn't even know you owned a suit."

"Well, both of your dresses are amazing," Kayla chimed in. "And, Em, I didn't even catch those stilettos until now." She gently turned her to look at them from the back and then whistled low. "You look like you're ready to stomp all over someone's heart."

As they laughed, Savannah and Kayla were pulled by Diana and introduced to a cousin of hers and his wife. Erica glanced between them and raised an eyebrow. "Wait a second, speaking of hearts…" She threw a look over Emersyn's shoulder and then glanced at her. "Did you and Savannah arrive together?"

Emersyn's cheeks burned as she grabbed her arm and guided her back to the bar, away from the rest of the group. "We…I mean, yeah, she kind of picked me up from my room," she said as she waited for a bartender to catch her eye.

Erica pressed her lips together and blinked. "Mm-hmm."

One of the bartenders tossed a paper napkin on the glossy bar and leaned forward. "What can I get you, señorita?"

Emersyn fixed Erica with a look before she turned her attention back to the bartender. "Vodka cranberry on the rocks, please," she said. "Twist of lemon."

As the bartender turned to make her drink, Emersyn rolled her eyes at her. "And stop trying to bite back your smile with whatever point you're trying to make."

Erica was clearly enjoying herself. "I don't know what you're talking about," she said. "Savannah hunts you down yesterday and demands to speak with you. But yeah, totally casual, right? Just two former teammates going to a cocktail party together dressed like absolute bombshells, no big deal."

Emersyn laughed as she shook her head quickly. "Erica, *everyone* is dressed up here," she said as she tossed her hair over her shoulder. "Besides, I told Kayla I'm positive Kay and Diana put her up to it. They didn't want us to feel out of place as the only two without a plus-one tonight."

Erica looked unconvinced. "Right," she purposely drew out the word.

Emersyn glanced around the banquet room as she gently stirred the tiny black straw around the ice cubes in her drink. *There she is*. Savannah was near the dance floor, deep in conversation with Arissa and a woman next to her that Emersyn didn't recognize.

As she glanced back at Erica, she startled as she realized Erica was still watching her closely as she sipped her Merlot.

"*What*?" Emersyn said. "You look like you have something you want to say."

Erica opened and then closed her mouth. "You look happy, Em," she said. "You really have been glowing, you know that?" She looked like she wanted to say more, but shook her head instead. "I'm here if you ever, you know, want to talk."

Emersyn arched an eyebrow, mildly confused. As she took another sip of her cocktail and wondered what Erica meant, Kayla rejoined them and slid her arm around Erica's waist. "Did you know Coach Connor just got engaged to her fiancée about a month ago?" She leaned in to Erica. "Sounds like we'll be doing this all over again once they set a date."

Erica laughed as her face lit up. "No way!" she said. "Jane finally made it official with Nora, huh? We should go congratulate them. Come on, Em."

As they found Jane Connor and her fiancée near one of the cocktail tables and excitedly shared their congratulations, Emersyn found herself half-listening and distracted as Erica recounted an anecdote about her toddler nephew wreaking havoc at the grocery store.

Emersyn's gaze drifted again to where Savannah stood near the dance floor. Behind her, the band adjusted and tested their instruments. The ache in Emersyn's chest deepened as she drank in the sight of Savannah, all effortlessly magnetic, as she held a glass of white wine and tilted her head back, laughing at something Arissa had said. Hundreds of tiny, twinkling string lights hung from the exposed ceiling beams over the dance floor and shimmered along her glossy dark curls, the gentle curve of her profile, and the defined lines of her smooth, bare arms.

"What about you, Emersyn?" Kayla's voice brought Emersyn back to the conversation in front of her. She flushed as she realized she hadn't heard a word they said.

"I…sorry," she said with a wry smile. "I didn't catch that."

Erica looked at her for a beat and then followed where her gaze had been. She shook her head as Emersyn felt her face burn. "It's okay," she said quickly. "Emersyn is a little distracted. Kayla was just asking how it was coaching high school girls and if there was a lot of drama with them."

"No, not as much as you'd think," Emersyn said honestly as she stole another glance at Savannah. "I mean, I'm sure there's a lot of drama that goes on with them that I don't even know about, but these girls are focused. Some of them are looking at pro ball as a potential career and all of them want to go on to college to play, so they understand the work that goes into it. And that doesn't leave a lot of room for extra drama. Besides, we emphasize *team* at Crestwood." She glanced at Jane Connor warmly. "I learned from the best. Playing for each other instead of for themselves is one of the biggest foundational pieces of my team. No egos allowed."

Jane grinned. "You'll see, Tanner, that's really the best part of coaching," she said. "When you see the values and ethics that you instilled in your girls living on and being taught again. Next time Nora and I are in Chicago during basketball season, we'll get in touch so we can catch a home game."

Emersyn nodded. "I'd love that."

As the conversation drifted to Jane and Nora's upcoming wedding planning kickoff, Emersyn swallowed as she found her gaze being pulled again to Savannah like gravity. Savannah leaned in slightly, her palm resting gently on Arissa's forearm, as she said something and they all laughed. The electric current running just beneath Emersyn's skin gave way to a pang of longing at the easy, confident way Savannah commanded the conversation.

As if reading Emersyn's thoughts across the room, Savannah glanced up. Their eyes locked across the cocktail tables scattered between them and lingered as the energy between them warmed to a penetrating heat that Emersyn felt low in her stomach. The rest of the party dulled and blurred around her. The lively, accordion-laden music from the band, Erica's laughter, and the story Jane and Nora were regaling them with about their recent couples' massage at the spa all faded to a low pulsing hum. Emersyn didn't look away. Neither did Savannah.

Savannah's full lips curled into a faint, devastating smile as Emersyn swallowed hard. Savannah's gaze, dark and smoldering, was telling her everything: *I want you. I remember it all. And you've made it impossible for us to ignore what's happening.*

The ache inside Emersyn spread like a slow wildfire as she forced herself to glance back at Erica, who casually pulled Kayla into her lap as they talked about their next planned vacation.

Emersyn placed her empty cocktail glass on the table and smoothed her dress. "I'm running to the restroom," she said. "I'll be right back."

As she turned and strode into the quiet hallway just outside the large double doors, she could feel Erica watching her curiously. *I need to stop staring at Savannah with, like, heart eyes or something.* Emersyn's pulse pounded as she pushed open the frosted glass door to the bathroom. *Or is that just how I've always looked at her?*

Emersyn stood in front of a wide gilded mirror over a porcelain pedestal sink and blinked back at herself. She carefully turned the faucet and ran her fingertips beneath the icy cold water in hopes of grounding and distracting herself from the undeniable pull she felt toward Savannah. It felt like a night that could change everything.

❖

Savannah leaned casually against a cocktail table near the dance floor and gently swirled the last of her Riesling with a slow twist of her wrist. Arissa stood beside her and shifted in her forest green silk wrap dress as she gestured to her date, a psychology professor from North Carolina named Zoe.

"That's really cool," Savannah said warmly. "You must be a saint to willingly want to get inside peoples' heads. I can imagine that helping people resolve their traumas and challenges is not for the faint of heart."

"Or I'm mildly delusional," Zoe joked. "But what can I say, I love it. It has been nice getting a break this summer though." She glanced at Arissa shyly. "I never expected to meet someone right here at the resort."

Arissa flushed as she nudged Savannah playfully. "Tell Zoe about your plans to expand the Vault. I know you're excited about it."

Savannah smiled down at the empty wine glass in her hands. "Nothing is confirmed yet," she said. "We're still very much in the planning stages, but the Vault currently has four locations around Phoenix and we're hoping to open another four soon. It's sort of my baby. The brand itself is a modern gym focused on body wellness, and it's the first of its kind because it blends expert physical therapy and professional sports training with your standard exercise gym that has all the equipment, group fitness classes, and one-on-one personal training you would expect. We focus on body healing, body training, *and* body maintenance, since all those things work in tandem together when it comes to physical wellness. My leadership team is in an exploratory phase now as we consider additional Arizona locations."

Zoe looked impressed. "I love that," she said. "It sounds like something you're incredibly passionate about."

Savannah nodded, but her gaze had already drifted across the room. It lingered on Emersyn and where she stood casually with Erica, Kayla, Jane Connor, and her fiancée. Emersyn giggled at something Erica said and Savannah could practically hear the soft, melodic sound over the upbeat norteño music just to her right. Savannah tried her hardest to stay engaged in the conversation around her as Arissa made a joke about exercise bikes and hamster wheels, but her focus kept pulling back to Emersyn.

It's always back to Emersyn. Am I that hopeless?

Emersyn gathered her hair over one shoulder as her gaze met Savannah's for a long, intoxicating moment. The warm tension and restless ache twisted together in Savannah's core. *God, if this were a real date...*

Savannah set her empty wine glass on the cocktail table next to her. She didn't want to get lost in the fantasy of what if; she already knew she'd stride across the room to Emersyn, pull her into her arms so it was clear to everyone who she belonged to, relish the feeling of her body pressed against her own, and whisper something sweet and teasing in her ear…

She swallowed hard as she tried to remember that Emersyn was engaged, though her ring was conspicuously missing from her hand tonight. Savannah wondered if that was intentional and then quickly shook the thought away. She looked over Zoe's shoulder just in time to see Emersyn slipping out the doors into the hallway. Before Savannah could think better of it, she straightened and smoothed a hand over her loose curls.

"Excuse me, I'll be right back." She leaned in and clasped Arissa's arm. "I'm going to run to the restroom."

Chapter Nineteen

Emersyn wiped her hands on a paper towel and surveyed the sink. She wasn't entirely sure how she was going to get through the rest of the evening, but she knew she couldn't avoid Savannah forever. Now that the door had somehow been wrenched open to everything she had tried so long to subdue, the pent-up emotion and desire seemed to flood her veins until she was so restless with her *want* for Savannah that she could barely focus.

She glanced up in the mirror as the bathroom door creaked open behind her. Savannah walked in, smiling at her in the mirror, and stopped short just behind her.

"You okay?" Savannah asked.

Emersyn nodded. Her heart thudded in her chest as her gaze traveled up Savannah's neck to her smooth profile and then finally to her eyes in the mirror.

"Okay, let me just wash my hands." Savannah laughed as she made a big show of adjusting her stance in her silver heels and turning on the faucet around Emersyn, who hadn't moved.

Emersyn laughed as she shifted in place with Savannah and relished the bolt of electricity that raced through her as she subconsciously eased back into her warmth.

Savannah dramatically shook her wet hands out, and Emersyn tried in vain to shield herself. She grinned as Savannah's cheek brushed her temple.

"Oh, sorry, did I splash you?" Savannah asked through her giggles. "I *definitely* wouldn't want to get even the smallest drop of water on that gorgeous dress. Even though you *are* blocking the sink."

Emersyn knew full well Savannah had and threw her a mock annoyed look in the mirror. As she wriggled around in Savannah's arms and turned to face her, they both seemed to freeze in place. Emersyn's breath caught as she registered just how closely they had been touching and shamelessly flirting with one another. She glanced up into Savannah's dark eyes and the sudden intensity behind her gaze sent a shiver down her spine as time seemed to stand still.

I should kiss her. The idea made her heart pound with excitement, but it also seemed like the most natural thing in the world. Memories of slow, sensual kisses many years before flashed in her mind's eye and reminded her with stunning clarity just how good of a kisser Savannah Sanchez was.

As her gaze fell from Savannah's eyes to her lips, Savannah took a breath. "God, I've missed you," she said. She tucked a soft lock of Emersyn's hair behind her ear, her gaze never leaving her face.

"I've missed you too," Emersyn said, her voice barely audible in the charged silence. "So much," she added as the full weight of that truth settled over her.

Emersyn wasn't sure who kissed who first, but the rest of the room faded around her and then she was lost in the soft lips gently exploring her own. Savannah deepened the kiss as Emersyn slowly wound her arms around Savannah's neck and pressed herself closer into her.

As Savannah's tongue met her own, the warm familiarity tumbled into Emersyn's consciousness. *Yes, this is it. This is exactly right.* The sizzling electricity of brand-new and *so* pleasurably familiar was enough to make her dizzy, but Savannah's arms were still surprisingly strong as they tightened around her.

"We should…" Savannah blinked but kept her arms firmly around Emersyn. "We should go outside, somewhere private, and talk."

Emersyn nodded slowly, dazed. "We should."

As they carefully smoothed their dresses and hair, exchanging charged glances and breathless laughter, Emersyn swung open the bathroom door. The hallway was quiet, save for the faint strains of a fast, lively song echoing from the banquet room. She strode toward the lobby, reaching back to lock her fingers in Savannah's, and glanced back at her.

Just as they passed the arched doors to the banquet room, they swung open and music swelled into the hallway.

"There you are!" Erica called out. "God, I thought you fell in or something, Em. Come on, get on the dance floor!"

"I..." Emersyn said as she glanced helplessly between Erica and Savannah.

Savannah nodded and squeezed her hand. "It's okay," she murmured. "Let's go dance first."

"Come on, come on," Erica said as she held the door open for them. "The band is just getting started."

The cocktail party had reached full swing by the time Savannah and Emersyn reached the dance floor, with Erica on one side as she waved to Kayla. The air buzzed with the sound of clinking glasses, cheerful laughter, and the lively music. Throngs of people had made their way toward the band as Erica slipped past them to gently place her hands on Kayla's waist and ease right back into the dance with her.

Savannah turned as she squeezed Emersyn's hand once more and glanced at her playfully. "Come on," she said as she tugged her toward the dance floor. "Dance with me."

Emersyn laughed as she followed Savannah through small groups of people. "I don't dance."

Savannah shot her a look. "You do too dance. I've seen it."

Emersyn rolled her eyes as she let Savannah lead. "Maybe, like, twice in college. And definitely not to this."

"Still counts," Savannah said as she held up their hands and spun her lightly. "You've always been a good dancer, Em. And besides, norteño isn't difficult. Just keep following my lead."

Savannah wrapped an arm around Emersyn's waist and interlocked their fingers with her other hand. Emersyn's other arm naturally slid over Savannah's shoulder, her fingers tangling in her hair, and she laughed breathlessly as they fell into a rhythm of gliding steps and seamless turns in time with the faster-paced beat.

Emersyn leaned closer to Savannah, their shoulders brushing, and her lips dangerously close to Savannah's ear. "Who knew Kay could dance like this?" She nodded toward the center of the dance floor. "I always knew she was a woman of many talents."

Savannah followed her gaze as she tightened her arm around Emersyn's waist and pulled her closer. "I'm convinced there isn't a thing she doesn't know."

Just then, the fast, upbeat song faded and the tempo dropped while the twinkling string lights faded into a darker, moodier ambiance. The band slowed into a softer rhythm, romantic and unexpected, as Emersyn glanced at the people around them instinctively pairing off. Erica and Kayla a few feet in front of them. Diana gazing up adoringly at Kay from the center of the dance floor. Jane and Nora somewhere on the edge slowing into a sway.

Emersyn hesitated. Even Arissa and her date had wrapped their arms around each other, their conversation softening into whispers, as their steps slowed. Swallowing hard, Emersyn turned halfway to leave the dance floor when she felt Savannah's fingers find her own, gentle but firm.

"You're not really going to run from a slow song, are you?" Savannah asked. The heat in her gaze was exactly the same as right before Emersyn had kissed her. Or had she kissed Emersyn? Either way, it sent a tingling thrill through her as she smiled.

"I guess I understand now why Kay and Diana wanted everyone to have a plus-one," she said.

Savannah stepped closer, their fingers still interlocked, and tugged Emersyn gently back to her. "I know," she said as the faintest hint of a smile brushed her lips. "And here we are. Again."

Emersyn closed the short distance between them until she felt herself melting further into Savannah's soft, tantalizing warmth. At that moment, the gentle melody sweeping around them, she acknowledged that she didn't care about anything except being with Savannah right now. She wound her arms lightly around Savannah's neck as her hands found the small of her back and held her like she belonged there.

Maybe I do. They swayed slowly beneath the darkened string lights as the rest of the dance floor faded into a muted blur. Right then, she felt certain she did. Savannah's hands left trails of lingering warmth along the small of her back through the light fabric of her dress.

Emersyn took a deep breath as her lips brushed Savannah's cheek. "If I haven't told you yet tonight," she said. "You're gorgeous. I haven't been able to stop looking at you all evening."

Savannah leaned in slightly as one hand swept over Emersyn's spine. Dark heat filled her gaze at Emersyn's slight shiver. "You have no idea what you're doing to me in this dress."

Emersyn pressed herself closer into Savannah and rested her chin lightly on her shoulder. Everything felt right about being there in that moment and locked in Savannah's commanding embrace. She took a deep breath and swallowed hard. Savannah's neck was right there, so close and tempting. It would be so easy to turn her face and press her lips over that gentle pulse point…

Just as the slow song had begun, it began to fade. The string lights rose, twinkling brightly once more from the exposed ceiling beams, and the band launched into another raucous, upbeat song. The couples around them gradually stepped away from one another as chatter filled the dance floor again. Still, Emersyn didn't move right away and neither did Savannah. They stilled, lingering for a beat in each other's arms, and Emersyn sighed in frustration at her reluctance to let go of the soft warmth between them.

Savannah leaned in, her hand still resting along the small of Emersyn's back, and her chin brushed her temple. "Come with me."

Emersyn nodded. It wasn't a command, but it wasn't a question either. She knew she would follow Savannah anywhere.

They headed down the hall, through the lobby, and paused at an empty outdoor gathering area around the side of the resort that Emersyn assumed was utilized for small, private parties. Heavy wooden chaises were scattered around a large stone fire pit, a sleek dark wood bar, and a small dance floor beneath a tall, covered wooden pergola. Spherical globe-shaped glass solar lights that were artfully cracked hung from the pergola and swayed in the gentle evening breeze, casting a soft, romantic glow over the space.

Savannah perched on the edge of an elegant wooden chaise and gently pulled Emersyn onto her lap so she was facing her. With the sky painted in deep indigo and tiny stars dancing above the tall palm trees looming around the private gathering space, everything felt slower and softer.

Instinctively, Emersyn leaned in and met Savannah's lips again, gentle at first, and tried to bite back her soft moan as Savannah deepened the kiss. Her fingers curled into Savannah's sides over the smooth silk of her dress and she melted into the kiss with an urgent, sensual hunger.

Emersyn was sure she could stay outside kissing Savannah forever, but she gently cupped Emersyn's face as they pulled back. She ran her thumb along Emersyn's bottom lip with a slow smile.

"So does this mean you're mine tonight?" The teasing lilt to her voice told Emersyn that Savannah was maybe partially kidding, but the suggestive nature of her question warmed Emersyn's core.

Emersyn shrugged. "I guess," she said cheekily. "I mean, I *am* your pretend date tonight, right?"

Savannah let out a shaky breath and raked a hand through her hair. "Is it ever pretend with us, Emersyn?"

Her heart thumped against her ribcage at the vulnerability in Savannah's low, soft voice. "I thought I had to move on," Emersyn said as she pressed her lips to Savannah's with gentle tenderness. "I thought I was supposed to. It was so easy to make up excuses rather than face everything I was scared of head on."

Savannah tightened her arms around Emersyn's middle. "I don't want you to move on from me," she said softly. "I want you with me. I just can't believe how quickly…" She bit her lip. "After so many years, and it's like none of that matters. It just *is* between us."

Emersyn nodded. "I want you too," she said and then opened and closed her mouth. "I've always wanted you. I was too scared to admit…" Emersyn took a deep breath as a group of loud, laughing resort guests meandered down the stone path. They didn't see Savannah and Emersyn as an older woman fished out a pack of cigarettes and her male companion dug into his pocket for a lighter, but they both quickly stood from the chaise at the unexpected interruption.

Emersyn sighed as she remembered there was an entire cocktail party they had mysteriously disappeared from, and it would only be a matter of time until one of their friends found them. She knew that to anyone who didn't know them, they looked every bit the passionate couple tucked away in their own private world far away from the rest of the bustling resort.

"We should go," she said reluctantly. Her lips were swollen from Savannah's deep kisses and her brain was hazy with desire. "If we miss Kay and Diana's toast, I think Erica will send out a search party."

Savannah nodded. "Let's go."

CHAPTER TWENTY

The air conditioner hummed gently as Emersyn padded barefoot across the cool stone tile in her room. The muted sounds of distant reggaeton and chatter from an evening beach gathering drifted faintly through the sliding glass door to her balcony, but she moved on autopilot as her mind replayed the evening. Her body was alight with desire as she recalled the heat of Savannah's gaze and the softness of her lips in excruciating detail.

Emersyn exhaled slowly as she tugged off her dress, realizing that it smelled faintly of coconut milk, and her pulse quickened. She could still feel Savannah everywhere and she desperately wanted to keep kissing her until the sun rose over the horizon.

Her thoughts were interrupted as her phone buzzed loudly on the bathroom vanity and the screen illuminated with a notification. A pit formed deep in Emersyn's stomach as she glanced at it. *Jared.*

Emersyn picked up her phone as she pulled on her yoga shorts and a soft cotton tank top, but stilled as her breath caught. Three missed calls from Jared. A missed video call. Then another. A series of unanswered text messages.

Have a great night, beautiful. Text me when you get back to your room.

How's it going? Did you make it back?

Where are you?

Call me when you get this. Can we talk? Just need to hear your voice.

Emersyn swallowed hard as the pit in her stomach cratered. She realized she hadn't been in touch with Jared aside from the occasional short one- or two-word text message in over twenty-four hours. She had been far too distracted and enamored with the woman she couldn't seem to stop kissing just hours before.

She sat heavily on the edge of the bed and quickly typed out a reply assuring Jared she was fine and had temporarily misplaced her phone at the cocktail party. The lie settled deep and uncomfortable in her chest, and Emersyn despised the icky feeling of not being truthful. Her fingertips hovered over the screen for another moment before she set her jaw and hit the call button instead.

Emersyn took a deep breath and tried to will the guilt away, as Jared answered on the first ring.

"Hey." His voice was clipped and distant. "You okay? I know you said you lost your phone at the cocktail party, but you kind of disappeared on me all day and the day before too."

Emersyn sprang up from the bed, unable to sit still. She paced over the cool tile and then slid onto the balcony. "Yeah, I…" She sighed. "Yeah, I'm okay. It was a long night. I'm sorry for not responding. The party was packed and I was catching up with a lot of old friends…"

Emersyn swallowed hard as the brief memory of dancing slow with Savannah, melting into her as she wrapped her arms around her, flashed in her mind. She hated how she sounded. She knew she was throwing bad excuses out to Jared, and she had a feeling he knew it too.

"We should talk, Jared," Emersyn finally said softly. Her gaze fell on a group of resort guests dancing on the beach with frosty drinks in hand, as the orange-gold flames from tall black tiki torches illuminating the stone path billowed in the night breeze. "I've been thinking about a lot of things."

"Okay," Jared said warily. "Like what?"

Emersyn sighed. "Really, I've been thinking about a lot of things since before I came to Cabo," she said truthfully. "Something about being able to step away forces you to confront a lot of the stuff I've been trying to ignore for a long time. Hide. Avoid. I don't know, all of the above." She blew out her breath as she watched one of the people dancing, a man in baggy swim trunks, dip a woman in an elegant one-piece as they shimmied to the music. "There's a lot I've pushed to the side for *so* many years. I just need to talk to you. Like, *really* talk."

Jared was quiet for a long moment. "Emersyn, I've got an early panel that starts at seven sharp tomorrow morning." His voice was cold and detached. "Can we talk another time?"

Emersyn's heart sank as she inhaled the scent of sea salt and lingering coconut milk lotion. "Sure. I guess. We'll talk later."

"Cool," Jared said. "Glad you're safe. Talk soon."

As they hung up, Emersyn gazed at the endless stretch of inky velvet beyond the beach. Its surface rippled gently beneath the pale silver moon and slow waves shimmered as they lapped against the shore. The heaviness in her chest weighed down like lead, though disappointment at not being given the opportunity to say what she needed to flowed around it. Emersyn thought of Savannah, radiant, devastatingly gorgeous, commanding and soft all at once, and the sudden contrast between what she felt when thinking of Savannah and what she had been trying to force with Jared was in vivid, undeniable focus.

She knew Jared was upset with her and she also knew he had every right to be. *Especially if he knew what I was really doing tonight at the cocktail party*. She had never been unfaithful to a partner before in her life and it felt gross and sneaky. But then her mind wandered to Savannah again—

Emersyn's phone buzzed loudly and she grabbed it quickly, expecting to see Jared's name illuminating her screen. The slow, fiery feeling in her core burned brighter as she blinked at Savannah's name instead. With an excited squeal, Emersyn opened the text.

Hey you. I know it's kind of late, but I couldn't stop thinking about earlier. I had an amazing time at the party. Sweet dreams, Emersyn.

The tightness in her chest softened into tenderness as Savannah's words wrapped around her like a soothing, calming balm. Emersyn quickly typed out a response and then set her phone down as she padded to the large bed.

You always know exactly what I need to hear. Sweet dreams, Savy—Good night.

Emersyn knew tonight would be another one when sleep wouldn't come easy, but for some reason the thought of being wrapped in one person's arms was the only thought that relaxed her as she flopped onto her back and gazed at the ceiling until it blurred—and that person was Savannah Sanchez.

❖

The bright afternoon sun hung high over the turquoise water as Emersyn dipped her paddle into the swaying sea. A brown pelican glided lazily above her as Emersyn and Erica kayaked several yards out from the beach as the resort loomed behind them. The water was calm and the steady rhythm of their paddles propelling their bright orange kayaks provided a soothing cadence as Emersyn squinted through her sunglasses and balanced the kayak paddle across her thighs for a brief moment to adjust her ponytail. Despite being only in her bikini under her thick yellow life jacket, her skin felt hot to the touch beneath the tropical sunlight bouncing off the surface of the ocean and her tantalizing thoughts of Savannah.

"Not bad for someone who always hated arm day," Erica said as she gently splashed Emersyn's bare legs with her paddle.

Emersyn laughed. "Kay's passion for endless bicep curls and push-up marathons during practice was the stuff of nightmares," she said. "This is nature therapy. Totally different."

Erica raised an eyebrow. "Convenient distraction." She blinked at the shoreline. "But I'll take it. Besides, Kayla had a little too much Merlot last night and didn't want to do anything except order room service and grunt-laugh at the *RuPaul's Drag Race* marathon she found on TV so I appreciate the invite out to enjoy the water."

The sun's warmth caressed Emeryn's shoulders as she dipped her paddle again. "Of course," she said. "Though those scratch-made pancakes and room service omelets *are* pretty spectacular. What will we ever do when we have to return home and start making our own breakfasts again?"

Erica snickered and then they paddled in companionable silence for a few minutes. Emersyn thought of how she had tried to call Jared earlier, but he had been conspicuously unresponsive. She couldn't help but feel annoyed, as though he was playing a petty game and trying to pay her back for disappearing the day and evening before.

Maybe I deserve it. I do *deserve it.*

As a seagull let out a long caw overhead, Emersyn glanced at her friend. "Erica, can I ask you something personal?"

"Sure." Erica shrugged. "I can't promise I'll answer, but you can ask."

Emersyn slowed her kayak as she bit her lip. A dragonfly landed for a brief moment on the tip of her boat before it flitted away on nearly translucent wings toward the horizon. "How did you know Kayla was the one?"

Erica grinned. "Oh, that's easy! It just *works* with her, you know? It feels right. More than anything else, ever."

Emersyn arched an eyebrow dubiously. "It just works?"

Erica laughed. "I mean," she said. "Energy doesn't need words. I feel that deep, amazing energy with Kayla all the time, every minute I'm around her, even when we're doing mundane stuff like yard work or grabbing groceries. I just look at her and I *know*. It's this pull that goes beyond attraction; it's love. And it's not always this clean, polished thing. Sometimes it's messy. Sometimes it sneaks up on you and exposes these parts of you that you wish you could hide. It makes you vulnerable. But with her, I feel like I've been found and seen every time we're together and I know I'm safe with her. *That's* how I've always known Kayla is the one."

Emersyn took a deep breath and glanced at her legs stretched in front of her. "I'm so happy for you, Erica," she said and then shook her head. "I...I've always wondered if I would ever feel something like that for someone. I've been trying—" Her throat unexpectedly tightened. "Like, *really* trying for a long time to feel something real for Jared. You know, to feel everything you described. To be excited, in love. Instead, it always feels like I'm pretending."

Erica glanced at her, but remained quiet as she listened with a nod.

"I don't know what I'm doing with him, Erica." Emersyn didn't take her eyes off the water. "I struggle to feel anything for Jared beyond an amicable companionship. Friendship, you know? And then I see—" She swallowed hard as she brushed a drop of water from her thighs. "I see Savannah, and I feel *everything*. It hits me all at once. This trip, being around her again? It's so different, and it's strong and overwhelming and *real*."

Erica smiled gently. "Em, I kind of figured. I'm glad you finally told me."

Emersyn chewed her bottom lip. "That deep energy and magnetic pull you were talking about? That messy vulnerability and being seen and found all at once? It's always there with Savannah, no matter how long it's been. I… Wait, did you say *finally*?"

Erica appeared to be trying but failing to suppress a knowing look. "Don't be shocked," she said. "I've seen how you are around her and how she is around you. The tension, the way you positively light up when she's around, this undeniable connection you two seem to have? It's not as subtle as you think it is."

Emersyn's mouth fell open as she nearly dropped her paddle into the ocean. "I had no idea you had it figured out."

Erica laughed. "Emersyn, you've never been able to hide how you feel about Savannah. Even now." She shrugged. "I always wondered why you disliked her so much our senior season. The way you avoided her, it was beyond just the challenges of reintegrating after an entire season recovering from injury. It was almost like you were fighting with yourself more than her." She guided her kayak around a wave rippling from a distant speedboat. "And then you both got so much closer toward the end of that year. You were inseparable. We all knew what it was. I mean, you can't hide a love like that even if you try. But neither of you said anything and the rest of us didn't want to dig into your business, so we left it alone. It was so close to graduation anyway. And then I learned Savannah went overseas to play and you disappeared into Chicago, and that was that."

Emersyn shook her head. "Was it that obvious?"

Erica rolled her eyes dramatically. "*Please*. Savannah would look at anyone that came near you like they threatened to burn down a yoga studio or something." She chuckled. "And when you'd get fouled during our last handful of games? Emersyn, I could *see* her going nuts behind that ultra-cool exterior she likes to put up."

Emersyn felt her smile fade slightly. "That was then." She sighed. "It's scary. And I have no idea what'll happen next, but I know when I'm with her it feels right. Like I don't have to pretend."

Erica gave her a sidelong glance. "And Savannah is the one who makes you feel…" She pretended to think. "How did you put it? Oh, yeah. *Everything*."

Emersyn trailed her fingertips in the water thoughtfully. "She is," she said. "It's terrifying. I don't want to hurt anyone. I'm afraid I'll disappoint my mom, break Jared's heart, face that vulnerable piece of myself that I've guarded for so long." She swallowed hard. "I may have played great defense on the court, but trust me, Erica. I've always played the best defense on myself."

Erica guided her kayak closer to Emersyn's until they were side by side. "It's brave is what it is, Em," she said. "You're finally listening to yourself and to what truly makes you happy. You deserve to be with someone who makes you feel *everything*. And honestly? You really do light up when Savannah is around. Even when you're trying your hardest not to. *Especially* when you're trying your hardest not to. All I see are two beautiful, accomplished women who are very clearly meant to be together if they'd just get out of their own heads for a second."

Emersyn flushed, but she knew it wasn't because of the sun shimmering along her face or the afternoon humidity thickening the ocean air. "Do you..." She thought of divulging how she and Savannah had kissed at the cocktail party the night before, but decided not to share that detail. "Do you think Savannah feels it too? This intensely?"

"Emersyn, she didn't let you out of her sight for one second last night," Erica said as they steered their kayaks toward the beach. "Don't run away from what makes you feel the most and from what makes you the happiest. You know that's Savannah, and I get it. She's amazing, Emersyn. You two have always complemented each other and that electricity, that tension? It's so obvious. Like it was meant to be or something."

Emersyn smiled as her kayak gently bumped against the wet, white sand along the beach. She felt stronger. Calmer. Grounded. "Thanks Erica," she said gratefully. "I didn't realize how much I needed to talk to someone about this."

Erica hopped out of her kayak and leaned down to pull it onto the sand. "I'm here for you, Em." She glanced up with an easy smile. "I always have been. You owe yourself your truth and pursuing what, or *who*, makes you happiest."

Emersyn stepped out of her kayak and walked through the knee-high water to the sand. Her mind went to Savannah, recalling her silky dark hair, her cool confidence, and the way her intense gaze seemed to burn right through her and past all the pretenses. "I appreciate it, E." She hesitated. "I can't wait to see her again."

As they padded across the sun-warmed sand to the small stucco boat rental building a few yards away, Emersyn allowed herself to consider a different future, one that was tantalizingly electric, vividly clear, bright, bold, beautiful, and *real*. Deep down, she knew that future meant belonging to Savannah Sanchez.

Chapter Twenty-one

The intimate open-air restaurant down the street from the resort was dark, low-lit, and chic, with tinted windows that blocked most of the golden-hour sunlight from the interior. The rich, savory aroma of garlic and fresh bread permeated the air. The soft hum of conversations in English and Spanish, alongside the gentle clink of glasses, filled the space. Savannah idly traced the rim of her wine glass as she gazed at the waves rolling rhythmically against the shore. Arissa sat opposite her at a corner table on the patio deck overlooking the ocean.

Arissa swirled her moscato and glanced at Savannah across the table. "Okay," she said, leaning forward slightly. A gentle Spanish guitar strummed near the wood-paneled bar as a solo musician played slow, mellow songs in the background. "I have to ask. I've annihilated my sea bass and you've barely touched your ceviche." She gestured at Savannah's picked over plate. "And you *never* let fresh ceviche go to waste. Spill it. What's on your mind?"

Savannah stared down at the Baja California-made sauvignon blanc in her glass as she let out a quiet sigh and shot Arissa a look. "I hate how well you know me," she said. "Even after all these years."

"Please." Arissa snorted as she sat back in her chair. "It has to be a woman, am I right?"

Savannah let out a slow breath as she considered her response. She wasn't sure how much she wanted to share, but Arissa's perceptive acknowledgement cracked something open inside her. "It's Emersyn," she finally said. "We've gotten…" She paused. "Close again. She's not straight, Arissa. At all. She's acknowledging it and what that means for her."

Arissa blinked but didn't look shocked. She nodded as she processed this. "Wow, okay," she mused. "That actually makes a lot of sense. I mean, there's always been this *thing* with you two. It's like you can't leave each other alone and…" she took a deep breath. "Look, I know you two fell in love our senior season. Everyone on the team knew it. But the way you look at her now, Savannah? It's like it never went away. You two have always had something. And if this is finally your time, I want that for you."

Savannah sipped her wine. "I know," she said. "You're totally right. There's always been something with us. It's magnetic. Even though I should know better, I keep *wanting* her. And what makes it even harder is that I know she feels it too. When we're together and she lets her guard down, it's amazing. It's *right*, like it was meant to be. But…" She felt her jaw tighten. "She's engaged."

Arissa reached across the table and gently squeezed Savannah's hand. "Savannah, you're falling for her all over again. Hard."

Savannah blinked and shook her head. "I…" She closed her mouth as the ache echoed in her chest. "I know," she finally said. "How can something that feels so right be this complicated? I don't know how to *not* want her. I've been trying and failing miserably."

Arissa smiled kindly. "As your friend, it's my job to support you but also to be real with you. And I want you to be careful, Savannah. Coming out isn't always this clean, simple thing. In fact, it's usually *not*. Emersyn has a whole life she's built for herself after Northwoods that she's been trying to live one way, and now it's shifting fast. People can freak out a little, especially when they're finally facing themselves for the first time." She squeezed Savannah's hand once more before reaching for her wine glass. "Or after sixteen long years."

Savannah nodded. "I know," she said. "Emersyn needs to figure this out at her own pace. But when we're together, it's like nothing else exists. I can't pretend I don't want her, Arissa. Especially after we kissed last night. It was *electric*."

Arissa's eyes widened as she dabbed at her mouth with a linen napkin. "Oh, Savannah, you have it *bad*," she said. "I love you and I love Emersyn, but I don't want to see you get hurt either. I mean, I think it's obvious that Emersyn wants you too." She pursed her lips. "*Especially* if she was kissing you. She looks at you like you're oxygen and she forgot how to breathe, by the way. You just have to let her come to the realizations she needs to arrive at, you know? If she's not fully sure, you both could end up devastated. Just remember, you can't control what you can't control, Savannah. And I know you *love* being the one in command." She rolled her eyes. "But I don't want either of you to get burned because the fire is too hot, too bright."

Savannah exhaled. "I understand what you're saying." She stirred her fork through her ceviche again. "God, you sound like my therapist."

Arissa smiled as she raised her wine glass in a mock toast. "Yeah, well, I also have a master's degree and I don't charge by the hour."

Savannah laughed, grateful for the moment of levity. "Regardless, I appreciate you looking out for me. For us."

Arissa tilted her head thoughtfully as she took another sip of moscato. "I mean, who knows?" she said with a casual shrug. "Maybe you two really are soulmates and this wedding is fate, bringing you back together for good. Believe me, I would love to see you and Em together, Savannah, and giving this a real, genuine try. We all would. You two have always had this inexplicable connection."

A waiter in a dark collared polo shirt approached their table for their dessert order. As Savannah glanced over the menu and pointed out the chocolate flan, the weight on her shoulders loosened slightly.

As the waiter ambled away, Arissa leaned forward again. "And seriously, Savannah, if this ends with you two living happily ever after and me giving the toast at your wedding, I expect an open bar with top-shelf liquor and a damn good DJ."

Savannah grinned. "Whatever you say, Arissa. Deal."

They clinked their wine glasses together under the soft glow of the brushed metal lanterns swaying along the deck's wooden ceiling beams.

"Enough about me," Savannah said playfully. "You've been awfully quiet about *her*."

Arissa blinked innocently as she feigned surprise. "Her? Who?"

Savannah gave her a knowing look. "You know exactly who I'm talking about. Zoe, the psychology professor from North Carolina? The one you keep disappearing with for long stretches of time?"

Arissa laughed. "Okay, fine." She held her hands up. "She's sweet. Smart. *Amazing* in bed. We met completely by chance after Mia helped me set up that dating app at El Gato Azul." Arissa rolled her eyes. "Who knew I'd find someone right here at the resort?"

Savannah arched an eyebrow. "That sounds promising. North Carolina isn't that far from Atlanta, is it?"

Arissa leaned back in her chair and waved a hand. "You know me, Savannah. I don't jump into things."

"Except for spending every spare second of your vacation with her."

Arissa bit her lip but couldn't hide her grin. "Touché. It just feels *right* with her, you know? There's this deeper connection that I didn't expect."

Savannah nodded. "Yeah, I know exactly what you mean."

Arissa met her eyes for a moment and took a deep breath. "Sometimes I suppose it *is* worth risking the harder, more complicated parts for a connection like that."

Savannah's chest tightened as she thought of Emersyn. "You're not wrong, Arissa."

They were quiet for a contemplative moment as the waves below crashed against the shore. They both looked up as the waiter returned with their desserts on a round black tray.

"Here's to us." Arissa raised her wine glass once more. "Figuring our shit out day by day, hour by hour."

Savannah laughed as she clinked her glass against Arissa's. "Minute by minute."

❖

Late that night, long after the resort had slipped into a peaceful quiet, Savannah was wide awake. The soft night and warm ocean breeze wrapped her in a heavy, comforting blanket as she slid through the long white pool gate.

Her bare feet were silent against the cool concrete and the silvery moon cast a glowing shimmer over the infinity pool's still water. Despite the relaxed dinner with Arissa, Savannah couldn't sleep. Thoughts of Emersyn lingered and the tension that had been building between them since they came face-to-face all over again had stretched taut over the days. All Savannah could think about was how *right* Emersyn's lips felt on hers, even after all these years in between.

Taking a deep breath, she sat on the edge of the pool and gently dipped her legs into the cool water before wriggling out of her gauzy brown swimsuit cover-up. *I need to talk to Emersyn. I need to tell her how I feel and I want to understand how she feels.*

As Savannah considered how she would corner Emersyn and what she would say, she slipped fully into the pool and inhaled sharply as the cool water surrounded her in just her dark brown-and-gold-patterned bikini.

Just then, the pool gate creaked open. Savannah glanced up as she wondered in mild annoyance who on Earth else would be hitting the infinity pool just after midnight. Savannah froze as Emersyn walked into view, the soft glow of the moonlight shining off her hair, and stopped short. She appeared startled to see Savannah, but a slow smile eventually lit her face and replaced the momentary surprise.

Savannah couldn't help it; she smiled right back at her. "Couldn't sleep either?" she asked.

Emersyn tentatively walked closer to the pool. Her soft white cami clung to her like a second skin as her loose olive-green sweatpants swayed with each step. "No," she said honestly. Their eyes met for a brief moment and then Emersyn glanced away shyly. "Mind if I join you?"

The air between them sparked with tension as Savannah shook her head. "Not at all."

Emersyn wiggled out of her loose pants and top, leaving them on a nearby chaise, as Savannah tried to look anywhere but at Emersyn in her black bikini. She grimaced and laughed at the shock of cold water as she waded into the shallow end of the pool. Savannah couldn't help but notice how the still water seemed to wrap around Emersyn's legs and waist like smooth silk and how the underwater lights illuminated just enough of her profile as she gazed at her.

"So why couldn't *you* sleep tonight?" Emersyn said. "Something on your mind?"

Savannah took a deep breath as she drank in the sight of Emersyn across the water. "Yes." She paused. "It's always been like this with us, you know?" Her voice was barely above a whisper and Savannah wasn't certain Emersyn heard her until she drifted closer.

"Like what?" Her gaze was steady but warm.

"This pull." Savannah's arms trailed languidly beneath the water. "Like gravity or something. No matter how long it's been or how hard I try to ignore it…" She blew out her breath. "You're the one I can't stay away from."

Emersyn swallowed hard. "I tried to tell myself it wasn't real," she finally said, her voice unguarded and trembling. "That maybe I wasn't really who I am. But every time I see you and every time you look at me like *that*… I feel *everything*, Savannah. You make it easier."

Savannah tilted her head. "What do you mean?"

"To breathe," Emersyn replied. She moved closer until just centimeters separated them in the water and Savannah could feel the warmth radiating off her. "To be myself. I mean, I do love myself, but you make it easier to live truthfully. I know I've said it before, but I've missed you, Savannah."

Savannah's fingertips brushed Emersyn's cheek as she met her gaze. "You have no idea how it feels to hear you say that," she said. "I've got you, Emersyn. I've always got you."

Savannah couldn't resist anymore. She wanted so badly to get beneath the layers of Emersyn's carefully constructed life, pull her open, uncover everything she was still too scared to say, and cover her with kisses and whispered reassurances that it would be okay, that she would be there for her and protect her. It was something she regretted being unable to fulfill when they were twenty-two, but now things were different. They weren't college kids anymore.

She met Emersyn's lips, soft at first, and then the kiss melted into something deeper. Emersyn pressed her body against Savannah's as their tongues explored with urgency and tenderness. Emersyn reached up, tangling her fingers in the low, loose knot that Savannah had tied her hair into, and the world around them disappeared.

All Savannah could hear was her heart pounding in her ears and the soft lap of waves against the tiled pool wall as heat began to spike between her thighs. Emersyn's wet skin was slick and warm beneath her fingertips and she let out a soft, barely audible moan as Savannah brushed kisses down her jaw, her neck, and to her collarbone.

"God, I want you so bad," Emersyn whispered breathlessly. "I want to be yours again, Savannah."

As tendrils of desire deepened the ache in her core, Savannah slid her hands behind Emersyn's thighs and lifted her in the water so she could wrap her legs around her waist. With their bodies pressed together, Savannah slowly guided them to the edge of the infinity pool and pinned Emersyn gently against the smooth wall without breaking their kiss.

"You have me." She pulled back to meet Emersyn's gaze. "I want to make you mine again. Now that we're here, I…I can't keep pretending like what we had wasn't everything I ever wanted." She bit her lip as she blinked at the velvety black ocean behind them. "Except now it's even better, because we grew up. We're steadier. *Ready*."

Savannah was momentarily surprised by the force with which Emersyn crashed her lips back against hers. She could feel her surrender in her arms and it drove Savannah wild. Her fingers tangled in Emersyn's hair as her lips explored her neck and shoulders again. She couldn't help the feeling of desperation to reclaim every inch of her body.

As the still night wrapped around them like a secret and the stars reflected off the water's surface, Emersyn moaned as Savannah roamed her hands over her back, around her waist, and along her stomach, lingering as they teased over her breasts. The thin bathing suit fabric was no match for Savannah's touch and she felt Emersyn arching further into her, desperate for friction amplified by the gentle water. She could feel Emersyn's thighs tighten around her as she pressed herself into Savannah's center, deepening the pressure building inside her.

"I've never wanted anyone like this," Emersyn said as she cupped Savannah's face in one hand. Her thumb brushed over her lips and Savannah could see the hazy desire clouding her expression. "That's how I know it's been true all along." She took a breath. "I'm gay, Savannah." The declaration hung between them. "And I know what I want."

Savannah gently slid her fingertips up Emersyn's palm until their fingers interlocked, Emersyn's back still pressed against the infinity wall. "And what is it you want?"

Emersyn lifted her chin, her voice vulnerable but steady. "You. I want only you. I want this."

Slowly, Savannah leaned forward as her lips found Emersyn's ear. She felt her shiver against her and tighten her arms around her neck as a thrill snaked up Savannah's spine. "You were always meant to be mine," she murmured. "Good girl."

Savannah brushed kisses along Emersyn's jaw until she found her lips again. After a moment and despite her body screaming at her to slip into one of the private cabanas with Emersyn and reclaim her until she was breathless and sated, Savannah took a small step backward. Her self-control was rapidly fraying, but she didn't want to put Emersyn—or herself—in a regrettable position by moving too fast. There were things that needed to be addressed first.

"Do what you need to do," Savannah said. "I'll be here when you're ready."

Emersyn searched her face for a long moment, heat, desire, and something deeper swirling in her gaze, before she nodded in understanding. As she wrenched herself free from Savannah and walked slowly out of the water, Emersyn turned once as she took her clothes from the chaise. Water trailed down her bare legs and pooled around her feet as she wrapped a towel around her shoulders. Her lips curved into a slow smile as the electricity between them sizzled.

"Sleep well, Savy."

CHAPTER TWENTY-TWO

The next morning, the first streaks of dawn cast a soft coral glow across the endless stretch of ocean. The rhythmic sound of waves rolling along the beach and the delicate, candy-colored shades of blush-pink, lavender, and pale yellow were breathtaking over the hushed resort. Emersyn sat stiffly at her balcony table as she took a deep breath, inhaling the scents of saltwater and hibiscus, and took a long sip of her sweet French vanilla macchiato.

Along the corner of the resort, Emersyn had a partial view of the infinity pool and how the water's still surface mirrored the colorful sunrise brilliantly. She recalled how, just hours before, she had finally spilled her soul to Savannah. Fully. Surrendered.

I want her so bad it hurts. The warm coffee grounded her racing pulse. The realization of surrender was delayed; Emersyn understood that she had already subconsciously been drawn like a magnet to Savannah since she first swung open the door to Kay and Diana's suite. *It's like it's not even up to us and never has been. Like she said, it just* is. *And I'm not going to let her slip through my fingers again.*

There was a sense of resigned sadness as Emersyn mourned the life she tried to have, but it was belied by the nearly overwhelming, undeniable connection she'd always had with Savannah. She steeled herself with another sip of coffee and blinked at her laptop glowing before her as she waited for Jared to connect to the video call. After another moment, his face appeared on her screen in his own hotel room. From what Emersyn could see, it was a lot larger than hers. His blond hair was rumpled against his forehead and she could barely make out the breathtaking New York City skyline dazzling in the early morning sunlight behind him.

"Hey," she said gently. "New York looks beautiful in the morning. You've got a great view."

Jared rubbed a hand over his jaw. "Not as great as the view in front of me right now," he said. "I know you're behind a few hours. You're up early today." He paused. "God, it's good to see your face, Emersyn. I've been missing you a lot."

Emersyn took a breath, but it caught in her chest as bolts of guilt ricocheted through her. "I'm sorry we haven't been connected lately." She was surprised how her throat tightened so quickly. "I…" She blinked rapidly, willing the tears to remain behind her eyes.

Jared leaned forward, concern all over his face. "Emersyn, you okay?" he asked. "You sound upset. What's going on?"

There was a beat of silence as Emersyn tried to compose herself. A few seagulls glided in the early morning breeze as their calls echoed across the beach. "We need to talk about us," she finally said. "I've been thinking a lot. Actually, being here is probably the first time I've allowed myself to pause and really think and acknowledge in years."

Jared's posture shifted as his shoulders bunched. "Okay," he said slowly. Frown lines crinkled around his normally bright blue eyes. "Acknowledge what?"

Emersyn took a deep breath. *Just spit it out.* "I don't think we should get married, Jared," she said quietly. "I can't marry you."

The silence seemed to stretch into eternity as Emersyn's heart pounded. She picked at a corner of the table as palm leaves rustled in the background.

"Wait, what?" Jared asked sharply, as the invisible wire finally snapped. "What the hell are you talking about, Emersyn?"

When she finally glanced at the screen, she wished she hadn't. Jared looked as though someone had slapped him. His face was filled with hurt and confusion as he stroked his chin anxiously. "You can't be serious. I know you were having some hesitance about setting a date before, but we're engaged. How can you just throw that away?"

"I'm so sorry, Jared," Emersyn said softly. She meant it in her very core. "I never wanted to hurt you. I promise. It's me…" Hot tears blurred her vision. "You deserve to marry someone who can love you completely."

"I don't believe you." Jared's voice turned accusatory. He flexed his jaw as he crossed his arms tightly. "Is there someone else? Because it really feels like there's someone else. Who the hell else is down there at Dulces Sueños or wherever the fuck with you?"

"I know you're angry," Emersyn said. "You have every right to be. I'm just…I'm not who I tried to make myself be. And it's not fair to either of us to keep pretending. We both deserve better than that."

Jared scratched his temple and shook his head. "After almost three years, Emersyn?" he asked coldly. "Now you can't marry me. Give me one good reason why not."

Emersyn opened and then closed her mouth. The words were so close, but felt trapped in her throat behind years of avoidance.

I'm gay. Just tell him. I'm gay and I've always known.

"I'm…" she said. The words were stuck in her throat as Jared shook his head in disgust. "I told you, I'm just not who I tried so hard to be."

"And what the fuck does that mean, Emersyn?" Jared shot back. "You know what, I can't do this. Not right now." He held up his hands and then reached toward the screen. "I need some time to calm down."

With a loud click, the video call flashed to black. Emersyn swallowed hard as she slid through the glass door back into her suite. The room felt too small, too hot, and too cramped. Her mind raced with things like Jared, the past, the present, her friends, her family, and Savannah. Always Savannah.

Emersyn tossed her laptop onto the small desk with a clatter and paced once, twice, over the cool stone floor. After a moment, she grabbed her room key and stepped into a pair of plain black flip-flops. She couldn't stay in this room a second longer.

Emersyn marched down the hallway, barely registering the suite door slamming behind her, and only as she paused in front of the elevator bank did she notice how wildly her hands were shaking.

Basketball. Go to the court. Shoot hoops. That always clears your mind.

A small trickle of relief washed through her at the thought of the empty half-court downstairs and only the sound of the ball bouncing on the hardwood to fill her consciousness. That always soothed away everything else until she lulled herself into a meditative rhythm with the ball in her hands. She hadn't even registered she'd hit the elevator button for Savannah's floor, as though her body and heart were on some kind of autopilot that her brain hadn't caught up to yet, until the doors gently opened into another quiet hallway.

Emersyn stepped out of the elevator and paused for just a beat as she wondered if she should turn around and go to the basketball court as planned. The overwhelming pull for Savannah was stronger.

Her feet moved on instinct down the hallway to her door. All she could think of was Savannah; her hands, her voice, the way she looked at her like she was already home, her full, tantalizing lips, the way her kisses lit up her entire body, and the way she moved with commanding confidence and composure.

Emersyn paused outside Savannah's door as her heart pounded. *Oh my God.* Understanding washed over her in crystal-clear waves. *I might love her. I might be falling for Savannah. Again.*

Emersyn knocked once and was momentarily surprised by how quickly the door opened. Savannah blinked at her, all soft and comfortable in a baggy cotton hoodie over tight yoga shorts.

"Emersyn?" she asked, surprise tingeing her sleepy voice. She gazed at her as her expression shifted to concern. "Baby, are you okay?"

Emersyn didn't answer; she *couldn't* answer. Her throat was tight and she knew if she tried to respond right then, she'd lose her increasingly fraught grip on the tears pressing right behind her eyes. Instead, she surged forward into Savannah's arms, winding her hands in her hair, and crashed her lips against hers. Emersyn could already feel her pulse slowing as she melted into Savannah's confident, sure warmth and the kiss deepened with urgency and passion.

"I couldn't do it," Emersyn whispered breathlessly between kisses. "I couldn't lie anymore. Not to myself. Not to anyone. It's over. I need to be with you."

Savannah pulled her in close and shut the door resolutely as she wrapped her arms tighter around Emersyn and kissed her again. "Come here." Her eyes were dark with emotion. "Be with me. You can try to shield yourself from the world all you want, but you know that doesn't work with me." She brushed her lips along Emersyn's jaw as she buried herself against Savannah's chest. "I've got you, remember?"

Savannah's fingers intertwined with her own as she pulled back slightly and met her eyes. She gently brushed a lock of hair behind Emersyn's ear as she glanced down at their hands.

"I mean, it's terrifying." Emersyn blew out her breath. "How I'm yours. Just like that. It's inexplicable, but it never goes away. From the second I opened the door at Kay and Diana's suite, it was there, like this giant magnet inside of me or something. No matter what I say to myself or how I've tried to rationalize things over the years, it's there." She met Savannah's gaze. "You're so beautiful and you've always, *always* been that way. I want to give this the chance it never really had before."

The look in Savannah's eyes brought Emersyn right back to their senior year of college. It was the same smoldering look that made her stomach do somersaults then and ignited the slow-burning fire between them now, with Emersyn sure she was going to launch herself again at Savannah any moment. Somewhere in the back of her mind, Emersyn knew they were about to cross a line that they once again couldn't uncross, but it only fueled the desire deep in her core as Savannah pulled her closer and met her lips with a slow, aching hunger.

Savannah brushed her thumbs down Emersyn's cheeks, tracing her jaw with the light, deliberate touch that she remembered so well, and then clasped her wrists in her hand as they collapsed onto the bed. She held them over Emersyn's head as she kissed softly along her jaw before finding her swollen lips again.

"Thank you." Savannah kissed her slower this time.

Emersyn blinked. "For what?"

Savannah was quiet for a long moment, her gaze filled with dark desire and unbridled longing. Emersyn pressed her thighs together in an effort to tamp down the heat that ignited there as she watched Savannah angle her body over hers.

"Thank you for being vulnerable with me," she said softly. "Again. Trusting me again. You have no idea how much it means to me that you feel comfortable and safe enough with me to let down your guard and be real."

Savannah ran her fingertips through Emersyn's hair and drew them along her jaw, affection all over her face as Emersyn trembled beneath her.

"You've always been the one, Savannah," she said. "It's always been you."

Savannah leaned down and claimed Emersyn's lips in a searing, slow kiss as her palm smoothed up her bare thigh and lingered just below the hem of Emersyn's white and blue floral print summer dress. As Emersyn shifted and tried to reach up to pull the straps down, Savannah placed a firm hand on her arm.

"Let me," she murmured. "I want to see you. I want to touch every inch of your body and enjoy you here with me."

A shiver snaked up Emersyn's spine as a gentle smile played at Savannah's lips. *She knows exactly what she does to me.* Emersyn understood just how much Savannah seemed to enjoy unraveling her. *Of course. It's always been Savannah.*

Emersyn sat up gently as Savannah shifted behind her and pulled the straps of her dress down slowly, planting soft kisses along her neck and shoulders, and then carefully slid it down her body until Emersyn could wriggle out of it and kick it to a heap on the floor.

Her skin felt electrified under Savannah's knowing touch. True to her word, Savannah continued planting kisses and touching her softly and reverently along her collarbone and down her chest, re-memorizing every inch of Emersyn.

Savannah's lips ghosted over her breasts as she gently unclasped her bra. Emersyn could feel her smiling against her skin as she squirmed impatiently. "Lie down." Her voice was low and tender. "Right now, you belong to me. And you *know* I'll take care of you."

Emersyn obeyed as she sighed and sank further into the soft comforter that smelled faintly of Savannah. Goose bumps rose along her bare skin against the cool fabric. As Savannah's gaze raked over her body, Emersyn felt exposed and open in a way that should have felt vulnerable. With Savannah's eyes on her and her fingers teasing her nipples, Emersyn felt safe instead. Cherished. And *oh* so deliciously turned on, as jolts of electric pleasure ached against her clit.

Savannah arched up to pull her hoodie off before leaning back over Emersyn and capturing her lips in a deep kiss. Her dark hair slid over her shoulders, creating a curtain-like effect around them, and Emersyn was sure Cabo had somehow become heaven as she relished the feeling of Savannah's smooth, golden-tan skin brushing along her own. Emersyn couldn't help herself; she traced her hands along the soft curves and toned muscle pressed into her, unable to quiet her moan.

Emersyn arched beneath Savannah as she dipped her head, her lips finding Emersyn's nipples and running her tongue over them again and again, eliciting breathless sighs. Every inch of her was being marked and touched with intent, and Savannah seemed to enjoy taking her time teasing Emersyn's body. Her fingertips skimmed along the curve of her waist as she languidly kissed down Emersyn's ribs and her hair tickled her stomach as her palms dug into Emersyn's hips with demanding urgency.

Savannah kissed along every inch of Emersyn's inner thighs as she shifted beneath her with need. She paused for a moment, her lips hovering just a few millimeters above Emersyn's tight, aching bud, and gazed back at her.

"You don't have to think." Savannah tilted her head to kiss her inner thigh again. Emersyn practically groaned with frustration. Savannah smiled as she gently slid a teasing fingertip along her slick folds. "Just feel. Feel everything." Her grin deepened. "You're already so wet for me, Emersyn."

As Savannah leaned down again, Emersyn let go. A loud moan floated through the suite—surely that couldn't be her?—as Savannah's tongue ran the length of her and then lingered around her swollen clit. She practically melted into the thick comforter and into Savannah's power and softness as she gently slid a finger into her, curling it just enough to find *that* spot inside her and tease it mercilessly. Emersyn let herself be claimed by Savannah all over again as her body reacted to her touch like it was made for her and had simply been waiting all these years.

"Tell me what you want," Savannah whispered against her. Her tongue gently massaged her clit in exactly the way Emersyn knew made her squirm the most. Savannah carefully slid another finger inside her as both stroked her from the inside out. "Tell me what you need."

Emersyn could barely form a coherent thought as her head fell back against the soft pillows and her thighs tensed with building pressure that felt *so* good. "You, Savannah," she moaned as the bright white morning sunlight blurred around them. "Just you, always."

Everything seemed to dissolve into warm puddles and bright fireworks as Emersyn's orgasm crested and crashed through her with breathless force. She rippled and shook against Savannah's fingers, still stroking each second of her orgasm out of her, and pressed further onto Savannah's tongue as she tightened her grip in her hair.

Her orgasm swelled into another as the sensation and sensitivity tingled into an intoxicating blend of electric jolts and deep coiling pressure. Emersyn's body tremored and her fingers slid down, clutching at Savannah's bare shoulders.

"*Savannah,*" Emersyn thought she heard her voice break as she shattered. "Yes, yes, Savannah," she panted as her heart pounded wildly in her chest. She finally collapsed, sated, into the blankets.

Savannah was next to her in a heartbeat and wrapped her arms tightly around her as Emersyn snuggled into her. As Savannah held her, she kissed her hair, her cheeks, and finally lingered on her lips. Emersyn could faintly taste herself on Savannah's mouth and a deep warmth ignited low in her stomach all over again.

I want to taste her. After a few moments of lying tangled together in the sheets, Emersyn skimmed her hand along Savannah's bare side.

"Savy?" she asked. She hadn't even realized she was using Savannah's nickname, the ones only those closest to her ever casually called her, until she heard her soft laugh.

"Yes, baby?" she asked.

"I want to taste you," Emersyn said breathlessly. "I missed you. Everything about you."

After what felt like an agonizingly slow moment, Emersyn momentarily distracted into a near-trance at Savannah's fingertips running lazy circles over her spine, Savannah finally nodded.

"Show me how much you missed me, Emersyn," she said. She met her gaze with a smile. "My girl."

That familiar pang exploded across Emersyn's chest. Savannah always knew exactly what to say and what to do to make her unravel completely—and she always had. Where everyone else had found carefully constructed walls, Savannah had always looked right past them with mild amusement and ease.

As Emersyn brought Savannah's nipple into her mouth and brushed her other nipple between her thumb and index finger, she felt Savannah arch into her mouth. She was blissful in her knowledge of the pleasure she was giving as she teased, gently tasted, and touched everywhere. As she scooted down the bed and found the soaked space between Savannah's thighs, she felt her fingers in her hair.

Emersyn glanced up at her, nearly losing her breath. Savannah's dark hair was tousled over her shoulders and her heavy-lidded gaze was filled with an intensity and devastating desire that made Emersyn's chest ache. She was sure she had never seen anything more gorgeous in her life.

Yup. I'm falling for her. I never stood a chance.

Savannah took a shaky breath as the muscles in her thighs tensed with anticipation. "I never, ever stopped wanting you."

Emersyn gently squeezed her waist in response and inhaled her scent as her own excitement began pressing between her thighs again. Today, it was just her and Savannah—and Emersyn was on cloud nine.

Chapter Twenty-three

Midafternoon sunlight poured in through the sliding glass door of Savannah's suite as the tropical rays filled the space with easy warmth. Savannah stirred, her skin still buzzing from an entire morning of passionate lovemaking with Emersyn. The white linen sheets were tangled around their bare legs and she swallowed hard. Soft golden beams danced over the sleek stone floor as she blinked and idly played with the ends of Emersyn's hair. She was curled into her chest, sound asleep, and looked impossibly peaceful. Emersyn was too warm, too soft, and Savannah knew the last of her resolve had crumbled like dust. Emersyn still fit as perfectly in her arms as she did when they were twenty-two. She still napped with one leg thrown over Savannah's like she had when they were twenty-two. It felt so intoxicatingly *right*. Still, it was all new between them too, and that deepened the invisible, tender layers that seemed to bind them forever; the settled stability, the careers and financial security, the composure and self-assuredness that could only come with growing up—and accepting your desires while knowing how to recognize what was real.

As Savannah's phone buzzed on the nightstand, Emersyn blinked but stayed firmly in place in her arms. After a moment, she gazed up at her as Savannah softly met her lips.

"Work?" Emersyn asked as she stretched languidly.

Savannah glanced at her phone and laughed as she shook her head. "No," she said. "Just my mom checking in on how things are going in Cabo."

Emersyn brushed another soft kiss to her lips. "You're very affectionate this afternoon," Savannah said as she pulled Emersyn tighter to her. "Not that I'm complaining."

Emersyn laughed as she rolled off Savannah. "Lazy afternoons are the best," she declared. "Lazy afternoons after spending all morning with Savannah Sanchez? Well, I think I've reached, what do they call it in yoga? Nirvana? That. I'm there."

Savannah burst into laughter as she tried in vain to smooth her hair. "You inflate my ego. But I'll gladly take it."

Emersyn pulled an oversized royal purple Phoenix Suns T-shirt over her head that Savannah tossed to her. "Go on, I guess you'd better call Lisa back," she said. "Is it cool if I take a quick shower?"

Savannah fixed her with a look as she pulled a black cami and matching pair of jogger sweatpants on. "Of course." She gathered her dark hair into a high ponytail. "Take your time."

Emersyn shot her a grateful look as she turned into the small bathroom. As Savannah grabbed two chilled bottles of water from the mini-fridge and poured one into the stainless steel coffee maker on the nearby desk, her phone buzzed loudly on the nightstand again. Savannah accepted the video call.

"Buenos tardes, Mami," she said, as Lisa's still-youthful face appeared on her screen.

"Buenos tardes, Savy," she replied warmly. "How are you? We haven't had hardly a chance to connect since you landed in Cabo, but something told me to check in with you." She shot Savannah a serene smile. "You know my sixth sense when it comes to you never leads me astray. So, tell me. How has it been in Mexico? You look incredibly well-rested, my dear."

Savannah fought the flush that threatened to color her neck. "Things have been well, Mami," she said amusedly. "I did just wake from an afternoon nap. It's been busy, but that's mostly because of Kay and Diana's wedding preparations and trying not to disappear off the work grid for too long."

"I know that smile," her mother said knowingly. "There is something you're not telling me. Have you tried the root chakra meditation I texted you the other day? The video is only about fifteen minutes, but it would be perfect to do at the beach. It will help ground and secure you with warm energy."

Savannah glanced up as Emersyn emerged from the bathroom. Her wet hair was pulled into a loose bun and the oversized Phoenix Suns T-shirt hung off her slender frame over a pair of Savannah's yoga shorts. Savannah grabbed two coffee mugs from a shelf above the desk and glanced back at the screen of her phone.

"No, I haven't had a chance to yet. I'll make time for it though." She met Emersyn's eyes across the room. "Cream and sugar?"

Emersyn nodded gratefully as she sat on the edge of the bed. "All of the above. Please."

There was a pause and then her mother hummed lightly. "It sounds as though you're not in your suite alone." There was a hint of knowing in her tone. "I didn't realize you had a guest."

Savannah rolled her eyes playfully. "No, I'm not alone. Emersyn is here."

Her mother squealed so loudly in delight that both Savannah and Emersyn startled. "Emersyn *Tanner*?"

Savannah laughed as she handed her one of the mugs. "Yes, *that* Emersyn," she confirmed. "From college. She's here for Kay and Diana's wedding festivities also."

Savannah met Emersyn's gaze as she took a slow sip of the steaming coffee. *Want to say hi?* She mouthed as she arched an eyebrow.

Emersyn nodded and grinned as she strode closer to Savannah and waved at the phone. "Hi, Lisa," she called. "You haven't aged a single day. You look radiant."

Her mother blushed as she waved back. "Hi right back at you," she said warmly. "It's wonderful to see you. I'm thrilled that you're there."

Savannah wasn't sure if her mom meant *there*, as in Cabo San Lucas, or *there*, as in standing in Savannah's suite fresh out of the shower with the golden afternoon sunlight shimmering off her damp blond hair. There was something natural and easy about being there with Emersyn.

"And I love your choice of T-shirt." Her mother arched a knowing eyebrow. "The only diehard Phoenix Suns fan I know is my Savy."

Emersyn's mouth dropped open and her cheeks flushed as they both realized they had been caught. *Nothing gets past Mami.* Savannah quickly cleared her throat.

"I just…" Emersyn began.

"She spilled a mimosa," Savannah said at the same time. "This morning. At brunch. On her dress. It, um, might need to be laundered at the resort."

Her mother gazed through the camera and Savannah shifted. She always knew when she wasn't being truthful.

After a moment, she pursed her lips and shook her head. "It's good to see you both," her mother said warmly. "I'll let you go so you can get back to your vacation. Keep me updated, Savannah." She smiled at Emersyn. "I hope to see you again soon, Emersyn."

❖

Emersyn sank onto the bed cupping her coffee mug as she watched Savannah wrapping up the video call. After they hung up, Savannah shot her a lingering look that made her stomach flutter. It was like watching a memory come to life before her that she didn't realize she'd been aching for all these years. Savannah's back was strong and elegant, the toned muscles in her arms flexing as she quickly rinsed out the coffee pot in the bathroom sink. She glanced at Emersyn again.

"I can't believe you made my mom squeal like that." She laughed. "She always liked you a lot."

Emersyn took another slow sip of coffee. Her gaze tracked Savannah with something between lazy satisfaction and reverence. "I always liked her a lot too."

As Savannah sat next to her on the bed, Emersyn felt a wave of something deep and tender wash over her as she realized she had never felt as seen, desired, and loved as she did when she was with Savannah.

Unable to help herself, Emersyn leaned forward, cupping Savannah's face in one hand, and kissed her slowly. After a long moment, she finally pulled back. Savannah's eyes remained closed for a beat, though her lips curved into a smile.

"What was that for?" she asked.

I think I love you. Emersyn answered in her mind. *And I'm not scared anymore.* She opened her mouth but faltered, and then glanced down at her phone as it vibrated with a reminder.

"I almost forgot," she said. "Early dinner plans with Kay tonight. It'll probably be the last chance we get to catch up before the official wedding events kick off tomorrow night with the rehearsal dinner."

Savannah nodded. "You definitely don't want to keep Kay waiting."

Emersyn laughed. "I'd better run to my room so I can change into something that isn't…" She gathered her dress from the floor. "Wrinkled and rumpled like I was having sex all day."

Savannah leaned back on her elbows. Their laughter quieted as Emersyn crawled over her and met her lips. "You definitely were, but I get it," she said. "Coach Hanlon always knows."

Emersyn rolled her eyes again as she pushed herself off the bed, afraid that if she continued kissing Savannah she would never, ever make it to dinner. "You're telling me. We'll talk soon."

She turned once, blowing a kiss at Savannah, as she slipped out the door and pulled it closed with a gentle click. Despite her quick shower, her skin still felt warm and flushed from the morning they'd spent tangled together. Emersyn felt as though she was practically floating, the faint taste of Savannah still on her lips and the weight of her touch lingering along her skin, as she waited patiently for the elevator.

As Emersyn stepped out of the elevator onto the sixth floor, her lips still slightly swollen with the memory of Savannah's mouth on hers, she headed quickly down the hallway. She stopped short as she spotted a familiar face walking toward her from the opposite direction, also headed to her suite.

"Hey, there," Kay greeted her. She paused, pushing her sunglasses onto her head, as she took in Emersyn's flustered expression, the oversized T-shirt and borrowed yoga shorts, the damp, messy hair, and the wrinkled dress in her fists.

Emersyn blinked. "Kay! What a surprise. I was just heading into my room to change for dinner."

"Mm-hmm," Kay said lightly. Her eyes sparkled, but she didn't give anything away. "I was coming by to ask if you'd rather do a casual dinner at that beachfront bar down by the pool."

Emersyn opened her mouth to agree, but Kay wrinkled her nose. "You know, Tanner, I always took you as a big Bucks fan." She nodded at her T-shirt.

Emersyn flushed as her mouth fell open. Kay held up a hand as something between a knowing smile and mild look of surprise crossed her face. "It's okay," she said smoothly. "You don't have to explain. Meet you downstairs?"

Emersyn nodded, her throat dry. "You got it." As she fumbled with her plastic key card, she stole a glance at Kay. Kay was whistling cheerily, her hands in the deep pockets of her cargo shorts, as she walked to the elevators.

Yup, she definitely knows.

Chapter Twenty-four

The wide bamboo tiki bar glowed with warm golden light as the sun began its descent beyond the horizon. Resort guests lounged at high-top square tables and chairs scattered around a concrete deck surrounding the bar and a small kitchen. Tall, swaying palm trees were planted around each corner of the concrete deck for shade and a semblance of separation from the nearby pool that shimmered under the setting sun.

Emersyn glanced at the bar, noting the rows of top-shelf liquor and flavored syrups lining the wall, as she waved at Kay, who was sitting at a small two-top near the corner of the deck. Upbeat tropical music drifted through hidden speakers and the mingling scents of fresh seafood, citrus, and charred pineapple lingered in the warm air.

"Hey," Emersyn said as she slid into her chair. "Sorry about that. I, um, needed a quick wardrobe change."

She flashed Kay a smile as she slid her sunglasses up her nose and prayed she wouldn't question her further.

"That's all right." Kay poured them each a glass of ice water from the sweating glass pitcher at the table. She opened and then closed her mouth before meeting Emersyn's gaze. "You know, Tanner, I've been around you a long time. Long enough to recognize that you have a look about you lately."

Emersyn shifted on the chair. "A look?" she repeated. "I suppose I needed this vacation more than I thought. It's been nice to take some time for myself in the off-season. I haven't really done that before."

Kay fixed her with a look that said she knew there was more to it, but didn't press. "You're glowing, Tanner."

Though Emersyn's first inclination was to brush Kay off and do what had become habit since she was young—scoff, insist that everything was fine and she had no idea what she was talking about, and swear that she was just imagining things; that she had this under control—but after a moment of quiet contemplation, Emersyn shook her head as if to shake the defense mechanism away.

"Thanks, Kay." Emersyn took a slow sip of her sparkling seltzer, enjoying the electric fruity bubbles exploding on her tongue. "It's complicated."

Kay shot her a soft, almost maternal smile. "Of course it is," she said gently. "It always is when it matters. Complicated doesn't mean wrong, though, Tanner. You know who you are, kid."

Emersyn took a deep breath and gazed at the ocean. "Savannah and I kissed in the bathroom at the cocktail party," she said. The confessions were tumbling out. "We slept together. It was amazing. I—"

Kay nearly choked on her sip of ice water. "Wait, you what?" Her eyebrows shot up. "You kissed in the bathroom? Or you slept together?"

Emersyn flushed and ran her fingertips along the smooth edge of the table. "Um, both."

Kay crossed her arms and blinked at a spot somewhere in the distance as she nodded, appearing to process Emersyn's confession. "Wow." She whistled low after a moment. "I'll be honest, Tanner, it's always been obvious how you and Savannah feel about each other. There's something real there. *You* know how you feel about her. You always have. You know that, don't you?"

Emersyn ripped off a corner piece of bread in a small wicker basket on the table and stuffed it into her mouth. She covered her face with her hands. "I know, I know," she groaned. "I didn't expect it to happen, I swear. It's just, like, when we're around each other…" She swallowed. "I'm scared."

Kay reached out, her strong hand warm and steady on Emersyn's forearm. "And that's perfectly normal," she said firmly. "Look, whatever it is between you and Savannah? It's real. You know that. Anyone who has been around the two of you for more than five minutes in the last sixteen years can see it. Don't be afraid of who you are. I know you've spent a long time trying to convince yourself otherwise, but you care deeply about her, kid. It's written all over you."

Emersyn took a deep breath. "I do."

Kay squeezed her arm as she smiled at her. "Then don't let fear keep you from the kind of thing that most people spend their lives searching for.

If you truly care about Sanchez, don't make her wait for a version of you that might never be ready to live her truth. Be the one who chooses her fully."

Emersyn bit her lip. "I understand," she said. "I do choose her. I just didn't expect it to still feel like this after all these years."

Kay patted her arm. "Love doesn't always go away just because time passes," she said. "Sometimes it gets stronger, better. And it sure as hell doesn't shrink once you finally let yourself feel it."

Emersyn nodded. "You're right," she said thoughtfully. "When I'm with her, it's *everything*. Like going into another world where I'm completely *hers*, mind, body, and soul. I can't explain it. I've been in this bliss bubble where I've been *letting* myself feel everything and now I can't stop. I can't go back and un-feel everything I've always felt for her, even the things I told myself I'd moved beyond."

"Why would you want to?" Kay asked with a casual shrug. She carefully buttered a thick slice of flaky bread. "I mean, especially if it feels like everything with Sanchez."

"I told Jared I can't be with him," Emersyn said. "I tried to force it with him for so long. He's not a bad person; he doesn't deserve this." She lifted her chin from her hand as everything she felt continued tumbling out, the words colliding and landing around each other. She met Kay's eyes. "But he's not Savannah."

Kay set her bread down and held Emersyn's gaze. "It'll be okay, Tanner," she said gently. "You're doing the right thing by being honest with him. What's stopping you from admitting it already?"

Emersyn watched a gray-blue tropical mockingbird loop over the water as its wings fanned out against the setting sun. "Admitting what?"

"That you're in love with Savannah," Kay said simply.

Emersyn blinked, unsure if she was more surprised by Kay using her first name or by the simple, soft declaration that echoed deep in her core. "I…I never…" She hedged lamely as she exhaled and stared up at the sharp angles of the palm fronds jutting above them. "I mean, I don't think we knew how to make it work back then, during our senior year. The timing was all wrong and our lives were already set in different directions." She blew out her breath and fiddled with a grape on the cheese and fruit plate the waiter had placed before her. "But now? I want to be the version of myself that I am with her. I know that's who I really am. And that's the future that feels right and *real*."

Kay grinned as she bit down on a forkful of crisp Caesar salad. "Then you know what you need to do, Tanner. Don't half-ass this. Don't make her wait around for someone who's unsure. Be all in. You're going to have to do hard stuff, and it's going to feel strange and uncomfortable at times, but you'll have to sit with it anyway." She took a long sip of ice water. "Remember, you have support. You have me, Diana, every single woman who was on that team. You have *Sanchez*, waiting to love you like you've always wanted. And the way I see how you two are around each other without even realizing it? It's going to be worth it, kid. You know Savannah deserves it. And maybe you don't realize it, but you deserve to be fully and completely happy too. And I think you know who that happiness is with." She shrugged. "When you're ready, stop running from what's right in front of you."

They sat in silence for a moment as the evening breeze tickled Emersyn's back and shoulders. A sense of calm settled over her.

"I know," she said contemplatively. "The only way to be with Savannah is to embrace who I am and what we have fully." She took a deep breath as she bit into a thick chunk of gruyere. "What we have is amazing," she admitted. "Why would I ever want to hide that?"

Kay leaned forward. "I'm here for you, Tanner," she said. "I think you know what you need to do."

"I'm finally going to come out, aren't I?" Emersyn said. "Well, besides to you. And Savannah. Obviously. And Erica and Kayla. And Savannah's parents…"

As she ticked off the growing number of people who knew who she was—and loved her still—Emersyn belatedly discovered maybe she wasn't as closeted as she'd thought.

Kay laughed. "Sounds like you're already halfway tumbling out of it." She shook her head in amusement. "Welcome to the out life, kid. It's wonderful, messy at times, deeply moving, and sometimes heartbreaking. But it's so freeing and sometimes you get moments like this." She gestured at the pool before them and the ocean beyond that. The rippling waves reflected soft pink and deep red brushstrokes from the clear evening sky. "Moments when you get to say 'I do' to the love of your life on a gorgeous tropical beach after forty-odd years together. And I'll tell you, Tanner, that authenticity is better than anything. Well, apparently besides mind-blowing sex with Sanchez."

It was Emersyn's turn to nearly choke on her mouthful of sweet, refreshing melon as she wondered if her college-aged self could ever imagine having this conversation over dinner with Coach Hanlon.

She squeezed Kay's hand. "Oh my God, promise she'll never know what I said." She giggled. "But really, thank you, Kay. For everything. Over *all* the years. I don't know where I'd be without you."

Kay smiled. "You'd be just fine, Tanner," she said. "Now, do what you need to do and get your girl. But first, pass me that bread plate if you're not going to finish the last of it. A retired athlete's got to eat, you know."

Emersyn laughed as she held up the plate so Kay could pick off the remaining wedge of bread. The pit of tension that had plummeted into her stomach after breaking off her engagement with Jared had temporarily dissipated and, though she knew she had more to do, the knot between her shoulders loosened. *Maybe it* would *be okay.*

The breeze ruffled her hair as Emersyn listened while Kay launched into her and Diana's morning brunch plans with Diana's two sisters who had arrived that afternoon.

I'm finally going to live my truth. And stop holding my breath. Savannah is so *worth it. She always has been. And Kay is right; I've always been worth it too.*

As she laughed at Kay's commentary about last New Year's Eve with Diana's two sisters, Emersyn knew at the back of her mind that she still wasn't exactly sure how it would all unfold. She didn't know when she would speak to Jared again, though she knew they would have to talk eventually if only regarding logistics. She didn't know how her mother might react, how a future with Savannah would look, or if the world would shift tremendously around her once she fully embraced who she was and stopped skirting around her truth. Still, Emersyn was certain what she wanted. Her chest swelled with anticipation and warmth as her face flashed in her mind: Savannah Sanchez.

❖

The next morning, Emersyn stepped into the hallway as the elevator doors quietly slid open. With an iced coffee from the resort's quick café in one hand, the cool condensation sliding down her fingers, she reached into the pocket of her loose black linen pants for her key card with the other hand. With a deep breath, she tried to shake off the lingering ache in her chest that was part nerves and part anticipation. Tonight was Kay and Diana's rehearsal dinner and she hadn't stopped thinking about Savannah—or how excited she was to see her later that morning, after she wrapped up her work check-in at the resort's business center.

The scent of espresso and sweet vanilla syrup drifted upward as she registered the sound of movement coming around the corner across the hallway. The distinct sounds of a rolling suitcase and heavy, shuffling steps made Emersyn glance up out of habit. Her stomach plummeted as she nearly dropped her iced coffee all over the immaculate hallway.

Jared grinned nervously, looking disheveled, jet-lagged, and exhausted, and he held out a stunningly colorful bouquet of tropical flowers. “Surprise?” he said sheepishly. “Thought I’d beat the wedding rush. This resort is amazing.”

Emersyn opened and closed her mouth as her gut clenched. “Jared,” she said as she blinked at him, her brain still not quite registering that he was there. Standing in front of her. With flowers. “What are you doing here?”

Jared’s face fell slightly, a sure sign Emersyn knew meant he was disappointed she didn’t run into his arms. “Em, I couldn’t stop thinking about you.” He shook his head. “I…I don’t believe that you really want to break things off. No way. I know things have been distant lately, and I thought maybe you were upset that I wasn’t here with you.” He swallowed hard and gestured at the flowers as a colorful peace offering. “I, um, left the think tank early. Took a red-eye from LaGuardia. I want to talk, Em. I want to fix this.”

Emersyn was stunned as her hotel suite clicked open. The words weren’t coming yet, and all she could do was blink at Jared while her stomach churned. “You didn’t have to do that.”

“I know,” Jared said. He gently brushed past her into the suite and whistled, impressed. “Hell of a view here, Em.” He turned slowly as Emersyn took a few steps into the room and gently closed the door behind them before setting her coffee on the desk. “But I wanted to. I thought if we had a real conversation, you know, face-to-face, we could fix this. Figure it out. I still want to marry you, Emersyn.”

Emersyn stood frozen next to the desk. Her heart felt as though it was simultaneously breaking while jumping into high gear with nerves and dread. “Okay,” she replied slowly, resting her hand along the back of the desk chair for support. “We can talk, Jared. We should. But it’s not going to change anything. I—”

Jared flashed her a hopeful smile. “That’s fine,” he interrupted her smoothly. “Just give me a chance. Hear me out. Please.”

“Like I said—” Emersyn said.

Jared dropped his rolling suitcase heavily near the sliding glass door to the balcony and ran a hand through his hair. "Hey, can I take a quick shower before we get into it?" he asked. "I feel disgusting. I haven't slept and I've been on a plane for hours."

Emersyn hesitated as her body tensed. Every instinct screamed at her to get Jared out of there now, to make him go into the lobby and get his own room. Still, a pang of guilt at the impending conversation flashed through her and she gave him a terse nod. *After everything I've done, the least I can let him do is take a quick shower.*

"Fine," she said tightly. She folded her arms over her gray ribbed tank top and nodded toward the bathroom door. "Bathroom is there."

"Thanks." Jared hesitated for a moment as he seemed to realize he was still holding the flowers. After a quick glance around, he gingerly placed them on the desk next to Emersyn's iced coffee. He paused for a moment next to her, as if waiting for a hug or kiss, and then sighed as Emersyn pointedly stepped backward once and trained her gaze at a spot on the wall just over his shoulder. Defeated, he walked into the bathroom and shut the door firmly behind him.

As the shower squeaked to life, Emersyn sat on the edge of the bed and pressed her index fingers to her temples. She knew Jared was confused and she knew he hadn't necessarily done anything wrong. She sighed, knowing she owed him an honest conversation but not looking forward to it nonetheless. The scent of her rapidly-melting iced coffee lingered in the room, but now she was anxious and overwhelmed as cold panic and curls of pressure settled deep into her gut. She wondered how exactly Jared would react once she told him the truth and how she was going to explain his sudden, unexpected presence to Savannah.

Chapter Twenty-five

Savannah paused outside Emersyn's door as her fingertips hovered over her phone, her focus on her final work email of the morning. A local luxury lifestyle magazine serving the greater Phoenix area had expressed interest to the Vault's marketing director for a feature on Savannah for one of their upcoming fall publications. As she quickly typed out an affirmative response to her marketing director's suggested date and time for the interview, Savannah quickly slid her phone into the pocket of her light blue chiffon maxi dress and ran a hand through her hair. It had been enough work for the morning. Savannah hadn't been able to stop thinking about Emersyn and the way she had looked at her the day before. The way she kissed her. The gentle, warm weight of her in her arms. The softness in her voice and the way she gazed at her as though she had loved her for her entire life.

Savannah had barely slept the night before and could hardly focus on work that morning; she had to see Emersyn. It had been nearly twenty-four hours and that was more than enough. She had to feel Emersyn's lips against her own and tease the soft, sensitive spot just behind her ear. *God, who am I?* She knocked on her door.

Savannah softened as she heard Emersyn pad to the door. As the door opened, Savannah's heartbeat quickened as she laid eyes on her. Emersyn was all sun-kissed, barefoot, and radiant with her hair in a messy, loose knot, leaving a few face-framing strands to shimmer in the morning sunlight that seeped through the suite.

"Hey, you," Savannah said. "Enough with the work for me today. Really, I could barely focus anyway because I just wanted to see y—"

The bathroom door opened next to Emersyn. A chiseled, muscular, blond, and unfairly handsome all-American-looking man stepped out barefoot and shirtless, his damp hair sticking to his forehead and just a white cotton towel slung low on his hips. It was only then that Savannah registered the look of shock and horror on Emersyn's face. Without a single word, Savannah knew exactly who it was. *Jared.*

The air seemed to crackle and spark, the tension so taut that Savannah knew it would snap any moment, and the crushing waves of disappointment, betrayal, and shock so overwhelming that she grappled at the doorframe with one hand for a steadying moment. The sharp weight of betrayal was practically suffocating as Savannah took a deep breath.

"Hey," Jared greeted her with an easy smile and a casual nod.

"Savannah," Emersyn said urgently as she stepped forward once. Savannah stepped backward. "Savy, please, I know what you're thinking and I promise this isn't what it looks like."

Emersyn's voice snapped Savannah back into the present and the shock of the moment coalesced into pulsing, hot anger coursing through her veins. She clenched her jaw and tried to rapidly blink away the growing pressure behind her eyes. She hated the panic etched across Emersyn's hazel gaze and the throbbing crack that seemed to permeate Savannah from the inside out.

"You've got to be fucking kidding me," Savannah said, her voice low. Somewhere in the back of her mind, even she was mildly surprised by the hard-edged ice in her tone. "I rushed up here to see you because I missed you already. And he's here?" Savannah gestured at Jared, who blinked as he glanced between them in confusion. *He has no idea.* The thought boiled Savannah's blood as she took another step backward. "I should've known you'd never be ready. Instead, I let myself believe you wanted this. That we had grown up. Still, Emersyn, I at least used to be able to tell when you were outright lying to me."

"Savannah, I swear to you." Emersyn's voice was thick as she swallowed hard. "I know how this looks, but I *swear* to you I didn't lie to you. I do want this, I want all of it, I…"

The pleading look on her face was too much for Savannah and she felt hot, angry tears snaking down her cheeks as she tried to quickly swipe them away. She hated the hurt in Emersyn's gaze, knowing she was now responsible for some of it. "You know." Her voice was cool and steely. "You *know*, Emersyn, that no matter how far apart we are or how long it's taken us to come back, that this is real. Whether you ever admit it or not, you've always belonged to me. *Always*."

Savannah shut her mouth tightly as her voice broke, hating how she felt herself unraveling right there outside Emersyn's suite.

Jared stepped forward as he tightened his grip on his towel. "Wait. What's going on? Who are you?"

Savannah glanced at him long enough to fix him with a sharp glare. *I'll tell him exactly who I am.* "You really don't know? You're that clueless?"

Jared turned to Emersyn, who was still staring at her with big tears threatening to spill down her face. "Em, what's going on?" He wrinkled his nose in confusion. "What the hell is she talking about? Do you know her?"

He really has no idea. The realization hit Savannah like a cold slap. *Emersyn lied right to me. I used to always know when she wasn't truthful, but I couldn't even tell this time. She's never mentioned me once to him.* She couldn't stay and watch Emersyn stumble through more lies. The hallway felt too hot, too stifling, and unbearably bright from the morning sun that bounced across Emersyn's suite and through the open door.

Without another word, Savannah turned and strode down the hallway. "Fuck you, Jared," she tossed over her shoulder, refusing to look back.

The pressure behind Savannah's eyes was nearly overwhelming and she refused to let herself cry any more until she was back in the private quiet of her own room, though she had to breathe to keep her long strides from breaking into a run for the elevator bank.

Savannah barely registered the loud slam of the hotel room door and Emersyn bolting barefoot down the quiet hallway behind her. Emersyn was still fast, but Savannah's legs were longer and she had gotten a better head start to the elevator.

"Savannah, wait!" Emersyn's voice rang out. She could hear the desperation, the panic behind her words. "Please, Savannah, talk to me!"

Savannah didn't stop. She stepped into the elevator, her spine rigid, and turned just as the doors began to close.

"Please," Emersyn said breathlessly. "Please don't leave like this."

Savannah swallowed hard as the elevator doors shut with a gentle whoosh. Emersyn's wide eyes were still shining with unshed tears, her face desperately apologetic, and her chest rose up and down rapidly from what Savannah assumed was a combination of sprinting after her and the sudden adrenaline at being unexpectedly caught in a massive, unbelievable lie.

Savannah felt sick to her stomach. The vision of Jared, shirtless, muscular, and wearing only a towel, in Emersyn's suite made her skin crawl and her chest tighten with dark jealousy. As Savannah silently reminded herself that she couldn't be jealous over someone who wasn't hers, the resort seemed darker and quieter. The world that just yesterday had felt so full instead muted around her as she walked down the hallway. She couldn't bolt to her room fast enough.

❖

Emersyn swallowed hard as she closed the door to her suite and leaned against it for a moment. Her heart pounded in her chest and it was hard to get anything other than ragged breaths that seemed to catch somewhere between her throat and her lungs.

Jared sat on the edge of the bed, now fully dressed in a pair of black basketball shorts and a white T-shirt, and had carelessly slung his towel along the edge of the desk chair. He stood, his expression a mixture of confusion and suspicion, and stopped short as he reached Emersyn.

"What the hell just happened?" he asked. "Who was that and what the hell did I do to her?"

Emersyn exhaled, but her breath was still shaky. It was now or never, and all she could think about was finding Savannah. "Jared, we need to talk," she said quietly. "We need to *really* talk."

Jared nodded, watching her curiously, as Emersyn sat in a chair near the small table and fidgeted with her hands. "I…I didn't ask you to come here, Jared."

"I know," Jared replied as he sat back down on the edge of the bed heavily. His face looked resigned as he scratched his chin. "I thought if I surprised you because maybe deep down you were mad that I wasn't here with you, it would help." He swallowed. "Help us get back on track, maybe reconnect, and figure things out. I hoped when you told me you couldn't marry me, it was a rough patch for us. You were having cold feet and punishing me or something for not being here with you."

Emersyn took a deep breath and shot him a sad smile. "I appreciate you dropping everything for me. And giving it your all to try to make this work. But, Jared, this isn't a rough patch or some kind of petty punishment, I promise. It's…It's a lot more than that, and it's me."

Jared opened his mouth, but Emersyn held up a hand. "I know everybody says that when they break up," she said. "The whole 'it's not you, it's me' thing. But this time? It really, *really* is me, Jared. You would have been the perfect man." Emersyn glanced down at her hands, fighting the tears that rose in her throat. "But that's the problem…"

Jared folded his arms. "Is there someone else?"

Emersyn met his gaze as Kay's words over dinner last night flooded back to her. *You're going to have to do hard stuff, and it's going to feel strange and uncomfortable at times, but you'll have to sit with it anyway.* This time, she didn't shy away from the confused hurt on his face or the hot tears snaking down her own. "Yes," she finally said. "But it's more than that, Jared. I'm…I'm gay."

Jared blinked, but didn't unfold his arms. "You're gay?"

"I'm so sorry for wasting your time," Emersyn continued after a beat. "I thought I could make it work. I thought it was all behind me, that if I buried it enough then I could want what I thought I was supposed to want. But it never really went away, even though I do care about you. I always will. But I can't pretend to be someone I'm not anymore."

Jared took a long, slow breath as he absorbed her words. "So, all of this," he said, his jaw tightening. "The refusal to set a wedding date. Never initiating sex or intimacy in nearly three years together; I always had to be the one to initiate. The emotional distance I was never quite able to cross with you. That woman…Is it her?"

Emersyn nodded, fresh tears filling her eyes as Savannah's face flooded her mind. "Savannah. We were teammates during our senior basketball season at Northwoods."

Jared rubbed a hand over his face as he nodded. "You know, I always kind of wondered why you never talked much about your life then. After all, you were, like, this hometown hero in Northwoods, going on to play for the local university on a full scholarship, fighting your way back tooth and nail after that accident." He shook his head again. "It's legendary stuff, Em. And you never, ever wanted to go deep about it. It's like you just wanted to forget that part of your life ever existed. Were you with, um, Savannah then?"

Emersyn nodded as she glanced down at her lap. "Yes. We were in love. We were too young and had too much ahead of us. Well, Savannah did. And I just wanted to get out of Northwoods."

Jared gave a small, rueful laugh. "God, I can't believe I didn't see it before. I can't believe I never put it all together or pressed harder."

"It's not your fault," Emersyn said softly. "I didn't want anyone to see it. Not even myself. I told myself over and over that maybe I wasn't really gay, but I was trying to mask the pain of losing Savannah. The hurt and the fear. And then it just became habit and I refused to look any deeper once I stuffed it all down far enough. None of this is on you, Jared. It's all me." Emersyn glanced at the firmly shut door of the suite, as if willing Savannah to come back. Her heart clenched as she wondered how and where she would find her and make her talk to her. "And I'm so sorry for that. I'm so sorry I can't be the woman I need to be for you."

Jared nodded, as though the pieces of a long unresolved puzzle were finally drifting into place. "I understand," he said finally. "It sucks. A lot. Especially for me, selfishly. But I understand that you're not doing this to hurt me. I'm sorry too, Em. I really am."

He stared down at his feet as he stood and paused for a moment before walking to his suitcase. "I'll get my own room tonight." He hesitated for a moment as he glanced at her. "I'll look into flights back to Chicago tomorrow morning and be out as soon as I can. I know there will be a lot to figure out with, um, the living situation and everything, but I'll give you space for now."

Emersyn rose to her feet too, walking with him to the door. "Thank you," she said softly. "For everything, Jared."

He turned to face her once more. "Are you in love with her?"

Emersyn took a deep breath and nodded. There wasn't a single doubt.

Jared watched her face for a long moment. "I'm not angry with you, Em," he said, a slight shake in his voice. "I just…I'm sad, you know? Sad that it wasn't real for both of us. But I care about you and I want you to be happy, even if that happiness isn't…" He took a deep breath. "…Isn't with me. I hope you stop running from yourself. This is a fresh start for you. Be honest with yourself and, um, with her." He nodded in the general direction of the elevators.

Emersyn blinked back her tears. "I will."

The echo of the door clicking shut sounded louder in the silence that followed Jared leaving. Emersyn stood in the stillness as the seconds stretched into minutes that felt like forever. After a few minutes, she slid onto the balcony and sat in a chair as she gazed out at the distant crystal-blue shimmer of the ocean beneath the cloudless sky. Everything felt raw, open, and exposed, the sharp emotions cutting right through her chest and coursing deeply into her core, as she let the tears fall freely for another moment and tried to even her breaths.

As the silent, shaking sobs subsided, Emersyn realized that beyond the raw sharpness she felt strong. Confident, despite the waves of long overdue emotion breaking free. Authentically herself and *real*. She stood after another moment, drinking in one last sweeping view of the white sand beach and the glittering ocean as she felt her nervous system begin to settle. She would talk to her mom next; she *needed* to talk to her mom, if only for the reassurance and comfort she so desperately hoped she'd receive from her only parent after what she'd tell her once and for all—but first, Emersyn was determined to find Savannah.

Chapter Twenty-six

The breeze in the resort's open-air lobby was balmy and warm as sunlight danced across the shining marble floor. Morning had shifted to midafternoon, and the lobby was abuzz with arriving guests and cheerful laughter as they were greeted by uniformed resort staff.

Emersyn barely registered any of it as she scanned the crowded lobby, desperate for any sign of Savannah. Her heart thudded against her chest as she looked across the expansive open space. She ignored the light scents of gardenia and hibiscus, but the subtle coconut scent in the air made Emersyn feel as though she might actually unravel right there in the resort lobby. She had spent the last hour scouring the entire space, from the beach and the pool to the walking paths, fitness center, business center, and even glancing around the restaurants and cafés. Her legs and feet were sore and she ignored the trickles of sweat that snaked down the back of her neck. There had been no sign of Savannah anywhere and if she was in her room, she wasn't answering the door. *Not for me, at least.*

Just as Emersyn crossed the large space and glanced along the throngs of people crowded around the small lobby bar, she caught sight of Erica, Kayla, and Mia. They were sitting along the edge of the bar sipping umbrella-topped spritzers and laughing at something on Kayla's phone. Emersyn took a deep breath and beelined for them as she sidestepped stacks of designer luggage on wheeled carts and exuberant guests in wide-brimmed hats and flowy sundresses.

"Erica," Emersyn called breathlessly.

All three of them turned expectantly and Erica's easy smile faded the moment she saw Emersyn's face. She turned to Kayla and Mia, murmuring something to them quietly, before sliding off the high-backed leather barstool and guiding Emersyn to a quieter corner of the lobby.

"Hey, you okay?" Erica asked, concern all over her face. "What's wrong?"

"Have you seen Savannah?" Emersyn asked, hating that her voice nearly broke on her name. She didn't want to sound as desperate and hopeless as she felt. "I need to talk to her. Jared came here early this morning. I…I didn't know he was coming, but she saw him in my room and it looked bad. Really bad, E." Emersyn took a deep breath, willing her heart to slow down. "I had broken things off with him. He thought maybe if he showed up and surprised me, then we could work things out. I should've just told him I was gay when I broke things off, but I told him now. And now I can't find her anywhere and she's not answering my calls or texts and—"

Erica placed both hands firmly on Emersyn's shoulders. "Em, breathe."

Emersyn took a deep breath and closed her eyes as Erica pulled her into a grounding hug. "Shit," she said. "I'm so sorry. You broke things off with Jared and he still showed up?"

Emersyn nodded. "I swear I did. But now Savannah thinks I lied to her. I tried to explain, but she left so quickly. I ran after her, but she got on the elevator before I could say anything." She sighed and bit her lip. "I wasn't even thinking about Jared in my room when she was there. All I could think about was running after her and trying to explain."

"Is he still in your room now?"

Emersyn blinked. "No. I…I finally told him the reason why I wanted to break things off. *Needed* to break things off. He knows I'm gay. He got a separate room for the night and I think he's trying to leave tomorrow." She swallowed. "There's more. Savannah and I…we reconnected during this trip, you know?"

Erica wrinkled her nose. "I mean, I know you can cut the tension with a knife between you two, but be specific, Em. What does reconnected mean?"

Emersyn stared up at the ceiling for a long moment. "We were intimate, Erica," she finally said. "But it was more than that. It wasn't just some fun experimental vacation fling with an old…ex, I guess. We *really* reconnected." Emersyn felt her throat tighten. "I want to be with her, Erica. There has never been *anybody* but her."

Erica sighed. "Savannah still loves you, Em. That's been pretty obvious from the second she saw you again. If I had to put myself in her shoes, which by the way I would never because those heels..." Erica grimaced. "But if I *did*, I would guess that seeing him in your room after you two have spent this whole trip falling back into each other probably gutted her."

"I know." Emersyn swallowed hard. "It kills me that I made her feel that way, because I don't want to be with Jared. I had no idea he was going to drop everything to make some last-ditch effort to fix things. I should've told him I was gay when I broke things off, but I just..." She chewed her lip as a tear ran down her cheek. "I did now, though."

Erica's expression softened. "That's huge, Em," she replied. "Don't forget that. How do you feel about it?"

Emersyn wrapped her arms around herself against the blast of air conditioning through the lobby. "It was time," she said simply. "I know coming out isn't easy, but I can't keep fighting myself either. Jared was as understanding as I could expect. He didn't fight me on it. He was just...sad. He asked me if I was in love with Savannah."

Erica raised an eyebrow. "What did you say?"

"I said yes." Emersyn's voice was barely audible over the din of the lobby. "Because it's true. It's always been true. And I've spent most of my adult life trying to run from it and trying too hard not to feel it."

Erica slung an arm around Emersyn and glanced at Kayla, who quietly approached them with concern etched across her face. "You need to find her," Erica said. "Not only to fix this, but to tell her everything you just told me. If you love her, Em, love her like you mean it. Don't just tell her that you care about her; tell her *all* of it. The real stuff. Tell her that you're not running from it anymore."

Emersyn nodded as she swiped at her cheek with her index finger. "I will. I just don't know where she is and I can't get a hold of her."

"Savannah?" Kayla asked Erica. Erica took a deep breath and nodded in response.

"We haven't seen her." Kayla squeezed Emersyn's hand. "But we just got down to the lobby bar about thirty minutes ago. I'm sure she's around somewhere."

Erica nodded. "Savannah isn't the type to just run away and blow off Kay and Diana's wedding. If I know Savannah, she's just hurting somewhere right now."

"That's the thing, I don't *want* to hurt her." Emersyn shook her head. "And somehow I already did." She blew out her breath in frustration. "I'm *so* ready for her to love me because her love is....it's *everything*. I'm ready to be hers. I just want to love her too."

"You always have," Erica replied with a grin. "And you've *been* hers, our entire senior season and from the moment you laid eyes on her again. Even all those times you were pretending it was something else."

Erica's words plunged deeply into Emersyn as she realized how right she was. She knew there was one more important thing to do if she was going to love Savannah like she meant it this entire time—with her whole heart—and then she'd resume reaching out to her, stalking her at the resort, whatever she had to do to get Savannah to face her.

"Can you let Kay and Diana know that I'm very sorry, but I won't make it to the rehearsal dinner tonight?" Emersyn asked. "I need to do this right and I'm not letting Savannah go. Unless she makes me." Emersyn's heart sank. She didn't want to think about the terrifying idea of Savannah being truly done with her. "But I need some time. I need to talk to my mom."

"Of course," Erica said gently. "I've got your back. You know I do. We're here if you need anything at all, Em, even just someone to talk to after you have that conversation."

Emersyn embraced Erica and then Kayla before walking to the elevators with a nearly suffocating ache in her chest that rose all the way to the lump in her throat. She may not have found Savannah yet, but Emersyn knew exactly who she was and what she wanted—and that was a good start.

❖

That evening, Emersyn sat cross-legged on the desk chair in her suite as the vibrant tropical sunset spilled dark gold across the floor. She had opened the sliding glass balcony door to let in the soft ocean breeze and enjoyed the way it swept over her shoulders and gently through her hair. Palm leaves swayed lazily outside the balcony. Their soft rustling alongside the waves rushing to the beach created a steady, calming rhythm that Emersyn desperately needed as she gazed at her laptop screen and waited for the video call to connect.

Within a moment, her mother appeared with a wide smile and a thin light pink cardigan wrapped around her shoulders. She was on her modest patio, surrounded by the dozens of impossibly green plants that Emersyn always teased her about, and held a large mug of tea in her hand. The thin string and small paper square at the end fluttered in the cool northern Wisconsin summer breeze.

"Look at you, so tan!" her mother greeted her. "Cabo looks like it's being very good to you. Have you been out on the beach every day?"

"Not every day," Emersyn said. "But enough to give all the Midwest winters I've experienced a good middle finger."

Her mother laughed as she sipped her tea. "And the wedding?" she asked. "That's coming up soon now, isn't it?"

Emersyn nodded. "Tomorrow evening," she said. "Everything Kay and Diana have planned has been beautiful. I never expected it, but the destination wedding actually fits them. Everything has been elegant but relaxed. And they both seem *so* happy."

"That's great," her mother said warmly. "I always liked Kay. She was good to you during those high school and college years. She made you work hard and take accountability, but in the right way. You learned a lot from her *and* you really honed your strengths on the court."

Emersyn nodded. "Kay always believed in me. Even when I didn't necessarily believe in myself." She paused. "Most of the old team is here, which has been really cool…"

Someone opened the sliding glass door behind her mother and padded barefoot onto the small patio, handing her a slice of cherry pie on a small white dish.

Her mother glanced up with a grateful smile as she took the pie, but Emersyn didn't miss the flush that colored her cheeks as a man's hand patted her shoulder affectionately before walking back into the condo.

"Mom?" Emersyn's eyes narrowed in suspicion. "Who was that?"

Her mother blinked as the color rose higher in her cheeks. She reached for her mug a little too quickly and took a slow sip of tea. "Oh, I… Well, I do have company over, Emersyn. His name is Peter."

Emersyn arched an eyebrow. "Peter?"

Her mother waved her hand in embarrassment. "He lives in one of the condos down the street, at the end of the cul-de-sac." Her voice was light and airy. "We've, um, just been spending some time together, that's all. He gets the best cherries from Door County." She gestured at the untouched slice of pie. "He and his late wife actually owned a bakery out there for a number of years; he loves to bake. The cherry pie is his specialty. In fact, we're hoping to plan a weekend trip there this fall."

Emersyn grinned before she could stop it. "Mom!" she exclaimed. "Are you telling me that you're dating?"

Her mother rolled her eyes playfully, but her cheeks remained flushed. "Don't act so shocked, Emersyn," she replied dryly. "I may be in an active adult retirement community, but I'm not *dead*. He's incredibly kind. We like to go for walks after dinner, attend the movie nights, spend afternoons at the golf course… He makes me laugh. I swear, Emersyn, I laugh harder than I ever have with that man. After everything with your father? I just…" She threw her hands up and chuckled. "Oh, why not? It took me long enough. And life is far too short to stay lonely."

Emersyn shook her head in amused disbelief. "I didn't see that one coming, Mom. But I'm glad you're happy."

"Neither did I," her mother said. "But it feels good to let someone in again, you know? We have a nice time together."

Emersyn swallowed hard as she nodded. "That's good," she said. "I'm really happy for you, Mom."

"Well," she went on, switching gears as she took a bite of pie. "Tell me, you mentioned most of the old team is there in Cabo?"

"Yeah." Emersyn's gaze fell to the edge of the desk. "I don't know if you remember her or not, but Savannah Sanchez is here too…"

Her mother gasped in excitement and Emersyn couldn't help but notice the gleam of happiness lighting her mother's face. "Well, of course I remember Savannah!" she exclaimed. "You two were inseparable during that last half of your senior years. I always wondered what happened to her after she went to play in Germany. I did always hope she was successful in whatever pro basketball career she pursued."

"Yeah, well, uh," Emersyn sputtered, slightly taken aback by her mother's obvious pleasure at Savannah being in Cabo. "She was. She owns a small chain of gyms in Phoenix now and mentioned that she hopes to expand them in the next year or so."

"Oh, so you two have been catching up!" her mother said excitedly. "I'm so happy to hear you're back in touch."

That's one way to put it. "I wouldn't say that we're back in touch," she replied quickly. "More like I was having lunch with Kay in her suite and had no idea Savannah would also be attending the wedding until I opened the door and she was standing right there." *Or that she's as devastatingly gorgeous as I remember.*

Even through the laptop screen, Emersyn couldn't escape her mother's penetrating, thoughtful gaze. *Damn it.* She had always been exceptionally bad at lying to her and fibbing through half-truths.

Her mother sat back against her chair thoughtfully. "You know, I always liked Savannah a lot." She shook her head. "You were such a shell of yourself after that accident. It was absolutely wretched as a parent to have to watch your scholarship get rescinded and you having to take out those loans just to graduate, all while trying to recover from the injury." She took a deep breath. "It was awful. I worried so much about you. It was like you just didn't care about anything anymore. You had no light behind your eyes. It felt like the more I tried to reach you, you just slipped further away."

Guilt poked at Emersyn's gut. "I'm sorry, Mom. I was just a kid, really. I didn't know how to—"

"No," her mother cut her off firmly. "No, Emersyn. You had every right to feel how you did, to be anxious about the future, to be angry and sad. But something changed when you became friends with Savannah. It was the first time I saw you with light in your expression again. That friendship brought out the best in you and I've always been so thankful to Savannah for it."

Emersyn swallowed hard. *She had to have known it wasn't just friendship. She must have known Savannah and I were never friends. It was always so, so much more.*

Her mother's smile didn't appear to reveal anything more about her thoughts on Emersyn and Savannah's "friendship," so she simply shook her head and glanced at the door. *Maybe Mom really is that innocent. After all, she thought I was pregnant the first time I tried—and failed—to come out.* It seemed funny now, though it hadn't then.

"It's been…a lot seeing her again," Emersyn said. "We've talked a lot. Spent tons of time together here. We even played some basketball. You know, like old times."

Her mother's silence stretched for a beat too long before she tilted her head. "And how has that felt?"

Emersyn looked into the screen, at her mother's relaxed posture on the patio with her mug in hand, and at the breeze that rustled across her silver ponytail. "Like something I never stopped feeling," she said after a heart-stopping moment. "Even when I tried really, *really* hard to bury it all."

Her mother's expression didn't change, though a gentle smile played at the soft corners of her mouth. "That doesn't surprise me, Emersyn. Not one bit."

Emersyn glanced out the sliding glass door at the darkening sky, wondering how the rehearsal dinner was going. A pang echoed across her chest as she thought of Savannah and how badly she wanted to storm the dinner, sit on her lap, and kiss her until they were both dizzy. "There's a lot I've been figuring out and finally facing, Mom," Emersyn said. "About myself mostly, but about her too."

Her mother took another sip of tea. "I'm listening, sweetheart," she said warmly. "Whatever is going through your head, you can tell me."

The lump expanded in Emersyn's throat. "I'm ready to say it," she muttered more to herself than her mother. "Actually say it." She took a deep breath and fiddled with the drawstring on her linen pants. "I'm gay, Mom. I'm in love with Savannah. I was then and I am all over again. I don't know, maybe I always have been."

When Emersyn finally got the courage to look at the screen, her mother's eyes were shimmering with tears, but she was smiling. Relief swept through Emersyn so quickly that she thought she might deflate in on herself. Her mom was *smiling*. She wasn't mad. She wasn't yelling. She didn't have a look of shocked disappointment or obvious discomfort narrowing her fine features.

"I'm proud of you. For knowing your heart and letting yourself love. You deserve to be happy, Emersyn, and if that's not with Jared or any man, then don't keep waiting to let yourself feel it."

Emersyn exhaled as the tension loosened from her shoulders. "I broke things off with him. He's been understanding. I just..." She swallowed hard. "I just know you liked him so much, Mom. I've always wanted to make you proud. It was never fair for you, having to deal with Dad leaving and then that accident that wrecked you as much as it did me..."

"Emersyn, honey, I have *always* been proud of you. Who you love doesn't affect that one bit; *how* you love is what I'm proud of." Her mother smiled. "You've always had such a big heart and you truly care for others. You put everyone before yourself, but you don't need to do that all the time, sweetheart. You deserve happiness for yourself too. You're my daughter. I am so proud of the woman you are and I will *always* be proud of you."

Emersyn grinned through her tears, feeling like herself for the first time in years. "Thank you, Mom," she said softly. "Though I may have already messed everything up."

As she launched into filling her in on the latest, her mother listening with occasional nods or quick shakes of her head, Emersyn felt the weight disappearing as she opened up and confided everything.

After a few moments, her mother leaned forward again. "Emersyn, I know things are messy right now. I know it hurts, but don't run from this."

Emersyn's throat tightened. "She wants nothing to do with me." She glanced at her silent phone as if hoping she had somehow missed a text or call from Savannah while chatting with her mom.

"Tell her how you feel," her mother urged her. "Stay for the wedding and see it through. It's just another couple of days, right? This is your chance to show her how you feel about her. Being honest with yourself is the hard part. Being honest with her is the brave part. And, Em, you have always been the bravest person I know."

Emersyn bit her lip. "What if she doesn't forgive me? Or hear me out?"

"She will," she replied without hesitation. "Savannah has loved you for a long time too, Emersyn. This is worth the fight."

Emersyn nodded. "You're right. I'll have to see her eventually. I'll tell her."

"Good," her mother said with a grin. "That's my girl. Now go wash your face, order some room service, and remember who the hell you are."

Emersyn laughed despite the nerves clenching her stomach. "Thanks, Mom. I love you."

"I love you more," Her mother said and then laughed. "And don't worry, Peter didn't overhear a thing. He's in the living room watching *Jeopardy*. Maybe you'll get to meet him sometime soon."

"I hope so, Mom," Emersyn said. Her heart felt lighter than it had in a long time. "I'll keep you updated."

Her mother looked directly into the camera and winked confidently. "You've got this, Emersyn. You love her and that's what matters now, sweetheart."

CHAPTER TWENTY-SEVEN

The soft hum of excited conversation and hair dryers over the gentle background of ocean waves in the distance should have been relaxing, but Savannah felt anything but. The salon inside the resort's upscale spa was airy and elegant, with taupe-colored walls, tall green plants in handmade clay pots, sleek white marble counters, and gilded gold-framed mirrors at each styling station.

Savannah crossed her legs resolutely in one of the buttery-soft cream-colored leather salon chairs, her hair half-styled with smooth, glossy curls cascading down her back and the rest still pinned up, and tried not to glance at her phone on the small, narrow countertop in front of her. She hadn't answered Emersyn's calls yesterday or responded to her texts begging to see her, yet she was slightly annoyed that her phone today was so silent. *And* she was annoyed that she felt annoyed by it. She took a deep breath and took a small sip of champagne from the glass flute in her hand before brushing an imaginary stray hair off her dark blue skinny jeans.

Arissa was perched beside her in the next styling station, a mimosa in one hand, as she flipped through a fashion magazine in her lap and waited patiently for her stylist to finish sectioning her hair for the elaborate chignon she'd requested.

"So," Arissa said carefully. She glanced in the mirror at Savannah and then at Mia, Erica, and Kayla, all at their own styling stations in varying states of wedding hairstyles. "I'm just going to address it. Has anyone heard from Emersyn?"

Savannah felt herself tighten reflexively, but she didn't meet her questioning gaze.

"Not a word," Mia said from across the small salon as her stylist clamped a hot hair straightener down sections of her brown hair. "I texted her last night after the rehearsal dinner just to let her know we missed her. I got nothing back."

"She's been radio silent in the group chat too," Arissa mused as she glanced down at her own phone.

Erica took a deep breath, and Savannah could feel her dark eyes land on her. "She was pretty shaken yesterday when I ran into her in the lobby." She paused, as if wondering how much to share. "Something happened and she's really devastated." Erica's gaze didn't leave Savannah's face in the mirror and she wondered if Erica was mainly talking to her or to the entire group.

"I hope she's okay." Mia wrinkled her nose. "Nothing with her mom or anything at home, right?"

Erica shrugged and sighed. "No, nothing like that. Nothing with Nancy."

Mia looked confused, like she wanted to ask more, so Savannah shifted slightly in her chair. "She's fine," she said flatly, keeping her gaze trained on the edge of the mirror. "Probably needs some space, that's all."

Arissa raised an eyebrow at her uncharacteristic tone. "You sure?" she ventured cautiously. "You two have been pretty inseparable most of this trip."

"That doesn't mean anything," Savannah said quickly and then bit her lip. "I mean, I think her fiancé is here now, so she probably just wants some time with him." Tendrils of jealousy wrapped around her heart as she tried to forget Jared's cluelessly handsome face when he looked between them, bewildered.

Erica met her gaze in the mirror and pressed her lips together. "From what I understand, he left today," she said evenly. "And she had no idea he was coming."

"That's sweet," Mia said. "He surprised her out of the blue? God, I wish I could meet a man with a romantic bone still in his body like that."

Erica grimaced as Savannah's gaze narrowed. "Well, whatever it is," Savannah said as she shrugged one shoulder and took a sip of her champagne. "That girl has stuff to figure out." She wished she felt as indifferent as the cool ice in her tone.

"That girl, Savannah, really?" Erica shot back. "Emersyn has talked to me a lot on this trip about a *lot* of things, but most of it has revolved around you. Stop pretending like you don't care."

A low murmur floated over the salon as Arissa squeezed Savannah's hand. "And Savannah has been talking to me too, coincidentally most of it revolving around Emersyn," she said coolly. "She's hurting, Erica. She's allowed to feel that."

Savannah reached over to the champagne bottle balancing precariously in a silver ice bucket on a tray between them and topped off her glass. "Of course I care, Erica," she said. "I'm just…" She clenched her jaw. "I'm not going to chase her. I'm pissed, that's all. I spent the entire afternoon yesterday hiking alone at Mount Solmar because I had to get out of this resort. Emersyn told me one thing and then a day later Jared is stepping out of her shower in a towel? Please. I'm done hoping she figures it all out. I actually let myself *believe* this time she was ready and that she knew it was real too."

The salon was quiet for a moment as Mia exchanged an incredulous glance of surprise with Kayla, who nodded in silent confirmation. Only the low hum of the hair dryers, the distant crash of waves through an open window, and soft, instrumental spa music filled the background.

"She *is* figuring it out." Erica's tone was gentler. "Emersyn had broken things off with Jared, and he flew out as a last-ditch attempt to salvage their engagement. She didn't invite him. She wouldn't lie to me about that and she *definitely* wouldn't lie to you. She's trying, Savannah."

Savannah leaned back in her chair and glanced in the mirror as her hairstylist returned with a steaming curling iron and a large can of hairspray. She realized too late that she was gripping her champagne glass so tightly, her knuckles were turning white.

I'm not going to cry. Not here. Not when all of my teammates and friends are sitting there looking at me in the mirror with that quiet sympathy. The soft smile of understanding that Arissa flashed her made it even harder to pretend she didn't feel everything all at once, and that beneath it she wasn't still aching for Emersyn in her arms.

"Emersyn has been hiding from it for a long time," Arissa said quietly, as the other girls turned back to their own phones and hushed chatter. "If we get a moment, you should talk to her tonight. You don't have to keep pretending what you two have doesn't mean anything."

"I'm not." Savannah's shoulders stiffened. No matter how hard she tried to put up the cool, composed, and totally in control front she usually perfected, she knew they could all see through the cracks and splinters around the edges. "Really, I'm fine," she said, softer this time. "It's Kay and Diana's day, and that's what matters."

Arissa glanced down at her mimosa but didn't say anything more. Instead, she trained her gaze on herself in the mirror. Savannah knew she was letting her carry her heartbreak with dignity until she was ready to say more, to stop pretending like her chest didn't pound with a slow ache and her heart wasn't shattered.

As the hairstylist unpinned the top layer of Savannah's hair and gently ran an organic smoothing oil through it, she tried not to wonder what Emersyn was doing, where she was, what she was thinking, or how she was feeling. She swallowed hard as she lifted her champagne glass and drained the last of the bubbly in one quick sip, as if to ward away the tiny shadow of something much deeper that wound itself around her chest. It kept whispering one thing over and over again:

I miss her already.

❖

That evening, Savannah nearly lost her breath as she strolled into the private outdoor ceremony space that had been roped off along a quiet stretch of beach around a corner of the resort. The setting sun was large and bold over the ocean, its rays flashing like molten amber across the horizon and settling over the still water. Rows of whitewashed bamboo chairs neatly lined either side of a light pink linen aisle stretched over the white sand. The bamboo arch, the rows of chairs, and the aisle were all somewhat shaded by a large, heavy light pink canopy that swayed gently in the evening breeze from where it was supported by four tall, narrow wooden beams. Large string lights hung from the breezy canopy and matching spherical-shaped golden lanterns lined smaller beams around the arch, as the floral scented candles inside them added a pleasant scent to the salty air. Blooming white orchids and bright pink hibiscus arrangements were hung from the back of each chair as soft, instrumental music emanated from hidden speakers designed to look like small boulders jutting from the sand. Everything inside the ceremony space was elegant but simple, classy, and immaculately arranged.

Savannah quietly took her seat in the second row next to Arissa and Zoe. They quickly whispered hellos and Savannah hoped she looked far more composed and controlled than she felt inside. She had opted for a tailored suit that evening, with her cropped, cream-colored skinny pants and sleeveless white silk blouse an ideal choice for an outdoor beach wedding. The ruffled collar of her blouse fluttered in the breeze as she turned to hang her matching fitted blazer around her chair. It was still so warm outside that she wasn't sure she would wear it at all.

"This is beautiful," Savannah whispered as she looked around once more.

Arissa nodded as she slid her fingers into Zoe's and rested their joined hands on her date's lap. Savannah felt a slight twinge of *something* at the casual show of affection and wished not for the first time that evening that Emersyn was there with her. Technically, she was but Savannah knew it wasn't the same. The iceberg between them was too massive. As others filtered in, greeting one another warmly and finding seats, Savannah's gaze kept straying to the stone path between the crop of palm trees that led to the roped-off ceremony space. Despite her best efforts not to think about Emersyn, Savannah couldn't help but notice that she hadn't arrived yet.

It doesn't matter. She turned, facing forward once more, as a light breeze brushed her loose curls over her shoulder. Nearly everyone had taken off their shoes once they reached the sand and Savannah had done the same. She gently nudged her brown leather stilettos, the gold buckle on the ankle straps glinting in the low light, beneath her chair and fought the urge to crane her neck as more guests entered the ceremony space.

I'm over it. I'm just here to support Kay and Diana, and then we'll all go our separate ways. We're adults. We can get through it.

Savannah felt the sensitive skin along the back of her neck prickle with knowing. Before she turned, she knew she was there. Erica and Kayla, who had just sat down two rows behind them, confirmed it when she heard Erica call out to her.

"Hey, Em!" Erica's voice rose above the gentle conversation. "We saved you a seat."

Savannah turned before she even realized what she was doing, and all her resolve shattered. Emersyn was positively radiant in an effortless short-sleeved peach-colored dress. Its neckline plunged just enough to tease soft cleavage and the hem fluttered around her legs just below her knees with each step. A thin gold choker glinted at the base of her throat and her brown slingback pumps barely sank into the soft sand as she strode down the aisle. For a brief, tantalizing moment, Savannah imagined Emersyn walking down the aisle to her, locking her fingers into her own like Arissa and Zoe, and greeting her with a wide smile and a gentle press of her lips to hers.

As Emersyn stopped short, hesitating as she glanced between Erica and Savannah, she appeared to realize that sitting with them meant sitting two rows directly behind Savannah for the entirety of the ceremony. She didn't meet Savannah's gaze.

The brief fantasy shattered and felt like a punch to her gut as she realized she had forgotten how to breathe. Emersyn's straight blond hair was half-up, with a few pieces curling around her face, and her sun-kissed skin appeared to practically glow against her dress and thin gold hoop earrings. There was something just slightly different about her. There was an emanating confidence and settled self-assurance that Savannah picked up on.

"You okay?" Arissa murmured as she leaned over.

Savannah swallowed hard, but she couldn't tear herself away. "Not even close."

Emersyn turned and sat deliberately in an empty chair several rows back, despite Kayla scooting over and patting the chair next to her. As she sat, her gaze dropped to Savannah. Their eyes locked and Savannah felt a warm, cresting wave rush through her all the way across the ceremony. Primal heat, regret, hunger, desire, and deep love all coursed through her veins at once and when Emersyn blinked and looked away, the flaring ache in Savannah's chest took her breath once again.

"It'll be okay," Arissa reassured her. "She looks beautiful."

Savannah's throat tightened as she nodded her agreement. There were no words, and as the music transitioned and swelled, she was relieved she didn't have to respond. Everyone turned expectantly as Kay walked down the aisle first in a neatly pressed white-on-white tuxedo and light pink silk tie. A boutonniere of white jasmine and light pink hibiscus sprayed across one side of her tailored jacket as she took her place barefoot near the arch and turned with an expectant smile toward the stone path.

After a few quiet moments, an instrumental version of "Here Comes the Bride" began slowly and then Diana emerged from the path. Savannah stood respectfully with the other guests and watched as Kay's eyes filled with tears as Diana slowly stepped toward her. They were only looking at each other, their gazes locked as Diana walked down the aisle, and Savannah realized she understood that exact love deep in her soul—because the only thing she wanted more than anything else in the world, the person she craved so badly it ached, was sitting several rows behind her. The heat inside her swelled, burning her with longing, as she realized everyone had been exactly right: She was in love all over again with Emersyn Tanner.

Chapter Twenty-eight

Emersyn stood to the side of the banquet room near the bar as she curled her fingertips tighter around the glass of pinot grigio she had barely sipped. The reception was in the same banquet room as the cocktail party, though the energetic, pulsing vibe was much different. Colored lights flashed over the dance floor as guests swayed to pop music and all the windows in the banquet room had been thrust open to let in the scents of salt, hibiscus, and coconut oil clinging in the air. Emersyn could see the dark shimmer of the ocean outside the large glass windows and she could hear the waves between songs from the DJ.

As Emersyn turned, feeling slightly out of place, her gaze landed on Savannah across the room. The slow-burning heat started low in her stomach again as she tried not to stare. Her sleeveless silk blouse emphasized her toned, golden arms and her loose curls cascaded down her back as she laughed at something Arissa's date said. She held her champagne glass close to her, the strong, confident curve of her spine practically begging for Emersyn's fingertips to trail along her warm skin, as she leaned in to hear whatever it was that Zoe was saying.

All night, it had been like this. Emersyn would spot Savannah and her gaze would linger. Savannah would glance over her shoulder slowly and deliberately, her dark eyes practically branding her, and the undeniable magnetic pull would tighten. Emersyn's chest would ache and the warmth would seep everywhere inside her, and then Savannah would turn away blinking, her jaw tight and her shoulders tense.

"You good?" Erica sidled up to Emersyn and followed her gaze. "You know, you're not being nearly as subtle as you think you are." She shrugged before shoving her hands into the pockets of her suit pants. "But

I'll tell you that when you walked into that ceremony, Savannah couldn't stop looking at you. Even a few minutes ago when you were ordering your wine, she was looking over here like she wanted to pin you to that big glass window." Erica gestured with her cocktail glass to the floor-to-ceiling windows.

"This is torture," Emersyn said glumly. "There hasn't really been an opportunity to approach her. And I don't want to cause any drama at Kay and Diana's wedding."

Erica smiled as she slid her empty glass onto the bar. "Look at all these people here." She gestured to the throngs of well-dressed guests throughout the banquet room. "No one is paying any attention. Asking Savannah to talk isn't causing drama." She paused again. "But, while you work up your courage, why don't we go dance for a little bit? Seriously, I can't get Kayla *off* the dance floor. And, really, anything is better than lingering around the corner of the bar looking heartbroken."

Emersyn followed Erica's gaze and burst into laughter. Kayla was at the center of the dance floor, blue and green lights illuminating her face, as she twirled along with Shania Twain's "Man I Feel Like a Woman."

"You're right." Emersyn took a long swig of her wine and set the glass back onto the smooth bar. "Is it that obvious?"

Erica laughed. "Girl, you've been undressing Savannah with your eyes since dinner. *Yes*."

Heat flushed along Emersyn's exposed neck as she shook her hair off her shoulders. "Fine," she said decisively. She grabbed Erica's hand and tugged her toward the dance floor. "Let's go dance."

❖

Mia rolled her eyes dramatically. "You have *got* to go talk to her already," she said pointedly as she followed Savannah's gaze.

Arissa nodded her agreement. "You know, the longer you wait, the more Emersyn is going to think you really *don't* care about her. We're all leaving the day after tomorrow. You're going back to Phoenix. She's going back to Chicago. And then what? You're going to stalk her on social media instead?"

Savannah took a deep breath. "I don't stalk on social media." She watched Emersyn on the dance floor as she tossed her head back and moved her hips against a laughing Erica behind her.

"All I'm saying is why wait until it's too late?" Arissa said. "Especially when you can talk to her in person, *now*."

Savannah tried not to feel everything at once as the music pulsed low and sexy, an old R&B song spilling through the tall speakers, and Emersyn laughed as she and Kayla swayed against Erica. Golden light danced across her flushed face, her peach dress hugged her curves snugly as she moved slower, more sensually, and her hair fell over her shoulders, nearly begging for Savannah to fist her hands into it and claim Emersyn with a searing kiss.

"I'm just trying to figure out what I want to say," Savannah finally said as she glanced down and took a sip of champagne.

Arissa threw her hand up in frustration. "I don't know, how about 'Emersyn, I'm madly in love with you and I want to know what happened and how we misunderstood each other'?" She grinned. "Or, you know, 'I've been dying to take you back to my room, slam you against the wall, and make love to you until the sun comes up'?" She tilted her head in consideration. "Oh, that's good. If you don't use that, I will. On Zoe, of course."

Mia snickered. "Wait, Savannah, are you scared?"

Savannah rolled her eyes as she crossed her arms coolly. "Of course not," she said, though her heartbeat quickened at the sight of Emersyn so radiant and carefree on the dance floor. "I'm not scared of her or anyone or anything."

Arissa and Mia exchanged a look. "Except risking getting your heart shattered," Arissa said. "But we all know Emersyn. She has it *bad* for you."

"She left her fiancé, Savannah." Mia shook her head in disbelief. "So what if he decided to show up and try to fight for her? That just means she's worth it. And she *still* left him. If that doesn't say she's yours, I don't know what does."

Savannah's gaze narrowed as a wedding guest she hadn't seen before drifted a little too close to Emersyn. He grinned, a trickle of sweat dripping down his temple, as he slid behind her and placed a firm hand on her hip. Dark possessiveness bloomed hot and low in Savannah's core as she watched Emersyn smile politely and then turn, slipping firmly out of his grip.

Savannah sighed as something sharp twisted in her chest. *She* was supposed to be out there on the dance floor with Emersyn. It was supposed to be *her* body pressed up against hers, *her* hand on her hip, and Emersyn leaning back into *her* as they laughed breathlessly along with the music.

"I hate this feeling." Savannah set her glass resolutely on an empty linen-covered table. "I wasn't supposed to want her like this *again*."

Emersyn moved sensually, her hips rolling slowly, as Savannah felt her control slipping. Emersyn had always been the greatest temptation, and now all she could do was stand there with her heart practically throbbing with equal parts jealousy and desire.

"Go dance with her," Arissa said. "I'll go with you. Once Zoe is back from the bathroom, we can all go so it won't be so obvious."

Savannah dragged her gaze away from Emersyn as she clapped, carefree and beautiful, at Erica spinning Kayla. Too late, she knew that she didn't just want to dance with Emersyn, she wanted to claim her. Heat and pressure spiked between her thighs as she wondered what Emersyn would do if she grabbed her hand and led her into the quiet hallway, pressed her up against the cool wall, and slid her hands beneath her dress. She wanted Emersyn to gasp and moan her name, unraveling for her the way she always did when they made love and the rest of the world melted away, and the thought nearly undid her.

"I need to clear my head. And then I'll talk to her, I promise." Savannah glanced between Mia and Arissa. "Can you guys cover for me while I take a few?"

Mia nodded. "We got your back, Savannah. Just don't disappear for too long."

Savannah smiled gratefully as she slipped through the throngs of people that migrated along the dance floor. She needed to get out of there and think through what she wanted to say, before she instead did everything her body and heart were screaming at her to do: march onto the dance floor, take Emersyn's hand, and make it crystal clear who she would always belong to.

Chapter Twenty-nine

Breathless, Emersyn followed Erica and Kayla off the dance floor for a short break. They had been out there with groups of other guests for nearly thirty minutes and, though she was sweaty and flushed, she was grateful to Erica for encouraging her out there. The thumping beat of the pop song faded as they dropped into chairs at an empty table.

Instinctively, Emersyn glanced around the banquet room. She hadn't looked around for Savannah since she stepped onto the dance floor, instead opting to float away with the music and the evening, and it had temporarily cleared her head. After a moment, Emersyn craned her neck. Mia, Arissa, and Zoe stood near the dance floor, but there was no sign of Savannah. Kay and Diana were seated at the brides' table, chatting over refilled champagne glasses with a few members of Diana's immediate family. Emersyn's heartbeat quickened as she realized Savannah was gone.

"Hey, Em, want another glass of the pinot?" Erica stood and slowly stretched her long legs. She nodded toward the bar. "I'm grabbing another drink."

Emersyn shook her head as she scanned the room. No sign of Savannah. "I'm good, thanks," she said distractedly. "Did you see if Savannah left?"

Erica squinted as she glanced around the room. "No, I didn't. But I don't see her anywhere either."

Emersyn stood resolutely. Enough was enough, and she was going to find Savannah and tell her everything. Everything that everyone had been encouraging her to tell her forever, starting with the undeniable fact that she was hopelessly in love with her. "I'll be back. I'm...going to do a quick walk around."

Erica grinned. “Finally,” she said. “Take your time. We’ll be here if you need us.”

Emersyn threw a grateful smile over her shoulder as she weaved through groups of guests, her gaze sweeping every corner and every exit, as she migrated toward the large, arched double doors. As her mind drifted to the last time they had found each other outside the banquet room—when Emersyn had crushed her lips against Savannah’s in the quiet of the nearby bathroom and felt fire everywhere—she was distracted by a familiar voice calling out to her.

“Hey, Tanner.” Kay’s voice was calm and knowing as she slipped through a group of guests and gripped her wine glass in one hand. She smiled as she reached Emersyn just inside the doors to the banquet room. “Tanner, I think I know who you’re looking for.”

Emersyn hesitated for a beat. “I…Yeah,” she said, blowing her breath out. “I think she left.”

Kay glanced around. “She did. But from what Mia told me, she just stepped out for a few minutes to clear her head.” Kay cleared her throat as the music swelled behind them. “She looked like she was holding it together, but I’ll be honest with you, Tanner. She couldn’t stop watching you on the dance floor. You and I both know Sanchez, and she’s pure fire when it comes to something.” Kay winked. “Or *someone* she wants. My guess is she’s trying to pretend like it doesn’t matter, but whatever happened is killing her inside.”

Emersyn’s heart thudded. “I know I messed up, but I’m going to find her.” Her voice sounded more confident than she felt. “I’m going to fix it. I’m going to tell her everything, including exactly how I feel, even if it’s a little…messy.”

Kay placed a warm hand on Emersyn’s forearm. “Tanner, she has *always* wanted you,” she said. “I’ve always known you two have had a deep bond, even way back when I was coaching you both. And if I may, if it helps you at all, Sanchez has always wanted all of you. Not just the polished version—the high school star, the college basketball hero, the grown woman who ran away and found herself, *or* the adult who tried really hard to put it all behind her and fit into something she didn’t belong in. She wants the *real* you, Tanner. So, find her, go to her, fight for her, and *show* her how much you want her too.”

Emersyn blinked as Kay held her gaze for a moment. She wasn’t sure if it was because she used the same firm, heartfelt tone that she had always used when guiding her years ago or because Kay was usually never one for big, overt shows of emotion, but the urgency sank deep into Emersyn as she nodded her understanding.

"I'll be right back," she promised and then smiled softly. "I hope."

❖

Emersyn's heels echoed loudly on the polished marble floor of the lobby as she glanced around. The warm buzz of the reception, still in full swing inside the banquet room, clung to her skin, though the music, laughter, and celebration had faded into the distance. She had checked the bathroom, searched the hallway, scanned the empty beach path, and didn't see Savannah anywhere in the lobby either.

Frustrated, Emersyn dropped into an upholstered wicker armchair opposite the elevator bank. *Surely she didn't go all the way back to her room. After all, Kay had said she'd be back.*

As Emersyn took a deep breath, crossing one leg over the other, she tried to imagine where Savannah could have disappeared. She wondered if she'd gone all the way down to the beach. It didn't seem likely, but it was one of the last places to check that was still somewhat near the banquet room.

As Emersyn uncrossed her legs and reached down to slip off her heels in preparation for a long walk through the sand, realization dawned on her.

"The basketball court," she said as she stood. She smiled as she glanced down the hallway leading to the corridor housing the fitness center, tennis courts, and half-basketball court. "Of *course*."

Emersyn walked purposefully down the hallway and paused as she reached the heavy door to the half-court. The loud, rickety air conditioning was still blasting the inside and the large overhead lights gleamed against the shining hardwood.

Emersyn pushed the door open and then stopped short as her breath caught in her throat.

Savannah had her back to the door as she stood just behind the free throw line. Her blazer had been tossed to the side and her hair had been haphazardly pulled into a messy ponytail, but she stood tall, controlled, and devastatingly gorgeous in her sharp stiletto heels as she swished a perfect shot through the bright white net. Her sleeveless blouse was still tucked immaculately into her cropped skinny pants as she caught the ball in one fluid motion and bounced it once, twice, off the hardwood.

Emersyn couldn't move and couldn't speak as she watched Savannah dribble once more and then arch into another free throw. Savannah cursed lightly under her breath as the ball spun lazily around the iron and then rimmed out before bouncing loudly across the hardwood. Emersyn was sure she had never seen anything more gorgeous in her life. She was taken aback by the warm tears gathering in the corners of her eyes as her chest tightened with slow-churning emotion. Savannah was everything she had ever wanted. It may have taken her way too long to realize it, but she wasn't going to let her go now.

Emersyn felt a hot tear run down her cheek and catch at her jaw, but she didn't wipe it away. Instead, she stood just inside the doorway and watched Savannah turn, momentarily startled, as the door clicked shut behind her. Their gazes locked as Savannah held the ball casually under one arm, her dark eyes burning into Emersyn beneath her long lashes, as her chest rose and fell with her breath.

"So," Emersyn stretched the word as she took a tentative step forward. "Are you going to invite me to play or not?"

❖

For one long, excruciating moment, Savannah was sure her heart had stopped. Without a word or a breath of hesitation, she let the basketball drop from beneath her arm and bounce across the hardwood. She was already crossing the court in long strides that quickly closed the gap between her and Emersyn. There was only one thing she wanted to do, and it wasn't playing basketball. Savannah pulled Emersyn into her arms and met her lips fiercely and desperately, undoing every last shred of restraint that she had, as Emersyn's lips parted easily and her tongue slid gently against hers.

Savannah gripped her waist tightly and refused to let go of even an inch of Emersyn, who melted into her as she wound her arms around her neck and buried her fingers in her messy ponytail. After a few moments, the kiss slowed but remained deep as Savannah felt Emersyn shiver against her.

"You know, someone should really talk to you about proper footwear for playing basketball," Emersyn murmured through her grin. "Trust me, sports injuries are no joke."

Savannah rested her forehead against Emersyn's and closed her eyes as she felt a smile tugging at her lips. "I'll manage," she said softly. "I know a handful of great rehab gyms." She blinked as she ran her fingertips along Emersyn's cheek. "I thought I'd lost you. *Again.* I was going to find you tonight and talk to you, I just needed a…" She gestured lamely at the basketball hoop behind her.

Emersyn leaned forward and brushed her lips against Savannah's again. "I get it," she said. "I need to tell you everything, Savy."

Savannah nodded but kept Emersyn wrapped tightly in her arms. "Then tell me."

Emersyn swallowed hard as her lips ghosted down Savannah's jaw. "I don't even know where to begin," she admitted. "I broke things off with Jared. *Before* he took it upon himself to fly to Cabo in an attempt to work things out. The only thing I didn't tell him straight away was that I'm gay." She met Savannah's gaze. "And I'm sorry for that. But I promise you I *did* break things off before his arrival, though I understand if I had been totally upfront with him when breaking it off then I could've avoided his, um, surprise visit."

Savannah nodded again as she searched Emersyn's bright hazel eyes. Her heart pounded louder as she realized she saw only raw vulnerability and bare honesty reflected back at her.

"I came out to him anyway." Emersyn's voice broke as she curled her fingers in the ends of Savannah's ponytail. "I mean, I should have to begin with but obviously him showing up like that and even just the *idea* of losing you…" Emersyn bit her lip. "And I had a long video call with my mom. That's why I wasn't at the rehearsal dinner. I…I didn't know if I could face you yet and I needed time and space to finally talk to my mom once and for all. I meant it when I said I didn't want to hide from people anymore. I told them both the truth."

Savannah's hands tightened around Emersyn's hips as she pulled her closer, desperately wanting to anchor and ground her. "Baby, I'm so proud of you," Savannah said as her lips brushed her ear. "Those are huge steps. I'm so sorry I didn't hear you out before. I was too stubborn and I'll do better. I would never, ever want you to feel forced to do anything you weren't ready for—"

Emersyn shook her head vehemently. "It was time, Savannah. You mean too much to me. And that's why I not only told them I'm gay, but also that I'm in love with you. That I've *always* been in love with you."

Savannah felt pressure building behind her eyes as she kissed Emersyn again, slow and searing, and ran her fingertips along her spine soothingly. Emersyn's body melted into hers like it was always meant to be there as Savannah kissed her. She moved her hands up Savannah's back, her touch sure and reverent, as she clung to her.

"I love you, Emersyn," Savannah finally whispered against her lips. "I've always loved you so much. I don't want to be without you ever again."

Emersyn cupped Savannah's face gently, meeting her tear-filled gaze, and traced her cheeks with trembling fingers. "Then don't be," she said simply. "After all, you were right. You were always right. No matter how far apart we are or how much time has passed, I've always belonged to you. I don't want to be away from you anymore. I want to be *with* you, completely."

Savannah kissed softly down the line of Emersyn's jaw, lingering at the spot just behind her ear, before she brushed languid kisses down the column of her neck. She could already feel Emersyn unraveling in her arms as she gripped at her blouse and tilted her head to give her better access. Slow waves of heat ached between her thighs as she kissed Emersyn's warm skin.

"You're all mine," Savannah said. "You always have been."

Emersyn nodded as she met her lips again, surrendering to Savannah's kisses, and curled her fingertips into her back. "And I always will be, Savy."

Chapter Thirty

The door to Savannah's suite quietly clicked shut behind them as Emersyn inhaled the scent of coconut milk lotion and closed her eyes slowly. She turned halfway and blinked as Savannah stepped forward, her movements slow and deliberate, as she kicked off her heels. Emersyn swallowed hard as the pulse began low in her stomach and jolts of electricity sizzled through her and landed between her thighs. Savannah gently slid open the door to the balcony just a few inches, enough so the cool evening breeze could drift into the room and bring with it the scents of salt and night-blooming jasmine. Walking slowly back around the bed, Savannah gently traced Emersyn's jawline with her fingertips before carefully tilting her head upward.

"You have no idea what you do to me," Savannah said. She held Emersyn's gaze for a long moment before raking it over her body. "You're so beautiful."

Emersyn grinned as she kissed Savannah. "I think I do," she said breathlessly. "Because I feel the exact same way about you." When Emersyn kissed her again, she was kissing Savannah like she knew exactly what she wanted and she let herself feel every moment, every sensation of her lips teasing her own and their tongues gliding together. Emersyn yielded easily as Savannah slowly walked her backward without breaking their kiss and she realized her walls had long since crumbled under the simple knowledge that she loved Savannah—and she didn't want to fight it anymore.

Savannah's hands roamed down Emersyn's sides and slid around to the small of her back as she pulled her closer. As the back of Emersyn's thighs bumped gently against the edge of the bed, she was practically begging Savannah to take her and was completely lost in the sensations of her soft lips exploring her neck, her collarbone, and around her jaw. Just as Emersyn was sure her legs were going to begin trembling, Savannah eased her down onto the bed. She hovered above her, her hands tangling in Emersyn's hair, as she pulled back for just a moment. Emersyn recognized in her expression the dominant, confident fire melding with deep, passionate love as her gaze swept over Emersyn's prone body. She was propped up by her elbows and she knew her own gaze was heavy with longing, her lips already swollen from Savannah's deep kisses.

"Take this off." Savannah's fingertips teased along the thin short sleeve of her dress. "I want you. All of you."

Emersyn reached behind her and tugged the tiny silver zipper down as the body-hugging fabric loosened and slipped around her shoulders and chest. Savannah's hands skimmed up Emersyn's legs and lingered around the hem of her dress before she gently pulled it up and over her head, tossing it to the floor in a heap.

Savannah's gaze was reverent and dark with desire. "God, you're gorgeous." She arched an eyebrow. "And lucky, lucky me, because you're all mine."

Emersyn's head swam with desire, love, and passion, as Savannah bent over her and kissed her slowly. As the kiss deepened again, Savannah's hands explored every inch of her gently but surely. She could feel Savannah's lips turn up as she coaxed breathy gasps and soft moans from her while trailing her fingertips along her sides and softly kissing her neck, moving ever so slowly lower around the sides of her breasts over her bra. Emersyn couldn't help it; she arched into Savannah as her fingertips and lips teased dangerously close to her nipples, desperate for her to touch her there. Savannah carefully unclasped her bra with one hand as she pressed Emersyn to her, and she gasped at the sensation of Savannah's cool silk blouse against her bare, sensitive skin. Emersyn wriggled slightly beneath her, craving more, but Savannah seemed perfectly happy to once again take her time as she languidly teased and confidently reclaimed every inch of Emersyn's skin.

Savannah's lips were *so* agonizingly close to her nipple and her index finger was making a slow, teasing trail over the underwear that Emersyn knew was already soaked, her fingertip stilling over her clit and then brushing gentle, feather-light circles around it. Emersyn bit back a groan as her hips twitched into Savannah, so in need of more pressure and friction.

Savannah's soft lips tickled over Emersyn's nipple and curved up into a smile as Emersyn felt it tighten into a hardened bud in her warm mouth.

"Savannah," Emersyn half-panted and half-whined as the tip of Savannah's tongue drew a slow circle over her nipple.

Savannah's fingertips stilled from where they had been gently teasing Emersyn up and down over her underwear. "Say please."

Emersyn's breath caught in her throat, but then she felt Savannah pull her head back just a few centimeters as she waited. "Please," Emersyn's voice nearly broke. "Please, Savannah."

Savannah softly kissed Emersyn's nipple. "Please what, baby?"

Emersyn groaned in frustration and threw her arms over her head. "Please, please fuck me, Savannah," she moaned. "Make love to me. *Please* let me come."

Savannah's other hand gently smoothed up Emersyn's arms, leaving a trail of goose bumps in its wake, and clasped her wrists over her head. "Good girl. Let go for me." She kissed her nipple again. "I've got you."

Emersyn nodded as she sank further into the bed, surrendering to Savannah's touch, her mouth, her command, and bit back a groan as she brought Emersyn's sensitive nipple into her mouth, massaging and teasing it with her tongue. Each stroke of her fingertips over her soaked underwear was deliberately meant to unravel her and the massaging pressure of her tongue on her nipple was slowly pulling her apart and making her come undone beneath her.

Jolts of pleasure from Savannah's tongue skyrocketed the pressure between her thighs, as Emersyn arched her hips further into Savannah. Still, she kept her fingertips just gentle enough over her clit to tease and unravel but not nearly enough to let her come. Emersyn let herself feel everything as she whispered Savannah's name like a prayer and wriggled out of her grasp just enough to free her arms and wrap them around Savannah's shoulders.

Savannah glanced up at her with a smile. "You're lucky I'm not staying right here for long." She glanced between Emersyn's thighs to let her know *exactly* where she was shifting next. "Next time, I might have to tie you to the bed."

Warm wetness pooled between her thighs at Savannah's suggestive promise. Somehow, the idea of her wrists being bound to the bed while Savannah took her time teasing every inch of her body made her wetter than she could ever remember being in her life—except the other times she was intimate with Savannah.

Before she could form a coherent thought, Savannah scooted lower, kneeling on the floor, as her mouth nibbled at the sensitive curve of her hip. Emersyn reached down instinctively and threaded her fingers through Savannah's hair as she brushed soft kisses over her inner thigh. Her lips grazed over Emersyn's underwear as she slid them down her thighs and tossed them somewhere in the direction of her rumpled dress. As Savannah's lush mouth hovered over her, her tongue slowly ran the length of Emersyn and teased her already swollen folds.

Emersyn desperately arched her hips at the same time that Savannah brought her clit into her warm mouth and slid a finger inside her. Emersyn realized too late that the desperate moans were coming from her as Savannah's mouth and tongue gently increased the tickling pressure, building coiled waves inside her. Savannah gently slid another finger inside her, curling it just enough to relentlessly tease that ultra-sensitive spot inside her, as her tongue teased her entrance before running over her clit and back again. Emersyn's thighs trembled with Savannah between them as the pressure grew tighter, feeling *so* intoxicatingly good as she realized her wetness was all over her thighs as Savannah's fingers teased a rhythm inside her.

As Savannah brought her clit into her mouth again, the sucking pressure combined with her soft, sure tongue sent Emersyn hurtling over the edge. Her entire body shook as she came, gasping Savannah's name and clenching around her until she was sated and soft, and she sank further into the bed as she tried to catch her breath. Emersyn was sure she saw stars as she gazed up at the ceiling and then at Savannah, who slid onto the bed to pull the sheets tight around them both.

Emersyn rolled over so she was facing her and buried herself in Savannah's chest as she traced her fingertips idly along the gentle line of Savannah's collarbone.

"I love you." Emersyn's voice was raw and she was dizzy with the warm afterglow.

Savannah gently tipped her chin up so Emersyn met her gaze, filled with unguarded tenderness. "I love you too."

She pressed a soft kiss to Emersyn's lips and ran her fingertips down her bare spine. "You're everything to me. I'll never let you go again."

Finally, Emersyn's breathing slowed. She was too warm, too comfortable in Savannah's arms as she understood it was the safest place she'd ever been. Savannah shifted so Emersyn was lying on top of her, her head curled into her neck, as the quiet sound of slow waves filled the still room.

After a moment, Emersyn shifted, her thigh arching between Savannah's legs, and she grinned at the heat against her bare skin through Savannah's pants. She shifted again, increasing the pressure, and heard Savannah's soft moan cut through the darkness of the room.

Emersyn hovered over her, teasing Savannah's warm skin beneath her rumpled, untucked blouse, and skimmed her hands along her bare stomach. Silvery moonlight spilled through the balcony door as she kissed Savannah's neck.

"You okay?" Savannah tangled her fingers in the ends of Emersyn's hair.

"So much more than okay," Emersyn said against her skin. She tightened her thigh between Savannah's thighs as her breath hitched. "But I want to make *you* come undone now."

Savannah smiled lazily as a gentle breeze swept through the room, though her gaze darkened with desire all over again. "Is that so?"

Emersyn nodded as she slid Savannah's pants and underwear down her smooth legs until they dropped off the edge of the bed. Savannah watched her quietly as she let Emersyn undress her. Emersyn moved up again until she was straddling Savannah's thighs and gently unbuttoned each tiny pearl button on her sleeveless blouse. The molten feeling of hot skin on hot skin, their centers gently gliding and pressing against each other, sent a surge of desire through Emersyn as she wondered how many orgasms Savannah would make her have that night.

As Emersyn finished unbuttoning Savannah's blouse, she pressed her palms flat against her toned stomach and kissed Savannah softly and then deeper, slower, as she rolled her hips against her.

Savannah moaned as Emersyn gently rolled her hips again. "Ride me." Savannah's voice was filled with need. "I want to watch you lose control on top of me."

Emersyn was no longer sure which slick wetness was hers and which was Savannah's as she shifted her hips and gasped as they glided gently together. Emersyn swallowed hard as she moved against Savannah with slow, intoxicating rhythm and felt her hips arch further into her.

Savannah gripped her hips, steadying her, as her head fell back onto the pillow. "That's it, baby. Just like that, love."

The tension was winding tightly between them as pleasure spiked in slow-building waves. They pressed and moved against one another, lost in the warm, slick wetness that slipped between them as their centers each massaged the other, and their low moans and soft sighs filled the air.

"Look at me." Savannah cupped Emersyn's cheek. "I want to watch you fall apart."

Emersyn, already sensitized, trembled as her gaze locked with Savannah's and she let go completely. Waves after endless waves of cresting pleasure coursed through her onto Savannah, who dug her fingers into her hips as she arched and shook silently against Emersyn. As the aftershocks dissipated, Emersyn collapsed onto Savannah and they tangled breathlessly in the sheets.

Savannah laughed lightly as Emersyn buried herself in her chest again and brushed her lips along the curve of her breasts.

"I can feel your heart pounding," Savannah exclaimed softly as she tightened her arms around Emersyn.

Emersyn shook her head slowly. "I've never…multiple times in a row…" she stammered, her head still fuzzy and her body sated. "Except with you…"

"It's okay, baby." Savannah smoothed her palm along Emersyn's bare arm. "You're all mine now, so you will. You'll get used to it."

Emersyn laughed as her eyes drifted shut and the gentle ocean breeze caressed her warm skin. "So sure of yourself, Miss Thing," she said. "But I think I can get used to that." She fought a yawn. "Besides, I always *was* yours."

Chapter Thirty-one

Early morning sunlight filtered through the still partially open balcony door and danced across the soft white sheets tangled around Savannah and Emersyn. The gentle hum of the ocean in the distance made it even more difficult for Savannah to wake, but she stirred after a long moment and blinked against the bright white sunlight. Emersyn was wrapped in her arms, her bare back pressed to Savannah's naked front, and their legs around each other. Savannah sat up slightly as her gaze swept over Emersyn, all blond hair spilling across the pillow and lips slightly parted in deep, relaxed sleep after a long night of release.

Savannah didn't want to move. She relished the feeling of Emersyn's slow, steady breaths against her chest and inhaled the faint scent of her jasmine-tinged perfume. Last night, the darker and more possessive part of her wanted to push just hard enough that Emersyn would finally let go and let herself fall into her, giving Savannah her heart, body, and vulnerability while trusting that she would love her and keep her safe. It had been intoxicating to feel Emersyn finally let go and the still-fresh memory rolled between her thighs with a soft ache.

After a quiet moment, Savannah dipped her head to brush a soft kiss along Emersyn's bare shoulder. Emersyn turned slightly, though her eyes remained closed.

"Morning, love." Savannah ran her fingertips along Emersyn's jaw. "You awake?"

Emersyn shifted again and blinked lazily. "Nope." She stretched and then tightened Savannah's arm around her middle. "What time is it?"

Savannah laughed as she reached for her phone and squinted at the small screen. "Oh, shit."

"What?" Emersyn groaned as she stretched back into Savannah. "Don't say 'oh, shit' like that unless it's an emergency."

Savannah dropped her phone back onto the nightstand and leaned over to press a kiss to Emersyn's temple. "We slept through my alarm. We're supposed to meet everyone downstairs for the farewell brunch in fifteen minutes."

Emersyn sat up quickly and pulled the sheet around her. "Oh, shit!"

They laughed as they breathlessly hurried around Savannah's suite and tried to get some semblance of ready while shaking off the heavy, relaxed sleep. Savannah's heart raced as she quickly tried to smooth her hair into a casual ponytail and then met Emersyn's gaze in the mirror.

"I don't suppose there's enough time to run to my room for clothes." Emersyn tapped her index finger to her lips. "But there's no way I'm showing up in the same dress I wore last night, only ten times more wrinkled and reeking of last night's perfume. I may as well tape a sign to my back that says 'I spent all night having amazing sex with Savannah Sanchez.'"

Savannah tilted her head and pretended to consider that. "I mean, I don't *hate* that idea…" She replied with a laugh as Emersyn rolled her eyes. "Okay, okay. Grab whatever you need from the closet or in my suitcases. I can't promise it won't be a little long on you, but it'll be better than wearing last night's dress." She quickly ran her mascara wand through her lashes. "Or a sign announcing all the non-sports cardio you did last night."

Emersyn grinned as she stepped forward, wrapping her arms around Savannah's waist, and pressed a quick kiss to the back of her shoulder. As she yanked open the door to the small closet and flicked through Savannah's neatly-hung clothes, she grabbed a brush and ran it through her hair with her other hand.

"I swear this resort is, like, magical or something," Emersyn called over her shoulder. "Dulce Sueños. No kidding. Now I get it. It's like time doesn't exist."

"I mean, we *did* do our very best to make up for all the lost time last night," Savannah said as she quickly stepped into a sleeveless tan floral sundress and buckled its thin belt around her middle.

Emersyn grabbed a bright red Ralph Lauren minidress decorated with splashes of bold tropical flowers. Savannah's minidress was long enough on Emersyn to brush her knees. "You're impossible." She tilted her head and softly brushed a kiss over Savannah's lips. "And I love it."

"And you're beautiful." Savannah paused to deepen the kiss. "If we're going to be late, we may as well be late together. Let's go show everyone what *finally* looks like."

As they slipped out of Savannah's suite a few minutes later, their fingers tangling together as they headed for the elevator bank, Savannah felt a flushing wave of something deep and content bloom inside her chest. She and Emersyn were real and this was their new, long-awaited reality. No more hiding. No more pretending they weren't meant to belong to each other.

Savannah pressed the elevator call button. A shiver raced up her spine as Emersyn casually leaned her head on her shoulder while they waited. This was exactly right.

❖

The private open-air terrace at the resort's other sit-down restaurant was surrounded on two sides by floor-to-ceiling glass walls, with the wall facing the beach open to the sea breeze and sounds of the ocean. The scent of strong, fresh coffee greeted Emersyn before they stepped through the entrance, drifting from slow ceiling fans that lazily rotated overhead, as she glanced over the long, white-washed communal wooden tables arranged in the middle of the private terrace. As expected, everyone was already there and a few people had plates stacked high with thick slices of mango and pineapple, soft round pancakes, crispy bacon, heaps of scrambled eggs, and chilaquiles smothered in queso and salsa verde. Emersyn's stomach growled loudly as she nodded at Kay and Diana sitting next to each other at the head of the table, their hands intertwined, as they fed each other samples of the food.

The low buzz of upbeat conversation seemed to still as heads turned expectantly at their arrival. Everyone appeared to blink at their hand-in-hand entrance as Emersyn and Savannah slid onto an end of the bench next to one another.

"Oh my God, *finally*," Erica crowed. "Come on, it took you two long enough. Now spill!"

Emersyn flushed as she squeezed Savannah's hand beneath the table. Savannah, ever unbothered, glanced around with an amused smile.

Kay raised her mimosa and winked. "We should've started taking bets on when you two would get it together already. Happy to see you both here."

Arissa sipped her mimosa and glanced over the top of the laminated drink menu. "Really, I thought it would take at least one more overly dramatic misunderstanding," she said dryly before meeting Savannah's eyes. "Proud of you, Savy."

Savannah laughed. "And here I thought we were so subtle."

Mia snorted as she bit into an oversized strawberry. "Not even close. And I would've figured it out a whole lot sooner if I hadn't been laid up with food poisoning for half the trip."

As the table erupted into laughter, Savannah rested her hand lightly along Emersyn's thigh beneath the table, sending sparks of anticipation through her veins.

"I can't believe I waited this long," Emersyn said, turning to Savannah. "It feels amazing. Being with you is everything I ever wanted."

Savannah leaned in close as her lips brushed Emersyn's ear. "You're here now. And we have forever to go."

Arissa, who had caught the last part of Savannah's words, glanced at her and shook her head as she took another sip of her mimosa. "Yup, you're definitely talking like someone who just had amazing sex."

Emersyn laughed as she gratefully accepted the glass of ice water that Mia had poured for her from a sweating pitcher. "No comment."

Erica, who hadn't heard Arissa's comment, rolled her eyes from the other end of the table. "Already with the whispering? So, tell me, Em. Did Savannah officially ask you out or was it more of a 'you're mine now' situation?"

Emersyn squeezed Savannah's hand again. "A little of both, honestly."

"Damn." Erica shook her head as she shoveled a forkful of scrambled eggs into her mouth. "Savannah, you do not play when it comes to what's yours."

"Never," Savannah said with a grin and then turned her attention to Arissa. "Speaking of asking out, where's Zoe?"

Arissa sighed as she twisted the stem of her mimosa glass between her fingertips. "Early flight back to Raleigh this morning. She's probably halfway there by now."

Savannah placed her hand atop Arissa's. "Tell me you two are keeping in touch. I know I'm not the only one who has it bad for someone."

Arissa's lips quirked up into a small grin as she squeezed Savannah's fingers. "Yes," she finally said, her expression giddy. "She was texting me from the airport this morning and we *might* have plans next month for her to spend the weekend in Atlanta."

Savannah arched an eyebrow. "You might or you do?"

"We do. She's amazing, Savy." Arissa sighed dreamily. "I'd be lying if I said I can't wait to see her again."

Savannah squealed with excitement as she rushed around the table and hugged Arissa. "Oh my God, that's amazing!" she exclaimed. "I'm so happy for you. We really did figure our shit out day by day, minute by minute, didn't we?"

Arissa laughed and leaned into the hug. "I guess we did." She glanced at Emersyn and grinned.

"All right, all right," Kay called out over the din of laughter and clinking silverware and plates. She paused as the buzz of conversation died down and then cleared her throat. "I wanted to say a few words on behalf of myself and my beautiful bride." She gestured at Diana. Her voice was warm, but still carried the confident, authoritative coach's tone that everyone at the table knew so well. Kay's gaze caught Emersyn's and the smile on her face deepened with something proud and tender. "I've had the privilege of being surrounded by such incredible women throughout my life. From coaching all of you as college kids to becoming genuine friends as adults, it has been one of the greatest honors of my life to guide you, teach you, and to now share these moments with you."

Diana gently squeezed Kay's hand. "You've inspired me, you've challenged me, you've kept my firm belief in the future of women's sports alive knowing it's in the best hands, *your* hands. There have even been times when you've driven me to an early happy hour." She looked at Emersyn pointedly as everyone laughed. "Now, entering this next chapter of life, I wanted you all to be the first to know that I'm announcing my retirement. It's official. This coming season will be my last."

Diana's mouth fell open and her eyes filled with proud tears as everyone around the table applauded and raised their glasses to Kay. Kay laughed as she leaned over to press a kiss to Diana's lips. "I mean it this time!" She wagged her finger warningly. "No comebacks. This is it. I have every confidence that the program is going to be in excellent hands with Coach Connor, who has been more than ready to step into this role for years." Kay raised her glass to Jane Connor, who raised hers back. "In fact, she's probably ecstatic now wondering if this day would ever come or if I'd be coaching until I'm in a wheelchair."

After a moment, Kay glanced affectionately around the table and Emersyn was wondering if a lifetime of memories was flooding her mind's eye as she looked around at them. "So, all of that to say," Kay finished, her voice soft but gruff with emotion. "As much as I may have helped you grow in certain areas of your life, you have all helped me grow too. Thank you for letting me be a small part of your journeys. You've made mine absolutely unforgettable."

As Kay eased herself back into her chair, grinning as Diana threw her arms around her neck and kissed her cheek, applause rose over the table again. Erica held a hand over her mouth and whistled before holding up her glass of grapefruit juice. "To Coach Hanlon!"

The rest of the table followed suit, lifting their glasses in near unison, and echoed Erica's toast. A dozen "To Coach Hanlons!" drifted across the terrace as Kay's face reddened. Emersyn couldn't be sure and it was far too quick to truly know, but she thought she caught a flash of something watery at the corners of her eyes before she turned to affectionately kiss the top of Diana's head resting on her shoulder. She met Kay's gaze once more across the table and they regarded each other for a long, fond moment that was filled with everything where the words stopped: Gratitude, celebration, pride, legacy, finality, and tenderness.

Emersyn leaned over slightly, out of earshot of the rest of the table, just enough that she knew Kay would hear.

"Thanks, Coach," she said. "For giving me everything."

As the conversation around the table swirled, Emersyn was still all too aware of Savannah's hand resting lightly on her thigh. She felt a swell of pride as she looked around the table. She would miss her friends immensely, the women who always knew who she was and loved her still, the teammates who had never given up on her, and the people who continued to have her back even after years of lost contact, as they all checked out later that evening to return to their regularly scheduled adult lives across the country. This time, Emersyn promised herself, she wouldn't lose any of them again.

She stole a glance at Savannah, her full lips curved into a smile as she listened attentively to something Mia was gesturing incredulously about, and fought the urge to plant a soft kiss on her jaw. *And I* especially *won't lose her again.*

EPILOGUE—ONE YEAR LATER

Emersyn padded barefoot onto the cool tile as she tied her hair up into a loose knot and surveyed the stacks of neatly labeled cardboard boxes before her. Her worn black Tegan and Sara tour T-shirt was already sticking to her shoulder blades in the relentless dry Arizona heat, but the scent of takeout sushi and tempura wafted through Savannah's house. *Their* house.

Emersyn glanced down at her old T-shirt with a smile as she recalled Savannah on the rideshare home from El Gato Azul, just over a year ago. *Weren't you wildly obsessed with Tegan and Sara?* It was a reminder that she had always known and seen Emersyn in a way that so few others did, and it still made her heart practically skip a beat that they had made it to here. Now.

Savannah took a sip of sparkling water from where she leaned casually against the granite kitchen island and strode over to her. "You know," she said as she brushed her lips against Emersyn's temple. "You could just let the movers handle the boxes while we enjoy this very delicious, perfectly prepared sushi."

Emersyn put her hands on the hips of her short denim cut-off shorts and looked around again. Boxes of all sizes displayed small white stickers with Emersyn's handwriting: Clothes, Electronics, Northwoods memorabilia, and more. "I *am* letting them handle the boxes," she insisted playfully. "I'm just…coaching in the background."

Savannah laughed as she slipped her arms around Emersyn's waist and rested her chin on her shoulder. "Coaching even when you're not coaching. How on-brand of you."

Emersyn leaned back into Savannah's arms. Her carefully curated ranch-style home was slowly being taken over by a storm of Emersyn, from her casual Nikes kicked off near the front door and her boxes slowly taking up an entire corner of the living room to the faint scent of her cherry-almond shampoo lingering along Savannah's smooth, satin-encased pillows. "You're sure you're okay with…" Emersyn gestured around. "All this?"

Savannah brushed a kiss over Emersyn's cheek. "Baby, it's been a year of back-and-forth long distance. I know you were able to spend a lot of time here last summer before the school year, but not being able to see you…" She trailed soft kisses down Emersyn's neck. "Or kiss you." She tightened her arms around Emersyn's waist. "Or hold you or laugh with you all the time has been torture. We'll figure it out. We always have."

Emersyn turned in her arms as her face lit up. "Speaking of coaching, my second interview with Eagle Ridge Prep is next week. I have a really good feeling. It's an assistant coaching position for varsity, but the head coach and I really clicked, you know? We debated over Steve Nash versus Allen Iverson versus Jason Kidd and who the *real* point god of the aughts was for almost fifteen minutes before we even got to the interview questions. Honestly, she almost reminds me of a slightly younger Kay."

Savannah grinned. "Then the position should be as good as yours. Any school would be lucky to have you."

Emersyn rolled her eyes but couldn't hide her grin. "You kind of *have* to say that, Savy."

Savannah kissed her lips. "Maybe. But you're brilliant when it comes to basketball and I love you way too much to *not* hype you up."

Emersyn met her lips again in a soft, lingering kiss that grounded her in a now-familiar cloud of peaceful bliss. The last year hadn't always been easy. The remainder of the previous summer break had been feasible enough, with Emersyn flexible to visit Savannah in Phoenix a handful of times before the school year began. Jared had moved into a long-term temporary rental near the hospital and Emersyn had stayed in the condo while they listed it for sale. Her half of the proceeds from the sale had given her enough to keep her secure for now and afloat financially, as the following summer rolled around and she and Savannah made the easy decision to merge their lives fully and completely. Resigning from her role at Crestfield Academy had been bittersweet but necessary if she was going to relocate to Phoenix and immerse her life into Savannah's, which was finally beginning to slow again after a rapid four-gym expansion throughout the Phoenix metropolitan area.

"Oh," Savannah said, as if remembering something. "Don't forget my parents invited us for dinner tomorrow night. Lisa Sanchez is ecstatic to see you again. Besides, it might be a nice break from all the unpacking."

Emersyn laughed. "You mean your *mom*?" she said. "I can't wait. She's the best. And so is your dad. Where are we meeting them again?"

"This new tapas place that opened downtown." Savannah poured soy sauce into a small dish and set it at the center of the tall, square pub-style kitchen table. "I think it's called Luna del Sol or something. You'll love it. The reviews say good sangria, intimate ambiance, and ceviche that will change your life."

Emersyn's face lit up. "Perfect."

The drifting scent of the takeout was too much to resist. She slid onto the chair as Savannah sat across from her.

"Your mom texted me earlier too," Savannah said as she popped a piece of her Philadelphia roll into her mouth.

"Wait, she texted *you*?" Emersyn asked incredulously. "Since when does Nancy Tanner reach out to you before she reaches out to me?" Her teasing tone belied her mock wounding.

"You mean your *mom*?" Savannah teased Emersyn back. "And isn't it Nancy Morris now, since she and Peter eloped last month?"

Emersyn shook her head ruefully as she took a slow sip from her glass of water. "I think you're right. I'm still getting used to the new surname. But really, they're too cute. Do you know he surprises her with fresh flowers every Monday morning? Like clockwork. He says he wants to give her a bright start to each week." Emersyn shook her head again, this time in amazement, as she smiled. "They really do adore each other."

Savannah laughed. "Of course they do. You were always so surprised by true love." She met Emersyn's gaze. "But it's good to see you coming around. *Finally*."

Emersyn couldn't help it; she leaned in and kissed Savannah's lips. "Coming around? I think I'm there. In case you haven't noticed, I'm completely in love with you."

Savannah squeezed her thigh beneath the table as she flushed. "I think your mom knew you'd be busy the last few days with the move. She just wanted to let us know that the closing on the condo in Sun City went well. I think they're going to fly out next month for a few days to start furnishing it."

Emersyn nodded. "I still can't believe they're splitting their time between here and Wisconsin now." That had made the cross-country move so much easier. "It'll be nice to have her close for at least half the year."

"Well, it *is* Phoenix," Savannah said. "Sunshine. Warm weather. Pickleball all day and wine tastings all night with the other retirees? Sign me up. I'd spend my winters here too if I were her. One Northwoods winter was enough for me."

Emersyn grinned. "As I recall, you didn't seem to mind the blizzards," she said softly. "At least you didn't once upon a time when you had to share a motel room with me."

Savannah's mouth fell open and she nearly dropped the sushi from her chopsticks as they laughed. After they finished their takeout and rinsed their dishes, Savannah tugged Emersyn to the living room sofa. "Come on. Unpacking can wait a little longer. Lie with me and enjoy the moment. You're finally home now."

Emersyn glanced once at the stack of boxes looming in the corner, but the idea of snuggling up with Savannah on the cool leather sectional was far more appealing. As she settled comfortably beside her, wedging herself under Savannah's outstretched arm and sighing happily as she rested her head in the crook of her shoulder, Emersyn knew it was true. She *was* home. Together, with Savannah. And this was just the beginning of their forever.

THE END

About the Author

Midwest-based Lissandra Rowe likes spicy sapphic stories driven by deeply sensual and well-rounded characters, richly descriptive settings, and emotionally charged plots. She’s never met (or written!) an ice queen she didn’t love and enjoys reading all types of stories authentically representative of our community.

When she’s not planning her next novel or diving deep into new characters, Lissandra works in communications, content strategy, and copywriting. She lives with her family, dogs, and entirely too many pairs of shoes and has an intricately crafted playlist for everything.

Books Available from Bold Strokes Books

A Million Dollar Marriage by Margo Glynn. Their marriage ended months ago, but with an inheritance on the line, Elsie and Petra will fake it until they cash in, or until their true feelings catch up. (978-1-63679-961-2)

Changing The Game by Lissandra Rowe. Two former college basketball rivals turned lovers are reunited at a luxury resort, where hot days, sultry nights, and undeniable chemistry ignite a second chance at forever. (978-1-63679-998-8)

I Hate You, Now Kiss Me by Kimberly Cooper Griffin. When family brings them home, childhood enemies Lena and Andy are surprised to discover not only are they civil, but they find the missing parts of themselves in each other. (978-1-63679-996-4)

Musical Theatre Mondays by Marie Incontrera. A messy, musical queer romcom about falling in love, falling apart, and rewriting your second act. (979-8-90035-014-1)

Shot Through the Heart by Claire Donniere. When a Secret Service agent goes undercover to protect a senator, she falls for the woman she's meant to investigate and must choose between breaking the rules or breaking her own heart. (978-1-63679-985-8)

The Girl Next Door by Georgia Beers. A witty, heartwarming enemies to lovers romance about falling for the girl next door that proves the best stories are the ones with endings we never see coming. (978-1-63679-933-9)

Experts Only by Kel McCord. Torn between comforting solitude and the irresistible pull of connection, Michelle and Cas begin to wonder if the life they thought they wanted is enough. (979-8-9003507-0-7)

Never Say Die by Meredith Doench. Detective Rory Scott's personal and professional lives converge as she races against time to find the connection between two crimes and bring a killer to justice. (978-1-63679-793-9)

Swept Away by Radclyffe. When ER physician Sloane Marshall is called in as a last-minute replacement for a federal outreach mission in the remote mountain town of Coulter's Gap, she doesn't expect to fall in love with a sharp-edged helicopter pilot. (979-8-90035-008-0)

When Hearts Collide by Renee Roman. A car accident isn't a likely way to meet the love of your life, but when Harlen's and Annie's hearts collide, they may not have a choice. (978-1-63679-923-0)

Yes, Honey by Claudia Parr. Four sexy couples break stereotypes about committed sex to explore lust and love when the honeymoon is over. (978-1-63679-992-6)

Hurricane Season Hustle by Greg Herren. Scotty must catch the killer to protect his nearest and dearest, before they strike again. (978-1-63679-882-0)

Royal Rush: 75 Days to Fall in Love by Lissandra Rowe. When a royal matchmaking scheme leads to a chance encounter with Isabella Acosta-Ramon, a slow burn sparks that neither can deny. (978-1-63679-965-0)

The Moon to Me by Ana Hartnett. Sometimes it takes traveling thousands of miles to discover what's been yours all along. (978-1-63679-918-6)

To Love Violets for Their Thorns by Rachel Sullivan. Forced to face the heartbreak they never quite got over, Elly and Sonia must decide: breathe fresh life into an old love or try again with someone new? (978-1-63679-928-5)

Virtually Perfect by Melissa Sky. If your AI flirts better, listens harder, and never ghosts you…does that count as love? (979-8-90035-005-9)

Brooke Takes Queen by Alaina Erdell. Brooke Staley faces personal and professional upheaval when Elizabeth Bettancourt, the emotionally scarred new owner of the resort she works for, considers selling. (978-1-63679-886-8)

Coda by Anna Gram. Parker is intriguing, magnetic, impossible to ignore—and completely wrong for Hannah. But sometimes love's melody refuses to end. (978-1-63679-926-1)

Secrets Under the Junipers by Suzie Clarke. Who killed Hallie Lynn Peeples? Cecilia McConnel needs to know. Bitsy Hanover holds the key. Can love uncover secrets? (978-1-63679-845-5)

The Debutante Dilemma by Jane Walsh. Two debutantes are engaged to wealthy and titled brothers…but discover they only have eyes for each other. (978-1-63679-896-7)

The Love Book by Gun Brooke. When literary agent Rowan Cross receives an anonymous manuscript that deeply resonates with her, Verity realizes she has accidentally sent her own manuscript, complete with her very real feelings for her boss! (978-1-63679-850-9)

Traveling Toward Forever by Erin Dutton. When almost-strangers take a road trip through America's national parks, love may be the final destination. (978-1-63679-894-3)

Beautiful Things by Emma L McGeown. A warmhearted romance of missed chances, undeniable chemistry, and a stubborn love that maybe, just maybe, can find its way back. (978-1-63679-934-6)

Love Takes a Village by Karis Walsh. As Lena Preiss struggles to manage a busy restaurant in the Bavarian Christmas village of Leavenworth, Washington, chocolatier Devin Meyer brings an unexpected richness into her life, along with her delicious desserts. (978-1-63679-902-5)

Secrets of the Heart by Jenny Frame. When a beautiful stranger starts asking questions about Nikki Sharkey, head of an infamous crime syndicate, Nikki will stop at nothing to protect her daughter Isla. (978-1-63679-653-6)

Talon and the Songbird by Julia Underwood. In a world where survival depends on strategic alliances, Makayla and Talon must navigate not only complex politics but also the dangerous territory of their hearts. (978-1-63679-970-4)

The Great Popcorn Romance by Georgia Beers. Opposites attract, and Riley Shaw stands no chance of resisting Hannah Kramer's magnetic pull. But opposites know just how to drive each other crazy… (978-1-63679-910-0)

Three Blissful Days by Dena Blake. Kendall Jackson attempts to make her ex regret dumping her by announcing she's dating beautiful park ranger Ivy Patterson. But there's nothing fake about how attracted Ivy is to Kendall. (978-1-63679-707-6)

Chasing Her Scent by MJ Williamz. When Sheridan Rousseau walks into Lisette Mouton's charming little bookstore in Quebec City, she unknowingly holds the key to a mysterious box hidden in a secret room. (978-1-63679-900-1)

Heart's Run by D. Jackson Leigh. Hoping to recover an escaped racing mare, stock transporter Tobie Mason locks horns with local wild horse advocate Maggie Wilkes. (978-1-63679-825-7)

Scandalous by Kris Bryant. When a Hollywood actress trades places with her twin sister, everyone's in an uproar about getting duped, but Lindsay's more concerned about finding out which twin she made out with. (978-1-63679-874-5)

The Art of Love by Ali Vali. When Mimi and Bianca both set their sights on Jolly, sparks fly, loyalties are tested, and hearts collide as they navigate the unpredictable nature of their hearts (978-1-63679-719-9)

The Other Side of Forever by Kel McCord. Will Kenzie and Rachel be able to make love work when Rachel's cozy suburban dream feels like Kenzie's worst nightmare? (978-1-63679-812-7)

The Secrets of Rhydian Hill by Ronica Black. A doctor in need of a new start. A woman running from a killer. A love story that could end in tragedy. (978-1-63679-880-6)

www.ingramcontent.com/pod-product-compliance
Ingram Content Group UK Ltd.
Pitfield, Milton Keynes, MK11 3LW, UK
UKHW011434080426
11738UKWH00004B/449